What others say

Set in the tempestuous South during a tempestuous time, Lydia Hawke's *Firetrail* finely blends historical action with romance. Through interweaving the passion of war with passions of the heart, Hawke offers a romantic story that will satisfy Civil War enthusiasts as well as romance lovers.

LivelyWriter Reviews
(c) 2004 Kathryn Lively

This book is long and wonderfully detailed, but it flows so smoothly that you'll be finished before you know it. *FIRETRAIL* proves that Ms. Hawke is a wonderful writer and a gifted storyteller. I look forward to reading more of her work.

Overall rating: 5 Hearts
Reviewer: Renee Burnette
The Romance Studio
http://theromancestudio.com

Georgia had *Gone With The Wind* Now, South Carolina has *Firetrail.* Never was there a time more traumatic in the annals of American history and Firetrail has captured it all.

Flushed out of their homes by Sherman's torch wielding troops, all of the state is swept before the unstoppable horde. The good and the evil, the truly heroic and the unspeakably devilish all people this epic book.

Ms. Hawke's characters rival her intriguing plot; a self-reliant young widow and a noble Confederate cavalry captain thrown into a hurried marriage and then swept apart by the tides of war.

At first thought you would believe General Sherman is the ultimate evil but *Firetrail* reminds us that sociopaths are not restricted to the present day. Beyond any evil inflicted by the armies and their commanders are the "bummers," those who preyed on either side and wrought havoc in their wake equal to or greater than the army they followed. Harry Bell is an accurate if horrific characterization of these parasites. He wears a Union uniform but his only allegiance is to his own vicious appetites.

Beware! Do not start this book unless you have time to finish it at one sitting. You will not be able to put it down until the last page is turned. This book is a must read for romance lovers, action adventure fans, Civil War buffs, students of human nature and anyone who likes to read a really great story.

"Kathleen Walls, author of *Last Step, Georgia's Ghostly Getaways, Kudzu, Man Hunt - The Eric Rudolph Story, Finding Florida's Phantoms* and *Last Step*

Confederate Captain Blake Winberry is on his way home for a brief visit after fighting in Virginia. He plans on convincing his fiancée that she really doesn't want to marry another man. Almost to his destination in South Carolina, he encounters a lone woman doing her best to ward off an attack by three renegades.

After rescuing her, he brings her to his family home. She has lost so much to the war already, her home, most of her worldly possessions, her husband. She cannot bear to lose anything more, but realizes her situation is probably hopeless. The arrival of the handsome soldier seems almost to good to be true, especially when he offers her a warm bed and a hot meal with his family after chasing off the outlaws.

Blake and Judith face the trials and horror of war as South Carolina is invaded by the Yankees. Though married within a few days of meeting, theirs is a love that grows and endures in the face of destruction and loss occurring all around them.

Lydia Hawke's debut novel is a Civil War story that will touch your heart on all levels. It is beautifully written and rich in historical detail with characters that are memorable. *FIRETRAIL* is a story definitely worth reading and will stay with you long after you have turned the last page.

By Romance Junkies Reviewer Brooke Wills

Firetrail

Firetrail
©Lydia Hawke 2005

Previously published in 2004 by Wings Epress, Inc.

ISBN: 0-9766449-7-5
Library of Congress Control Number: 2005929072

Published by Global Authors Publications

Filling the GAP in publishing

Edited by Lorraine Stephens
Interior design by KathleenWalls
Cover Art by Christine Poe

Printed in USA for Global Authors Publications

Firetrail

by

Lydia Hawke

Dedication

To my patient husband Larry, my supportive mother Marilyn King, my encouraging daughter Jennifer,and critique partners Judy Dobrie, Ted Stetson, Carol McPhee, Carla Hughes, Mary Veele, Tim Conroy, and the late Clyde Rogers.

A Note From the Author

My fascination with the War Between the States dates back to fourth grade. A classmate had a book open to a map of the divided nation of that period. I noted that Florida was among the Confederate states. I came home and asked my mother about it. She informed me that "we" were defeated, and I felt an inexplicable sense of loss.

Much later, I spent a few months in Columbia, South Carolina because my husband's army reserve hitch sent him through training at Fort Jackson. Occupied with temporary jobs and competing with the army for my husband's time, all I knew of Columbia was that it was the state capital, I felt at home there, and the winter of 1969-70 was the coldest this Florida girl had ever experienced. Later, as I found out more about the War Between the States I learned that the city was burned during that conflict.

In Sherman's March through the Carolinas, by John G. Barrett, I read of the three regiments of Butler's South Carolina Cavalry arriving in that city a few weeks before Sherman's troops swept in. I wondered what those men were thinking, at least the ones who understood they were hopelessly outnumbered yet expected to defend their state from the coming invasion.

So I created Captain Blake Winberry, who came home to find all that he cherished in deadly jeopardy. I set out to write a story about him, and other characters rode in on their horses, or in Judith's case behind a mule, to help out.

After the first or second draft was written, I did a bit of research on my family history. I discovered that my great, great grandfather, John Hardy Bolton, fought in the Fifth Georgia Cavalry. Grandpa's regiment was in Wheeler's cavalry division during Sherman's march through Georgia and the Carolinas, opposing Sherman's army the whole distance. John Hardy Bolton was from Screven County. The county seat, Sylvania, was for a time occupied by Sherman's army. Thus my great, great grandfather experienced a similar ordeal to the one endured by the character I had already created, that of watching the enemy capture his home town. Genetic memory? Past lives? Scrambled brains? Who knows? (Hey, let me tell you about another great, great grandfather, the one I discovered was a partisan ranger who rode with Captain J. J. Dickison. Never mind, that's another story. Later.)

Whatever the inspiration, I owe a great deal to the resources made available by those who work to preserve voices of the past. Jim J. Fox, a South Carolina historian, locates rare old books and reprints them to widen their availability. Through him I was able to acquire Butler and his Cavalry During in the War of Secession and other first hand accounts of the campaign. Especially helpful were the libraries at the University of North Florida, University of South Carolina, University of North Carolina and the Museum of Southern History in Jacksonville. I mustn't forget the living historians who still hear the guns and fire them from time to time at battle reenactments. Picking the brains of Civil War reenactors yielded nifty factoids that found their way into my novels.

In Firetrail, I have striven to maintain historical accuracy in a fictional setting. Enough books have been written about famous generals and politicians. My interest was to experience what life must have been like for ordinary people during the great conflict that tore our country apart.

Lydia Hawke, Orange Park, Florida

Chapter One

Five miles south of Columbia, South Carolina
February 2, 1865

So far Judith Rogers had managed to stay well ahead of the advancing enemy. She felt safer on the move, away from peril, though the zone of sanctuary was continually shrinking.

The rains had ceased, clearing into a mild spell. The good turn of weather and the high clay road helped her mule-drawn wagon roll along easily. She expected to make Columbia well before dark. Only then would she worry about finding accommodations, or whether she could even afford them.

Pine, scrub and red maple just starting to bud covered the gentle hills. She had not seen a drive or a farmhouse for the past mile or so, nor much traffic.

When three men on horseback neared her wagon, she was not immediately alarmed. She had encountered plenty of men during her flight, mostly Confederate soldiers, and had never experienced trouble from even the worst looking of them.

The three men ranged across the road and stopped, forcing her to rein in her mule.

"Howdy, ma'am," the nearest one said.

Judith nodded a curt acknowledgment, hiding her annoyance. They sat on their horses, looking at her and grinning, yellow tobacco juice staining their matted beards. The closest man wore a filthy gray army jacket, another a denim-patched black coat. Both carried army revolvers in their belts. The third wore a torn, faded blue coat of Union army cut but lacked a gun belt. A Yankee? Not necessarily. These days Confederates wore whatever they could

1

get.

Why wouldn't they let her by? Something was wrong with the menacing way they looked at her, but she tried not to let her rising sense of danger show. "Excuse me, gentlemen. I must be on my way."

The man in the gray jacket grabbed her mule by the halter. "Where's a pretty gal like you headed to all by yourself?" He drew back wolfish lips and exposed three random teeth.

Judith lifted her chin, thoroughly alarmed, and invented a hasty lie. "I'm expected at the Smith place and I am overdue. I'm quite certain they've sent out a search party by now."

He glanced down the road. "That so? They ought to be along directly."

The black-coated man picked up a corner of the oilcloth tarpaulin that covered her belongings. "Trunks, Dink. She's got two trunks. Been on the move awhile. Lady, you got anything to eat?"

"Get your hands off my things," Judith snapped.

His gaze whipped to her face and swept downward. "A looker, too."

Dink licked his lips. "What a find."

The nearer man smelled of sweat and sour liquor. A shiver rippled through Judith, the habitual fear peaking to a new level. She raised her hand to her throat. Would she have to show them the shotgun she had hidden under the wagon bench?

"What's in them trunks, missy?"

"Clothes, a few dishes, nothing you would want."

"What you waitin' for, Snipes," Dink said. "Have a look at what she's got." He threw a glance at the man in the blue coat. "Bell, you be on the lookout."

"So long as I get my share." His way of talking was rough like Dink's, but oddly clipped.

Dink laughed. "You get what I say you get, you damn Yankee. You're lucky we let you join up. You would've starved on your own."

Bell's eyes narrowed but he said nothing.

The shotgun was under her seat, ready. Judith slipped her shaky hand down to grasp the breech. Thank God it was there. The feel of the cold metal against her palm steadied her. If only she had the courage to shoot a man.

Snipes started to dismount.

Judith snatched up the shotgun and whipped the stock to her shoulder. She pointed it at his midsection, like her husband George had told her. "Go away or I will shoot."

Snipes sat back in the saddle. His grin faded and he glared at his snickering partner. "What's so funny, Dink? She's got two damn barrels."

Bell threw back his head and laughed. "Go ahead, sugar. Use it up on them dumb mule turds. Then we can have our own fun."

She trembled so hard the gun wavered. Snipes backed his horse. "Mind that piece, missy. It might go off."

"Go away."

Snipes nodded, staring at the shotgun. "Anything you say, ma'am."

Dink let go of the mule's halter and all three men rode around behind the wagon. Judith set the shotgun within reach, popped the reins and shouted, "Git!" The beast shambled into a sluggish trot.

Judith glanced over her shoulder and saw the men following, stalking her. She grabbed the switch and lashed the mule's back. Just like a mule, Fancy would not go faster.

So much for outrunning them. She hauled the wagon to a stop, snatched up the gun, whirled, and whipped it toward them.

"Stop," she yelled. "Leave me be."

They kept coming, pistols drawn, making their intentions clear. They meant to rob what little she had, and she feared even that would not satisfy them.

She pointed the double barrels at the nearest man, the one in the gray jacket. All three men closed in, laughing, not believing. The movement of the approaching men and her own shakiness made her aim waver, but she took a chance and squeezed one of the triggers. The shotgun spat fire and a puff of smoke. The full-charge explosion sent the butt ramming into her shoulder. Dink yelped-- his horse squealed and reared--but he clung to the saddle.

The startled mule lunged forward and Judith lost her balance. She threw a hand out on the bench to keep from pitching to the floor of the wagon. Gripping the weight of the shotgun with her other hand, her fingers convulsively closed around the second trigger and the remaining charge went off skyward, wrenching her arm.

She dropped the shotgun, grabbed the reins and tried to whip up Fancy. But before the mule got into stride Snipes and Bell were riding alongside.

Snipes brandished a pistol toward her face. "Stop that critter, bitch."

She looked past the weapon at the man's triumphant grin. She twisted to jump off the other side and run but Dink was right there, holding his hand over his cheek. "Goddammit." Blood seeped through his fingers and dripped onto his sleeve. Through clenched jaws he said, "You gonna pay for this, goddammit."

With his free hand, Dink wiped at the weeping round hole in his cheek and smeared blood into his beard. He stuck his fingers into his mouth and pulled out a tooth, then a bit of shot. He spat. "You won't be so feisty when I get done with you. Get down."

Judith climbed out of the wagon, legs set to run.

Dink didn't give her a chance. He jumped down from his horse and grabbed her by the wrist.

She stared at his filthy hand, understanding how a trapped animal could chew off its own limb to free itself.

Snipes told Bell to stand lookout, tied the horses and climbed into the wagon. "Don't start with her here, Dink." He pulled up the tarp. "Somebody might come along. Bring her with us, then we can take turns."

They were going to take her somewhere, beat her and have their way with her. Kill her too? She threw her weight sideways but couldn't break his grip.

"Quit." He balled up his fist.

Judith raised her free arm to protect her face and tried again to twist away. The blow glanced alongside her head and clipped her ear, smarting. She exhaled sharply, letting out a short, involuntary cry.

Snipes spat over the side of the wagon. "Damn you, Dink, help me get whatever is worth gettin' and pack it on the mule. You gonna help or you gonna stand there sweet talkin' that wench? Let Bell take care of her. He can have her shotgun."

"Yeah." Bell looked down from his horse and licked his lips. "Let me take care of her."

Dink pointed to his cheek. "She shot me!"

"You ain't hurt. You'll never miss a few teeth." Snipes manhandled a trunk open, pawed over the neatly folded bedclothes and threw them aside.

An embroidered pillowcase, a wedding gift, fell into the dirt. How dare he desecrate… "Get your nasty hands off those things. They are mine. You have no right."

Snipes just laughed, digging deeper into the trunk. Her china shifted and clinked under his hand.

"Stop. You're breaking it."

"Hell, we gonna take those and you too," Dink snarled. He balled up his fist again.

"Turn me loose!" Judith clawed at his face, attacked his eyes, ripped at the wound on his cheek. He yelled and lashed out. The blow clacked her jaws together and she slumped to the ground.

Judith groped for a rock--anything--to strike at the cursing, kicking Dink. Then she heard shooting and yelling and drumming hoof beats. Bell hollered, "Rebs! It's the Rebs." He whirled his horse around and fled. Snipes scrambled off the wagon onto his horse and raced after him.

Dink pulled out his revolver and raised it to fire at whomever had sent his friends running. She found a rock and threw it at his back with all her strength. He grunted and spun around, confusion on his face.

A rider closed in, greatcoat spread behind him like a cape. His revolver flashed and barked. Dink gasped and staggered backwards. His gun fired into the ground. He collapsed next to Judith. Blood spread through the front of his coat from a little fountain in his chest. His breath expired, a gurgling groan. His legs jerked, then it was over.

She reached over and grabbed Dink's smoking gun from his flaccid grip.

The rider galloped past her then doubled back, slower. She looked up and cocked the revolver, trying to decide whether to aim the gun at the newcomer. Did he just want her for himself? She cast about for others. Could he have caused such a ruckus all by himself?

He reined his horse to a stop. "You hurt?"

Though wary, Judith kept the barrel pointed down. She shook her head, then rubbed her sore jaw, tasting blood. Her ribs pained, but she did not believe they were broken.

He jumped off his horse, tossed the reins down and bent over Dink, revolver still in his hand. Blood flowed in a small stream over the hard-packed clay. A blank stare was frozen on the clawed face. The newcomer picked up the wrist and felt for a pulse. "Dead." He threw the hand down, straightened and looked directly at her.

He was tall and fit, lean face weathered and sun-darkened. His fair hair fell collar-length, cavalry fashion, his beard neatly trimmed. He wore a military coat with captain's bars on the collar. A South Carolina palmetto badge caught up one side of his hat. His gray eyes crackled, still full of fight, but when they met hers they softened.

She fought down a wave of lightheadedness, clutching the revolver, determined to reveal no weakness. "Where did you come from?" she finally asked.

~ * ~

Blake Winberry ran his gaze from the woman's pale, strained face to the weapon in her hand, hoping to God his meddling was not a huge blunder.

He had acted on his best instincts honed by his experience at war. He had expected thieves to cut and run at the first sign of a threat, but this man had chosen to stand and resist. Had he misinterpreted the situation, which had seemed clear cut before? Did he kill the woman's husband, for God's sake?

"People warned me of bushwhackers in the area, and it appeared... I saw them abusing you, and I..." Blake nodded toward the dead man, fearing to ask. "Did you know him?"

"Not until he accosted me." She let out a shaky breath. "I believe you saved my life. Thank you, Captain--"

Relief flooded through him. "Winberry. Blake Winberry."

"I'm Mrs. Rogers." She swayed on her feet.

"Better sit down." He stepped forward to take her arm but she backed up a step. She moved without his assistance to a grassy spot at the road's shoulder, where she folded to the ground.

"Why don't you give me that revolver?" he asked. "You might set it off by accident."

She stared at him and gripped it even tighter, if that was possible. "What if they come back?"

"Mind where you point it. Please."

The trace of a smile crossed her face. Now that he had the situation in hand, he took notice that she was the loveliest vagabond he had ever seen. Her heavy dark hair, undone, framed her upturned face. Her plain widow's weeds did not entirely obscure her fine figure. "Are you afraid I will shoot you, Captain Winberry?" she asked.

"Should I be?"

She did not drop her smile, nor did she reply, but met his gaze straight on, letting him make his own conclusions.

He reciprocated the paltry smile, respecting her reasonable fears. "Stay there. I'll put your things in order."

He tethered his mare, Magic, to the rear of the wagon and looked over the dead bushwhacker's horse. The chestnut gelding had taken a few pellets in its neck, but the trickle of bleeding had slowed. Blake raised his hand to rub the animal's nose but it snorted and backed away as far as the rein would let it. "Easy there," he said. "You'll be all right. We'll turn you into a good honest cavalry horse."

Next he reloaded his own revolver, a detail he dared not overlook in case the bushwhackers scraped up the courage to return. Then he gathered the woman's possessions from the ground and set them back into the wagon. He hefted the shotgun and checked the breech. Empty, but it stank of freshly burnt powder.

Finally he directed his attention to the dead bushwhacker. It wouldn't be right to ask Mrs. Rogers to carry it in her wagon. Tomorrow would be soon enough to send men to throw dirt over the body. He went through the dead man's pockets as any good Confederate would, but did not find identification or valuables. He rolled the body into the ditch where it flopped in a tangle of arms and legs.

He stared at the dead heap for a moment, reflecting that he felt nothing. No regret, anger, pity or revulsion. Nothing. He had already exhausted such feelings on dead friends and a dead brother. He had none left over for dead vermin.

Mrs. Rogers still sat quietly on the grass, legs tucked underneath her skirts, watching him. He had seen many female refugees like her, in both Virginia and South Carolina, wandering about in their wagons carrying all they had left. God forbid his own family should ever have to go through that.

He walked over to her and hunkered down so he did not force her to look up at him.

"I gather you were headed toward Columbia," he said. "So am I. My home is there, and I will escort you in."

Relief gave her dark eyes a soft glow. "That is kind of you, Captain Winberry. I don't know how to thank you for all you've done."

"If you have need of it, my family has a spare room."

A rush of color came to her cheeks, and she glanced away from him.

"It is proper enough. My father, my mother and my sister all live there."

When she looked back at him, her eyes were moist. "I had not made any prior arrangements. If it isn't an inconvenience..."

"It's settled then. Let's go." He stood up, offered his hand and this time she accepted it.

Blake handed her up into the wagon, seated himself, chirped at the mule and popped the reins. The woman sat on the narrow bench beside him, only a hand's breadth separating them. She had finally given up the revolver, setting it under the seat near the shotgun.

He studied her surreptitiously. She appeared no longer in danger of fainting, though an occasional tremor betrayed her remaining fear. The folds of the coat she had drawn about her shoulders obscured the curves of her breasts he had noticed before. Her faded mourning dress was as much a uniform for Southern women these days as gray or butternut was for the men. Her chin was red and puffy where the bastard had punched her. She gripped her shredded hat in her lap, down on her luck but not her pride.

She finally spoke her mind. "Captain Winberry, aren't you worried they might ambush us?"

"It's Blake. Those cowards are halfway to the high country by now."

"I hope you are right." She scanned the woods, then turned back to him. "How did you happen to come along just then?"

"I heard gunfire."

She nodded. "They didn't think much of my shotgun."

"I took it to be somebody shooting his supper at first, but the country people had warned me about thieving army deserters hiding in the woods. They told me to watch my back because that lot wouldn't mind killing a soldier for his horse and weapons. So I scouted them out, saw what they were up to, and couldn't let them have their way."

This time her smile was warmer by degrees. "That was a brave thing you did."

"It's an old trick, making noise and shocking them. We are used to being outnumbered and having to bluff the enemy. I figured they would panic because their kind hates getting caught out in the open." If he had guessed wrong, he would be the one dead in that ditch. "It's a shame you have to travel alone."

"I was not always alone. My companions dropped out. One took ill, another had a wagon break down. Anyway, I never had this kind of trouble before."

"Once is too often."

"I am so sorry you had to get mixed up in it." Her smile dissolved away. "You might have gotten hurt for my sake."

"Good thing you threw that rock just when he was drawing a bead."

"I would have fought him with my last breath." She bit off the last word.

The more he talked to her, the better he liked her. "Where did you drive up from?"

"Near the Georgia line. People passing through said the Yankees were coming, so I left. They have taken enough from me as it is."

"See any lately?"

She sat up straighter, thoughtful. "One of those men was a Yankee."

"This far behind the lines?"

"Strange, isn't it?" She tilted her head to one side. "The others called him a Yankee. They ordered him around, treated him like they were barely tolerating him."

"Maybe he escaped from a prison camp and took up with home-grown renegades. Have you seen any others?"

"No, thank goodness." She retreated into her coat and made

herself small. "I heard the Yankees were all the way to Robertsville. They follow me wherever I go."

"Anything else? Maybe you have information that would--"

"Just rumors." Her hands tightened in her lap. "They were bragging they have lots of matches and plan to use them in South Carolina."

Uneasiness gnawed at his gut, a knowing of what was to come. "We have to stop them." Though spoken with conviction, his words sounded as vacuous as the feeling at his core.

"Whether or not they can be stopped, I am headed to Fayetteville to live with my aunt. Maybe they won't follow me there."

"North Carolina? That's another long haul."

"I was born there," she said. "My father moved us to Tennessee, and my husband and I lived in Atlanta. My house was blown up by an artillery shell."

"Is it your husband you're mourning?"

"George was captured and died in prison. Typhoid--"

"Sorry. I didn't mean--"

"It was a year ago." Her controlled expression did not change. "My brother too, just last summer, during the fighting around Atlanta."

"I lost my brother at Trevillian Station." The stab of memory made him sorry he had brought up the subject.

She let out a long breath, apparently feeling the same way. "Let's talk about something that isn't so gloomy. You haven't told me anything about yourself. What about your family? I take it you're not married."

"I'm detached."

Her voice turned quizzical. "Detached?"

"Disengaged, then." He shook his head, then shook it some more. "It wasn't my idea. Guess I've been away too much to suit her so she found somebody more convenient. A Mr. Randolph." Conscription-dodging lardass government lackey.

For the last four years, since college and through the war, he had courted no one but Sally. The only payoff was a letter breaking their engagement. A message like that in between bullets on the picket line. Would getting shot have hurt that much?

"You're still mad at her, aren't you?" She gave him another

faint smile.

"There's still hope, now that I'm back in town." If only Sally would agree to see him and talk to him face to face. "I spent the past eight months in Virginia and my division just transferred back to protect our state from Sherman's army."

"I know what you are facing." Her voice was sad. "You'd better have a lot of men."

No use insulting this lady with false optimism. It wouldn't fool her, in many ways a fellow war veteran. "I'm trying to do some recruiting while I'm waiting for orders. Not much luck so far. It seems just about everybody worth shooting is already in the army."

She looked away. "Or dead."

He kept his voice flat. "We lost some of our best men in the fighting around Richmond."

"Not all of them."

Neither of them spoke for a little while.

The mule was poky but he didn't rush it.

Federal Vanguard
About sixty miles south of Columbia, South Carolina

Lieutenant Andrew McCord sat on his horse next to General Howard, the commander of Sherman's right wing. He had claimed a good vantage point to watch General Mower's troops rush across the Salkehatchie River bridge with their usual ferocity and storm the Rebel position. The vanguard must open the road for the wagon trains and thousands of men stretched behind them in a 25-mile-long queue. He lifted his field glasses to his eyes and panned the wet pine and cedar landscape, locating the Rebel artillery on a bluff.

This was only the latest of many delays and annoyances the army had faced since crossing the Georgia line into South Carolina. Winter rains worsened the swamp, a morass of quicksand that swallowed mule legs and wagon wheels. Even the causeway, which looked solid on the surface, was a slough underneath. Foot soldiers fared better than mounted men.

At least the spill McCord had experienced had not broken any bones. He brushed dried mud off his faded blue coat skirt. He was only bruised, and had provided the troops with a diversion of sorts.

He lowered his glasses and looked at General Howard. The general rubbed his beard with quick, nervous strokes of his left hand. He had lost his right arm during the Peninsula Campaign, over two years ago. The boys called General Howard "Old Prayer Book" behind his back because he liked to distribute religious tracts. Mercifully, he didn't realize they used the paper for tinder, or worse.

McCord shifted in the saddle. Was Mower wise in executing a frontal attack? No one could be sure of the strength or the tenacity of the Rebels here. An assault would draw their fire, reveal the enemy, and sacrifice a few lives in the exploration. With any luck, the enemy would give up their position easily. The whole stubborn lot should see the light and quit their futile resistance.

The assault began with a cheer and a crackle of rifle fire. Supporting artillery boomed from his side of the bridge and lobbed shells into the Confederate stronghold. The vibrations pounded his chest and his horse shied. He coaxed it back under control and fixed his glasses onto the blue backs surging across the bridge.

Puffs of smoke erupted from the other side as the enemy replied with artillery fire. Punched by the big guns, caught on the narrow bridge, the leading edge of the Federal line crumpled. Blue figures broke the line to jump or fall into the swamp, splashing water as high as the bridge. Rebel shot pounded and tore at the attackers, clearing the bridge of anything erect. Bodies floated in the river, shrouded by drifting smoke. Peppered by rifle fire, survivors made it back through the water as best they could, and those still on the causeway ran for the safety of their own lines.

McCord felt ill at the apparent cost of the failure. General Howard's lips moved. Praying? The entire staff remained quiet except for mumbles.

"Lieutenant McCord," Howard finally said. "Find General Mower and tell him to call off further frontal attacks. We must cross at some other point and flank those Rebels instead."

They would. It might take a day or two, but they would find a way to work around the Rebels, kill and capture some of them, scatter the rest, then continue their march deep into the center of South Carolina. McCord was privy to what the generals had decided, what the rest of the army did not know. They were aiming for Columbia, capitol of the most treasonous of all the Rebel states.

~ * ~

Judith had stopped trembling by the time they crossed the covered bridge over the Congaree River and rolled into Columbia. She did not have anything to be afraid of for the moment. Not with her rescuer right next to her, enduring and tough, that big army revolver at his waist. Perhaps she should have felt bad about his

13

killing Dink, but what else could he have done? Given the chance, Dink would have murdered both of them. Captain Winberry had earned her trust for the time being. She had even told him her given name.

She was sore from the beating, but bruises would heal and she had not lost anything. Perhaps her narrow escape had taught her something of value and had clarified her outlook. For the first time she realized her life had been reduced to a simple, animal struggle for survival. She must take refuge where she could and accept whatever solutions presented themselves, even if it cost the indignity of accepting the charity of strangers.

In truth, she hadn't felt so protected since George had left. She made herself relax and enjoy the temporary sense of safety. For one night at least, she knew in advance where she would be sleeping, and she wouldn't have to keep her shotgun within reach. The young cavalry captain was a pleasant companion, cultured and attractive. She was mindful of her vast good fortune that he had come along and had chosen to act decisively on her behalf.

His hometown was a busy place crammed with traffic. Yellow dust stirred by hooves and wheels thickened the air. Winter-bare trees lined the wide streets. The houses were spacious and genteel, even if some of them wanted for paint and repairs.

He turned the mule onto a side street, into a residential district, then looked at Judith. "When I got off the train I was amazed to see so many strangers in town. Refugees from the low country, and they moved the Confederate mint here from Richmond. The textile and war factories are going full steam."

"You have a pretty town," Judith said. "I hope Sherman doesn't come here and destroy everything, like he did in Atlanta."

"Some people claim he won't make it through the swamps, but nothing has stopped him yet. In the end it will be up to us."

To get killed. Judith wondered why the thought touched her with concern. One advantage to not having any male friends or relatives left--all the soldiers perishing these days were strangers.

She turned her attention back to the houses, wanting to banish thought. "Which is yours?"

"That two story over at the corner of Gervais Street."

His house occupied a big lot. Peach trees, live oaks, outbuildings, a chicken coop and a garden plot gave it the look of a country place.

"My father is a doctor," he said. "Presently he is working as a government contract surgeon. If you wish, I shall ask him to examine you, just to make sure you are all right."

She shook her head. "Don't bother him. I'm fine."

"He practices at South Carolina College. After the war commenced they converted the DeSausseur Building into a military hospital. No students left. We all quit to join the army." He halted the mule in front of the gate. "Here we are."

Blake introduced her to his sister Lexi, who met them on the front porch. She was a slim blonde girl, with a boyish grin, around sixteen, Judith supposed. Dressed in black like herself, doubtless for the dead brother.

He said to Lexi, "Mrs. Rogers had a nasty run-in with bushwhackers down the state road. She will be spending the night with us."

Lexi's eyes widened. "Who won?"

"Your brother did." Judith touched the bruise on her chin. She must be a sight, still wearing his coat, hair in disarray, hat ruined.

Lexi didn't outshine her by much, not with sun-streaked hair knotted under a homemade palmetto hat and fingernails bitten to the quick. But she had clean facial lines like her brother, and Judith thought her ordinary good looks could be transformed into something fine if she made the effort.

"Did you get any good licks in?" Lexi asked her.

"Licks?" Judith blinked. "I shot at them, but all that did was make them mad. Then your brother came along and saved me."

"Sounds exciting. Tell me--"

"Where's Mama?" Blake asked.

"Inside."

Blake opened the door. Judith stepped into the welcoming warmth and Lexi slipped through behind her. A conservative fire heated the parlor. Cordwood must be as costly here as anywhere else. Throw rugs on the hardwood floor added to the sense of warmth. The sofa and chairs were not new but looked comfortable. Volumes filled the bookshelves, and the top shelf displayed a daguerreotype of a much younger Blake, clean-shaven, beside another youth who resembled him. Both wore new uniforms and bristled with swords, pistols and do-or-die expressions. In the corner stood an upright piano.

They still had what she had lost, family, connections, security, and a place to call home. Maybe at least she could play that piano before she had to leave.

A woman glided into the room, an older, tidier version of Lexi.

"Mama, this is Mrs. Rogers," Blake said. "She will spend the night with us."

Judith gave her a tentative smile, aware of her bedraggled appearance, wanting a way to explain herself. "Pleased to meet you, Mrs. Winberry."

"Welcome, Mrs. Rogers." Blake's mother said it as though hospitality was a habit, but when she glanced toward him, Judith caught the question in her eyes. Wondering where her son had found this stray and why he had brought her home.

"I hope it isn't an imposition," Judith said. "I expect to pay for a room."

"No. You are my guest," Blake said.

"You've done so much for me as it is."

He waved his hand dismissively.

"She can use Justin's room," Lexi broke in.

Mrs. Winberry's face betrayed a hint of strain as she said to her daughter, "Show Mrs. Rogers her quarters." To Judith she said, "Lexi can get you water and fresh towels so you can refresh yourself. Supper will be ready soon."

Judith's eyes stung and she blinked back a mist of tears. "Thank y'all so much," she murmured.

"I'll get your trunk and take care of the animals," Blake told her. "Do whatever Mama says."

He said it bossy, like an order, but just now she did not mind being told what to do. It simplified things not to have to make decisions. Besides, she owed him her life and he had been nothing but kind. Certainly assumption of command came with the captain's bars on his collar.

What did it matter? She'd be continuing on her way to Fayetteville after she found people to travel with.

She would never see him again after that.

~ * ~

As Blake expected, Mama followed him outside. Naturally she would want to know from him about the stranger he had brought into her home. He led her out into the yard so their voices would not carry from the porch ceiling into the house. He stopped beside Judith Rogers' wagon and faced his mother, considering what version of today's events he could safely tell her. He knew his own homecoming had made Justin's death more real to Mama and Papa. Justin should be here too, but he was not, and never would be home again. Blake did not wish to add more worry to her burden of grief.

"What sort of trouble is Mrs. Rogers in?" Mama was not one to dither about. She stood only a few inches shorter than him, hands on hips, demanding eye contact, a woman who had never suffered foolishness gladly. "Who put those bruises on her face?"

"I found her on the Orangeburg Road, being robbed by highwaymen. I ran them off and thought it best to bring her home." He realized she would eventually find out about the dead man. His body, whether buried or not, would not be kept secret by soldiers or townspeople. Better she learned it from him. He took a deep breath. "I had to kill one of them."

She paled and her shoulders sagged almost imperceptible, but kept her gaze fixed on his face. "Are you all right, son?"

"I don't take chances, Mama," he said softly. "I take care of myself."

"Did you report it to the sheriff?"

"The sheriff?" He pressed his hand to his temple, feeling the sense of dislocation that had hit him often since he had left the war zone. In this world where his family lived, violent death was a matter of significance. In the other world he knew, life held trifling value and was bartered cheaply. "I'll take care of it, Mama. There won't be any trouble. Mrs. Rogers will confirm it was self defense."

"I am not questioning that you did the right thing." The concern in her eyes had not diminished. "That poor girl still looks frightened. I suppose it will do no harm to let her stay on until she can find something permanent. So many people have been put out of their homes. I would never abandon my home unless it burned down around my ears."

"That's why I took the liberty--"

"I'd better hurry to the kitchen and tell Chloe to set another place." Mama seemed to relax a little, now that she turned her attention to mundane matters. She even smiled. "I'll tell her she needs to put more water in the tea."

Left alone with the animals in the gathering dusk, he led them each in turn to the stall, rubbed them down, watered and fed them. The bushwhacker's skittish beast danced about too much for him to see to its wounds. He would ask his father to help him later.

He lifted Judith's trunk from the wagon and picked up her weapons to take them into the house for safekeeping. Grim though the task had been, he was glad he had been able to help her. Were he not clinging to hope that he could win Sally back, he would be inclined to court the young widow. She was easy on the eyes, he sensed a core of steel under her softness, and he wanted to know her better. Was that disloyal of him when he still loved Sally?

For the time being, he didn't see any harm in enjoying her company.

He had tried to see Sally often since his return to Columbia, but each time her mother had told him she was busy or else with the new beau. Mrs. Dubois had seemed cool to him, and Blake suspected she had failed to pass on his messages to Sally.

Or had Sally gotten the messages and chosen to ignore them?

~ * ~

Judith washed and changed into fresh clothes in the privacy of her own room, a great luxury. She pinned her hair back into control, then joined the family at the supper table. Blake sat across from her, Lexi beside her, the elder Winberrys at each end.

Blake's father greeted her cordially. Apparently someone had already informed Dr. Winberry of her presence. The trim, graying man with kind vague eyes accepted her without fuss. Through the polite dinner conversation she was obliged to tell her history to Blake's family as she had related it to him.

She ate everything the cook Chloe set before her, a steaming portion of turnip greens flavored with ham, sweet potatoes, corn bread, and drank sassafras tea sweetened with sorghum syrup. Hungry enough for seconds, she did not want to appear famished and greedy.

After supper she felt weary and ached from the bruises. She ought to go straight to bed, but the piano and her hunger for companionship lured her into the parlor with the family instead. Besides, she ought to act sociably and honor the hospitality.

Her own piano had perished with her home. Not since leaving Atlanta had she run her fingers over ivory keys to make music. It had always helped her forget her troubles and losses, at least temporarily.

Judith stroked the dark wood of the instrument and asked Lexi, "Do you play?"

"Mama and Papa make me take lessons so I'll be a proper lady." Lexi cut her eyes at her parents, who had sat down on the couch together.

"She's very musically inclined," Mrs. Winberry said. "Despite her lack of discipline."

"Practicing is a bore." Lexi shrugged grandly. "I'd rather listen to you play, Mrs. Rogers,"

"We would enjoy hearing you play," added the courteous Dr. Winberry.

Judith glanced at Blake, who gave her an encouraging nod.

"I hate to make you suffer. I'm so out of practice," she demurred as she sat on the bench and lifted the cover from the keyboard. She leafed through the sheet music open on the stand and found "Amazing Grace," a hymn she knew but had never memorized.

Blake fetched a tallow candle and held it so Judith could see the written notes. She faltered, unsure, over the familiar tune, then she ran through an arpeggio, banged out an assertive series of chords, and looked up at Blake.

"Now I know why I lugged my own sheet music over all creation and made my poor mule pull the extra weight! I'm going to go get it!" Energized, she stood up and started toward the door.

Blake followed her. "You are not going out there alone. There's no gas for the streetlights and all kinds of bad characters--"

She paused, her hand on the doorknob. "You'll go with me, then?"

"I'd better bring a light."

She humored him, enjoying the fuss. "Whatever would I do

without you?"

The night had turned cold. Wrapped in a coat, clinging to Blake's arm, Judith let him escort her to her wagon, a dark shape beside the horse shed. The only light available besides the lantern he had provided was the dim glow from the house and other windows in the neighborhood.

She lifted the cover to expose the crate she kept her papers in and riffled through them. "Oh, here they are." She grabbed a handful of sheet music and gathered it against her bodice.

He held the light close to the music. "What have you got there?"

She flipped through, showing him the titles. "'Drink to Me Only With Thine Eyes,' 'Annie Laurie,' hymns, a few patriotic airs. Do you sing?"

"Of course. They don't let you in the cavalry if you're tone deaf. You see, there's an audition." He said it seriously, but his eyes were alight, crinkling at the corners.

The man had a sense of humor after all. "It is indeed a comfort the men protecting our country have such high standards." She smiled, tilting her head. "Or is it just a fib you're telling me?"

"You decide. Shall we go in?"

He offered her his arm again and they started toward the house.

"Fayetteville." He shook his head. "You can't be serious about going there."

"I told you my aunt--"

"Anything could happen to you between here and there."

"I'll go with a lot of people. I've done that before, and we never had any trouble."

"You did today. Don't you know how far it is?"

Judith shrugged. "About the same distance as Atlanta."

"You had better reconsider."

At the top of the porch steps, she faced him. "Are you telling me what to do?"

"Somebody needs to."

She reminded herself he had fought for her, killed for her, saved her life and brought her into his own home. She settled her arching back. "Good of you to care."

"Then you're staying."

She said, "I'll need a few days to find some folks who are going my way, then I'll see."

A slow smile crossed his face. "You sure do have a mind of your own."

"Good thing, isn't it? I haven't been able to rely on anyone else's in quite a while."

The lantern light reflected from his eyes. "It doesn't have to be that way. You are among friends."

"I am nothing but a burden on your family. I know how scarce food is, and your mother refuses to take--"

"That's not your concern. I just got paid, three months worth. I'll buy more provisions tomorrow. Besides, I can sell that bushwhacker's gun and horse for you, then we'll be even."

"You really want me to stay, don't you?"

"You catch on quick."

He gazed into her eyes, his expression intense, and the astonishing thought that he might kiss her crossed her mind. Her cheeks tingled when she realized she wanted him not only to kiss her, but to take her in his arms and hold her. Not daring to reveal the bold thoughts going through her head, she lowered her gaze. She still felt the crackle of his animal vitality, held in check under the genteel surface.

He did not impose his will on her, but said softly, "Let's go in." She was relieved and disappointed at the same time.

"Lordy, Blake. What took you so long?" Lexi said as they walked into the house. "We were about to send out a search party."

Judith flashed the sheaf of music. "Took us a minute to dig it out." She glanced at Blake and met his level gaze.

She sat down at the piano and he stood over her, holding the light. She snatched up the top piece, "Drink to Me Only With Thine Eyes," and started to play, her mind racing ahead. Sensing Blake's attraction challenged her. She, who had only been courted by one boy all her life and married him as a matter of habit.

She had loved George, still did. And she had liked being married. Besides, in those days she didn't have to worry about where the next meal was going to come from or where she was going to spend the night. This home was so pleasant, so welcoming. Could she possibly drop her burdens and live here, safe and secure?

Blake was singing in a clear baritone. She had not caught him in a fib after all. He had a fine voice. He had removed his hat, and his hair was mussed into a sandy storm. Relaxed, the edge off, he looked more his age, a hard-tested young man. She saw much to admire in him. Given time, she might grow to care for him.

Given time? Ha. She was utterly taken with the man.

Then she remembered that he was a soldier, and too soon he had to go away, back to the killing. Time was short.

And she recalled his wild charge, one man against three, all for the sake of a stranger.

The next fight would likely be in defense of his home and family. How reckless would he be then, a man likely to act on his convictions?

If she had any sense she would leave before she got too attached.

Chapter Three

Blake took the next morning off, having convinced himself that the Confederacy would not fall as a direct consequence. He reported the events of the previous day to the civilian authorities. They took him at his word, allowed as how there had been trouble with such human rodents lately and didn't seem to mind that he had exterminated one of them. The sheriff promised to send a crew to dispose of the body.

That chore accomplished, he walked Judith to the post office and tacked up a recruiting poster he had picked up at headquarters.

A forlorn hope. Nobody had to read a sign to know that every able-bodied man must rise to South Carolina's defense. The word was in every mouth, on every newspaper, in every barroom. It came by way of refugees and retreating soldiers bringing tales of brutality and destruction. It even seemed to hang in the wind.

Sherman is coming.

Last night he had managed to forget the danger for a little while. Judith had played just about every song he knew. She was warm and attentive, and he felt a touch of guilt that he had put Sally out of his thoughts for a little while. After he turned in, he slept little knowing that Judith was in the next room.

She seemed to be recovering from her ordeal. Today she smiled easier, and the bruise on her chin didn't show as much.

She had made a notice soliciting other parties who wanted to caravan toward Fayetteville. He started to post it on the wall, then lowered it and let it dangle between thumb and forefinger.

"You can stay with us as long as you like."

"Not forever, not as a guest." She tilted her head to one side.

"But it's liable to take a few days to raise a traveling party."

"Good. I'll post it where nobody can see it."

She snatched at the notice, laughing. "Don't you dare, you scoundrel."

He shrugged and tacked it up. "What does it matter? Nobody will look at anything this close to a recruiting poster."

~ * ~

Judith strolled with Blake to the grocery and general merchandise store a few doors down. He introduced her to the owner, Mr. Frank, whose son was a sergeant in his troop. Mrs. Frank had the worn look of a woman who uses her imagination mostly to worry.

The place smelled musty, of feed and croaker sacks. Judith picked over the scanty goods strategically spread on the shelves. She found little to buy, and the city prices were an outrage.

She touched a bolt of light blue calico, lingering by it. She longed to replace one of her worn-out dresses. But even the ordinary cotton material was prohibitive, probably off a blockade runner. "Look at that," she said to Blake. "Scandalous. Who can pay that much?"

"Did you want to buy it?"

She turned away from the fabric and picked up a bag of dried apples. "These ought to travel pretty well."

"I wish you would quit talking travel."

"I will when I am somewhere safe."

She looked at a two dollar per pound price tag tacked to an empty shelf marked "SOAP". She could make it for practically nothing, sell it here and make a profit. But she dared not tell him how often she had perspired over hot lye to support herself. Then he would know how desperately poor she was.

She handed Mr. Frank three dollars in Georgia shinplasters. He pursed his lips, laid the bills down on the counter, and rubbed his hands across his smudgy grocer's apron. "Haven't you silver, or at least South Carolina money?"

"Why? This is perfectly good."

Blake leaned over the counter. "What's the matter?"

"Georgia currency." Mr. Frank shrugged. "That place is a shambles, you know."

She stared at the dried fruit and the money she had laid beside it.

It had never occurred to her that her money might not be good here. Was there never going to be an end to her string of disasters?

Blake reached into his pocket. "Never mind. I'll pay for them."

"No. I won't let you do any such thing." Judith picked up her worthless currency. At least it would make good tinder. What did she have that she was willing to give up for trade besides the horse and revolver?

Blake dug out a wad of cash. "I want to."

"Really. I couldn't take your money."

Mr. Frank held up his hands, laughing. "Enough. For you, madam, since you are a friend of my boy's captain, I will accept your Georgia money."

Grateful, she handed over the bills once again.

After they left the store Blake said, "You should have let me buy them for you."

"Your connections were enough. I never noticed how much they mattered until I lost them."

"Don't you have anything but Georgia notes?"

"Nobody else has given me trouble about it."

"Things are liable to get tighter. What are you going to do then?"

Drat. Her poverty was an open topic, thanks to the storekeeper. "I just didn't want to spend my silver yet."

"Prices might be better in the country. I was going to ride up Dent's Mill way to pick up some provisions for Mama. Come along with me. It'll be proper enough. We'll have Chloe pack us a lunch and we should be back before dark."

She hesitated. "Bushwhackers?"

"Are you afraid? I wouldn't blame you."

"Not with you there." His confidence reflected in her eyes.

~ * ~

Blake entered the crowded shed to fetch the mule, which was sharing a stall with the family cow. In the adjoining compartment, the deserter's wounded horse rolled its eyes and backed up until its rear bumped into the far wall. Earlier this morning he had used a twitch to control the horse while his father washed and examined the pellet holes on its neck.

"Haven't forgiven me yet, have you?" He offered it a handful of corn. The horse warily extended its head and took a few grains, the warm breath sweet on his hand. The wounds were draining but didn't smell foul.

"You'll be all right." He lifted his hand to pat the horse, but it snorted and threw back its head so violently its forelegs lifted off the ground, then it whirled into the corner.

"Head-shy. That bastard liked to punch you, didn't he?"

Magic stuck her head over the rails, and he paused to rub her muzzle. He was thankful she had survived the fighting, the harsh Virginia winter and the scarcity of food. She was skinny, but in tolerable condition. He had worked hard to keep her that way, buying and begging fodder wherever he could, keeping her hooves dry on boards he had foraged. It was good to have her stabled in clean-smelling quarters.

"Don't look at me like that. You get today off to hang around and fatten up. Before long we'll be so busy you will wish you were back in your nice warm stall."

He looked from Magic to the mule and noted the contrast-- Magic's clean limbs, high head and tall grace inherited from her thoroughbred sire, next to the knobby kneed, dumpy, long-eared mule.

Judith had told him she had named the beast Fancy to give it a sense of pride. But a mule was still a mule no matter what she called it. Still, it looked sound enough. He gave Magic a final pat then snapped a lead to the mule's halter.

His sister sauntered in, looked over the railing and made kissing noises at the wounded horse. She rested her chin on the top board. "I want to keep him. Lightning is so old, and he's Papa's horse anyway."

Blake shook his head. "The cavalry needs him more than you do. Besides, he's so spooky he's liable to hurt you."

"Aren't you afraid he'll hurt one of your boys?" She extended her hand to the horse. To Blake's surprise, the animal let her stroke its muzzle.

"They don't ride sidesaddle." He led Fancy outside.

Lexi followed him. "I'll have you know I ride straddle, brother dear."

"Not very ladylike."

"Who wants to be a lady? Ladies don't have any fun. They don't get to do anything." She crossed her arms, lifted her chin and leaned against the wall of the shed. "What you doing?"

He slid the bit into the mule's mouth. "I'm taking Judith out to Dent's Mill."

"Good. It's boring around here. I'll go with you."

"You will have to be bored."

Lexi grinned. "Got a new sweetheart?"

He gave her a sharp look. "You got any of your own business to mind?"

"Some of yours, if you want to know about it." She grinned wider, tantalizing him.

"Lexi, don't play games."

"Sally's mother came calling while you were out."

Hope fluttered in his chest. "What did she want?"

"She made an announcement. You won't like it much."

The fluttering stilled. "Out with it, little sister."

"Sally is getting married to that Randolph fellow in just two weeks."

He rested his hand on the mule's withers and gripped a handful of stiff mane. Couldn't Sally stick the knife in any deeper?

Lexi's wild laugh interrupted his thoughts before he could feel too sorry for himself. "Ain't he the prettiest thing you ever did see? Top hat, patent leather boots, riding crop. Like he knows how to ride."

Blake smiled grimly "I would love to recruit him."

"You mean you would love to get him killed off."

"Not a bad idea."

Lexi glanced at the holster on his belt and grinned. "Why don't you just call him out and shoot him?"

"Tempting, but not practical. Wouldn't Sally love me for shooting her new beau!"

"She'd be thrilled to see somebody die for her sake."

"Lexi, that's mean."

"It's all right with me if she marries Randolph. I never did want her for a sister in law."

"I can't allow it." He dropped the bit back out of the mule's

27

mouth. "I'm going to go see her, right now. Tell Judith I'll take her to Dent's Mill whenever I get back. Just tell her I have some business to see to."

"Sure, leave it to me." Lexi rolled her eyes. "Why can't you let it go? Sally's done with you."

"We'll see about that."

"I used to think you had good sense, big brother."

~ * ~

Judith went to the kitchen to ask the cook to pack them a lunch as Blake had suggested, and found Mrs. Winberry seated at the little worktable conferring with the servant.

Judith greeted Blake's mother, nodded at the cook, and said, "Blake wants to go a little ways out of town so we can buy provisions. What would you like for us to look for?"

"Chloe?" Blake's mother turned to the cook. "Perhaps it would be simpler to tell Mrs. Rogers what we don't need."

The wiry, tea-colored cook answered immediately. "We got plenty rice, Ma'am. Field peas, sassafras root and sorghum. We got greens and sweet potatoes in the garden. Whatever else y'all can find, I can cook for sure."

It was reassuring to know they were that far away from starvation.

Mrs. Winberry gave Judith a weary smile. "It's been getting worse lately. This war…" She trailed off, shaking her head.

Judith could have finished the statement for her. The war was ruining their lives, smashing their dreams, killing their hopes along with their loved ones. But nobody needed to voice the obvious. "If it's not too much trouble, Blake wanted us to pack a little something for lunch. Do you have any of those corn biscuits left over from breakfast?"

"Yes, Ma'am. I'll see what I can scare up." Chloe got up and moved to the pantry. "We got peach preserves from our own trees."

Lexi appeared in the doorway, crossed her arms and leaned her shoulder against the doorsill. "Mrs. Rogers, Blake wanted me to tell you he's going to be late."

"I wish you would call me Judith. How much longer did he say he would be?"

Lexi shrugged. "No telling. He went to see Sally."

"That Sally has been leading that poor boy around by the nose since he was nothing but a baby," Chloe snorted as she wrapped the biscuits in a white finger towel.

"I don't know what he expects to accomplish," Mrs. Winberry said. "She's getting married in two weeks."

"Maybe he'll shoot Mr. Randolph." Lexi grinned.

"Don't even joke about such a thing!" her mother snapped.

"Why not? He wouldn't be any loss, except to Sally. She thinks she's found a gold mine. He bought up all those dry goods when they were cheap, and he's been selling them off little by little as the prices go up. He stands to make a fortune, and he'll be able to keep Sally in fine style."

"He's a speculator?" Judith asked.

"So is Sally, in her own way. She dropped Blake the minute she found old Randolph, and I'm glad she did." Lexi thumped her hand over her heart dramatically and feigned a swoon. "But he's sooo heartbroken!"

Judith pressed her hand over her mouth to hide a grin, but Chloe laughed out loud and Mrs. Winberry appeared to be struggling to keep a straight face.

"I take it Sally isn't popular in this household," Judith ventured.

"Not to be unkind, nor to make light of Blake's discontent," Mrs. Winberry said, "We all think he's better off without her. The best thing for him would be a clean break and to forget about that girl."

"He's a fine man," Judith said. "I shouldn't think it would be difficult for him to start over with someone else."

Mrs. Winberry gave her a speculative look that wasn't friendly, and Judith realized she had said too much. She had not meant to imply that she wanted to be that someone else. Nor had she meant to stir his mother's protective instincts.

She glanced at Lexi, whose grin had broadened.

Chloe thumped a wicker basket onto the counter. "Here's your picnic lunch. It's ready whenever Master Blake finishes his business with Miss Sally."

"Thank you, Chloe." Judith picked up the basket. "I think I'll wait on the front porch. It's such a lovely day out." She tried to make her retreat an orderly one.

~ * ~

Blake hustled Magic into a blood-warming trot, weaving through the traffic. Sally's house was located at the northeast end of town, not too far to walk under less urgent circumstances.

Through all that long, bloody summer in Virginia, knowing she was home waiting was all that sustained him. Then came that letter breaking their engagement, a blow to the gut.

His orders back to South Carolina came just in time, so he thought. He came home determined to straighten things out and get her to marry him right away. That was before he knew about Randolph.

In two weeks Sally would be sleeping with the bastard. Before Blake left for Virginia last May, he had taken her. Just that once, when her mother was asleep upstairs. A goodbye present. Both of them were fevered and apprehensive, but they figured it out.

He had fearfully searched each of her letters for weeks after that, for a hint that he'd planted something in her. She would have married him then, and the gossip wouldn't have lasted long. Everybody loosened up with the war going on, even good girls like Sally. She'd be due right about now and he would live on through son or daughter in case the Yankees killed him. But nothing had come of it. Nothing at all.

Mrs. Dubose answered the door but did not appear glad to see him. "What do you want, Blake?"

"Is Sally home? I would like to speak to her."

Mrs. Dubose watched him guardedly. "I wish you'd tell me what you want of her."

He took a deep breath and tried to be tactful, even if it meant a lie. "I heard some news about her and Randolph. I came to offer my congratulations."

Mrs. Dubose brightened. "Why, yes. They're getting married two weeks from Saturday. And I'm so fond of him. Such a darling young man, so thoughtful. He always brings the most precious gifts."

Suddenly aware of his empty hands, Blake felt awkward, as though he had failed some test. He had rushed here, didn't even stop to pick up a bauble or a sweet for the ladies who were so important to him. Nor did he have a plan, or rehearsed arguments, just his raw longing and blasted hopes to bare before Sally one more time.

He shifted on his feet. "Would you please tell her I'm here?"

"Certainly." Her tone was friendlier. "Wait right there, Blake." Mrs. Dubose disappeared up the stairway. He looked around the interior of the house, at the couch where he had sat with Sally so often. The same place they had made love.

He heard Sally's voice, excited and happy. Then she appeared at the top of the stairs, holding onto the railing, looking down at him. "Oh, Blake! What a lovely surprise!" Her eyes a lustrous jade, lips parted in a dazzling smile. Her creamy complexion carefully protected from the sun's exposure. Full breasts, tiny waist set off by a flaring skirt. The sight of her affected him as it always did, holding him spellbound.

He let out his breath and said, "Sal, you are a beautiful sight."

She laughed gaily and glided down the stairs, strawberry blonde sausage curls springing. Thank God, she was glad to see him. She couldn't possibly be serious about marrying Randolph.

He met her at the bottom and held out his hand for her to catch. The light pressure of her fingers triggered a tickle of wanting. She brushed closer, skirts rustling. He clasped her hand in both of his and brought it to his lips. Oh, God, how he wanted her.

"You sweet thing," she breathed, her voice low. "Mother says you were good enough to come pay your respects."

"We need to talk, privately."

She ran the tip of her tongue over her upper lip and looked around. "Mother is still upstairs. We can go to the front porch. Nobody will overhear us there."

He led her out the door and faced her. "I heard you're marrying Randolph. Tell me it's a lie."

She gripped his hands, cheeks aglow. "I'm truly sorry you're so upset about this."

"Do you love him, Sally?"

"Not the same way I love you, dear Blake."

His hopes rushed upward. "Then don't do it. Marry me instead."

She sighed, dropped her gaze, and shook her head sorrowfully. "No. I'm going to marry Mr. Randolph. I promised." Then she raised her face to his, lips twisted into a crooked smile. "I hope it doesn't break your heart too bad."

"Why are you doing this, Sal?"

"Lots of reasons. I'll never see his name on a casualty list, for one. And Mr. Randolph is, well, established--"

"He's a stinking profiteer."

She laid her fingertip over his lips to shush him. "--a very clever man."

"I suppose doing my duty makes me not so clever."

She laughed. "Mr. Duty and Honor. You'll remember I tried to get you to resign your commission--"

"Damn it, Sally. You know that's impossible."

"Hush! Watch your language, dear. Here comes Mr. Randolph into the yard now."

Sally edged away, and Blake turned to face the enemy. Randolph strutted toward the porch, frowning. His soft body was stuffed into a broadcloth suit, ferocious moustaches covered his mouth, cheeks pink and fresh-shaved.

Blake forced a tight smile, hating him. "Hey, Randolph." Then he winked, letting hostility fly. "Done any good speculating lately?"

Randolph paused at the foot of the porch steps and drew himself straight. He threw Sally a questioning glance, then glared back at Blake, scowling. Measuring him? Maybe the bastard would call him out and he'd have an excuse for the murder he'd cheerfully commit.

But if Randolph was inclined to take insult, he prudently buried the impulse in studied politeness. "I don't believe we've been introduced, sir."

Blake hooked both thumbs on his gun belt. "Sal and I are old friends. And I've been admiring you from afar. Nice duds."

Sally coughed into her hand, but didn't mask the laughter in her eyes. "Blake, don't be such a beast. Mr. Randolph, this is Captain Winberry. We grew up together."

Randolph climbed up the steps and extended his hand stiffly, a flaccid grip. "To what, sir, do we owe the pleasure?"

Sally said, "Captain Winberry came to pay his respects and offer us congratulations."

Randolph inclined his head. "How nice."

"Know what?" Blake smiled, showing his teeth. "There's an opening in my troop. You can join the cavalry. Help us lick Sherman, protect our homes and our people."

"I don't own a horse." Randolph shrugged complacently. "Besides, I'm exempt. I am employed by the state."

Blake ran his gaze down Randolph's soft body. "No matter. We even let cripples in the cavalry. General Butler himself lacks a foot. Doesn't look like your leg's broke, and I've got just the horse for you. Gentle as a lamb, and not a skittish bone in his body."

With any luck, the crazy animal would kill him.

Randolph said in an affable voice, "A kind offer, but I must decline." He turned to Sally, dismissing Blake. "My dear, are you ready to go?"

She sighed. "It's so much fun seeing how well y'all are getting along." Then she snuggled up to Randolph and kissed his cheek, saying, "Come on inside and wait for me."

She slipped her hand under Randolph's arm, glanced over her shoulder at Blake, smiled, and waggled her fingers goodbye. "I'll be sure to send you a wedding invitation, Captain Winberry. See you then."

Blake stood still for a moment, staring at the closed door. Then he squared his shoulders, turned and left the Dubose home, knowing in his soul he was beaten.

Randolph would go on making a fortune off the war while Blake faced the bullets. Then for years to come, Sally would bear Randolph's children instead of his.

Most likely he'd be rotting in an unknown ditch by then, leaving nothing behind but an empty chair at the family table, a second spare bedroom, and a likeness of him posing with his also-late brother in their Hampton Legion uniforms.

Chapter Four

Judith rested in the rocking chair, enjoying the view of the quiet street. Down the block two small boys were running with an energetic dog at their heels. She closed her eyes, listened to the barking and laughter and relished the illusion of safety. Sitting here in the soft winter sunshine, she could almost make herself believe she was safe from the war.

Her hosts were good people and had made her welcome. This clean and comfortable home had the feel of sanctuary. Perhaps she should tarry a while, as Blake had invited. Although he had put off their excursion and gone to see another woman, she recognized she had no claim on him. Complaining would be childish.

Eyes still shut, she pictured Blake, recalling the tact and consideration he had offered her. Sally was stupid, blind or both. Judging from what she had just heard, he would likely not be successful in winning the silly girl back. From what she had heard, he would probably be the only person in the household to regret it.

Scanning the street again, she spotted Blake riding back to the house. She watched his approach, glad to see him. The little catch in her throat surprised her.

Blake dismounted at the street and led his bay mare into the yard. By the time he had tethered the horse, she knew from the set of his shoulders and the defeat in his face that he had failed with Sally. She sensed his pain, and recognized a chance for her to repay Blake's kindness by offering him a sympathetic ear.

"I'm sorry for the delay." At the foot of the steps he stopped and faced her, hat dangling from his hand. He gave her a tentative look, as though unsure of his reception. "I had business to tend."

"It didn't go well?"

He regarded her thoughtfully. "Just exactly what did Lexi tell you?"

"That you're better off without Sally."

He tapped the hat against his thigh. "My sister… She would say that. She and Sally never did get along."

"Yesterday you told me you were detached. So, nothing has really changed, has it?"

"Sally has been avoiding me ever since I've been back. This morning she finally agreed to talk. And I met Randolph." He gave a short laugh. "I was tempted to shoot him, but I didn't."

"I admire your restraint." Judith smiled at him and gestured toward the basket. "I believe we were going somewhere."

He nodded, and she could have sworn he didn't look quite as lost as before. "I'll hitch your mule to the buggy. My mare isn't trained to pull."

Judith stood up, basket in hand. "I'll come with you."

~ * ~

Blake's notion that marrying Sally was a life-or-death matter subsided in Judith's company. Her dry humor and easy acceptance lifted him out of the worst of his despair. Although he'd known her for less than two days he was quickly coming to value her friendship.

Sally was as unlike Judith as a woman could be. Sally had constantly pushed and tested him, demanding his indulgence in matters small and large. Even after the heat of the lovemaking she had allowed him, he had sensed a certain calculation behind it. Judith, however, asked nothing of him, although he suspected her wants were just as great.

He freed Magic of the saddle and staked her to graze while Judith led Fancy from the stall. Blake walked over to help her harness the mule to the family buggy.

Judith rubbed the mule's neck while he buckled the straps. "I know Fancy isn't a stylish beast, but she always gets me there."

He paused to study Judith. Smiling and relaxed, her dark eyes alight, she did not seem at all conscious of her own beauty. It occurred to him that, if they happened to meet Sally on the street, his ex-lover would be more inclined to notice the young woman within the buggy than the creature in front of it. If the sight set Sally to wondering, so be it.

Judith met his gaze. "What is it?"

"I was admiring you."

She lifted an eyebrow. "Comparing me to my mule?"

Caught short, he blinked. Then he found himself smiling, something he had hardly believed he would ever do again. "Most favorably, I assure you."

She stood on her toes and whispered into the mule's ear, "Don't listen to him, Fancy. You're the best-looking mule I've ever seen."

"Let's get this magnificent animal moving, then." Blake handed Judith up into the buggy, savoring their brief contact. He swung himself onto the seat, shook the lines and urged Fancy down the drive and onto the road.

He watched for Sally on the way out of town, but did not see her. Being spared the sight of her with Randolph was a good thing.

He let the mule plod along lazily, which would make the trip last. Eventually they rolled past houses and businesses into fallow fields on either side of the road. If Judith was worried about encountering bushwhackers, she did not let it show. Blake took her lack of fear as a confidence in his ability to protect her.

He took advantage of the privacy, rested his free hand next to hers in companionable contact. She did not move hers away. He asked her about herself and her family, and her mood shifted into seriousness.

"I married George right after my father died. We always had an understanding, ever since we were little. Things were so simple and life chugged along like a locomotive as long as you stuck to the track."

"Right. And didn't get derailed," he added.

"Derailed. Exactly. You know how it is." She gripped his hand and he linked her fingers through his. "I must be boring you."

"Not at all. What about the rest of your folks? Are they behind Federal lines?"

"My stepmother and two sisters. My brother Richard was a lieutenant, First Tennessee. I was still in Atlanta last July, helping in a hospital. They took Richard out of that ambulance…" Her voice caught. "Two attendants lowered him to the ground. They weren't gentle about it, because he wasn't protesting. He had blood all over his mouth, his shirt, all dark over the hole in his belly."

She swallowed hard, and her hold on his hand tightened.

"Judith," he said softly, "I know what it's like. You don't have to--"

She kept on as though speaking of something that had to come out. "He even had blood from other men that had dripped onto his trousers. I said his name, but he didn't answer. I shook his shoulder, but he flopped like a doll. He was already gone. First George, then Richard." She inhaled, stifling a gasp, and covered her mouth. Tears welled in her eyes, and she looked down, blinking hard.

He let the mule find its own way down the road. He touched one of Judith's tears, took it onto his finger, stroked it away from her cheek. Bitter things. "I know. I was right next to my brother when he got killed. Held him while he took his last breath."

"I felt as though, if I'd been there, I could have saved him," she said.

He shook his head. "I couldn't save Justin."

"I'm sorry. It's hard to talk without--"

"You've earned the right. Grown men also weep." Blake had wept. He knew she would understand, and in that moment he loved her for it. He checked the mule so he could give Judith his full attention.

She murmured, "I'm such a bother. Thank you for being so good about it."

"You were saving up from yesterday," he said.

She nodded, regaining some of her composure. She gave him a damp smile. "I'm all right now. I don't want you to think I'm some weak and weepy female."

"You are beautiful and valiant."

"What a dear, sweet man you are." Her eyes shone with tears and sincerity.

He slipped his arm around her waist, wanting to console her, and she nestled against him. Her vulnerability touched him. Her warm weight gave him a good feeling, not Sally's lightning heat, but comfort, a rightness, as though she belonged there.

As he had the night before, he felt the urge to kiss her. Last night he had restrained himself, because she had tacitly shown him she would not welcome such boldness.

This time her face lifted to him and he bent his head lower. She parted her lips softly, accepting him. Sweetness and salt. Her hair smelled of lavender. Aroused, he drew her to him and her full, firm breasts crushed against his chest. He nuzzled and kissed the warm curve of her throat. He worked his lips down to the dip between her breasts, felt her breath catch, her fingers dig into his arm. God in heaven, did she want him, too?

She squirmed against him and gently pushed against his chest. "What are we doing, Blake?"

His breathing came deep. His physical and emotional needs were at the boiling point. With difficulty he forced himself to draw back.

Judith laughed softly. "I'd say you got over Sally right quick."

He stared at her, confused. Dry-eyed now, she reached into her purse, pulled out a handkerchief and wiped her still-damp cheeks. He envied her calm. "I'm sorry," he said. "I'm not trying to take advantage--"

"I would never think that of you." She rested her hand on his, still smiling, letting him know she was not offended. Letting him know she was open to his advances, provided he showed her proper respect. "Don't you think we'd better get Fancy moving again?"

He urged the mule forward, thinking about what he wanted, and it was not merely physical release. He had ached to marry Sally so she could provide him with a sense of permanence and the hope of continuation. He yearned for a woman to care for him and to help him keep his sanity in the aftermath of so much terror and killing.

Along came Judith, who knew how to touch his heart and heal it. He wanted desperately to keep her close. He did have something to offer her. A place to live was a start. Would not any woman in her situation want to give up her refugee status?

Could he survive two rejections in one day? He had felt less frightened over the prospect of battle than his endeavors with women. Apparently he was better at fighting than at making love.

Still, she had made it clear she was fond of him.

Was that enough?

~ * ~

Judith watched him pick up the reins with both hands, breaking the contact between them. Though she felt bereft, she should have put a stop to his advances more quickly. She was just getting herself in trouble, letting him start loving on her like that. No matter how much she wanted him to, she would have been a fool to let him continue.

She studied his finely chiseled profile, blurred by the short beard, liking the way he looked. Straight nose, sensitive lip line. Shoulders high, back straight, just like a soldier. To her that was his worst fault. These days, men had a way of going off and getting themselves killed. Columbia could be Atlanta all over again.

Just thinking about it threatened to bring fresh tears to her eyes. She hoped he wouldn't notice. Breaking down in front of him was bad form, and she must not do it again. To this end she confined her conversation with him to matters of small importance. He had pulled into himself, preoccupied, and she worried that her gentle rebuff had dampened his interest. Perhaps it had, if his only interest was getting her to lie down with him, but she did not believe he was that simple. Even for a man, and Lord knew they were simple creatures.

The trading post at Dent's Mill was a cabin at a crossroad that offered little more than the store in town, but the prices were slightly better. Blake purchased a side of bacon, a sack of Irish potatoes, and five pounds of light flour. Judith bought a little corn meal and a bag of pecans for herself, goods that would store indefinitely. She hoped she wouldn't have to leave Columbia and the Winberry home for a while, at least.

On the way back, Blake mentioned he knew a good place to stop for lunch. He turned off the road and down a secluded drive to an abandoned pecan grove. The trees were bare and the ground not too overgrown at the spot where he halted the mule and set the brake. He smiled, his gray eyes fixed steady on her face. "Hungry?"

"Famished." She reached for the wicker basket and set it on her lap.

"What did Chloe pack for us?" he asked.

She lifted the lid and examined the contents. "Those corn biscuits from breakfast, a smidgen of ham. Apples. Peach preserves."

He spread a blanket under a tree and she settled onto it. When he sat Indian-style next to her, she was aware of him watching her pick through the basket as she removed the food. She started to smear preserves on a biscuit. Glancing up, she met his eyes.

"You must be hungry." She handed him a biscuit. He took it without looking away from her face. She reached into the basket and got out an apple. She handed it to him and realized the hunger she saw in his face had nothing to do with the food. She looked away, her cheeks tingling.

Instead of eating, he watched her fix the next biscuit.

Hadn't the man ever seen anybody prepare lunch before? Was some part of her showing that was better left covered? "Is something bothering you, Blake?"

"I was just thinking."

"I wouldn't have believed thinking was such an effort for you." She bit into her biscuit, noting that he had not yet taken his first bite.

"We have to talk."

Talk was better than his acting on what she knew he wanted to do to her. What she secretly wanted him to do to her as well. She swallowed the bite of biscuit and waited.

"We're good for each other. Don't you think so?" he asked.

"You've certainly helped me," she agreed.

"What I mean is…" He took off his hat and rubbed his temple, looking lost. "We've been taking care of each other."

"It's been you solving my problems, Blake. What have I done for you?"

"Made me see that losing Sally isn't the worst thing that ever happened to me."

She was already sick and tired of that girl, even though she'd never met her. "Might be the best thing, from what I've heard."

"I want you to marry me," he said in a rush, as though it was something he had to get through.

"Us? Marry?" She stared at him. "Why, we are practically strangers."

"We understand each other too well to be strangers. There is already a great deal between us."

She shook her head, not believing. "Surely you mean after the war is over, if things go well enough. Don't you?"

He held his features controlled and tight, but she caught the flicker of desperation in his eyes. "That could be too late. I mean let's get married right away. Before I have to go back to the fighting."

Slowly she said, "You're not joking, are you, Blake?"

Now his eyes were pleading. "I am dead serious."

She wished he wouldn't have put it that way. "I need time. I have to think."

"I realize it's a little sudden," he gave her a tense smile. "Think of the advantages. You will have family, a place to live--"

"There's always my aunt in Fayetteville." She shook her head. "You certainly move fast. One day we meet, the next day you're--"

"I know what I want when I see it." His voice softened. "The present moment is all either one of us can be sure of, and together we can make the best of it."

She swallowed past her dry throat, wishing she could think more clearly. She tried to come up with objections, why she shouldn't agree to marry him. Of course, she hardly knew him. Because he was a soldier, the grim possibility existed that she would never get to know him well.

On the other hand, his offer would solve most of her immediate problems. What would she have to sacrifice for the commitment he was asking? She could think of nothing besides a compromise of freedom, and considering her circumstances, freedom held few advantages.

If she married him, she would have a home and she wouldn't have to depend upon her own precarious means of support. He had shown himself to be a generous man, willing to share.

He would share his bed with her, too. She considered his taut good looks, how delicious his arms had felt holding her tight against him and how that kiss had stirred her to her core. Lying with him would be no sacrifice at all.

She reached out and touched his cheek, stroking fingertips tenderly downward through his beard, the vital look and feel of him driving out the dark thoughts and fears. He wanted to marry her. Cherish and protect her. How could life possibly turn around so fast? She was almost afraid to breathe, afraid she'd wake up and he'd be gone, just like everybody else. Everyone she had ever cared about.

"Dear Blake, how could I refuse you anything?"

His features relaxed into a smile. He took her hand in both of his, brought it to his lips and kissed it. "You honor me."

~ * ~

Hunter Lightfoot and his fellow scout, J. C. Cooper, spent the morning on the Federal fringes, disguised in blue uniforms. They amused themselves watching supply wagons bog down in the muck. No wonder this part of South Carolina was called the low country. It was nothing but scrubby trees, rice fields and swamps.

He sure wasn't getting much accomplished. Last night he and J. C. had sneaked into a Yankee camp and had listened to the men bragging about how they'd outflanked the Confederates at the Salkehatchie. But none of them knew where they were headed, although they offered enough theories. Charleston, or Augusta, or Columbia, but no information definite enough to send up the courier line to General Hampton.

Hunter had to learn to stalk different Yankee commanders, corps and regiments since coming south with Wade Hampton and Butler's Division. But he'd always been a quick study. Besides that, if he stayed in Virginia he would be working for that pompous ass Fitz Lee. And he couldn't ever go back to Mosby's battalion. Not after what happened.

Down here, most likely he would not run across any more Maryland relatives who were fighting for the North. He'd like to forget, but he never would, all his days.

His empty stomach turned his attention to the mundane. "Let's go find some grub, J. C."

"About damn time, Lieutenant."

Hunter overlooked the insubordinate tone--an independent streak came with the best of the scouting breed. He took a bridle path toward friendly lines. Soon he came to a log house. Smoke drifted from one of the chimneys. "Somebody is home," he told J. C.

The scouts hid their horses in the woods and walked to the house. Hunter glanced into the window, but a curtain blocked his view. He knocked at the door. A woman opened it a crack, took one look at his Union blue coat and tried to slam it shut. But he was ready for that and forced the door wide. "We don't mean you any harm, ma'am, but we are coming in."

She backed away. Let her think they were Yankees. What she didn't know she couldn't tell anybody.

The house was dark like a cave, spare of furniture, warm, and smelled of baking sweet potatoes and corn bread. They had come at the right time. Three tow-headed children stared at him. The smallest wiped his runny nose.

Hunter took off his hat and bowed to the woman, now that he could afford to be polite. "We'd like something to eat. We don't mind paying for it."

She made the oldest child take the rest of her litter somewhere to the back of the house and rushed to get food. Hunter sat down at a rough oak table in the front room, facing the outside door. He pulled out his pipe and stuffed tobacco into the bowl.

He had plenty of time for a good smoke. Eventually the woman brought their plates and scurried back into the kitchen. He lifted a steamy bite of sweet potato to his mouth then held it still, listening. Horses.

"Who's that?" He set the forkful down uneaten.

J. C. tipped the edge of the curtain and peeked out. "Two Yanks. Should I take 'em now?"

"Just two?"

"That's all. Coming up like they own the place."

"Nothing to it." Hunter smiled. "I want them in talking condition. Let's get the drop on them as they come in."

J. C. stationed himself by the door, revolver ready. Hunter kept his seat at the table and held his two Navy pistols out of sight under it.

The Yankees probably wouldn't bother to knock. They didn't. The door crashed open and two men stomped in. J. C. jabbed his weapon toward the nearer man's head and Hunter showed his pistols. "Put up your hands."

They froze, eyes wide.

"Now!"

The hands flew up.

Hunter relaxed, just a little. "Smart boys. Didn't make us get blood all over the nice clean floor."

The woman started into the room, then hesitated, open-mouthed, shock on her face. Hunter said, "Lady, go to the back and stay there until I say different. J. C., get their guns."

He stood up, moved around the table and strode closer to his prisoners, pistols pointed toward their chests. Their eyes were round with fear. Good. Keep them frightened and they'd be easier to control.

The taller one asked, "What are you going to do with us?"

"That depends. Do you want to live?"

"I do."

"Tell us everything we want to know, then we'll send you into our lines. Alive."

They looked at each other. Better interrogate them separately. Hunter said, "Cause us any trouble, any trouble at all, and it'll be your last act on earth. Got it?"

The taller one had gone pale. "I got it."

"Lie down on the floor. Face down. Are you expecting any friends?"

"No, damn it all," the stocky Yankee said.

"Better hope nobody shows up. We'd shoot you first then take care of the others. J. C., go through them."

J. C. piled the contents of their pockets on the table and rifled through their wallets. Then he let out a whoop.

"What did you find?" Hunter kept his attention on his prisoners.

"Federal money, but that's not the best thing. Passes, Lieutenant. They got passes, signed by Major General Judson Kilpatrick, no less."

Hunter smiled again. He had plenty of use for passes signed by Sherman's cavalry chief. They would reproduce into good counterfeits, too. What a capture. It almost made up for his recent frustrations. Passes, two horses complete with equipment, weapons, and ammo. And prisoners, probably scouts or couriers who knew a useful thing or two.

"Very good, boys." He sat down at the table, picked a U. S. dollar out of the loot and laid it aside to pay the woman for their food. He was always careful about such amenities--the legal training. "Now lie very still while we eat. I don't want to take the time to shoot you. My dinner would get cold."

After they returned to Columbia, Blake bought the calico cloth Judith had coveted and she selected bone buttons and factory thread that wouldn't break in his mother's sewing machine. They posed for a Daguerreotype and ordered three prints. He spent freely, saying he was flush, having drawn several months' back pay before he left Virginia. Besides, Mr. Frank gave him a discount. They conferred with the pastor of Blake's church, and he reluctantly agreed to perform the hasty ceremony.

Judith entered the study, hand in hand with him, and found his mother sitting at a desk, writing in a journal. The older woman looked up and smiled, then her expression went guarded. What did Blake's mother see in their faces?

His mother said, "Blake. Mrs. Rogers. Did you find what you needed at Dent's Mill?"

"I left it in the kitchen with Chloe," Blake said.

Judith felt him shift from one foot to another. "Mama, Judith has decided to stay on with us."

His mother's brow etched deeper but she said politely. "Stay as long as you'd like, Mrs. Rogers."

Judith gripped his hand. Wouldn't his mother have a conniption when he told her they were getting married?

Blake glanced around the room. "Where's Papa? Is he back from the hospital yet?"

"He doesn't usually come home until six or so."

"We'll just tell him when he gets back." He pulled himself straight. "Mama, Judith and I are getting married."

"Married?" His mother's mouth stayed open.

"Right away. In a couple of days."

Mrs. Winberry closed her mouth and shot Judith a sharp look. No doubt questioning what evil she'd done to her innocent boy on the way to Dent's Mill. Ha. It had taken all the persuasion and tact she could muster to keep him from consummating their plans on the spot.

Mrs. Winberry cleared her throat. "So soon?"

"We have to get it done before my troop is sent down state," Blake said.

His mother sat up in the chair and pointed to the sofa. "Sit, both of you."

Judith sat. Mrs. Winberry looked right through her. Judith held her head high, returning her gaze. His family's disapproval was one complication she hadn't considered.

"This certainly is sudden. Unheard of. It's hardly proper. Scandalous. People are going to talk--"

"Let them talk." Had he really expected his mother to be delighted? "Mama, I don't have much time."

"On the contrary, you have plenty of time. You're very young."

"It's settled. Please, Mama." His tone was firm, matter of fact. "You might as well accept Judith as your daughter, because that's the way it's going to be."

Mrs. Winberry leaned back, speechless. Though uneasy, Judith felt a thrill of gratitude that Blake continued to fight for her.

~ * ~

That night, after taking care of business at the courthouse and parsonage, Blake walked into the study and sat across the desk from his father.

Unlike most contract surgeons, Dr. Winberry wore a plain black civilian coat instead of an officer's uniform. He wasn't much on decoration and ceremony. Blake counted on Papa's unconcern for the earthbound to work in his favor.

Mama must have gotten to him first. Papa gave him a disappointed look, reminding him of that day almost four years ago when he'd announced that he was dropping out of college to join Hampton's Legion. And before that, when he'd told Papa he didn't have the stomach to be a doctor.

But he wasn't about to back out on his promise to marry Judith, no matter what objections his family offered. She was warm and giving and let him know she cared for him, and he was glad to provide her support.

With any luck, he'd also provide her with the beginnings of a child before he had to leave for the front.

"Son, what has gotten into you? This Mrs. Rogers is practically a foreigner."

Blake smiled, hoping it was disarming enough. "Thanks for doctoring that horse. He's already healing up."

"The horse? Good." Sidetracked, his father took on the pleased, absent look he got whenever he discussed his main passion. "I'm afraid it was impossible to remove the shot. It is embedded in the muscle and luckily missed the arteries, esophagus and trachea. I'm sure he'll recover and I hope the metal causes no problems." He looked off. "If only all my patients were so uncomplicated."

"I guess they keep you right busy down at the military hospital these days." Blake feigned interest. "Any unusual cases?"

"I should say. But not many fresh wounds. The men we treat are sent down from Virginia by rail to relieve the crowding up there. Mostly long-term convalescents."

Blake pretended to pay attention to another dissertation on the horrifying variety of wounds and disease his father treated. When he was a boy he had accompanied his father on his rounds. Papa planned for him to apprentice and follow up with medical school in Charleston. That didn't work out. What good was a queasy healer? Odd--now that he inflicted pain more often than he succored it, grisly sights affected him hardly at all.

Papa trailed off and shook his head. "Son, what about this young widow?"

Blake grinned. "Isn't she fine?"

"I hope your disappointment with Sally hasn't clouded your judgment."

"Sally who?"

"Don't be flippant. This is a serious matter. Surely Reverend Reynolds wouldn't go along with--"

"He's agreed to waive the banns and marry us day after tomorrow. I gave him to understand if he wouldn't we'd find somebody who will."

"Mrs. Rogers seems to be down on her fortunes. Are you not concerned that she wishes to marry you for pecuniary reasons?"

"I'm not rich, but I don't expect you to support her. All I ask is that she be allowed to move into my room afterward."

"Of course you haven't known her long enough to get her in trouble. Have--?"

"Sir, I won't dignify that with an answer." Blake stood and leaned forward, bracing his hands against the desktop. "She is a lady, and you will treat her like one."

His father frowned and took a long time to answer. "Son, you're being rash. Give this time."

"That's how I'm supposed to do things. Goes with my line of work."

"You haven't been yourself since you returned from Virginia."

"That's right, sir. I'm a whole new man." Blake forced himself to smile. "I cuss and lust and kill people."

"Son, son. Let's pray about this."

"Fine. Let's pray. I suppose it is possible God hasn't renounced me entirely." He sat down. "Papa, I am going to do this--with or without anybody's blessing."

~ * ~

The next morning, hugging her shawl around her shoulders, Judith stood inside the stable watching Blake saddle his mare. "I'll be gone overnight," he was saying. "Stay over with my ex-captain, Mr. Hughes, for convenience. Anyhow, I'll be back in time for the formalities."

She had known all along what situation she was accepting. He was bound by duty and it was her duty to support his endeavors. Her safety was tied to the army's success in repelling Sherman's hordes. His success in gathering reinforcements was part of that effort. Besides, she believed the more men he could surround himself with, the safer he would be.

She realized they had stolen the time he had taken with her yesterday and he could afford no more dalliance, though she was going to be lonesome without him. "I'll miss you," she told him.

"Everything is arranged, is it not?" He kneed Magic in the belly and hauled up on the girth strap.

"I suppose. Your mother is making all the plans." Not

enthusiastically.

He buckled the cinch. "Then all I have to do is show up tomorrow afternoon."

She punched him lightly on the arm. "You better show up."

He grinned at her. "Are you forgetting this was my idea?"

She let her hand rest on his arm, enjoying the firm muscular feel of him under the coat sleeve, wanting him to understand she would be ready for him when the time was right. "We do need to get to know each other better."

"If I stay around here we sure will, sooner than we agreed." He slipped his arms around her waist and pulled her to him. She kissed him lightly and broke off.

"Come back here," he murmured.

She shook her head, smiling. "It wouldn't be fair to send you off in a state."

He grinned back, real affection in his eyes along with desire. "You already have me in a state. We could make this straw floor our marital bed."

Laughing, she punched him on the arm again. "I love you, Blake, I really do."

She expected him to make his own declaration. Instead, he said, "You are really making it difficult for me to leave."

"I'll still be here tomorrow," she assured him.

"That thought will sustain me." He let go of her, gathered the reins and led his horse outside, where he swung lightly into the saddle. He turned back toward Judith and threw her a salute. She lifted her hand and blew him another kiss. He urged Magic into a trot, through the gate and onto the road. She watched his back until he rode out of sight.

~ * ~

Blake rode up Richardson Street to catch Two Notch Road toward Camden. He spotted Sally walking along the sidewalk toward him, arm in arm with that damned Randolph. He slowed Magic and reined in close. Wouldn't hurt to tell her the news.

Her burgundy velvet dress looked new, and so did Randolph's tailored black coat and trousers. With such new clothes, they must be the best-dressed couple in Columbia. She turned to him and he caught his breath, still aching at the sight of her, despite his realization that he didn't need her any more.

Randolph just scowled.

"Congratulate me." Blake drew himself up in the saddle. "I'm getting married tomorrow night."

Sally's mouth formed a pout. "Married! You?" Then she put on a smile. "What a surprise. Anybody I know?"

He shook his head. "She's new in town."

"A refugee?"

"A very beautiful, refined lady."

Sally wrinkled her nose and laughed. "I'm sure."

What was she picturing? A desperate female who'd say yes to just anybody? This wasn't turning out to be quite as satisfying as he had anticipated.

Randolph said, "I congratulate you, sir. Now please excuse us, we must be going."

Blake nodded curtly and watched them go by. After they passed, he headed Magic away from the sidewalk and continued on his way.

Sally's implied slur on Judith offended his sense of fairness. Judith hadn't lost her home through any fault of hers. Sally ought to try refugeeing and see how she liked it.

He glanced over his shoulder for a last look, but Sally was gone.

~ * ~

Judith returned to her room, then picked up the new picture and studied their images. She sat in a chair with Blake standing behind her, earnest and protective. After tomorrow night, she would no longer be alone and adrift. The war had shifted her fortunes frequently and without warning but then, she wasn't used to having things improve.

The arrangement wasn't perfect. Stunned at how swiftly he'd proposed, Judith had accepted so quickly she'd even surprised herself. Also, his parents were only going along with the marriage because he was so adamant. She would do her best to earn their esteem.

Judith turned to more immediate problems, such as her limited wardrobe. She did not have enough time to make the new dress by tomorrow night. How could she wear mourning clothes to her own wedding? She opened one of her trunks and rummaged through it. She pulled out bits of cloth she'd saved, George's papers, a pair of his old socks, a pair of corduroy trousers.

She was relieved to lay her hand on the only dress that she hadn't dyed black, a yellow silk. It would do. Besides, it was time to put away her mourning clothes and get on with her life.

Still, she would not ever abandon her past. She looked over the other things she had brought from Tennessee, to Atlanta, and carried ever since. Silverware she'd inherited from her grandmother. Fine linens her mother gave her. A couple of shards of broken china and a smashed teacup. The fragments took up space and added weight to her wagon, but they were wedding gifts, they were hers, and she'd hang on to them forever. If she ever had to sell her silverware and what was left of her china so she could live, part of her would surely die.

She picked up a likeness of George and kissed it, her eyes stinging. Wherever he was, would he understand that saying yes to Blake wasn't a betrayal of his memory? But if he had not died she would not be in this fix, either.

A rap at the door made her jump. "Who is it?"

"Lexi. Can I come in?"

She set down the portrait. "Door's open."

Lexi strolled in and flopped into a chair. "I'm going to go help at the hospital this morning. Thought you would like to come along."

"I worked at a hospital before, in Atlanta."

"It's a sure way to Mama's heart." Lexi grinned, the only one of Judith's soon-to-be in-laws who wasn't fit to be tied over the sudden affair.

Judith sighed. "That's something I'd like to do. I'll go with you." She touched the blue calico that Blake had bought. "Do you think she'll let me use her sewing machine?"

"What are you making?"

"A dress for me, a shirt for Blake."

"She'd never refuse anything for her boy." Lexi laughed out loud. "Once you prove you aren't going to break the thing, she'll let you use it to make your dress too. See if I'm right."

"I won't break it."

"Mama always liked her boys. She should have been smart enough not to bother having a girl." Lexi bit her thumbnail again, then looked at it and picked at the ragged edge with her finger. "Ready to go? Of course, they won't let us do anything but write letters, read tracts, fluff pillows. Boring. Wish I could do what Papa does instead."

"Surgery? Cutting off legs and things?" Judith shuddered.

"Or else what Blake does. He's a hero. But he's the one who used to faint at the sight of blood. I roll bandages and knit socks and take piano lessons. See what I mean?"

"Doesn't sound so bad to me."

"Boring." Lexi reached into her bag and pulled out a gaudy orange book. "This time I'm bringing a story about an Indian princess who runs away with a frontiersman. I'm going to read it to the boys. Sure beats reading a religious tract. Don't tell Papa."

Judith flipped through it, glancing at the crude woodcut illustrations. "The Indian princess favors you. If you had dark hair--"

Lexi laughed. "You won't faint like Blake did, will you? And it doesn't smell too flowery in there either."

Judith slammed the book shut. "I'll have you know Blake is a hero. He didn't faint when he shot that renegade and saved me from a thousand deaths. And I know full well what hospitals are like."

Lexi surprised her with a wide grin. "Bravo, sister-in-law. You'll do."

~ * ~

At mid-morning Blake rode into the Hughes yard. The farm looked like failed prosperity: sagging fences, falling down buildings, fields in overgrowth. Quarters boarded up, vacant and hollow-eyed. Common knowledge had it Mr. Hughes was rich. Blake knew that was a lie. The old man had spent everything on the troop he had recruited, now Blake's command.

He called to the chuffing old watchdog that met him in the yard and knocked at the door. Mr. Hughes' light-skinned servant, Sam, greeted him like an old comrade. He still wore a cavalry private's uniform same as he did during the coastal service. Sam let him in and hurried to fetch the old man.

The inside of the house was much the same as the last time Blake had visited, plain but reasonably clean. Sam had always taken good care of both Mr. Hughes and his home. Blake paced around the sparsely furnished room, remembering. By the time their original enlistments expired in '62, he and his brother Justin realized they'd be privates forever if they stuck with the elite Hampton Legion. But they had ambition. They came home seasoned veterans from Virginia, bought horses with their bounty money, and helped Mr. Hughes raise a troop. They got their commissions, all right.

Mr. Hughes shuffled from the rear of the house. "Ho, Blake," he said, grinning. His shoulders rolled forward around his concave chest and his belly was paunchy despite his thinness. Dry skin stretched over knobby joints and stick limbs. Face long and gray, wispy white hair framing a high forehead. He sat down heavy, breathing hard. "I heard the boys was coming back, but I was feeling poorly and couldn't get out to meet the train t'other day."

Sam perched on the arm of a chair. As always, Blake noted the resemblance between the servant and his master, the forward set of Sam's eyes and the squareness of his chin. "It's just you two?"

"That's it. Sam, go fetch us that corn whiskey." Mr. Hughes's eyes glittered. "How was Virginia, my boy?"

"Between May and October, hardly got through a day without fighting. All the pressure on Richmond, Petersburg and the railroads."

"Glorious, weren't it? Better'n the coast, where we had more skeeters than Yankees to kill. Sorry I couldn't a joined the fun."

"It wasn't any oyster roast."

"Sorry about your brother." Mr. Hughes shook his head in sorrow.

"I was with him. He didn't seem to suffer much."

Sam poured whiskey from a ceramic jug into a mug and gave it to Blake. It tasted strong and raw. He swallowed and said, "We didn't have to fight as often after winter came, but that didn't make it easy. Cold hell. So cold pickets froze to death."

Mr. Hughes took a rasping breath, hanging on his words.

"Relieved a post one morning," Blake continued. "I thought--hoped--they were asleep. But they were stiff."

"Good lord."

"We had orders against fires, but we built them anyway on account of wanting to stay alive. Dead pickets don't do much guarding, unless you prop them up to fool the Yanks. Like scarecrows."

He smiled at his own brutal joke, but Mr. Hughes only stared at him. "You disobeyed orders?"

"Yanks zinged a little shot our way, punched a hole in my spider pan. Colonel Aiken called by. He warmed up by the fire. Afterwards he told me to put it out. I told him I'd just as soon be shot as freeze to death, but he didn't press charges."

Blake took another swallow of whiskey. Mr. Hughes was asking to be thrilled with tales of valor, but the ghosts of dead friends and his brother clung to him like cobwebs. He didn't wish to stir them up by speaking of them any longer. He shook off the weight of grief, coming back to the urgent present. "We need horses. I'm authorized to pay with government vouchers."

"Don't have nothing you'd want. All I got is a mule, only good for plowing."

"I brought my mare back with me, not everybody managed it."

"You better look out for bushwhackers," Mr. Hughes said.

"I know. I had to kill one."

"Did you now?" The old man sat up straight. "Ought to get a medal."

"Three of them, abusing a lady. Two got away. She said their names were Snipes and Bell. The one called Bell was wearing a Union coat. Look sharp for them."

"Sam wants me to let him carry a gun."

Sam leaned forward and their eyes met. Blake judged the resolution he saw there, and nodded. "He knows how to use one."

"Folks round here might object to a negro carrying a gun," Mr. Hughes said.

Blake nodded at Sam and turned back to Mr. Hughes. "To hell with them."

The old man shrugged and changed the subject. "The lady all right?"

"We're getting married tomorrow."

Mr. Hughes swatted him on the back. "Great God, boy. You don't waste no time."

Blake's face went hot. "My folks think I've lost my mind."

"Have you?" The old man grinned slyly.

"Just wait'll you see her. Come to the wedding. It'll be at the house tomorrow night."

"If I'm up to it, I'll be there."

"We need more men for the troop. Know any?"

Mr. Hughes considered, then said, "Try the Stewart place. The twins are sixteen, big strapping boys. Then there's Mrs. Caldwell's son, Jimmy. He's kind of a runt, but maybe he'll grow."

"Just what I need." Blake shook his head. "A mama's boy."

"You weren't but eighteen when you joined The Legion, nineteen when you made lieutenant."

"It's a different war than the one you remember."

"If you don't get them, somebody else will. Wish I could join up. Volunteered for the militia, but can't even keep up with that sorry outfit." Mr. Hughes' breathing became noisy again, eyes moist. "I always did want to go out game. Kill a few Yanks for me, will you, boy?"

Blake emptied his glass in a single gulp. If he took it fast, his mind would numb that much quicker. In the unlikely event he lived through this war, he would never speak of it again. Not to anyone. Give his memories the decent burial too many men didn't get.

He held out the glass to Sam for a refill and forced a laugh. "Say, you ever hear about the twenty-four hundred head of beef we rustled right out from under Grant's nose last fall?"

Next day, Blake turned his new recruits in to the sergeant major and reported to headquarters. Cold rain pattered on the tent and he sidestepped drips from the leaky roof. The last of the water slicked off his poncho onto his jeans but it didn't matter because they were already wet and clinging to his boot-tops.

The only staff officer on duty, Captain Causey, looked up from his desk and returned his salute. "Find any horseflesh, Winberry?"

"Six head. Three with riders."

"Anything promising?"

"Not especially. Sixteen-year-old twins. They think they're so hot the rain sizzles on 'em. And Jimmy Caldwell. A little boy with a pet pony."

Causey grimaced. "I hate to say it, but you have done better than most."

"Pitiful. Good thing Jimmy's mama isn't here to see her little darling's new home." Blake shook his head. "He cried, then I had to make the other boys lay off calling him names. After that, he stuck to me like I was his long-lost daddy." He shook his head again. "Any orders? I've requested tonight off. And tomorrow morning."

"What for?"

"It's personal."

Causey shot him a curious look and consulted a roster. "You're scheduled for Officer of the Day tomorrow. Report at five a.m. Nothing till then."

He had time for the ceremony and what came after, but not much time for sleep.

"Don't like it?" Causey smirked. "Take it up with General

Butler. I'm sure he would be delighted to discuss it."

"Very funny." Blake didn't smile. "Anything new? Where is Sherman headed?"

"There's been some fighting in the swamp country near the Georgia border. Sherman keeps getting by Hardee's defenses. But everybody thinks he'll bog down in the swamps with all this rain."

"When are we going to go down and hit him?"

"No telling. We aren't in fighting trim yet. Not enough remounts."

"Not enough anything."

Causey shrugged.

Blake continued, "But we aren't going to stop Sherman by sitting here and talking about it."

"Go get him, then. You're the one who's sizzling." Causey laughed. "You bucking for major?"

"I just want to do what's got to be done."

Blake went home, where his sister met him at the door. "About time you showed up. I thought you got scared and took off."

"I was busy saving civilization. Where's Judith?"

"In her room. You're not supposed to see her until the wedding. It's bad luck."

"Guess I don't need any of that." He stood in front of the fire and warmed his hands. Steam rose from his wet trousers. "You look nice, little sister."

"Judith's been working on me."

"What do you think of her?"

Lexi grinned. "I kind of like the idea of having a sister-in-law that takes shots at bushwhackers."

"You would. How's Mama doing?"

"She'll get over it. You can get away with just about anything 'cause you're a boy."

"I stopped to see Matt Kirkland and he asked about you. He's coming tonight. Best man."

"Best man?" She knitted her brows. "What's he good for?"

"Please, just be nice to him." He looked toward the kitchen. "I'm starved. Has Chloe got anything cooking?"

"She's scraped up enough ingredients for a wedding cake."

"That so?"

"I made up a dried flower arrangement."

"Fine." He nodded vacantly, glad the women were taking care of whatever details a wedding involved.

"That horse you brought home takes to me. I want to keep him."

He shook his head. "I need him for a remount."

"He doesn't like men. He likes me."

"I'm going to get something to eat."

He paused in the kitchen door, felt the delicious heat on his face. A loaf-shaped mound of yellow cake rested on the worktable in the middle of the room. Chloe bent over the stove and chucked in wood chips. She straightened, turned around and squinted at him. Her high cheek boned brown face, shiny from the fire, crinkled into a smile. "Bout time you be showing up, Mas' Blake."

"Mama hoping I'll get cold feet?"

Chloe's opaque look belied her smile. "I wouldn't know about none of that, honey."

"I'd like something to eat."

"You'll spoil your appetite."

He stared at the sweet mound atop the worktable. "That cake would be good."

"It's for your weddin'. You don't get no cake 'til tonight."

He laughed. "All right. It's your kitchen."

Chloe's smile broadened. She had always liked anybody acknowledging her domain.

He nodded toward a pitcher on the sideboard. "How about some of that buttermilk?"

"A little buttermilk won't hurt you none." Chloe reached for a glass and poured the thick white liquid from the pitcher.

He took a swallow of the buttermilk and it coated the inside of his mouth, sour but nourishing. "You doing all right, Chloe?"

"Yassah. I be just fine." Her smile was fond and guileless.

He had an impulse to ask her what she'd do if the Yankees came, but didn't. She'd been with the family, all his life. To his recollection, she'd never acted unhappy with the arrangement. She might take a question like that for distrust.

~ * ~

That night, Blake stood next to Judith, dressed in his good uniform jacket and trousers, cravat, and freshly blackened boots. His hair and beard, still damp from his bath, were neatly combed. He had thought Judith striking even in black weeds, but the yellow silk set off her classically pleasing features and the rich dark hair cascading over her shoulders. Sally had nothing on her for looks. And her warm smile was genuine, and all for him.

He repeated the vows after the dubious Reverend Reynolds. "Till death do us part." He slipped his late grandmother's ring onto her finger, a perfect fit. That was that, he was a married man.

He kissed his bride, staking his public claim, anticipating the private one that would follow.

His papa embraced Judith and his mama gave her a stiff hug and a peck. Then they moved off to talk to Reverend and Mrs. Reynolds. They were the only guests besides Matthew, his best man, who was trying to make conversation with the unresponsive Lexi.

Judith whispered, "Your mother didn't invite a soul."

"Looks that way. I guess she didn't exactly shout it from the rooftops. I asked Mr. Hughes, but he must not have been up to it."

"The most important people are here. You and me."

She looked so happy, just to be married to him. He smiled and slipped his arm around her. Let Sally have her dandy. He felt generous and expansive, willing to grant Sally her own preference. Maybe they were all better off this way.

His father broke out a bottle of wine and made a few toasts, enough for a glassful each. Soon after the wine and cake ran out, the minister and his wife left. Matt didn't stay long either, having had no luck with Lexi. Social obligations done for, Blake led Judith to his room.

They paused at the door and he picked her up. She circled her arms around his neck and snuggled her face against his shoulder. He carried her into the room, kicked the door closed, and set her down on the bed. She pulled him on top of her, laughing, and they sank into the deep mattress. This time, she would not push him away, but would freely welcome his ardor. "Hold me tight," she said. "I'm afraid this is just a dream and I'll wake up to the same old nightmares."

"No, it's real. Everything's going to be fine." He covered her mouth with his and worked on her blouse buttons while she unbuckled his belt, unfastened his buttons and freed him.

He suckled at her breast. Inhaled the warm scent of her skin. Pushed up her skirt, parted her thighs and didn't wait to undress her before he mounted her, exploring the feel of their bodies flesh to flesh. She relaxed and sighed, liking it. Wanting him.

He made himself pause to take his pants all the way off, heard the rustle of her skirt dropping away. He crawled back into the bed and found her waiting under the covers, reaching for him. He came down on her and she arched up to receive him. He entered, thrust deep into her warmth. She let out an earthy little cry, moved with him, her fingers digging into his buttocks. Her insides closed around him, rippling, coaxing him to pleasure so exquisite it pained. He groaned with the sweet effort of releasing his seed into her core.

Spent, he rested on her, kissing and fondling her. She buried her hands in his hair and held his head to her breast. "Oh, Blake, I'm so happy."

He murmured, "Yes, Sally, yes."

Her fingers froze on him, but hanged if he could figure out what was wrong.

Chapter
Seven

Judith awoke snug and warm against Blake, sheltered there ever since she had fallen asleep. She ran her thumb over the ring. She sure had her connections now.

But last night he'd called her Sally, and didn't even seem to notice. How could he say such a thing? Was he still in love with his old fiancé?

Maybe it wasn't really a disaster. He'd married her, hadn't he? Besides, Sally was going to marry someone else, the sooner the better.

In the meantime, Judith had what she wanted, a home and a husband to love. In time, she would make him forget Sally and she would have his whole heart, just as he had hers. Picking a fight with him over it would not further her cause. She'd be smarter to ignore his slip.

Blake reached for her, rested his hand on her hair, stroked down the length of it and fingered the ends. Then he chuckled. "Who's this sleeping in my bed?"

She frowned, not enjoying the joke. "Don't you know?"

He gathered her into his arms. "Ah, Jude, you're everything a man could want."

A tingle of desire crept through her. She snuggled close, reveling in the feel of his strong male body. She craved to hold him inside her again. It was more than pleasurable sensations she wanted. She longed to join his body, his very spirit. "Love me," she murmured.

He pulled her even closer. "You sure know how to make a man happy."

Afterwards, she rested under him, feeling his long breaths, his heart beating over hers.

Then he kissed her and lifted onto his elbows. He said in a drowsy voice, "Have to get up."

She tightened her arms around his back, even though he'd already warned her he had to report this morning. "What do you have to do at camp?"

"Make supply requisitions, see how the new recruits are doing. Things have been going slow, so I'll be back tonight." Blake laughed softly. "You'd better let me go."

He lit the lamp on the bedside table and dressed in the smoky light, quick about it in the cold. Cord like muscles rippled under the tight skin of his back. Fascinated with the sight of him, she reached up and touched his hard shoulder.

He bent over and kissed her. "Keep that up and you'll make me late. Don't want to get me in trouble, do you?"

"Maybe they'll kick you out and you won't have to fight any more."

He shook his head, smiling, then peeled himself away from her and picked up a boot.

Last night they didn't bother with lights, so his room was new to her. It was sparsely furnished, only the bed, the chest and window curtains. Of course, he had been away, leaving it vacant. Now he was going off again. She said, "I'll miss you, darling. Be careful."

"There's no need to be careful. Will you be all right with my folks?"

"They're just skeptical, and you can't really blame them, can you? They are good people. I shall win them over by and by."

"Just like I told you." He sat down on the bed and pulled on his boots. "They will come to trust my judgment."

"Today I'll move my things in and decorate a little," she said. "Make your room mine."

"It already is. What's mine is yours."

"I'll go downstairs and find you something for breakfast." She swung her legs into the cold and groped for her dressing gown.

"We'll go together."

She found cornbread and buttermilk in the kitchen. After they shared it he kissed her goodbye. "See you later, sweetheart. We'll pick up where we left off." He disappeared into the dark.

George said something like that the last time she'd seen him. She hugged herself, aware of the damp chill seeping through her gown.

~ * ~

Sam drove the provisioned wagon back up the farm road. He felt happy because he had combined his errand with a visit to his girl friend Roxie, on a neighboring plantation.

He could talk the old man into buying her for him, but he'd be smarter to bide his time. After the Yankees came, nobody would have to buy nobody and they could get married like white folks. What was that going to be like? He could sure stand to find out.

As soon as he drove onto the main road he saw two white men sitting on their horses watching him.

"Hold up there, boy," the one in the dirty black coat said. "I wanna talk to you."

Sam hid his dislike of white trash his people called buckras after the shoddy buckram clothes they favored. He let his shoulders droop, put on an idiot grin. Most white men expected him to be a chucklehead and he'd spent his life acting like one. He had to if he wanted to live a long time. But he could still laugh at them inside. "Yassah."

He reined in, glancing at the revolver Black Coat wore. The other mean-looking devil sat on his horse watching him. He was wearing a Yankee coat, but Sam didn't see a gun on him.

"What you doin', boy? You got a pass?" demanded Black Coat.

"Yes, sah."

"Where the hell is it, then?"

Sam took his time, reached into his shirt pocket, pulled out the paper and handed it over so the writing was turned around.

The buckra stared at it, didn't fix it right to read it. Sam hid a grin at his private joke. He had more letter learning than this sorry piece of white trash, the sure-thing chucklehead. Black Coat handed it back. "Where you goin, boy?"

"I be goin' home, boss."

"You're Hughes' nigra, ain't you?"

"Yassah." Sam drew the leather reins through his long brown

fingers, not daring to let on how superior he felt.

"Howcum you wearin' that army jacket?"

Sam couldn't help sitting straighter. "I used to be with the army, sah."

Black Coat laughed at him. "You hear that, Bell? The nigra says he used to be with the army."

The one named Bell guffawed. "The Reb army? That's a good one."

Sam masked his anger behind a stupid face, recalling the name Bell. Captain Winberry had said one of the bushwhackers he'd warned them about was named Bell. What was the other name? Shakes? Sikes? Something like that.

"What was you hiding in yonder woods?"

Sam let his lower lip hang slack. "Sah?"

"Tell me, boy. Where'd you stash it?"

Sam wrinkled his brow. "Stash what, boss?"

"Everybody knows Old Man Hughes is rich. I heared it up to Dent's Mill."

Sam stared at him, marveling at the persistence of that stupid story.

"You're dumb as shit, ain't you?"

Sam scratched his armpit like a perfect chucklehead, thinking Black Coat was way dumber. "Yassah."

"Damn you Snipes," Bell said, "How come you wasting so much time with that mule turd?"

"It's my call," Snipes snapped at his partner. Then he turned back to Sam. "Look at here. Let's go pay the old man a visit. Come on, boy."

Sam drove the mule and racked his brains for a way to warn the old man. He held onto the whip, the nearest thing to a weapon he had, and daubed it at the mule to give himself a good excuse to carry it. He recalled the signal he had used at Adam's Run to let the pickets know he was coming through.

Back then the soldiers treated him like a comrade, especially after they found out how well he could forage and cook. He never had so much fun before or since. He would go over to the Yankees and get his plunder and information, then return to the old man and the Winberry brothers. They always had a good laugh about his tales of outsmarting the Yanks. He had enjoyed status like never before or since. The old man even taught him how to use a gun. Too bad he didn't have one now.

They came into sight of the house. The old dog wasn't much help. He didn't raise an alarm. Sam started to whistle "Listen to the Mockingbird." Then he raised his voice, sang loud and strong.

"Shut up, nigra," Snipes said.

He sang louder. Would the old man hear and know something bad was afoot?

"I said shut up." Snipes made a threatening move to his holster.

"Just shoot the dumb black bastard," Bell grunted. "That's what I'd do if I had a gun."

"He's still useful," Snipes said.

The door to the house opened. The old man stood in the doorway, army revolver in hand, alert. "Good afternoon," he said. "What can I do for you gents?"

Snipes eyed the gun, suddenly respectful. "We was lookin' for a Mr. Hughes."

"You found him. Who might you be?"

"Lem Snipes. This here's Harry Bell."

Sam shook his head just a trifle at the old man to warn him to be careful, not to ask the bushwhackers in. If only the old man remembered the names Captain Winberry mentioned.

The old man kept his revolver ready, must be onto them. "What's business you got with us?"

"Lookin' for work," Snipes said.

The old man shook his head. "Don't have no work Sam and I can't handle."

Snipes scratched the back of his neck. "Then we'll just water our critters, it's all right with you."

"Go ahead." The old man grinned like a fox. "Now you better be careful. I hear they's bushwhackers around. Captain Winberry shot one dead t'other day."

Snipes' eyes narrowed, and he and his partner gave each other a sharp look. "Do tell," Snipes said. "We'll watch ourselves."

"Sam, take that rig around back and get on in here."

"Yassah." Sam clicked up the mule, leaving the buckras staring after him.

If he carried the revolver, he'd be able to defend himself. Wouldn't have to bring that trash home with him in the first place.

~ * ~

Harry Bell kicked his horse in the flank and followed Snipes away from the Hughes place. "You sure that old man got money? His place don't look like much."

"Everybody that's from these parts knows it." Snipes shot Harry a scornful look over his shoulder. "You game, Yank, or you yella?"

Harry scratched the itchy place under his waistband, hating Snipes. "I ain't yella. You wouldn't a had the balls to jump out a moving boxcar like I did."

"That don't take nothing."

"Hell it don't. Armed guards all around. It was dark, too. How'd I know I wasn't gonna fall down a trestle and break my neck?"

"You're all brag, Yank." Snipes turned his back on him.

Harry wished he had a revolver. He wanted to plug Snipes for insulting him, or maybe just for being a Southron. He wished he had never taken up with Reb deserters. But this far into enemy territory, he wasn't able to pick better company, and he still hadn't managed to get his hands on a gun for his own defense.

But he was getting along a damn sight better than he had in prison. He was eating better, he had picked up a few pounds, regained his strength, and his teeth were tighter in his head.

Maybe he would chance getting rid of Snipes soon. He had learned enough about the lay of the land by now to go it alone, maybe even get back to the good old Union Army lines. They would welcome an escaped prisoner of war. Maybe they would call him a hero. He was captured in Virginia, a long way from here, and nobody in Sherman's army would recognize him, or know he'd jumped bounty twice before the Rebs captured him.

Snipes looked around at him. "You hear that old man say a Captain Winberry was the one that killed Dink?"

"You gonna do something about it?"

"Get the drop on him, I'll shoot his balls off."

"Yeah. I sure wanted a go at that wench," Harry said, licking his lips.

"We'd a let you have a little. After we got enough for ourselves."

Harry studied Snipes' back. Soon as he got himself a gun, he'd give the mule turd a little something.

~ * ~

After he checked in at camp, Blake sat on a log making out requisitions for socks, swords and other items for his troop, a mindless activity that didn't disturb his serenity. He ought to feel belligerent, keen to throw himself at his enemies. Instead, he had gone tame, was not mad at anybody. Amazing what a night of lovemaking could do for the disposition.

He was actually content, picturing his wife home waiting for him. Eventually, swelling up with his child. The pain of losing Sally had dulled, and thoughts of death driven to the back of his mind.

Captain Causey strode up. "Heard a rumor about you, Winberry. Is it true you got married last night?"

Blake smiled and tapped the pencil on his knee. "That's so." He'd kept it quiet to put off the ribbing.

"You have to report to General Butler."

"For congratulations?"

"Orders."

Blake laid aside his paperwork and followed Causey to the headquarters tent. Major General Matthew Calbraith Butler told him to sit on a campstool across from his desk. The general, a lean, handsome aristocrat with an aggressive jaw, lounged back in his chair. His cork foot rested on a stool. The real one had been blown off at Brandy Station. Blake had overheard Butler comment after a recent fight that he had taken a bullet in the fake limb and it didn't hurt a bit.

"Any luck rustling up horses, Captain Winberry?"

"Yes, sir. I found a few, so did some of my men."

"Enough to mount your troop?"

"No, sir. About half."

Butler scowled and reached for a glass of something that might have been whiskey and took a swallow. "This country is too picked over. I even advertised for horses in the newspapers, can't hardly find any."

"Yes, sir," Blake agreed. "First string got killed off long ago."

Butler handed him a piece of paper. "Captain Causey said you were the right man for this job. You are to take a squadron and proceed as soon as practicable to Branchville and report to General Stevenson. Assist him in watching the river crossing, the railroad junction." He waved his hand. "And whatever else he needs."

"I am honored, sir." Blake scanned his orders, realizing that peace was over for him. "When are the rest of our horses expected from Virginia?"

"Not for another week. Take such men as are mounted to make up a squadron. I'll have Colonel Aiken prepare a list."

After discussing logistics with General Butler, Blake reported to Colonel Aiken and sent off runners to round up men. Then he slipped off to town, making an excuse that he needed supplies.

He hurried home instead to tell his wife goodbye and settle his affairs, just in case. He had promised her a home and support, and he meant to hold up his part.

Judith had spread the fabric over a table and she was humming while she cut the pieces for her new dress. She looked up from her work and smiled, dark eyes alight. "Oh, darling. I didn't expect you so soon. Are you off duty?" She set down the scissors and hurried from behind the table to meet him.

"Not exactly." He took her in his arms, touched by her happy welcome. Her beauty seemed to radiate from the goodness within. He felt a fresh rush of affection for her.

"Sweetheart, I have to go down to Branchville, won't be back for a few days."

He felt her arms tighten on him. Her body stiffened. "You won't have to fight, will you?"

"I doubt the Yankees will give in peaceably." He reached into his pocket. "I'd better give you this because you're more likely to need it than I am."

She took the currency and frowned at it.

"I want to make sure you're all right if anything happens to me. You can stay on here. My father has agreed."

Her smile vanished and her eyes took on a hurt, scared look. "I wish you wouldn't talk that way."

"I said I'd take care of you."

"Didn't expect--"

"I'll be back before you know it."

She slipped the money into her skirt-pocket and gave him an unhappy smile. "Take off your jacket and hold up your arms."

"Why?" He grinned and patted her behind. "Are you going to disarm me and take me prisoner?"

"I'd like to." She rummaged through a workbox and pulled out a tape measure. "I can't very well make you a shirt without taking your measurements, can I?"

"Oh, the shirt."

"Your mother's been trusting me with her sewing machine, so I'll have it ready for you by the time you get back." She tugged at the front of his jacket. "We'll be a matched set, us two."

He started to unbutton his jacket, then grasped her hands instead and gathered them to his chest. She cuddled against him lovingly. The feel of her firm warm body stirred him. "Wait," he said. "To really get this right, we have to go up to our room."

~ * ~

That night Sam didn't go to bed. Not after the old dog didn't show up for supper. The buckras must have killed it to keep it quiet. He didn't tell the old man, who was too feeble tonight to be much good for anything.

After the old man was snoring he took the revolver off the table by the bed and made sure it was loaded. He crept into the front room and raised the window so he could hear outside noises. Blowing out the lamp, he barred the door and sat with the weapon in his lap, shivering in the draft.

He sat quiet, listening to the night noises. Every so often he got up, carrying the revolver, and prowled around the house in his stocking feet and looked out every window.

Once he nodded off, then jerked awake. Had to do better than that. Those were two mean looking white men. What if they caught him napping? Skin him alive, that's what they'd do.

What was that sound? He froze and listened. A bang, like the mule hitting the side of the shed. He started to relax. That's all, just the mule.

~ * ~

Harry Bell walked behind Snipes toward the house. Dark

windows, nobody up. With any luck they'd surprise the old man in bed, then find out what they wanted to know. He wasn't worried about the nigra, he was too stupid to offer much trouble.

Snipes stepped onto the porch, but Harry hesitated. Better let Snipes take the risks before he stuck his own neck out.

~ * ~

A board creaked. The porch, just outside. A footstep?

Sam knelt behind the sofa and cocked the revolver. He wiped sweat out of his eyes. His gun hand shook. He brought the other hand up so he could hold it steady. Couldn't stop shaking.

The doorknob grated. The door thudded softly against the bar, but didn't open.

Then a man's shape blotted out the little bit of light showing through the window. The sash scraped as the intruder pushed it higher. A leg swung into the open space and the rest of a man above it.

Sam fired into the man's middle. The bang echoed loud against the walls and the flash showed one of the men he had been expecting, revolver in hand. The intruder jumped and shrieked and sent the window squeaking higher with his back, then hollered some more, fired his gun and lit himself up all over again, caught in the window frame. Sam heard the bullet hit the wall.

Sam fired again. The man fell forward this time, half in and half out the window, not yelling now, making gurgling sounds. Sam shot again and the buckra jerked, letting out a long wet groan, twitching like a snake that wouldn't quit.

Sam crouched in the quiet, the room stinking of powder smoke, burnt sulfur and sweat, cradling the hot revolver.

Where was the other one? He heard horses, lifted his head, listening. Must be running off.

"What the hell? What the hell?" The old man came stumbling out of his room. "Sam, what the hell?"

"He was comin' to get me so I kilt him." Shaky, Sam sat down on the floor.

The old man lit a candle, showing the mess. The man he shot hanging down through the window, not moving any longer, coat blotched with blood. Blood on the floor and spattered on the wall around the window. That buckra wouldn't skin nobody alive now.

The old man stood over the body, blowing hard, like he did every time he moved too fast. He picked up the head by the hair and looked at the ugly dead face. Blood dripped from the mouth and nose. "It's one of them fellers came by today up to no good. Snipes."

Sam stared at the body, counting bullet holes. One in the chest and one in the belly.

The old man let the head drop, and Sam spotted the third hole between the shoulder blades. "Fine shooting." The old man gave him a strange look, like he was wondering if he was still the same Sam.

"I done it. I killed that white man. He'd have got you."

The old man nodded, frowning. "You seen the other one?"

"I heard him run off. I better go make sure he didn't steal the mule."

"You done right. You always take care of me."

Sam cradled the revolver in his lap.

The old man said, "Come daylight, you can lay him in the ground where nobody will find him. Clean up the blood."

Sam stroked the warm gun barrel. "I want to keep it from here on out."

"Negros ain't supposed to carry guns. Folks'd hang you, they ever found out you killed a white man, even a varmint like that."

"I'll keep it under my coat, nobody'll even know."

The old man didn't answer for a while, just looked at him. Then he said, "What you going to do if the Yankees come, Sam? You fixin' to leave?"

He'd thought about it. Plenty. He was already free. But maybe they'd make a real soldier out of him, let him carry a gun.

"I need you, Sam."

Sam drew himself tall. "I keep the gun, I stay."

The old man had new respect in his eyes. "I'm sure not trying to take it away from you."

Chapter
Eight

Judith woke up and sleepily reached for Blake, but her arm slid across the blanket without meeting his muscular body, and she remembered the army had sent him away.

She shivered and dragged the blanket closer around her chin. Better get up soon. Blake's mother had promised she could use the sewing machine and Lexi wanted her at the hospital. She planned to see about hiring Fancy to the livery stable so the mule would earn its keep. And she could teach piano lessons if only she could scare up any students.

But the hearth was full of cold ashes, and outside the wind was blowing a norther. Thanks to Blake she was sheltered in a secure home, but he would have to spend his nights in the open and his days in the saddle. No telling when she would see him again.

Her in-laws were coming around to accept the marriage. Genteel, mild mannered folk, they would not risk estranging their son by rejecting his bride. Besides, her campaign to convince them she was cultured, capable, and an asset to the household seemed to be making progress. They were more than civil.

Still, she liked it best in the room she shared with Blake, where his scent lingered in the bed sheets. He had left some of his belongings behind, a couple of old shirts and a holey pair of jeans that needed a new seat, assurance that he expected to come back soon.

~ * ~

Blake emerged from General Stevenson's headquarters at Branchville and paused on the wooden porch. The morning drizzle had stopped and a sharp north wind had freshened. He pulled on his gloves and surveyed his squadron, 43 men drawn from different units in Butler's division. He knew most of them at least slightly, a dozen pretty well. He had Matt Kirkland and David Frank along, old hands to help things run smooth. It wouldn't take much posturing to convince the balance of them that he was in charge.

A whole week of rest had eased a little of the perpetual tiredness from their faces. Most conserved their energy, lounging under whatever shelter could be found clear of the dripping trees. But the falling temperature made others frisky. A couple of men sparred while a cluster of their fellows watched and offered jeering advice. Of course one of the scrappers was Simmons, number one troublemaker.

Blake had sprung him from the bullpen for the expedition. The fool was arrested for drinking a snootful of whiskey, riding his horse into a saloon, firing his army revolver and scaring prominent citizens.

The three new boys were conspicuous with their full faces and bright eyes. Caldwell, the mama's boy, had not yet lit out for home. Maybe he would work out all right. Cliff Stewart's identifying pimple was fading so Blake was starting to have trouble telling the twins apart. Their flesh and innocence would soon melt away, cheeks would hollow and expressions would turn wary. He shook off a touch of guilt for being a Fagan who would teach them things they'd be better off not knowing.

The horses stood tethered head to head along a fence rail. Fresh off the cattle cars, they switched their tails, stamped their hooves and chewed on the frayed ropes, their dull winter coats rough from the rain.

Matt looked up at him from the porch steps. "Well?"

"We're to patrol this side of the river beyond the picket line, watch for any Yanks trying to cross. A little skirmishing south of here a couple of days ago--the general had the bridge torched after he got his men across."

A few minutes later Blake led the squadron through the railroad village in columns of two. Shod hooves thumped in the mud, leather squeaked and buckles rattled. A musically inclined trooper began to sing "Oh! Susanna," and others joined in like they were going to a picnic.

The sky cleared by the time they passed an infantry picket-camp that smelled of wood smoke and rancid bacon. Ragged and hairy foot soldiers lolled about scratching themselves like hounds. Their weapons, polished and stacked under fluttering tent-flies, were the only military-looking things about them. They lazed to their feet with long-jawed grins as the horsemen rode by, looking for amusement.

"Hey, boys, when ya gonna jine the army?"

"General Stevenson put up a five dollar re-ward for a dead critter soldier. Reckon we'll collect?"

"Don't worry, gals! We'll save ya, darlin'!"

A trooper behind Blake retaliated, yelling, "Saved yourselves pretty good up Nashville way! Finally stopped running did'ya?" Blake recognized Simmons' voice.

That insult was too much for the infantrymen, feelings raw from their recent disaster. They surged forward with a collective snarl to drag the loudmouth from his saddle. Blake wheeled his horse, shouted a warning, drew his saber and swiped it to get their attention. Matt moved up alongside him, cursing.

The show of authority scattered the pack. But Simmons drew his revolver and hooted, "Better duck, webfoot! Before I pop a cap!"

"Put that away, Simmons." Blake stood up in the stirrups. "I ought to let 'em tear you apart, idiot."

"Who, me? I was only funnin', Capt'n." Simmons affected aggrieved innocence.

"Hoping I'll send you back to jail so you won't have to do any real fighting? Bad idea. You just bought yourself extra picket duty."

Blake didn't bother to note Simmons' reaction. He settled back, jammed his saber back into its scabbard, brought his horse around and called out, "Forward by twos. March." He held up his hand and signaled forward.

A few hundred yards further they reached the South Edisto River. Blake and Matt rode close to the bank and looked out across the expanse of brown water. All that remained of the bridge was a broken framework of charred timbers. The water lapped high, covering the bottoms of tree trunks above the banks.

The swift current swirled and tugged at the pilings. Dirty smoke polluted the sky to the southwest.

Blake pointed out the smoke to Matt. "There's Sherman, across there. Got through the swamps, didn't he?"

"Doesn't matter," Matthew said. "He's got to cross this here river. Won't be easy."

"Pontoons. They've got pontoons."

A flash and a plume of smoke broke from the underbrush across the river. A ball whined by and split through the brush behind him. He jerked Magic's head around, dug his heels into her sides and headed into the woods. Another ball clipped a tree, showering bark onto his thigh. Two more shots followed before his men answered, peppering the opposite bank with carbine fire. Blake whirled and brought up his revolver, but couldn't make out any target.

Matt rode up behind him, grinning with tension. "I hate to give way to that bastard. But he's got a repeater."

Blake adjusted his hat and peered through the screen of underbrush at the gun smoke and smoke from the burnings. "At least they won't be hard to spot."

~ * ~

Harry Bell skirted Columbia, pushed through the rain all night, and did not stop to rest until daylight.

First Dink, now Snipes. Suddenly the life of a bushwhacker seemed a little too chancy. Now that he was on his own, unarmed at that, he'd better head for his own lines and turn into a good Union soldier again.

Just keep moving south, he would run into blue coats in a few days. Maybe it wouldn't be so bad. He wouldn't have to reform. In Sherman's army, Union soldiers were expected to live off the land. He figured an army like that was just to his liking.

~ * ~

Blake squinted into the morning glare and made out two mounted figures riding across the field toward his squadron.

"They're wearing blue," Matt said. "Don't they see us? We ought to be plain as day on this here hill."

"Maybe they're deserters. Or scouts."

"Or just plain stupid."

75

"We have to find out." Blake unsnapped his holster stay and drew his Colt. "At least they aren't asking for it, no damn fool demonstrations."

His men cocked their weapons, menacing clicks. He said to them, "Hold your fire 'til I say different."

One of the bluecoats waved a white handkerchief over his head. "Ho, friends!" the Yankee yelled.

"What the hell?" Matt said.

"Just two of 'em, and we've got the drop on them." Blake made a sweep with his arm and called out, "Come on in! Keep your hands in sight!"

The one with the handkerchief shouted, "Hey, Winberry! It's Lightfoot and Cooper!"

Blake whirled to his men, "They're ours! Put away your weapons!"

"Lightfoot's going to be plugged by his own side one of these days," Matt said.

Blake raised a sardonic eyebrow. "Looking for an excuse?"

"One is as good as another. He won all my back pay. Cheated."

"Your mistake. I don't play cards with him."

Matt leaned over and spat tobacco juice. "How did you ever get so smart?"

"Maybe the Yanks will hang him for you. That won't get your money back, though."

"Maybe I can." Mathew looked thoughtful. "I hear they got a price on his head."

"Tell him that." Blake grinned. "I dare you."

"I just don't like the cold-blooded bastard."

The scouts rode up. Hunter Lightfoot slouched on his Morgan, wiry, compact and neat in his dark blue uniform. Controlled expression, eyes giving nothing out. The tough kid with him had the hard look of a killer who might just enjoy his business.

Blake holstered his revolver. "Wish you would wear the right color."

Hunter smoothed his moustache. "So do the Federals."

"At least get yourself a bigger handkerchief. Where you headed?"

"Back to Columbia." Hunter dug his pipe out of his pocket and stuck it between his teeth. "General Hampton wanted to confer," he said around the pipe stem.

"We're covering Stevenson's rear," Blake said. "I reckon we're going about the same direction. Ride with us if you want."

"Not this time." Hunter struck a match and lit his pipe, sucking in his cheeks. "Change of base?"

"Yanks crossed the South Edisto somewhere west of Branchville. We're providing them with an escort."

Hunter smiled, but it hardened his appearance even more. "Hope they appreciate your trouble."

"When you get to Columbia, would you please take a note to my wife?"

"Your what?" Hunter's right eyebrow shot up.

"Ha. Got one up on you for a change." Blake grinned with satisfaction. "Given your talents, you should have sniffed it in the wind."

"It's so," Matthew chimed in. "He got married."

Hunter took a thoughtful drag on his pipe. "You do have a smug domesticated look about you, old chum. Congratulations. I think."

Blake fished a notebook and pencil from his saddlebag and threw his leg around the pommel of his saddle, using his boot-leg as a desk. Magic lunged forward and dropped her head to snatch leaves off a bush. The J in Judith shot off the top of the page.

"I hope you have somewhere safe to send her," Hunter said. "Yanks are planning to take Columbia."

Blake hesitated in his scribbling. "You sure?"

"I've been listening. They mean to make an example out of your town."

Blake's stomach tightened. He looked past Hunter, toward the smoky sky to the south. "Seems like whenever they run out of houses, they torch the woods. Always have to be burning something."

"They're punishing the trees for growing on South Carolina soil," Hunter said. "Not exactly in love with your state, I gather."

"Aren't we going to concentrate and check them?" Blake asked.

"We're too scattered." Hunter's shoulders jerked in an impassive shrug. "Trying to cover every place from Charleston to Augusta doesn't cover any place."

Blake considered the ineffectualness of his troop's rear guard action. "There ought to be something better we can do."

"They torched Barnwell, renamed it Burnwell. A hilarious crew, that. We surprised a few of 'em lighting up a house yesterday." Hunter turned to the other scout. "Won't ever do that again, will they J. C.?"

"Sure won't, Lieutenant." The boy smiled, his eyes cold as a reptile's. "They did burn pretty good."

Blake tore his gaze from the savage young face and stared at the paper. "There's likely to be fighting around Columbia."

Hunter nodded. "Can't see Hampton letting the Yanks walk in peaceably. He's got property there."

"Charlotte. That's it. I'll tell her to take the train to Charlotte. The rest of my family, too. They need to stay out of what's coming." He finished writing the note, folded it and handed it to Hunter. "You'll respect this letter is private, of course."

Hunter nodded and stuck the note in his shirt pocket under his blue coat. "Anything else you want me to tell them?"

"To get out before all hell busts loose."

~ * ~

The big house seemed to be deserted, but Harry Bell hung back in case any Johnny Rebs waited in ambush. He hid behind a tree until the other soldiers bounded up onto the veranda. Let the heroes draw fire. Just because he was back in the army didn't mean he had to get himself killed.

Kramer flung open the door and flattened himself next to it. Nothing happened. Harry strolled onto the porch, his rifle ready, Morrison behind him. He scuffed the mud off his boots onto the rug in the entrance hall. A white rug. Fancy that.

Mahogany furniture, paintings of damned Southerners on the walls, a curved staircase leading up to the second floor. The snobs that owned the place would never have invited the likes of him through the front door. Not until he convinced them it was healthier to let him do whatever he pleased.

A movement. He started and ducked. Then he realized that it

was a mirror, and he had caught sight of his own blue image.

Morrison laughed at him. "What's the matter, Harry? Afraid the Rebs will catch you again?"

"Go to hell."

Kramer and Schultz left them to work outside, sticking their bayonets into the ground to hunt for buried treasure. Morrison found a trunk of women's clothes. He tried on a bonnet and a skirt in front of the mirror, preened and posed like a freak in a sideshow.

Harry picked up a chair and threw it into the mirror. The glass exploded into splinters. "I like that better." He nodded, satisfied.

He knocked out a window with his rifle butt and Morrison laughed. Then Harry wandered off on his own to see what else he could get into. A fine, big house, and he got first dibs.

Hardwood floors and frame structure, the place would go up hot after they took out everything worth having. He had found out straightaway he had heard right about his new cronies. Now that they were in South Carolina, Uncle Billy Sherman wouldn't bother to stop them from having just about any kind of fun they wanted. South Carolina had started the fight, and the Union army was going to finish it. Harry was glad to help.

They even let him keep his horse to ride. Most of the men in this unit confiscated critters and rode, even if they were supposed to be infantry.

Gunshots. Rebs? If they caught him they'd mulch the ground with his carcass. He looked out the window and almost peed with relief. One of his comrades was killing off livestock that the owners were dumb enough to leave behind.

He climbed the stairs, found a bedroom, a chest of drawers nobody had gotten to yet. He yanked out a drawer and rifled through it. He found a gold ring, wiped it on his sleeve and tried to stick it on his finger. Too small, so he dropped it into his pocket. Another drawer brought him real loot, necklaces. Gold and pearls. He hung them around his neck and the pendants jingled as he poked around for more.

Bell heard a weak cry. Sounded like a baby in the next room. A baby would have a mama close by. He followed the muffled sounds to a wardrobe and yanked the door open.

A darky woman was folded like a spider in the corner, clutching her brat hard enough to squash it and shaking like she was going to have the fits.

"Come out, sugar."

She wouldn't move.

He dived into the wardrobe and grabbed one of her skinny wrists. "Don't you understand American, wench? Come out. Now."

He peeled her out but she turned away, head high like she was better than him. A cuff or two would fix that, then he would show her how a real man could stir up her blood. He grabbed her chin and yanked her face toward him for a better look. She squirmed away but he snatched her blouse. His hand brushed her milk-heavy breast and he got hard.

Whitfield came in. Still in the house. Shit. But he wasn't carrying a rifle. Must have left it stacked outside, stupid bastard.

"What's this, Harry?"

Harry let go of the woman. "Uppity nigra and her brat."

"We won't hurt you," Whitfield said to her. "We're Union soldiers and you're a free woman now. Go outside."

Harry watched his lost opportunity scurry off. "Ain't you the fine gent. 'You're a free woman now.' Them nigras is the cause of all our troubles. Wasn't for them, I wouldn't have gone through hell in a Reb prison and we wouldn't be down here fightin'."

Whitfield cocked his head and looked him up and down. "I've been noticing things, Harry. You seem to disappear when there's any chance of fighting. And who did you steal that jewelry from?"

"Finders keepers."

"I don't hold with out-and-out thieving."

"It ain't thieving. I hear Uncle Billy says any house that's deserted is fair game. Army policy, he says."

"It isn't quite deserted."

"You talkin' about that wench? Goddamn. This house ain't hers. She don't count."

"Get out of here."

"Go to hell. Just cause you're a corporal, you think you're the next best thing to God, lording it over me and kissin' the sergeant's ass."

Whitfield took a step forward and balled up his fists, threatening.

Harry lifted the rifle the army had issued him when he rejoined. "I wish you'd try it."

Whitfield backed off, glaring at the rifle. "You're worthless. I wish the Rebs would have caught you and cut your damn throat." He left the room.

Harry watched the door close, then lowered his rifle. Whitfield could have him arrested. Probably wouldn't have the balls. Harry muttered, "Watch your back, bastard. I get a chance to plug you, I'll sure take it."

He'd have the next woman if he could get around prigs like Whitfield. Wasn't for the Rebs dogging the army and hunting the hides of Union soldiers, he would free lance again.

He struck a match and lit off a curtain. The bright flames danced and leaped upward with a whoosh toward the wooden rafters. Nobody'd give a damn. The house was deserted and he was just following orders. He watched it, whistling "John Brown's Body," until the smoke got too thick and he had to leave.

Chapter Nine

The terrain lifted a little from the low country flatness as Blake continued to move his squadron north ahead of the enemy. Whenever he turned to face the rear from a rise, he spotted Federal infantry mounted on stolen horseflesh. Beyond that on the road and as far as he could see on either side of it, many blue-coated soldiers spread over the land like a dark plague. Feeling impotent, a mere witness, he continued going northward.

He led his troop past a big prosperous farmhouse. Half an hour later, he looked over his shoulder and saw smoke billow from the spot.

On the approach to the next town, just beyond a field, a small collection of Confederate troops hunkered behind plank breastworks. A demolished shed nearby must have provided the timber. A fat militia major waddled out into the road and flagged him down.

"Captain, dismount your men and get them on into the breastworks." The major waved his arm toward the clutter. "We've been ordered to make a stand, and I order you to assist."

Blake sent two vedettes back to watch the road and told his men to dismount. The horse holders, every fourth man, took their charges behind nearby shacks for safekeeping. The remaining three quarters of his squad filled in with the infantry stragglers and home guards behind the barricades.

Then he rode up to the major, who sat on a stump resting, elbows on knees. Broken veins in the officer's nose made his red face resemble a relief map.

Blake saluted. "My men are in place, sir."

The major nodded. "Right, then. Very well." He started to rise, then sat down heavily, swayed and righted himself by sticking out his hand.

"Don't you feel well, sir?"

"Fine. Fine." The major blinked up at him. "Do you know what this is all about, Captain?"

"Might help if you told me, sir."

"We're supposed to give people time to skedaddle." The major unstopped his canteen and took a long swig. "Haven't you seen what's coming at us?"

Blake shifted in the saddle, controlling his rising anger. "We've been watching them all day, sir."

The major started to get up again. This time he succeeded. "I'm sick." He picked his way toward the remaining shacks.

Matt rode up. "What's the matter?"

"Major's sick," Blake told him.

Matthew squinted toward their superior officer. "You mean drunk."

"That too."

The major bent double and heaved into the bushes.

Blake shook his head, disgusted. "With any luck, he'll pass out and be out of the way. Are we the only officers besides him?"

Matthew nodded.

"Then it's up to us to run this thing. Hold them off as long as we can."

The major lay down on his back, a plump gray mound.

Matthew said, "We ought to get drunk too."

Easier to keep on going and forget the major ever flagged him down. He wouldn't be sober enough to register a complaint until after they were gone. No, better not behave that way. Might be a good reason for the stand, something worth risking their necks for, somebody really needing to buy time.

"Pick a couple of men," Blake said. "Ours, not the home guards, to take him back to the horse-holders. Tell them to keep quiet about his condition."

"Leave him to the Yankees, he'd sober up right quick."

"Don't tempt me. Let's get this mob in order."

Blake rode down the line to inspect. His men were ready with the

Enfields that had served them so well in Virginia. The handful of infantrymen also had good rifles. Most of the home guards, young boys and old men, carried fowling pieces or shotguns, useless for long range.

Aim from the untried men would be high and nervous. He called out, "Hold your fire 'til I give the order. Pick your man. Aim at his shoes!"

He checked the charges in his Colt, dismounted and had Magic led off to the protected area. Then he stationed himself behind the wood and dirt barricade. Aware that he was being watched, he schooled his face and swallowed an excess of saliva. The cornbread and bacon lunch was not necessarily his for keeps.

He rechecked his revolver and found it loaded and ready.

The vedettes galloped in. "Yanks are three jumps behind us, Cap'n," one of them hollered.

"Just exactly how far is that, private?"

"Half a mile. They've formed in a skirmish line."

Must be expecting trouble. No surprises for the enemy today. "Take your horses to the rear then come back double quick and get into the line." He turned to the entrenched soldiers. "Attention! Don't shoot until I say, then aim low."

A few minutes later blue figures advanced across the field, rifles ready, hunters stalking game. They came in a serrated line, just like the book called for. Uniforms faded and dingy, most wore slouch hats like those favored by the Confederates. He couldn't see their legs from the knees down for the stubble on the field.

Bully boys, tough and handy, shouting and taking potshots at the breastworks, trying to bluster the defenders out of the way. The first few bullets sang by without doing any damage.

None of his men broke. Quiet, they waited for the signal, rifle barrels poking from the works like steel fingers. The home guards held fast, steadied by their example.

"Fire!"

Rifles crashed in a deafening racket. Smoke enveloped the line.

To a man, the bluecoats dropped to let the volley fly overhead. Then they scrambled up and charged, cheering.

The Yankees weren't following his program. They were good.

So much for low aim. "Fire at will!"

The crack of revolvers from his men, the boom of shotguns from the home guards and the high-pitched yells from the whole line hit the enemy. Some dropped, others turned back, and a few kept coming through the smoky haze.

One ran straight toward him. Blake raised his revolver with both hands over the barricade, sighted and fired. The grip thudded against the heel of his hand.

The Yankee shrieked and stumbled to the ground, writhing, only a few yards away. His hand moved to his chest. Blood gushed through the spread fingers. He rolled onto his side, tried to get up, collapsed.

Blake swallowed bile. He tore his gaze away from the man he had shot and scanned the rest of the field. No other Federals made it through the barricade. Not so far. Drifting smoke raked his throat and made his eyes water. He needed to relieve himself. His heart slowed its pulse. Couldn't tell how many of the enemy were hiding in the brown stubble, getting ready for another rush.

"Come out where we can see ya, Yank!" Simmons shouted.

Others took up taunts and whoops, a grim minstrel show in burnt-powder blackface. One of the old men had collapsed. Blake did not see any blood. Too much excitement? A trooper near Blake lay curled on his side, eyes fixed, blood draining from his forehead and nose. Shea, from Company B.

Controlling the tremor in his hands, Blake reloaded his Colt, didn't quite remember emptying it. He only recalled shooting that one man, who had since quit struggling and lay still.

"Should've stayed up north where you belong, Yank," he told the dead man.

He bit off the paper cartridges and the astringent saltpeter tainted his mouth.

At the far end of the field he glimpsed more blue, clots of it, moving to his right. So what if his little band was more stubborn than the Feds expected? There were enough bluecoats to entertain them in front while others surrounded them and shot them from every side.

~ * ~

Judith walked with Lexi to the hospital, carrying books under her arm. She had taken up reading to the sick and wounded men. She liked staying busy, and the invalids appreciated the attention.

Earlier that morning she stopped by the post office to mail a letter to her aunt in Fayetteville. She had found three names and addresses written on the notice she had posted, people who wanted to travel with her. She had left the notice in place even though her plans had changed dramatically.

Lexi pointed out a soldier riding by. She said, "I'd like to be in his place. Men have all the fun."

"Being shot at isn't any fun," Judith said.

"Neither is knitting socks."

Then Lexi gripped her arm, just as she stepped off the sidewalk to cross Sumter Street. "Ooh, look at that. Sally Dubose and Mr. Randolph."

Judith stopped at the edge of the street and glanced around. "Where?"

"Right in front of you. In the carriage." Lexi grinned and waved at the girl riding by. A pretty girl, wearing a green velvet dress waved back, looked hard at Judith, and turned away.

"So that's the memorable Sally Dubose." Judith walked across the street, watching the carriage until it disappeared around a corner.

"I'm glad Blake married you instead," Lexi said. "I never did see what he liked about Sally and I'd sure hate to have her for a sister-in-law. Did you see the look she gave us? Could've killed a snake."

Judith grasped the gate to the hospital yard and opened it, feeling relieved. The girl was only flesh and blood, not a goddess, and about to marry besides. She had nothing at all to fear from Sally Dubose.

Then why did she suddenly feel queasy with dread?

~ * ~

Firing slowed, and Blake's men noticed the Federals getting ready to flank them and pointed it out to each other. Busy maneuvering, the Federals popped off a few ineffective long-range shots. Now was the best, maybe the last time to get out.

"Attention!" he yelled. "Fall back to the shacks and rally there!"

He waited until his men cleared the works, then ran, crouched, toward a building. The Yankees increased their fire at him. He gained shelter, peered around the corner. Here they came, closing in.

Blake heard a thump of lead hitting flesh, a yelp of pain. Pinckney reeled and slunk off cradling his bleeding arm.

"They're really pouring it on now," Matt said. "God, look at 'em."

"Fire at will!" Blake yelled. He couldn't hear himself through the ear-numbing noise around him. The shacks offered almost no protection, bullets popping through the walls as though they were made of paperboard.

"Ow!" He jerked his hand away from the wall. A splinter stuck between his knuckles. A man dropped near him. A pain-cry keened.

He pulled out the splinter with his teeth. Blood welled out of the slit. He glanced up, noting the Yankees were closing in.

He couldn't be expected to hold off Sherman's whole army with less than a hundred men, and damned if he was going to sacrifice his little band for no good reason. "Fall back!" he screamed. "To the horses!"

He looked for the drunk major but couldn't find him. Then he ordered the home guards to start toward town while his squadron mounted. He wouldn't let them turn tail, made them give ground slowly instead. They shot and yelled like wild Indians as they backed through the streets.

By the time they cleared the town, the home guards were as scarce as their major. None of the enemy in sight, only a few of the usual refugees in wagons and carriages and buggies and on foot.

Blake made Pinckney as comfortable as he could. Fortunately, he found no broken bones. He stanched the bleeding, bound the arm and fashioned a sling from a strip of blanket. Pinckney was too faint to sit a horse, so Blake commandeered space on a refugee's wagon.

He had to leave a few casualties behind, two still alive that he knew of, home guards. Maybe their captors would treat them all right. He let infantry stragglers ride the horses belonging to Shea and Pinckney so they could keep up.

Blake picked the rest of the wood out of his hand and washed off the blood. He felt very tired. He always felt drained after a fight, especially when he got whipped. The failure stung, but he couldn't have won this one. Too many Yankees. Always too many goddamn Yankees.

Behind them, columns of smoke shot skyward. He didn't expect pursuit. Why should Yankees go after armed men when they could sack and burn a helpless town?

~ * ~

Harry Bell rode into town, saddlebags jingling full of silver and jewelry.

Although he had lost his place in an organized foraging party because Whitfield told tales on him, he had figured out he could show for roll call every morning, then skip off on his own and avoid the spoilsports. It was the best deal since he enlisted for his first bounty.

If only his pappy could see him now. The toad had said he would never amount to nothing and would most likely swing from a gallows. He'd like to stick his gold and silver up the old fart's nose. But it wouldn't ever be enough to make up for the beatings.

Earlier that day he had heard sounds of skirmishing ahead and took his time, avoiding getting into it with the Johnnies.

He stopped his horse at a likely house, broke the door down with his rifle butt and walked inside. Nobody was home, too bad. Great fun it was, roughing up a South Carolina aristocrat and stripping him of his valuables, almost as much fun as finding a woman.

He wandered through the house looking for loot, whistling "Yankee Doodle." Others had gotten there first and the pickings were slim, but nobody cut him out of the fun of torching the place.

~ * ~

Judith took the note from Lieutenant Lightfoot's hand. She ripped open the proof that Blake was all right, at least during the moment he wrote it.

Blake's mother said to the lieutenant, "Is that the only letter he sent?"

"Yes, ma'am." The lieutenant stood relaxed, as though at home anywhere. "His duties are demanding."

Judith squinted at the atrocious handwriting to make it out. "Oh, no."

"What's the matter?" his mother said.

"He says the Yankees are on their way. He wants us to take a train to Charlotte."

"Charlotte?" Mrs. Winberry repeated it as though Blake had suggested they take a boat to China.

Lieutenant Lightfoot said, "I give the Yanks two days, outside, before they're on the outskirts of Columbia."

Judith wished he would say he was only joking, but he stood indifferent, plumed hat in his hands. "But we heard they were going to bypass Columbia."

He shrugged. "I can't help that."

"What else?" Blake's mother asked.

Judith stared at the letter. "He expects to be back in town soon. He'll have further word then."

It was happening all over again. The Yankees were coming to ruin her life. She had settled into a home, hers because it was her husband's, more secure than she had been in two years. But it seemed she'd been trying to build on quicksand.

Must she pull up stakes and run again?

Most likely she'd better plan on packing that wagon and driving to Fayetteville after all. Oh, God. What if she ran into more bushwhackers?

Maybe she'd be better off in town. Surely the Yankees wouldn't harm her in a town.

No, they'd almost killed her in Atlanta. What if they bombarded Columbia, too? They would rob her. Take her mule and wagon and all the other things she'd managed to keep. She would have nothing.

Her notice was still pinned to the post office wall. She would be safe on the road if she could gather enough people. She had her shotgun, still had that revolver, and others would be armed as well.

Blake's mother shook her head. "Charlotte. I don't think so." Then to the soldier, "Lieutenant Lightfoot, won't you stay for supper?"

He bowed. "I'd be honored, ma'am."

~ * ~

After supper, Hunter stuffed his pipe bowl and smiled across the table at his hosts.

Winberry hadn't done too badly in the marriage business. His good-looking wife actually seemed competent, might fall into the asset side. Good thing, he liked Winberry about as much as anybody.

Winberry's mother was handsome, though middle aged. Her husband, the senior Winberry, was sitting at the head of the table.

Something about Winberry's sister interested him. She was attractive in an unaffected way, but that wasn't all. Maybe it was her frank gaze and unpretentious manner. She didn't stare demurely at the floor as well-bred young ladies were schooled to do. Disdain for convention, and he enjoyed that.

"Lieutenant Lightfoot, you in my brother's troop?" Lexi asked.

He shook his head. "I work for General Hampton and General Butler directly. I'm a scout."

"What do you do?"

"I gather information."

"How?"

"I watch. I listen. I trick the Yankees into telling me what I want to know."

She leaned forward and grinned. "Perfect. That's what I want to do."

He ran his fingers over the pipe stem. "Not too unrealistic. Young ladies are more than a match for homesick Yankee officers. They can get anything they want."

"I'd rather be a scout. A real scout."

"Only one drawback." He smiled, amused. "They don't let girls into the army."

"Stupid, isn't it?"

Amazed she would want that, he focused more closely on her eager face. "Tell me, can you ride a horse?"

She stuck out her chin. "Like an Indian. I have a good horse, too."

"Judith's horse," the mother said. "Blake is going to use him or sell him."

90

"He likes me better than Blake."

"Good taste on your steed's part," Hunter said. "Can you shoot and hit anything?"

"Like Daniel Boone."

He sat back and shook his head. "Nonetheless, it's too rough a game for a girl."

"I could do it."

"Don't be ridiculous," her mother said.

"I could."

"Tell you what, Miss Lexi." Hunter said, intrigued. "I'll take you riding tomorrow, if it's all right with your folks."

"Mama?"

"I don't see any harm in it." Her mother looked pleased. Most likely beaus didn't come knocking for this girl. But Hunter wasn't put off by her individuality. He found her interesting.

He smiled at both of them. "I'll be by first thing in the morning." The girl was fun, worth the trouble to wangle a couple of amusing hours.

"Where are you spending the night, Lieutenant?" Lexi's mother said.

"I don't rightly know, ma'am."

"Surely not on the street?"

"I hope not." He glanced around the comfortable home, considering his chances. "Could you recommend a place?"

"There's no sense in you're having to look for a place at this hour. We have a spare bedroom," Mrs. Winberry offered.

Hunter gave her a smile. "Much obliged."

"You aren't from South Carolina, are you?" Lexi said. "You don't talk--"

"Maryland," he told her.

"Oh, that's so far away."

"Behind the lines. I'll never go back!" He didn't intend for it to come out as snappish as it did. He smoothed his voice. "I guess you could say I'm an exile."

"I know how that is," Judith said. "I can't go home to Tennessee, either."

"Your people in Tennessee?" he asked.

"My stepmother and sisters." She looked wistful.

"You on speaking terms?"

"Oh, yes. I wish I knew when I could see them again."

"That's where we differ," he told her. "I've burned my bridges."

Chapter
Ten

Within a couple of days Blake's squadron had retreated with Stevenson's Division clear to Columbia. Matt covered for him so he could slip home.

Judith met him at the door. Her face lit up with surprise and relief and she threw her arms around him. She didn't seem to mind that he smelled of horse and used bullets. She touched his cheek. "Poor darling. You're cold."

He grinned and squeezed her. "Think you can fix that?"

"The Yankees aren't coming here, are they? Please tell me they're not."

He looked past her shoulder, around the inside of the house. Wood frame, wood walls, wood roof, wood floor. A firetrap. He said, "We have to talk."

Then Lexi and his parents came into the room, interrupting them. At least everybody was present to hear him out. Mama patted his shoulder. "Are you all right, son? You look so tired."

"Listen. The Yankees are on their way. There's going to be a fight."

Papa shook his head. "I heard they were going to bypass Columbia."

"Didn't Hunter Lightfoot tell you?"

"He did." Papa wrinkled his brow. "But the newspaper quoted General Hampton saying the enemy won't be able to take Columbia. He ought to know."

"When did he say that?" Blake waved his hand. "Never mind. The situation has worsened. We've been skirmishing with them a little, but there are so many... not enough of us. Even if we succeed, the Yankees might shell the city. They don't care if they kill civilians. Y'all need to go somewhere else."

"Son, even if Columbia falls," Papa said, "My duties will keep me here. I have respon--"

"Not after we evacuate the hospital," Blake said. "Stay, and the Yankees could take you prisoner."

"I cannot believe that even the Federals would have the temerity to do that. Some of the wounded cannot be moved, so I must stay. As a surgeon, I'm not subject to capture. Now, it is a good idea to pack off the ladies."

"I won't leave without you, Thomas." His mother's voice was strained, her hands clasped in front of her waist. "We can stay at the hospital. They wouldn't touch the hospital, would they?"

"I should hope not, Martha dear." His father looked vacant. "You know, my father came down from Connecticut. I went to school with Northerners in Philadelphia. Made some friends there I haven't heard from in years. This war is unnatural."

"Papa, those fine fellows you knew back then aren't running this thing. A lot of thugs are. They sack and burn and Lord knows what else." Blake glanced at the women. "At least send Mama and Lexi away."

"If we leave the house vacant, they'll burn it for sure," Mama said.

"For God's sake." Blake tried to keep his voice under control. "You can rebuild a house, but you can't--"

"They wouldn't harm women, would they?" His mother looked incredulous.

"Mama, why do you want to put them to the test?"

"Not so loud, son. We'll just stay at the hospital. We'll be safe."

"I hope to heaven we can keep them off so you don't have to find out what they're all about." Blake turned to Judith, who was hugging herself, anxious-eyed. "At least you will leave."

"How soon do I have to go?"

"Tomorrow."

"If I must."

"You must." He let his breath out between his teeth. At least his wife understood the danger, and she would obey him. "Get rail passage to Charlotte."

"But I'm going to Fayetteville. To Aunt Mary's house."

"No. Absolutely not. It's too far, and you can't get there by rail."

"But I don't know anyone in Charlotte," she objected. "Do you?"

"No. Doesn't matter."

"Not to you, maybe. It matters to me. I'd be all alone."

"Jude--"

She gripped his arm. "I have weapons. Besides that, several people have asked about a caravan toward Fayetteville. Two gentlemen with their families."

"How old are they? 75 or 80? Won't they be looking to you for protection?"

"I'll be fine. And you'll know where to find me."

He felt the anger rise in his chest. "We'll discuss it when we're alone."

Judith looked down, a stubborn set to her jaw.

"We don't wish to add to your burdens, son," Papa said. "I do agree that it would be best to send the ladies to Charlotte."

Mama threw up her hands. "Then we would be refugees."

"There is always Fayetteville," Judith said. "Y'all can come with me."

Blake shot her a warning look, but she wouldn't meet his eyes.

"Thank you for inviting us, my dear, but wouldn't your poor aunt be thrilled to have three guests instead of one?" Mama said. "Besides, I'm not up for such a hard trip. I'll just have to sit tight and hope for the best."

Judith turned to Lexi. "Want to come with me?"

"I'd rather fight them." Lexi said to Blake, "I'll join your troop and fight."

"Talk sense, little sister. I would like for just one person in my family to talk sense."

"Blake--" Papa began.

"Then I'll go with Judith." Lexi crossed her arms. "Never been to Fayetteville before."

"You're going nowhere," Mama said. "You'll stay with us."

"But Mama--"

"It's final. I won't have you running all over the country, and that's that. What Judith does is between her and Blake, but you are our responsibility, young lady."

Lexi tore upstairs and slammed her door.

"Oh, that girl," Mama said. "She's just impossible. Two boys were easier to rear than that one girl."

Blake took Judith's hand, holding onto his temper as well, and whispered, "Let's go talk."

~ * ~

After their lovemaking, Judith clung to him, fighting tears, her head pillowed on his shoulder. The secure corner of the world she had shored up was caving in. Shortly her husband would leave her again, and she would have to abandon her newfound home, or else face the Yankees.

What a fool she had been, letting herself believe she was safe here. Marrying Blake hadn't changed a thing.

No, that wasn't true. She kissed his neck and gently bit his ear lobe. He was part of her now, and she had more to lose.

He picked up a strand of her hair and lifted it off her forehead. "Do you think I might've got you in a family way?"

"It's too soon to know. Is that what you want?"

He laughed softly. "Who wouldn't?"

"I want your children. A light-haired boy that looks just like you. But it's a bad time."

"Might be the only time."

"Don't talk that way. You will be careful, won't you? We'll be out of touch, lord knows how long. What if you get hurt?"

"If I get hurt, Papa's here to patch me up. If I get killed, there's nothing anybody can do."

She shuddered. "Oh, please."

The corners of his mouth deepened, pained. "I wanted to do better by you."

"I knew in my soul the Yankees would mess up everything," she said. "I just didn't want to believe it."

"Sweetheart, don't drive to Fayetteville. Take the train to Charlotte instead. There's a run on mules and wagons right now, everybody trying to get away. Papa can sell that ratty old rig and get enough money to buy a ticket."

"It may be ratty, but it's mine." She sat up and hugged herself. "What would I do after I gave it up? I'd be stuck in Charlotte."

"That's the best I can do."

She drew up her knees and buried her face in her arms. "No."

Temper crept into his voice. "What's gotten into you? Why can't you just do what I say?"

Calm down, she told herself. He's bossy, but surely he'll listen to reason. She lifted her head and looked at him. "Even if I went to Charlotte, the Yankees are likely to go that way, aren't they?"

"We don't know which way they are going."

"See there? I might as well go to Fayetteville."

"It will take you at least a week."

"I'll be with a bunch of people."

"Jude, for God's sake--"

"Please, Blake. I don't have much left. Don't make me give up anything else."

"I can't let you drive to Fayetteville. It's too dangerous."

He just didn't get it. He was not going to be able to protect her, so she had to do the best she knew how for herself, just as she'd done before she married him. She looked away.

He reached under her chin and turned her face back toward him. "Jude--"

She balled up her fists, suddenly furious. "Are you going to make me? Tie me up and throw me on that train?"

His face darkened. "Is that what it'll take to get you to mind?"

"Mind? Ye gods and little catfishes. Mind? I'm not one of your troopers."

"You're my wife. You have to do what I say."

"I do not! You are leaving, and I'll have to manage the best way I see fit. Don't worry. I've had lots of practice."

"Damn it, Jude! I'm responsible for you."

"Responsible, my foot. You won't even be here. Maybe you'll even get yourself killed." Tears streamed down her cheeks.

"Yes," he agreed. "I might get killed. All the more reason to make sure you're safe."

"Don't bother." She was spitting out things she'd never intended to say, but couldn't seem to stop herself. "I've had lots of practice at being a widow, too."

Blake gripped her shoulders. Defiant, she met his eyes with her damp gaze. He checked his urge to shake her until her teeth rattled. Where was the agreeable woman he had married to soothe his aching heart? Now she was defying him. Worse, she was accusing him of not living up to his obligations.

And there wasn't a thing he could do to make her obey. He couldn't even march her to the depot because he was already overdue at his command post.

He let go of her and snatched for his clothes. "Have it your way. I can't stay any longer."

Judith threw her arms around him. "I'm sorry I said that. Please forgive me."

"Then do as I say."

She buried her face in his chest. "I can't."

What did husbands do to make wives mind? He couldn't raise a hand to her. He would never strike a woman.

He didn't know what else to with his arms, so he slipped them around her. He felt tense, and so did she.

"I finished your shirt," she murmured. "Don't you want to try it on?"

He nodded, teeth clenched.

"There is room on the wagon," she said. "I can take your things so the Yankees won't get hold of them."

He laughed harshly. "You might as well, since I can't stop you."

Then she broke down, sobbing bitterly.

Still angry, he softened a little. He held her to him, stroked her back, shushed and gentled her as he would a frightened colt, until her sobs trailed off and she rested hot and damp and quiet against him.

~ * ~

Next morning, Blake sat on his horse, shivering under his poncho. Though no order had passed down the ranks to maintain silence, most of the men were too cold to sing anyhow. They sneezed and coughed instead. Ice formed knives in the trees and crunched under Magic's hooves. The beast in front of him lifted its tail like a banner and plopped out balls of manure without missing a step. Steam rose from the shit-trail.

Ah, glory.

His troop marched directly behind General Butler's escort company. At an open field Blake spotted Butler's soggy hat plume.

"Halt," someone in front called out.

The command filtered back. "Halt." He lifted his hand and reined in.

"Whoa, you son." Matt stopped abreast of him, lumpy and round-shouldered in his wet greatcoat. Drooping hat hid his eyebrows, breath condensed white. He wiped his sleeve across his nose and pointed toward the field. "Fresh fish."

Beyond Matt's gloved finger, mounted men wearing Federal greatcoats approached, leading four riderless horses, driving four blue-coated men on foot ahead of them.

The mounted men brandished revolvers and sabers. "Keep going! Git! Go it, Yank!" The bluecoats cringed like dogs guilty of forgetting their housebreaking. They glanced about as if looking for a whipping.

"It's Hunter again," Blake told Matt. "Living up to his name."

The scouts herded the prisoners to the general for interrogation. Blake leaned forward, listening, but he was too far away to hear. He gazed across the field and into the stand of woods beyond. No sign of a Yankee infestation, but he imagined the mass and power of them, coming on.

This morning his division came back down the Charleston road toward Orangeburg to feel for the progress and strength of the enemy. The mission felt like poking barehanded under a log to check for snakes. He was glad the scouts had already flushed a few.

Judith sure had picked a miserable day to travel. If she would just do what he said and take the train out of town, at least she wouldn't have to endure so much exposure to the weather. She was liable to catch her death on the way to Fayetteville. It was too hard a trip for a woman to make by wagon. The headstrong, willful, disobedient female. God protect her. The same God that protects drunks, fools and soldiers.

Today he wore patched trousers and a threadbare old jacket because he expected to fight. Filthy business, fighting. He had folded the new shirt in his saddlebag to keep it from getting messed up. Maybe he would get a chance to wear it someday. It did look fine, and the workmanship expressed Judith's care. It fit just right.

Hunter rode up to him after finishing his business with Butler and said, "Howdy, old chum. We bagged ourselves some bluebirds."

"I took you for one myself," Blake pointed out. "If the Yanks don't get you, our people will."

Hunter chuckled, lit his pipe and shielded it from the drizzle with his hands. "That Yank lieutenant threatened to report me for insolence. Was he ever mad when he found out what was what."

Matt scowled, didn't bother to hide his dislike. Still believed in fighting fair.

Hunter tossed the match aside. "Unhealthy weather. Can't even keep my pipe lit."

"What does it look like down the road?" Blake said.

"Whole right half of Sherman's army is coming this way."

"How far?" Blake asked.

"Couple of miles. Some of their infantry are mounted on stolen horseflesh, like these lads." Hunter looked over the prisoners and their horses. "My, didn't we make a nice haul?"

The tamed Federals, still blown from their run, walked toward the rear between the columns of cavalrymen. Uniforms stiff with grime and soot. From campfires or arson? The captured officer kept his eyes straight ahead, humiliated, ignoring his own men as well as the guards.

Blake kneed Magic to one side, making room for them to pass. The Yankee lieutenant gave Hunter a withering look.

The Stewart twins shook their fists at the prisoners. "Yankee scum!"

"Bastards!"

"Shut up," Blake said.

The boys looked at him open mouthed.

"Aren't you brave!" Blake snarled. "Pick on somebody who can fight back."

"Did you get your folks to leave?" Hunter asked him.

"Nobody but my wife."

"I thought they'd be impractical. Where'd she go?"

Blake looked off so Hunter couldn't read his face. "We decided she'd better go to her aunt's place in Fayetteville."

"File right by twos!" someone ahead of him shouted.

He passed the command back and nudged Magic forward. Wouldn't be long before they pitched into the bluecoats. A tic started jumping underneath his left eye.

~ * ~

Judith drove to the rendezvous near the railroad depot. She was so early none of the other people in her traveling party had arrived yet. She hugged the waterproof cape her father-in-law had given her around her shoulders. Lexi sat beside her--she'd come this far to keep her company. Fancy stood, head and tail drooping, shivering in the freezing rain. Judith wasn't any happier about the situation than the mule. She grieved almost as deeply as she had when each of the men in her life had died. The enemy had snatched loved ones and security away. Hope was such a traitorous friend.

No trains in sight, but plenty of people stood waiting for the cars to come, so many they would be fighting for seats. The exiles huddled inside the station and under eaves dripping with frozen tears.

She was pretty well undone when Blake left last night. In the end he was kind, despite a stiff-lipped controlled anger.

But she couldn't do it his way. She just couldn't.

How did she ever let herself believe that marrying him would improve anything? She wasn't any better off. Maybe worse, after sampling a few days' happiness and having it snatched away again.

Lexi said, "Where are the others?

"I must be early. We ought to reach Camden tonight. Then we'll take the stage road to Florence. Fayetteville after that."

"Wish I was going with you. I've never even left the state."

"I wish I didn't have to go anywhere," Judith said, shaking off a shiver. "Are you afraid?"

Lexi shook her head, then drew a dagger from a pocket in the fold of her skirt and held it in front of her face. "If any Yankee tries to hurt me, I'll sure hurt him back."

"If I wasn't so afraid of them, I'd be staying, too. I'll try to write, but I don't think we can count on mail getting through."

"Look at all the people wanting to leave town," Lexi said. "Hey, there's Sally!"

"Where?"

Lexi pointed toward the depot. "She's wearing that tan coat. Her mother is standing right next to her. Where's old Randolph?"

Judith stared, studying the few men standing about, mostly old fellows. "Can't make him out."

"I'm going to go talk to her." Lexi flashed a wicked grin. Be right back." She climbed down from the wagon and hurried to the depot.

Moments later Lexi returned bringing Blake's ex-fiance, whose sausage curls frizzed in the dampness. Sally carried a parasol unfurled over her head. Her otherwise pretty face was compressed, lips pouting.

Sally looked down at the brown puddles in the road, frowned and stopped at the edge of the sidewalk. Then she stared at Judith, appraising. Judith returned the look.

Lexi grinned, pleased with herself. "Judith, Sally wanted to meet you. Sally, this is Blake's wife." She placed cheerful emphasis on "wife."

Judith could have stood living her whole life without ever meeting Sally face to face, but nodded and smiled anyway. Sally put on a smile, too.

Lexi said, "Sally's fiance left her at the depot."

"Mr. Randolph is not my fiance any more." Sally lifted her chin and a frown clouded her pretty forehead.

Judith blinked. "He's not? What happened?"

"Doesn't Sally go through fiances in a hurry?" Lexi laughed out loud. "Left her on the platform."

"To fend for myself." Sally twirled her parasol, furiously shooting droplets of water off the edges. "Only one place left on the train, and he took it. Told me he was in more danger than I was. Nobody treats me like that."

"Somebody just did," Lexi said.

Sally didn't act like she had heard. "Where's Blake?"

"Fighting the Yankees," Judith said.

"I knew it." She made a tsk sound. "Mister duty-and-honor. Wherever are you headed?"

"My aunt's, in North Carolina."

Sally tilted her head, green eyes gloating. "He left you too."

"He couldn't very well take me with him," Judith pointed out.

Sally laughed, not a pleasant sound. "I guess he figures you're used to being on the run. Used to refugeeing aroun--"

"Leaving was my choice," Judith snapped.

"I don't blame you for marrying him." Sally's claws were fully bared now. "Quite a step up."

Judith clenched her hands on the waterproof, wadding up the rubber material.

"You know why he did it, don't you?" Sally's eyes narrowed. "He wanted to make me jealous."

"That's ridiculous. How can you--"

Lexi took a step toward Sally. "Stop it. I didn't bring you over here to insult my sister-in-law."

Sally placed her hand on her hip and faced Lexi. "Be sure to tell your brother his little tit for tat game backfired. The joke is on him." She spun her parasol again and strode away.

Judith sat still in the wagon, watching the sway of Sally's hoop skirts as she hurried back to the depot, thinking of all the brilliant things she should have told her.

Lexi made an angry face. "Witch. Never could stand her. We ought to fix her. Roll her in the mud or something."

"Blake liked her just fine." Judith hugged herself. Suddenly it seemed important that he had accidentally called her Sally on their wedding night.

A boom, and Lexi jumped. "What is that? Thunder? Guns?" She stepped into the street, looking toward the sounds.

Another boom. Judith felt it more than she heard it. "Might be artillery."

Was it the sound of her husband being blown to bits?

Chapter Eleven

Blake guided Magic around the soggy piles of wood and resin on the narrow bridge. Her shod hooves cleared the icy timbers without a slip. Gray infantry and three artillery pieces with their tense crews waited behind the earth and timber works along the creek.

He'd been at it all morning and part of the afternoon. Four or five miles of dismounted Indian fighting from behind trees, peppering the bluecoats from every scrap of cover. They'd failed to turn them away. Again and again the Federals used their mass of troops to outflank the Confederates, forcing them to give up one position after another. Predicting what the Yankees were going to do didn't mean they could stop them.

If he had to yell "fall back" one more time it would stick in his raw throat.

His men looked weary and frustrated. Faces gray with cold, pinched and hungry under the powder stains. Fighting and falling back were damnably hard work. Plenty of bullets issued today, but no bread. Casualties were light--most of his men knew from experience how to take care of themselves while inflicting damage on the enemy.

But he had a few next-of-kin letters to write. In the noise and haze he saw both Stewart boys go down. Cliff forgot the instructions to stay low and took a bullet. Then his twin brother ran to him and got shot too. They crawled to safety and an ambulance wagon carted them away. He had an impression that Wilcox was killed, but he wasn't sure.

A courier rushed up to him and saluted. "Sir, General Butler sends his compliments and directs you to take your troop to the end of our left to protect our flank."

Blake led his men along the bank. The line of defense dwindled away almost a mile from the bridge. A few infantrymen at the end formed an oblique to the main line and faced the outside, a hedge against more flanking. The foot soldiers turned around from their breastworks of logs and dirt and eyed the newcomers. They were fresh out of cavalry jokes today.

After a brief conference with the captain in charge of this sector, Blake gazed across the creek over the gray backs. Thick woods, enough to hide the movements of the bluecoats on the other side.

He said to Matt, "They're coming again, I feel it." His voice sounded husky--all the shouting. "Not straight on, where they have to cross the creek in our faces. They'll go around the long way. Same old trick, attack from the side and roll us up."

Matthew sneezed. "They have to cross the creek first."

"They'll just wade. I used to swim it, not over my head anyplace. If they fell a big tree across it, they won't even get their feet wet. Let's extend the line a little, watch down this side of the bank. Stay mounted."

After he repositioned the troop, enemy artillery opened up. Shells landed and exploded far behind him, near the bridge. Concussions vibrated in his chest. He looked over his shoulder but couldn't see much through the trees. Friendly artillery--the battery at the bridge--boomed in reply. Rifle fire crackled, sounding like a burning field. But his part of the line wasn't under attack yet.

A long time seemed to pass, the rattle of rifles and the heavy boom of artillery marking seconds. Inactivity made him feel the cold more. His stiff hands ached. If he stayed still, he felt he might freeze to the saddle. Around him nervous men chattered and laughed. He pulled out his watch, checked the time. 4:43. Not much daylight left in the overcast sky. An hour, hour and a half at most.

Was that a movement through the trees? He averted his eyes to catch it. Nothing. He started breathing again.

The rain finally stopped. Wind crackled the ice in the trees--a shard dropped and flicked Magic's rump. She snorted and trembled; he stroked her neck to calm her.

He lifted his head, stiffening like a bird dog on point. Shadowy blue figures moved along the bank, right where he'd expected.

Murmurs of outrage, the hostile snicks of weapons cocking. He glanced around at the hard young faces. Like him, his men were fed up with being pushed clear to their own doorsteps. They looked to him for the word.

Poor ground for a cavalry rush. The woods would impede them and help the Yanks. He couldn't see beyond the first few skirmishers, couldn't be sure what he was getting into. He looked around at his troop. Only 25 men left out of the hundred who went to Virginia less than a year ago.

But a few men on horses, tons of barely controlled animals with yelling riders, ought to make somebody want to get out of the way.

"Let's go get 'em, Capt'n," a trooper said.

"We can take 'em," David Frank added.

Matt grinned, nodded. "Let's send 'em back to hell where they came from." He wiped his runny nose with his sleeve and smeared the powder stains under his eyes.

Blake glanced around at the wolfish faces and feverish eyes. If they didn't attack, take the initiative, they would lose faith in themselves.

He nodded and drew his revolver. "Attention."

They looked to him, weapons ready.

"Let's go. Charge!"

He kicked Magic and she lunged forward. He yelled from the bottom of his gut, couldn't hear himself for all the noise his men made. Colts and carbines spewed fire. Men and horses hit the jagged skirmish line and startled bluecoats scrambled for cover.

Blake gave Magic her head, guided her with his legs, trusting she would have the sense not to scrape him off on a tree trunk. A bluecoat fell in front of him. The crack and gleam of a rifle shot to his left, and a bullet zipped by his head. He swung his Colt toward the rifleman and squeezed the trigger. Blue appeared and vanished into the bushes. A riderless horse galloped by. A bough swept Blake's hat off and the strap burned his neck. Trees rushed past in a blur.

He spotted a full regiment of solid blue filling the woods behind the skirmish line, weapons ready and jerked Magic to a skidding stop.

"Halt," he screamed. He lifted his hand. "Fall back!"

Rifle explosions, bright through the smoke, confirmed he was right to call off the attack. He ignored a sting in his forearm, wheeled his horse and took a sullen backward look as he whirled away.

~ * ~

Clockwork.

Lieutenant Andrew McCord rode across the bridge at the head of General Howard's escort.

The rebels had tried to burn the bridge, but it must have been too wet to catch. Failing in that, they tried to knock down the supports, but Federal sharpshooters put a stop to that. Alongside the bridge stretched something that looked more like a saturated gray log than a freshly killed human being. The torso lay on the bank and the legs floated in the creek.

In the end, the Federals did not need the bridge anyway. Howard's engineers threw pontoons across the creek upstream, which allowed the usual flanking action against the rebels.

When were his misguided countrymen going to figure out they were licked and quit? He was willing to keep it up as long as they were, until the last one dropped with a Federal issue bullet in his body.

"Hail Columbia, happy land!

"If I don't burn you, I'll be damned!"

He turned to locate the voices, a knot of laughing soldiers on the bank. General Howard shook his head. Somehow, the general ought to show more disapproval than that.

McCord didn't like what he'd been hearing. The boys really were going to be hard to hold in this town. He didn't believe in making war on civilians, and he had been seeing more of it these days.

~ * ~

Blake stood on the north bank of the Congaree River watching the bridge burn. Unlike the bridge over the creek, this one had caught. The shooting flames made a dazzling display against the night sky, then the structure collapsed, hissing and steaming into the river. The Congaree was wide and swift, a fine natural barrier.

God, he was tired. The rage had gone and left a hole in the middle of him. He sat down. Didn't want to move or do anything. The smells of wood smoke, cooking bacon and cornbread made him dizzy.

"You going to get that thing seen to?" Matt asked. "You ought to go find the doc."

Blake looked at his arm. "It's nothing. Hardly touched the meat." It did pain. An annoyance.

"We had 'em runnin' for a little bit," Matt said. He leaned against a tree and sliced a plug of tobacco with his pocketknife. "Fun while it lasted."

"Your turn to write the letters."

"David took roll. Two killed and three wounded bad enough to hospitalize. But we gave better than we got."

"What did you hear about the Stewart boys?"

"Nothing since this morning. Jones got a finger shot off. I made him go back and get it looked at. You ought to get your arm done too."

"Quit pestering me." He rotated his wrist and flexed his hand. "See? Perfectly sound." He draped his poncho over it, hiding the dried blood.

David came up with supper. He handed a tin plate to Blake, one to Matthew, and kept one. Fine soldier, deserved a commission. Maybe someday, if he lived long enough.

Blake picked up a piece of bacon. The grease clinging to it congealed on the way to his mouth, but he didn't care. It tasted good and salty. The cornbread was soppy with grease, just what his stomach had come to expect.

Matt removed the plug from his cheek, saved it in a twist of paper, and devoured his supper. Then he stretched out on the wet ground. "My folks thought it would be a good time to visit some upland relatives."

"What did yours do, David?" Blake said.

"I told my father he'd better clear out, but he won't leave the store."

He wished his family had as much sense as Matt's did. And he hoped Judith found a safe stopping place for the night.

Jones weaved up, his hand bandaged, and threw himself on the ground. He smelled of whiskey.

Blake stood. "I'm going to see about the Stewart boys."

"Better get your arm looked at too. Get yourself some pain-killer." Matthew grinned. "Bring me some."

Blake found the regimental surgeon near the field headquarters. He was still working by lantern-light, standing at a table made from a door laid across two sawhorses. The place smelled of blood, like hog-killing time. Wounded lay nearby. One of them, his arm a bandaged stump, sobbed quietly, his face turned away from the others. Blake spoke to the torn men and looked at their faces but found none from his own troop.

He waited until the doctor was between patients, then said, "I'd like to find out about three of my boys we sent back."

"We packed off a bunch to the hospital in town." Dr. Thompson wiped his hands on his bloody butcher's apron and turned to his burly assistant. "Get the next one up here. How many more?"

"This bluebelly is the last one."

"Damn, I'm fast. Maybe we'll get some sleep tonight." Dr. Thompson swayed and rested his hand on the table.

"Twins. Don't you remember seeing twins?"

The doctor looked off and rubbed his stubbled chin. "Come to think of it."

"How are they?"

"One was shot in the face. He got a few teeth knocked out and his tongue cut up," Dr. Thompson said. "He'll do. The other one is critical with a penetrating lung wound that looked bad to me." He tapped himself on the ribs, showing where the wound was. "Kind of low. He'd have a good chance if it hit higher, but he wasn't that lucky."

"Colonel Aiken lived through being lung-shot. So have some other people I can think of."

Dr. Thompson grunted.

"If they went to the college hospital, my father will be taking care of them."

The surgeon turned to the prisoner, who sat on the table, cradling his bloodied foot in both hands. His toes curled with muscle spasms, his face twisted with misery. Blake recognized him. His men had hauled him in from the skirmish line they'd hit. He was from an Iowa outfit.

"I'd like to send a note to my father. Any more ambulances going into town tonight?"

"I reckon we'll make one more run." Dr. Thompson examined the bloodied foot in the dim light. "Hold still. Won't do a thing for you if I can't have your foot."

Blake asked the prisoner, "What's your name, Iowa?"

"Anderson." The Yankee looked at him suspiciously from the corner of his eye.

"Did you volunteer, or were you drafted?"

"I volunteered. Why?"

"A little hobby of mine. Find out what you people think you're doing down here."

"The right thing." The Yankee took on a stubborn look. "To preserve the Union."

Blake snorted. "Maybe I ought to feel flattered that the Northerns want me back in their country bad enough to kill me."

Loud and close by a cannon boomed and made all three of them flinch. A round screeched overhead and detonated across the river, a distant boom.

The surgeon poured water over the wounded foot, flushing away dirt and clots and blood.

Blake took a pencil and scrap of paper from his pocket and scrawled out a message for his father, making no reference to his own slight wound.

Dr. Thompson said to his assistant, "Hold his leg still."

The assistant clamped his huge hands around the ankle and leaned his weight on it. Anderson's eyes widened. "What you gonna do to me now?"

Dr. Thompson said, "Behave yourself, sonny. Don't want the knife to slip, do you? Lie back."

Anderson yelped at the first thrust of the surgeon's finger into the bullet hole, wriggled and arched like a fish being scaled alive. Blake tensed, feeling squirmy inside.

Finally Anderson's eyes rolled back and he went limp. Blake relaxed a little.

Dr. Thompson felt around the instep, his eyebrows drawn together, picked out bone splinters and dropped them into a pan.

Fresh blood oozed forth with every poke.

Blake held his hurt arm protectively close to his body. Another boom followed the last. He nodded toward the battery. "I hope none of those things fall short. Some of our artillery boys aren't such good shots."

The bullet from Anderson's foot clanked against the metal pan. "If they keep that up, none of us will get any sleep tonight," Dr. Thompson said.

"Neither will the Yankees." Blake smiled grimly. "Won't that make it easier to stand?"

"We're only going to make them mad." Dr. Thompson packed lint into the wound.

Anderson came to, blinking.

"Let them be mad," Blake said.

"They'll want to take it out on somebody. If they can't get to us, maybe the townspeople."

Anderson elbowed himself up and inspected his foot. Then he shut his eyes and lay quiet while the surgeon finished dressing the wound.

"There. Done." Dr. Thompson wiped his hands on his apron, then poured from an amber bottle into a mug and gave it to Anderson. "Here's your medicine, sonny." The surgeon took a swig straight from the bottle and swished it around his mouth before swallowing it.

Blake's mouth watered. "Aren't you going to offer me any?"

"It's for the wounded."

Blake lifted the poncho and showed him the injured arm.

The surgeon took another pull at the bottle. "Want me to have a look?"

"I took care of it myself."

Thompson handed him the bottle.

He took a large, warming mouthful, then handed it back. "My father wanted me to go to medical school, but I didn't. Too squeamish."

"Not so I noticed."

"I guess you get used to it."

"We could use more surgeons to clean up the messes y'all make. Maybe you should go medical school when the fuss is over. Ought to study on it."

"If I'm still around." Blake felt very tired. He wandered off to find his own piece of ground for the night.

~ * ~

Adrift again.

Heavy of heart, Judith shivered inside her blankets. She stared at the campfire and listened to Mr. Bagley's consumptive cough. He couldn't be very old, but he looked it. Amazing today's freezing rain didn't kill him. All of them, for that matter. At least the rain quit, but she and her companions still had to face a whole night out in the cold

After a late start, they hadn't made Camden by nightfall, and shelter was sparse in this region. They found none before night forced them to stop, just a clearing off the road.

She shifted on her aching buttocks. The springless wagon was mighty hard to ride in. Maybe the road would dry enough tomorrow for her to walk part of the time, leading Fancy.

The shelling was well under way when she'd rolled out of Columbia. She'd heard no news since, nothing. Was she a widow for the second time? Please, no.

She prayed Blake was safe, that they'd find each other again soon. If only she could talk to him, he'd confirm everything was all right between them. Assure her that Sally's poisonous words had no truth in them. Even if something was still wrong, she could figure out a way to make it right.

She looked off to the southwest, where she'd last heard the guns.

~ * ~

Next morning, Blake sat on the porch of a vacated house, cleaning his fingernails with his penknife, his legs swinging off the edge. His position gave him an excellent view over the boxwood hedge. All that was left of the Congaree Bridge were the brick piers sticking up like tombstones. From relative safety he watched the Federals milling about beyond the opposite bank. Somewhere among them a band thumped the bass rhythm of "Rally 'Round the Flag." Sun glittered on Yankee bayonets.

Sharpshooters on the near bank hid behind cotton bales and traded shots with their enemies. But distance reduced the deadliness--

didn't amount to much more than a reminder to keep one's head down. He'd counted three bullet thwacks on the deserted house, nobody in the way of any of them.

All day Butler's Division had waited in the streets at the edge of town, ready to contest any Union attempt to cross. Sustained gunfire indicated serious fighting northwest of town involving other units. It ought to be his fight too, but orders had placed him here.

His sore arm galled his nerves as much as the idleness did. This morning he had rinsed blood from his jacket sleeve and diluted the stain from dark red to rust. The damp fabric dulled the pain and cooled the inflammation but made him shiver. At least he wasn't sick from it. Matt's cold had worsened. He lay on the porch, flushed and feverish.

Wheeler's westerners were in town, swaggering and bragging how they had run the Yankee cavalry out of Aiken and saved the town. Almost caught the commander, a house burning general named Kilpatrick. Good for them. Maybe they would help save Columbia too.

Unfortunately, Wheeler's men held reputations as horse thieves that exceeded their reputations as soldiers. Blake did not want to help them prove they had come by the fame honestly, so he had placed the horses belonging to his troop in the back yard, under guard.

He heard the chuff of horses approaching along Huger Street and turned toward the sound. Hunter, this time in his fancy gold-braided gray coat, with a girl. Blake looked closer. Lexi, riding that spooky animal he had captured. Why was Hunter bringing her to the battle-zone?

He slipped off the porch and reached for the halter, but the horse shied from his hand. Useless animal, wouldn't ever make a decent cavalry horse.

But Lexi brought him back into line and grinned down from under her palmetto hat. "Aha! Found you."

"Lexi, what the hell are you doing here?"

"I brought you something to eat." Lexi untied a basket from the saddle and handed it to him. "Chloe is cooking everything in the house in case she can't later on."

He glanced down at the basket, aware that he was hungry, and the food had to be better than the bacon and cornmeal the army offered. "Thanks. What about Judith? Did she get away all right?"

"I rode with her as far as the depot. Good thing she didn't try for a train. One pulled up and you wouldn't have believed all the fighting and scrambling and carrying on. People hanging off the cars when it pulled out, I saw--never mind." She took a quick breath and continued. "The door was blocked with passengers, so somebody stuffed a woman through a window. Her feet stuck out for the longest time. Kick, kick, kick. You should have seen it. I like to died laughing."

"Did Judith team up with her party?" Blake asked. "How many in the caravan?"

Lexi nodded. "Five families, in all. She ought to be all right."

"Does Mama know where you are?"

"Course not." Lexi swung one leg around and lit on her feet as skillfully as a boy, even with her skirts in the way.

"Turn right around and go home." Blake whirled on the scout. "Hunter, what in God's name did you bring her here for?"

Lexi laughed. "Really, Blake. Don't have a conniption fit. Lieutenant Lightfoot came because I was going to find you with or without him."

Hunter smoothed his moustache. "That's so, old chum. You have a very resolute sister."

"How is it you are free to go joy-riding with my sister during a military emergency, Lightfoot? Doesn't General Hampton have a job for you?"

"My post is over there, old chum." Unruffled, Hunter jabbed his pipe stem toward the Federal army. "Since there is a bit of water in the way, I have no station for the time being."

He pointed to a dime-sized hole in the front door. "Those are real bullets they're shooting."

She stood her ground and looked across the river. "That's them? The Yankees?"

"Only a sample. They stretch for miles. Go home. It's too dangerous here."

"Just as dangerous for you, and I don't see you leaving."

"It's my job." He grabbed her hand and led her and the horse behind the house.

She hung back and looked over her shoulder. "What's that music? Do they have a band?"

"A band, artillery, bullets, pontoons and a horde of men," he told her.

Blake asked Hunter, "What's that fighting to the northwest? We can't see a thing from here."

"The Feds are trying to force a crossing of those two rivers at the fork--"

"The Saluda and the Broad."

"Yes, those. They are operating on the perfectly sound theory that two small rivers are easier to negotiate than one big one. Wheeler's men are disputing the point."

"And here we sit--"

"In case they change their minds and try the Congaree."

"What's the matter with your arm?" Lexi pointed to the rusty stain on his sleeve.

"Nothing."

A boom across the river made him start--artillery. The frame house would be no protection at all. "Get down!" he yelled. Then he pulled her to the ground with him.

Deceptively slow, the shell seemed to hang in the air over an intersection. Soldiers scattered out from under it. The bomb hit and detonated, sending dirt and debris hurtling upward. One soldier fell, thrown from his bolting horse. He got up, shook off the dirt and limped away.

Lexi popped to a sitting position. Her mount pelted toward home. Hunter held his own dancing horse steady, reins tight.

"That was exciting." Lexi laughed the fear away from her eyes.

The violent movement had reopened the arm wound. It hurt and throbbed and felt damp from fresh blood.

Another round plowed into the street and exploded a little farther north of where they huddled.

"All right, all right. I'll go home." Lexi stood up and dusted herself off. "See? No harm done."

Hunter slipped his boot out of the stirrup. "Ride with me."

Blake gave Lexi a leg up behind Hunter. "Go into the house and don't come out for anything."

He watched them ride away, not the way they had come, but a circuitous route away from the enemy artillery, using Hunter's evasive tactics. Lexi hugged against the scout's back with her arms around his waist. Her skirt hiked up enough to show some ankle.

Matthew walked up and blew his nose into a handkerchief. "Can't get any rest around here. Is that Lexi with Hunter?"

"He's taking her home."

"I'd be worried if that was my sister with him."

Chapter Twelve

Hunter felt Lexi lean into his back as a shell screamed overhead and exploded in front of them. Into his ear she said, "You going to lecture me too?"

"What's the use? I'd be wasting my breath."

She laughed. "You sure would."

"I hope you learned your lesson."

"What was I supposed to learn?"

He was aware of her arms around him, small breasts pressed to his back, her breath warm on the nape of his neck. Probably didn't have any idea what she was doing to him. He didn't mind physical arousal. But he'd vowed never to get attached to another living thing, and he didn't want to care for this girl.

He said, "You need to learn a little healthy fear. At the very least, respect."

He stopped in front of her house and she pointed to the horse cropping the dry winter grass in the front yard. "See? Scout knows where home is." She grinned. "I named him after you."

"Now stay home like your brother said. I have to go see General Hampton."

She jumped off Hunter's horse and turned her eager face up to him. "Let me go with you." Her breathless voice tumbled out. "I've worked it out. I've got my own horse. Judith didn't take him with her, and Blake doesn't want him because he doesn't like men. I'll cut my hair and wear a uniform, and they'll think I'm a boy."

"Would they really?" Hunter smoothed his moustache, liking her too much, trying to keep from laughing from sheer enjoyment. He ran his gaze over her slim figure. Maybe she could pass, not that it was ever going to happen. "I would know better. So would your brother. You don't want him to call me out for corrupting his little sister, do you? I'd hate to have to hurt him."

"He wouldn't--"

"Lexi, seriously." He lifted his hand, cutting her off. "We can't possibly hold this town. Just don't sass the Yanks when they come in."

"I'd like to crack a few chamber pots over their heads. Brim full."

"Don't give them any excuses to mistreat you." He paused, making up his mind. "Tell you what. Know how to use a revolver?"

"I told you I shoot like Daniel Boone."

"Then I'll leave you my Colt navy. I can always get more from the Yanks. He unbuckled his gun belt, slid one of the holsters off and handed it down to her. "Careful, it's loaded. Don't get yourself in trouble over it. You must never, ever use it except to save your life."

She hefted the revolver, reverently turning it in her hands. Finally showing respect for something.

"Take care of yourself, Lexi." He turned his mount and rode away, figuring that was the last he'd see of her, and both of them were better off for it.

~ * ~

Well after midnight Blake slipped home to tell his family goodbye.

Mama and Papa stumbled into the hall, sleep wrinkled, Mama carrying a candle. He embraced both of them. "We're leaving at first light. They're going to surrender the town."

Mama started to cry, and it unnerved him. He wasn't used to seeing her weak.

"At least there won't be any more fighting," Papa said.

Blake took a deep breath. "The Federals have crossed the Saluda and there isn't much keeping them from crossing the Broad. No good choices. If we don't give it up they'll reduce the town to rubble."

"They won't harm a surrendered town," Papa said.

"I hope." Blake looked down the hall to his sister's closed door. "Better wake Lexi, tell her goodbye too."

He knocked and called her name.

She slipped out and closed the door behind her. "What is it?"

Papa told her what was going on. Good thing he did. The words would have stuck to the roof of Blake's mouth like bad medicine.

"Goodbye, little sister."

She hugged him. "Take me with you. I have a horse and I can ride."

"Go to the hospital with Papa. The Yankees will leave you alone there." Blake turned to his father. "Papa, how are the wounded from my troop? Never had a chance to see about them."

"Two will recover. The third cannot."

"The Stewart boy with the chest wound?"

"Yes, son. I'm sorry."

Blake gazed around the dark house. No use staying any longer, drawing out the pain.

~ * ~

At dawn Blake got the order to abandon the town. He led his sullen men through the streets. Farewell, Columbia.

His edginess had been worsened by a terrific, ground-shaking blast an hour before. He had ordered his men on alert until he found out what the explosion was about. He later learned looters in the railroad depot had found kegs of gunpowder with their torches. The depot was disintegrated along with the looters.

He picked his way through the chaos. An overturned wagon lay on its side. Tangled in the traces, still harnessed, lay a mule with a broken leg and a blood-encrusted bullet hole behind its ear. The bed of the wagon was empty, picked clean. So were the stores. A powder trail of flour led from a grocery store into the street. Blake steered Magic around window glass that littered the road.

At the government storehouses along Main Street, authorities supervised the loading of commissary goods onto wagons. The workers shuffled as though they'd been at it all night.

Mr. Frank sat in front of his store, a shotgun across his lap. David started to dismount, then glanced at Blake for permission. "Sir?"

"Take a few minutes," Blake said. "Then catch up."

"Wait," Mr. Frank stood up and set down the shotgun. "I got something for your men."

Blake called a halt and watched the storekeeper lead his son into the shop. They came back out, each carrying a wooden crate. They set the crates down and broke them open.

Matthew sniffed and grinned. "Cough medicine. It'll do me good."

Mr. Frank handed Blake a bottle of red wine. "I might as well let you boys have it, even if you are throwing us to the wolves."

Blake frowned, needled. "We did all we could. Now we're ordered to skulk off, not even allowed to return fire. Don't want street fighting."

"A villain in a gray coat made me take no-good lead coins at gunpoint!" Mr. Frank shook his fist in fury. "I don't want his kind to get nothing more, and I don't want no drunk Yankees in my store either."

Blake stuffed the bottle into his saddlebag, squashing the food he had hoarded from Lexi's basket. "Didn't you report that soldier to the provost marshal?"

"It's no use, they don't do nothing. Even my own son don't do nothing. Soldiers are supposed to protect people, not run away."

"I'd fight them here, anywhere." David studied the ground.

Blake understood the boy's humiliation. He felt the same, but couldn't indulge his feelings. "Mount up, Sergeant Frank. We have orders."

A few blocks further, he came to Sally's house. He had not seen her or spoken to her since he told her he was going to marry Judith. The sight of the white wooden house brought up memories of their courtship and his love for her, come to nothing.

She was standing on the porch, alone, watching the soldiers go by. When she saw Blake she cried, "You're not leaving us!"

He reined Magic over to the steps. "Where's Randolph?"

She crossed her arms over her full breasts. "Didn't Lexi give you my message?"

"What message?"

"I'm not engaged to Mr. Randolph any more. It's all off."

"What? He stared at her. "You're not getting married?"

"Not to that poltroon."

His mouth went dry. "Matt, take the men on. I'll come after."

Matt gave him a disapproving look.

"That's an order."

Matt moved away, his forehead knit in a frown.

He dismounted, tied Magic to the rail and stepped onto the porch where Sally stood, small and scared. Her moist jade eyes looked at him with appeal from under long lashes.

"What are you doing here, Sally? You should have gone somewhere safe."

"I tried to, but Mr. Randolph..." She started to cry and fell against him. He wrapped his arms around her and she trembled in his embrace. "Oh, Blake, what am I going to do?"

"I can't very well bring you along on the march."

She lifted her head from his shoulder, looked at the dusty soldiers riding past and wrinkled her nose. "No. That wouldn't do." She gripped his arm, fortunately the unhurt one. "Can't you come inside?"

"Only a minute." He followed her into her house, to the parlor. She sat on the couch where they had made love, patted the cushion next to her and smiled through her tears.

He looked around. "Where's your mother?"

"She's so upset she took to her bed. We can talk."

He sat down and removed his hat. She laid her hand on his thigh. "Hold me, Blake. I'm so scared."

"Hold you? I'm a married man."

She ignored his protest. "I want you to understand." Her warm, frightened little body pressed closer. "That I never loved Mr. Randolph the same way I loved you."

"Fine way you had of showing it." His arm slid around her as though of its own will. "Why'd you throw me over?"

"I made a mistake." She brushed her lips against his ear, whispering. "Remember those times, before you left for Virginia? Wasn't I sweet to you? Remember what we meant to each other? You were everything to me, and I was your first love."

He certainly did remember, and the old longings returned full force.

Outside, an officer shouted a command. In the distance a rifle shot cracked. Another shot.

He looked toward the window, blinking. "Good Lord." He shook off her spell and struggled to bring his body under control.

Gently he pushed her away and rocked to his feet, amazed at his own lapse.

She pouted. "Oh, go on, then. Go ahead and save your carcass."

"I'll get back to check on you, somehow."

She turned away. "Just see if I'm waiting."

He snatched his hat and hurried out the door onto the porch. Bluecoats were marching up the street, just about in rifle range. Not a Confederate in sight. He snatched up Magic's reins and leaped into the saddle.

"A Reb! Shoot him!"

A couple of shots, and two minie balls sang by. He wheeled Magic around the corner of the house, shielding himself from their sight, and he was away.

He let out a shaky breath, ashamed. Lord, that was close. His idiotic behavior could have gotten him killed. Guiltily he thought about his near-betrayal of Judith.

He caught up to his troop and halted them on a hill outside of town. From there he watched the blue columns fill the open streets. Watchdogs passed the alarm from one end of town to the other.

Cheney looked ludicrous in a tattered greatcoat several sizes too big that fluttered around him in the rising wind. He balanced his bottle of wine on the pommel of his saddle and wiped tears from his cheeks. Matt coughed and blew his nose and swore.

Blake tried to pray, but his bankrupt faith carried his thoughts no higher than the top of his skull. His sore arm started to throb again. He supported it by hooking his thumb in his gun belt.

The sight of invaders taking his own hometown stirred his gut like ipecac. His mother, father and sister left to their mercy. And Sally.

An aide brought him orders to proceed up Winnsboro Road and rendezvous with the rest of the division at the village of Killians. He led the troop away from the hilltop.

~ * ~

Sally stood at the window and watched the Yankees boil through the streets, taking over the town. She shivered, a chill of fear. The men in her life had left her to the mercy of her enemies.

All her nineteen years, she'd never lived through such miserable days as the past two. How could Randolph humiliate her so, leaving her stranded at the depot? He'd sure had her fooled. She had never taken him for a coward who would let her down when things got difficult.

Her heart had lifted at the sight of Blake and she turned to him for help. But he left her too. At least he'd responded to her, she felt it just as surely as the desire he kindled in her. And he was still in love with her. She was sure of it, even if he did marry that widow creature just to show her up.

A fat lot of good that did now. He was gone, and the Yankees were here.

Her mother came down the stairs, clinging to the banister. "The Yankees! I heard shots and saw them outside. Oh, Sally! What are we going to do?"

Sally peeked out the window at dirty blue-clad men as they stacked their weapons and walked off or lounged around. A clump of them eyed her house and talked among themselves.

"Get away from there!" her mother cried. "What if they see you?" Ma threw herself down on the couch, burying her face in her hands. Her voice was muffled. "Oh, what are we going to do? Yankees plunder and steal and burn houses."

"And rape." Sally laughed, feeling mean. "They'll probably rape us both."

Ma went pale and stared at her, mouth open. Then she said, "Young lady, you shouldn't even know of such things."

Sally rolled her eyes. "Why don't you go back to bed, Ma. You're no good out here."

"I don't dare let them find me in bed."

Sally glanced outside again. She had mentioned rape just to tweak her mother, but wasn't it a real possibility? Another shiver ran through her. The thought of one of those filthy animals clawing at her made her stomach turn. Up to now, she'd been able to maintain power over men. Never before had lust been turned as a weapon against her.

But the Yankees were only men after all, and she would know how to handle them. "Know what, Ma? I'm sure some of them are gentlemen."

"They're Yankees. No Yankees are gentlemen."

Sally picked at her sleeve thoughtfully. "We'll find the nicer ones. Officers. They'll want to stay in our house where they'll be comfortable. If we're hospitable, surely they won't be too hateful."

"Yankees! In my house?" Ma's eyes widened in horror.

"That's right, Ma. And you'll be nice as pie." She laughed, liking the idea. "Tell Sophie to cook up a big dinner, the best she can hunt up. We're going to have lots of company."

She flew across the floor and raced upstairs to her room. She threw open the cedar chest by her bed and tore through the old linens stored inside. Underneath the bedclothes she found it.

She lifted the flag, unfurled it, and waved it over her head. Old Glory. She had put it away forever, she once believed, but it sure was going to come in handy now.

Her days as a Confederate were hereby finished. As far as the Yankees were concerned, she had always been a staunch Unionist trapped in a Secessionist city.

Smiling, she draped the flag over her arm and prepared to meet the conquerors.

~ * ~

Andrew McCord rode through the streets and viewed Columbia through victorious eyes. The cradle of secession, fairly won.

Dark-skinned people danced and clapped their hands and sang strange wild songs and flashed strong teeth in jubilant grins. He waved at them. They surged forward, jabbering, patting his horse and his blue pants legs. He laughed, heady with heroism. Behind him the band tooted and banged "Yankee Doodle."

One of the coloreds handed him a gourd. "For you, sah." McCord sniffed the contents. Whiskey.

He handed it back and told the colored man, "I don't use this stuff. You'd better not give this out to the soldiers. They get drunk, no telling what will happen."

The Negro just laughed. McCord watched him skip straight to a group of soldiers who were loitering on the sidewalk. One of the soldiers snatched it and upended it into his mouth. The others shouted and tried to grab it away from him.

McCord rode over to the soldiers and reached down for the gourd. "Let's have it."

Rebellion flicked across the soldier's coarse face. He clasped the gourd to his chest. "Aw, come on, Lieutenant."

"Now."

The soldier glanced around at his comrades. Was he expecting support for his little mutiny? McCord suggestively curled his hand around his saber grip.

A tall soldier finally said, "You might as well, Harry. Not like there's a shortage."

Without allies, Harry handed the gourd up to McCord.

"That's better, private." McCord turned it upside down and emptied it. Licking their lips, the soldiers mournfully watched the liquid splash and soak into the ground.

"We won't have any drunk and disorderly conduct in this town," McCord told them. "Is that clear?"

"Yes, sir. Anything you say, sir." Good-natured grins from all but the soldier named Harry.

He rode further, scouting the northeast side of town, where he spotted Old Glory fluttering from the balcony of a house. He slowed his horse to enjoy the inviting sight.

Even more delightful, a very pretty girl stepped out onto the porch and looked right at him. She gave him a demure smile.

He turned his horse toward her yard. That house was going to make a fine headquarters.

Chapter
Thirteen

Sam spent the morning leaning against the fence, watching soldiers march by. Squads of them left Columbia behind all morning and headed north. First came the foot soldiers, then the horse soldiers. Looking downcast, they paid him no mind. He was mostly invisible because of his color. Besides that, he reckoned they had their own problems right now.

He and the old man were going to be in for it soon. He had done all he could to get ready, buried food and valuables in the woods, even hid the pistol under his coat. He slid his hand underneath, stroking the handle.

More horsemen approached. He climbed up onto the fence for a better look, recognizing a few. He grinned and waved his hat at the men who used to be in the old man's troop.

Captain Winberry lifted his head. "Hey, Sam."

"Look at you, Sam," Lieutenant Kirkland said. "How's the Old Man?"

"Tolerable. How come y'all are leavin'?"

"Change of base." The captain smiled bitterly. "Get your mule and come along with us."

"Yeah, c'mon, Sam," the lieutenant said.

Sam felt a tug, longed to skip off and join them. He longed to brag about how he killed the buckra. But he better keep his mouth shut in front of these white men. "No sah. Have to stay, take care of the old man."

The captain nodded. "All right, Sam. I know you've got to do that."

He watched them file by. It didn't take long. He could cipher well enough to tell that the troop was a sight smaller than it used to be when it was based on the coast.

~ * ~

Harry Bell got himself away from that damned lieutenant and his brass-kissing buddies and found more free whiskey anyhow.

The whiskey made him drowsy. He tethered his horse and stretched out on a bale of cotton left by the street. He lit a cigar and dropped the match, still burning, onto the cotton bale. It smoldered and smoked as it caught a few of the fibers.

Ought to be better things to do in a town this size. He picked up his rifle, heaved to his feet, and mounted his horse.

He rode to the state house. Some of the boys were tearing up the place. Official-looking papers had been carried by the stiff wind littering the park. He scratched under his armpit and watched soldiers tear up a battle-flag from some war or another. Let them waste their time. He would hit the stores and get some loot.

He rode the horse into a grocery store. Others got there first. Busted glass, counters broke open and knocked over, merchandise mostly gone. A kid in a blue uniform scooped hard candy off the floor and stuffed it into his pockets. Emmett, the half-wit from his own company.

"Hey, Harry." Emmett grinned and tossed him a piece of red candy. Harry let it fly past his head and out the window. "How come you bringing that critter inside?"

"That's it? Nothin' left but candy?" Harry looked around at the rubble.

The boy stuffed candy into his mouth until his cheeks bulged. He looked like a squirrel, even to the buckteeth. He couldn't close his mouth all the way, so some syrupy spit oozed from the corners and stuck to the sparse whiskers he'd managed to raise.

Harry snorted. "Why you wasting your time on that stuff? Don't you want nice things, like watches?"

Emmett adjusted the candy in his cheek with his tongue. "S-sure." More spit sputtered out.

"C'mon."

It'd be fun to show off his skill to a pupil, even dumb little Emmett. Harry dismounted and walked along the sidewalk, leading the horse, scouting for a victim. Not many prospects. Most civilians were afraid to walk the streets this day.

But a few wary men in civilian clothes walked the streets on some business or another. He spotted one, handed Emmett the horse's bridle and stepped out in front of the old bugger. Harry pointed across the street. "What building is that?"

The old man obliged, pointing. "That's the state arsenal." As the arm went up, gold glinted.

Harry snaked out his hand and snatched a watch from beneath the coat. He let it dangle from its chain like a pendulum. "A very pretty little watch. He, he, he. Just to my liking."

Emmett made a snorting giggle. The old man's face went red and he lunged for the watch. "You give that back!"

Harry shoved him aside and swaggered away, his capture cradled in his hand. The old man had enough sense not to follow him. Ought to count himself lucky he still had two good pins to stand on.

"That was the slickest thing I ever seen," Emmett said.

Harry thrust out his chest. "Just my way!"

Further on he spotted a slim man about fifty years old, walking down the sidewalk toward them like he didn't have enough sense to be scared of all the Union soldiers. "Now, boy, why don't you go over and ask that mule turd what time it is?"

"But you already got a watch. Can't you tell time?"

"Sure I can tell time, stupid. Just do what I say. Then when he pulls it out, swipe it."

Emmett giggled. "Yeah, I can work that." He intercepted his victim and asked him for the time.

The civilian backed up a step, glancing from Emmett to Harry. "I have no watch."

Harry stepped in. "Now, don't lie to us." He looked over the man's tailored black coat and the felt hat with a medical insignia on it. "You a sawbones? Don't tell me you don't have a watch."

The sawbones looked down his nose at Harry like he was the mule turd. "I left it at my house."

"Where's your house?" Harry shifted his rifle in his hands. If a nearby office weren't eyeing him, he'd have used the butt of it against the man's skull.

The sawbones looked smug, like he had a joke on them. "All

right, then."

He led them to a white wooden house. Two Union soldiers sat on the front porch. The sawbones pointed at Harry and Emmett and said, "These men are pursuing me."

The guards stood up. One of them said, "Go inside, Dr. Winberry. We'll get rid of these fellers."

The other said to Harry, "Go on down the road, bub." Then to Emmett, "You too, boy."

Harry hefted his rifle. "You fellers ain't protecting this Reb, are you?"

"Yep. Orders."

"I'll be damned." He glared at the sawbones they called Dr. Winberry standing inside the open door, looking at him with his arms crossed, smiling. Then he remembered where he'd heard that name before, from Old Man Hughes. A Captain Winberry had busted up his fun and killed Dink. Must be a relative.

Emmett tugged on his coat. "Let's go, Harry."

"We'll be back, bastard," Harry said under his breath. "We'll be back."

~ * ~

Lexi started to gather her things. The Yankee guards had disappeared right after sundown and she took it as a bad sign.

She squeezed into several layers of underclothing and stepped into the hoop skirt. She had prepared it for emergencies by tying pouches to the wire framework and filling them with small treasures. Pictures, a gold chain, coin and other valuables. Over that she pulled on three blouses and four skirts.

How could she hide the revolver Hunter had given her? She studied it, examining the cylinder. It was crammed full of powder and shot, just like he had said. It was as dangerous as Hunter. She wrapped it in a scarf so she could carry it undetected.

She adjusted her laden hoop skirt, heavy enough to cut her in two if she had to wear it for a long time. Good thing the weather was cold. Otherwise, the layers of clothing would suffocate her. She slipped her dagger into her pocket.

Try something, Mr. Yankee.

~ * ~

To Harry, routine signal flares shooting from the camps

surrounding the city marked the opening of the ball. He figured on a rousing good night.

He stationed himself in front of the Winberry house, waiting for his chance, armed with a bottle of turpentine and pockets full of cotton balls and matches. An incendiary through the window didn't seem personal enough, like a letter instead of a visit. He wanted inside.

He didn't see the guards. They might be in the house, and they had guns. No sense tangling with them.

Part of town was already ablaze and fugitives stumbled down the street carrying their belongings. To a woman who brushed by with her brood in tow, he called out, "What do you think of the Yankees now, rebel bitch!"

She gave him a dirty look.

"Give it here!" He grabbed the carpetbag out of her hands and threw it to Emmett.

She reached, imploring. "Please. That's all I was able to save from the fire!"

He and Emmett tossed it back and forth, playing keepaway until he got tired of the game. He tore it open, but found only a few pieces of clothing. He pulled them out, one by one, and shook them. The woman watched, her eyes watering. Her brats hid behind her skirt.

Harry stowed the plunder back inside. "You want it?"

The woman nodded, her chin quivering.

"What you think, Emmett?"

The boy jerked his skinny shoulders. "Aw, give it to her. Nothing for us, Harry."

Harry threw the carpetbag down. She reached for it, and gold glinted on her neck. He grabbed it. A necklace broke off in his hand.

"Pretty. It'll do."

He let the woman run away, her carpetbag clutched in her hands, her brats trotting after her. She looked over her shoulder once, and he laughed.

Harry turned back to the house. "Oh, hell, Emmett. What're we waiting for? I don't see no guards."

He stomped onto the front porch and tried the door. It was

locked. He broke in one of the windows with his gun butt. Then he and Emmett beat the broken glass away from the ledge and climbed inside.

The sawbones met them in the front room. He didn't look so smug this time.

Harry grinned. "Where'd them guards go?"

Winberry looked from him to Emmett. "They are in the back."

Harry glanced down the hallway. "Hell they are. I come for that watch."

A woman's voice came from another room. "Thomas, what's the matter?"

"Never mind, Martha. Stay where you are."

Harry grabbed him by his collar. "The watch, bastard."

Emmett stood by, all excited, mouth hanging open.

Harry brought his bayonet up to Winberry's neck. "I'd just as soon kill you. Won't hurt my feelings."

Winberry's eyes crossed, focusing on the bayonet. "I'll get them."

"I'm goin' with you."

Winberry led him to a trunk in a bedchamber. Martha came into the room. Good, a bigger audience. And she wasn't bad looking. He'd never done it with a woman old enough to be his mother. Not yet. But he never knew his mother, who she was or what she looked like. She'd been useless to him all his life. And he hated her for it.

"You got any relatives that's a Reb captain?" Harry said.

Winberry and his wife looked at each other, unnerved, then he said, "Just about everybody I know has relatives in the Confederate Army."

"Not everybody, bastard. You."

"My son," Winberry said. "How do you know of him?"

"I owe him one." Harry grinned. It was going to be fun making the doctor and his wife pay what their Reb sonofabitch son did to poor old Dink. Not that he gave a damn about Dink, but he'd avenge him anyway.

Winberry took too long opening the trunk, so Harry shoved him aside, raised his gun and blasted the lock open. The room echoed with the gunshot and fogged with smoke. The woman covered her ears and the sawbones held onto her.

Harry ripped the lid open and rummaged through the trunk. Found a few trinkets under the bed linen, but nothing worth his trouble. He reloaded his rifle and pointed it at Winberry's head. "You lied! Where'd you hide your valuables?"

"For God's sake leave us alone."

"Not till you give us what's ours!"

Winberry sighed defeat and pointed toward a black box on the bookshelf. "There. Take it and get out."

Harry tossed the box to Emmett. Then he spotted a chamber pot. He had to take a leak, so he pulled his pisser out right in front of Martha dear and whizzed into the pot. Then he set the pot on the bed, stood back, raised his rifle to his shoulder and took aim.

The pot shattered and slopped piss onto the mattress. Emmett held his sides for laughing so hard. Martha shrieked and Winberry said, "Lord help us," under his breath.

~ * ~

Lexi heard a gunshot. She picked up the revolver, unwrapped and unholstered it. She opened the door as quietly as she could and edged down the hallway. She moved too slow, hampered by all the clothes.

She heard voices and harsh laughter, another gunshot, and a scream. Mama. Oh, no. Yankees must have broken into the house. What were they doing? Murdering her parents?

She drew back the hammer on the heavy revolver and started down the stairs. Couldn't see anybody. Then she spotted a man in a blue coat coming out of her parents' bedroom, rifle balanced in his elbow. He struck a match on the wall and held it to a cotton ball. She couldn't see the Yankee's face. He was busy setting his little fire, his back to her. She smelled turpentine.

She raised the revolver and held it out with both hands. It stuck out, seemed like a mile, weighing down her arms. She took aim along the wavering barrel. Steady, steady. The target wasn't very close, and she wasn't a practiced shooter. Her brag to Hunter was just that.

She squeezed the trigger. The revolver barked and jerked, setting her ears to ringing.

The Yankee yelled and bounded for the front of the house. She drew back the hammer and fired again, but he was already gone, out of sight. Another Yankee darted out of the bedroom and looked up at her as he ran by. She saw his panicky face. She shot at him too, but he kept running. Didn't even try to shoot back.

Cowards.

She almost tripped running down the stairs. Then she grabbed a pillow from the sofa and beat out the fire.

"Lexi!" Papa staggered out of the bedroom. "Did they hurt you?"

She shook her head. "Mama? She all right?"

"She's shaken, but that's all." He stared at the revolver. "Where in heaven's name did you get that?"

"Lieutenant Lightfoot thought we might need protection. Guess he was right."

He embraced her, but she freed herself and said, "No time for that, Papa."

She stalked through the front room along the path the Yankees had fled. No blood. She looked out the smashed window. They were gone. She frowned at the revolver. "Some Daniel Boone. How could I have missed three times?"

Papa said, "They followed me home this afternoon. I believed we were safe to stay here, with the guards."

"A Yankee lie," Lexi said.

He looked uncomprehending. "I never thought--"

"Those guards were Yankees too," Lexi said bitterly. "Just like the ones I ran off. Cut from the same bolt."

"I am thankful nobody is hurt."

"I wish I killed them both," she snapped.

~ * ~

After Harry got his breath back, he asked Emmett, "Who was that tried to plug us?"

"A girl."

"A what? A girl?"

"She had a pistol. Think we better tell somebody she shot at us?"

Harry shook his head. "Too much trouble." Too much explaining. He stopped to reload his rifle. He had messed up, not reloading it right after he blasted the chamber pot. "Damn. I left that box full of loot."

"Want to go back for it, Harry?"

"Probably Confederate money. Not even good for a bottle stopper. Besides that, she'll be laying for us. A girl, for Christsakes. Shit, shit, shit."

~ * ~

Lexi moved through the house, gathering whatever seemed important. From time to time she paused to look out her window at the coppery sky and the pulsing glare. The house next door was ablaze now, wind blowing flaming debris in her direction. Glowing embers flew to the window, fell, and died in the grass.

The roof of the shed where the horses and the cow were usually housed, started to smoke. She had already talked Papa into taking the animals to the campus common. Hunter's idea, so they were less likely to get stolen.

She snatched a picture of Justin and Blake off the shelf and threw it into her carpetbag. She sniffed--smoke, not the powder smoke from the shooting--wood smoke, thicker than before. She climbed the stairs, spotting the smoke curling down between the rafters. The roof must have caught. She called out a warning to Mama and Papa and waddled her overstuffed way down the stairs.

Mama hadn't recovered yet. Shaking, pale, eyes glazed over. Lexi saw her like this just once before, when they got the news about Justin. She took to bed for a week then. Couldn't afford that luxury this time. "Where's Chloe?" Mama cried.

Lexi shrugged. "Bet she's run."

"Run? Where?"

"Mama, don't be so slow. Run away. That's that." Lexi dusted off her hands. "Let's get out of here before we are roasted."

Mama closed her bundle and picked it up, set it down, picked it up again. It was frightening to see her unnerved. Lexi knew it was up to her to get them to safety. "We have to go, Mama. It's only a house."

"No it isn't. It's part of my life."

Papa came from the back of the house carrying a trunk on his shoulder. "Lexi, what did you do with that pistol?"

"It's under my coat."

"You had better give it to me."

"No. If they catch you with it, they'll hang you. I'm a girl. What are they going to do to me?"

"I don't know, daughter, and I don't want to know."

"If the same men are out there waiting for us, they will know I am not afraid to shoot."

He didn't argue after that. They left the smoking house. She stumbled and lost a shoe, but kept going.

Mama held onto her arm and Lexi clutched Papa's coattail so they would not get separated. Outside, the blaze roared and crackled around them, a tunnel of hell. Hot wind blasted her face. Soldiers jostled and shouted. Lexi remembered Hunter's warning to keep her mouth shut. She bit her lip and glared at the Yankees, only daring them with her eyes.

Slow going, smoke swirled in the hot wind, filling her lungs, making them ache, blinding her. She looked around, disoriented, coughing. They had to pass through an inferno of blazing houses. A roof crashed down through a two-story building, shooting sparks skyward. Points of fire rained down, burning holes in her wool coat. She let go of Papa to swat them. Her bare foot came down on a stinging ember.

She squinted through the smoky haze, trying to locate the college. Then a terrible thought came to her. What if it was burning too?

Only one way to find out. She kept on walking.

Chapter

Fourteen

Sally sat listening to the crackle and rush of fire and the noise of the mob. The Yankee officers she had invited into her house had gone, attending to whatever business Yankee officers did. Probably helping their men burn down Columbia.

She shivered, knowing her hometown would never be the same after the Yankees were through with it. At least her house had not caught fire yet. One thing in her favor, the wind wasn't blowing the embers her way. And she didn't believe even Yankee heathens would deliberately burn out their own officers.

So far her strategy was working. The Yankee officers were pleased to hear her Unionist sentiments, and even more pleased to enjoy her home. She found herself surrounded by ardent male admirers, and discovered she didn't mind a bit that they wore blue uniforms. Yankees were just as susceptible to her charms as Southern men.

Boot steps and laughter sounded on the porch. Maybe the Yankee officers were coming back. Maybe that handsome Lieutenant McCord. He was nice, for a Yankee, even if he did talk through his nose. She preened and arranged a welcoming smile on her face.

The locked door broke open and two filthy blue-coated men kicked inside, strangers. "Ha! Nobody's got into this one yet," one of them boomed.

She jumped to her feet and cried, "Get out of here at once!"

"That's not the Southern hospitality I been hearing about." The burly soldier advanced toward her. "Emmett, this is the best scenery yet in this sorry town."

Sally whirled to flee, but collided with the other Yankee soldier, who circled behind her in a few strides. He grabbed her arms and held her fast. She twisted her head up to look at him. He was young, grinning foolishly, buckteeth sticking out. He smelled as though he'd been swimming in whiskey.

The burly soldier leered at her, licking his lips. "Hold her there, Emmett, till we see what they got. Then we'll take her upstairs and have us some real fun."

Cold fear coursed through her. Suddenly the teasing she had given her mother about rape was not funny.

The burly soldier jabbed his bayonet into the back of the sofa and ripped it open from one end to the other. "Shit. Nothing in here," he growled. "Where'd you hide your valuables?"

"You better get out," Sally told him. "Union officers are staying here, and they'll fix you when they see what you're doing."

"Damn officers," he grunted. "We'll just take you with us. Emmett, you better not get no ideas, not before I have my turn."

He peered up at the portraits on the wall, grinned, then snatched graphite off the desk and started drawing a moustache on her grandmother.

Where were those officers? Weren't they ever coming back? She had invited them in for her protection, but they weren't even around when she needed them.

She'd better do something, or these stinking creatures would have their filthy way with her. She flailed from side to side, she tried to break Emmett's grip, but he clamped his arms around her and squeezed, giggling like an idiot, his breath rotten.

She screamed for help at the top of her lungs, but Emmett said, "Shut up," and stuck his hand over her mouth. She bit into it. He howled with pain and yanked it away, still holding onto her with the other hand. She screamed, "Help! Murder!" and struck at him. He ducked his head away, then grabbed her wrist and held her fast.

Her mother appeared at the top of the stairs and took in what was going on. Her eyes rolled up and she collapsed.

Then another blue coated soldier burst in, revolver drawn. McCord, his face and clothes sooty. "What's going on here? Release her at once!"

Emmett dropped her as though she had stung him. The burly soldier turned, graphite in one hand, bayonet in the other.

McCord pointed the revolver at the burly soldier, his face twisting in fury. "Get out or you're dead."

Suddenly docile, both intruders slunk out.

McCord closed the door and turned to face Sally. "I'm truly sorry that happened. Did they hurt you?"

Shivering, she brushed off her sleeves where Emmett had touched her. Then she whirled to McCord, furious. "Where were you all that time? Those men could have killed me! And lord knows what else."

"I had to organize a bucket brigade. The whole town's burning up. I came back to check on your house. It's a good thing I got here when I did."

"Not a moment too soon." Catching a movement, she glanced up the stairs.

Her mother sat up, recovering. "What happened?"

"It's all right now. Lieutenant McCord finally showed up to run those men off." Sally turned back to him. "My mother about had a stroke, and those nasty men wanted to do something unspeak--"

"Pretty rough treatment for a good Union girl." He smiled, holstering his revolver.

"That's right." She pointed to the portrait. "Look what they did to my grandmother. And the couch."

He grinned wider. "I should have shot them dead, just for you."

"They deserve it."

He crossed the room and touched her hand. "I won't let it happen again. I won't leave your side, the whole time we're here."

She lowered her eyes modestly. Why, the man was already falling in love with her. How sweet, and useful besides. She looked up into his soot-blackened face and gave him a tentative little smile. "Promise?"

"Promise. I'll be your personal bodyguard."

"How gallant of you."

~ * ~

Fire had not yet reached the hospital. Lexi shed her overloaded hoopskirt in the hospital office and set it down in the corner, where it collapsed under the weight. She rubbed her waist and hips, glad to free herself from the stifling weight. She hid her revolver in the desk but kept the dagger in her pocket.

She wandered up to the wards, restless and looking for something to do, anything to work off her nerves. The retreating Confederates had taken all the sick or wounded that could stand to ride in an ambulance, leaving the dire cases behind. Mama and Papa were busy with the few patients remaining in the hospital.

She found the room that housed Stewart, the boy from her brother's troop. Shouts and the noise of gunfire filtered in from the street. Smoke masked the hospital smells.

"Hey, fellas," she called out.

The men who were able murmured greetings. One of them raised a bony finger and pointed toward Stewart's bed. "He's gone up."

The light from the fires leaped through the window, dancing on Stewart's face, giving him false animation. Eyes dull, mouth slack. She touched his cheek. Cold. She reached under the covers, found his wrist and sought a pulse, a knack she'd learned from Papa. Only the marble feel that came when the blood stopped moving and the nerves quit working and nothing was going on under the skin any more.

She aligned his arms with his body so they would stiffen into a natural pose. Then she closed his eyes and mouth.

Too many of them ended up dead, all because of the Yankees.

She wiped her hands on her skirt, strode to the window and opened it, letting in the hot smoky draft. She looked for her house, but couldn't distinguish one blaze from another.

An ember blew in. She stomped it out and slammed the window shut. Hundreds of Yankee soldiers milled on the streets below. She prayed heaven would divert the flames to consume them in a writhing, screaming mass. She would like to use that revolver on them, but she would never get away with it.

The man on the next bed said, "What's goin' on out there, miss?"

"Yanks are burning up the town. Our house, too."

"What if this here building catches?"

"I guess we'll go somewhere else."

"Can't walk."

"Somebody will have to carry you, then."

A soft bump sounded from the hallway. She jumped, startled. Another thump and a groan. "What's that?"

The patient said, "Spook."

"I don't believe in spooks."

"I do. This place is full of 'em."

She picked up a candle and opened the door. A soft grunt came from the stairway. "Who's there?" she called out.

"Strickland. Help me," came the weak answer.

Strickland must be a patient. She didn't know many of their names. She carried a candle into the hall and found a man sitting four steps down the stairs, leaning against the wall. He turned his pain-pinched face to her. The bandaged leg was about a foot and a half too short. The dressing over the stump was dark with blood.

"What you doing? You ought to be in bed."

"Ain't gonna burn." The man panted. His eyes rolled, crazy. "Hear 'em screaming?"

"Burn? Is the building on fire? I don't hear any screaming."

"They're burning. Brush fires. They can't get away. Oh, God. Make 'em stop screaming."

"You're delirious. You'll hurt yourself. Look. You're bleeding, too."

"For God's sake, make 'em stop." His voice was tortured.

"Fall down the stairs, you'll kill yourself for sure. I won't let you burn. Come on."

Fortunately, he was skinny, wasted from the sickness brought on by his wound. She pulled up on his arm, hauled it around her neck and worked down the stairs, supporting most of his weight while he hobbled on his one leg. How much did an amputated leg weigh, how much lighter was he for the lack of it? His sour, sobbing breaths filled her ear and nostrils, sweat from his face wet her cheek.

She helped him to the bottom of the stair, then out the front door. She let him down next to the wall and propped him against it. His head lolled forward in a faint, so she laid him on his side.

She could see him pretty well. A burning city made plenty of light. The bandage at the end of his stump was only damp with fresh blood, no gushing. All right for the time being. She wasn't so sure about his brain.

Yankee guards were still on duty at the gate and no troublemaking soldiers had come inside yet. But the fire was sweeping closer to the campus. Men on ladders threw buckets of water onto the hospital roof. She spotted Papa among them. Maybe the one-legged man wasn't so crazy. He was right about the building being in danger.

She hurried to help.

~ * ~

Before reveille Blake went to the whitewashed Baptist church General Butler commandeered for division headquarters. During the night the wind had shifted and brought smoke and spent ashes into camp from the south, from the direction of Columbia.

He didn't sleep all night, worrying about the glow in the sky. He imagined his family in trouble, and cursed his duty for forcing him to stay where he could do nothing for them.

Captain Causey stood leaning against the wall by the door drinking from a tin mug. He returned Blake's salute without much snap, tired eyes ringed dark like a raccoon's.

"I need to see General Butler. Is he in?"

"Can't go disturbing him unless it's an emergency."

"It's gotten past an emergency. More like a disaster."

"What's your business, Winberry?"

"Volunteering to go back to Columbia, find out what's going on."

Causey shrugged. "We have scouts."

"They don't know the town like I do. I was born and raised there."

"How do you expect to get in and out in one piece?" Causey's smile was grim. "Last I saw of the place, it was crawling with Yankees. It's nothing to me if you want to get yourself killed, but we're short on able-bodied officers."

"I'll wear a Federal uniform. Lightfoot does it all the time."

Causey took a thoughtful sip from his mug. "If it comes up I'll mention your name."

~ * ~

Harry woke up on the street, a throbbing head and a bellyache plaguing him. He gagged on smoke and the stench of Emmett's vomit. His stomach turned somersaults.

Before they'd gotten sick from last night's whiskey, he and

Emmett had a couple of goes at a darky wench. She was so much fun that after they'd finished he let her run off with only a few slaps to hurry her.

Emmett lay flat on his back, his fly and his mouth wide open, making enough noise to wake the dead.

Harry poked him in the ribs. "Time to get up."

Emmett groaned.

"You stink. Gonna throw you in the river."

Emmett sat up, held his head in his hands, sank back down. "Oh, God, Harry." Then he leaned over and puked again.

Harry booted him on the butt.

Emmett gagged. "Can't help it."

"Why did I ever let you kick in with me?"

"I'm sorry, Harry. The whiskey. Must've been bad. Rebs poisoned it."

"Let's go."

Emmett lurched to his feet and stood swaying, his chin on his chest. Harry shoved him along, shuffling through the still smoking town. He stepped around a soldier lying in the road. He noticed the blood clotted all over the soldier's mouth, nose and back, and the red-black dirt around his body from the death wound. He paused and scratched under his coat. "Jesus, Emmett. That was some helluva party."

He passed a park where townspeople had camped in the open, hovering over whatever they'd kept. A woman stared at him through red eyes. He called out, "Howcum you Southrons run up your chimneys before you build your houses? Ain't that bass-ackwards?"

Emmett giggled. "Lord, Harry. That was a good 'un. You're the beatinest ever."

"He, he, he. That's my way, boy."

"Sure liked laying that wench, Harry."

"We'll find more of that stuff by and by." Harry scratched his itchy balls. Damned graybacks were eating him alive.

"Tell you what. When the army pulls out we'll get up a gang and slip around the back trails and have us some fun. We can do what we please if we just stay away from the damned officers. And I know where we can get some real loot."

~ * ~

McCord stood with Sally on the porch, looking toward smoking, debris-filled lots where houses had stood just yesterday. Smoky haze dulled the longer view, but he had told her the truth, that at least half of the city was destroyed. "We never intended... I personally did what I could to stop it..."

"How shall we eat?" She shook her head and caught her pretty lower lip between her teeth. "And people have nowhere to live. They'll all be wanting to pile into our house!"

"I'm sure General Sherman will leave some food behind for the citizens. And the insane asylum has been opened--"

"The crazy house?" Sally raised both eyebrows. "Isn't that truly fitting!"

Suddenly tired of apologizing, he said, "Your soldiers left out all those bales of cotton. Fine tinder. And I saw people passing out enough alcohol to pickle our whole army."

"Ha. The simple fact is, Lieutenant McCord, the fire didn't start until your soldiers came."

"The wages of rebellion, I'm afraid. 'Sow the wind, reap the whirlwind.'"

She pouted. "Are all Yankees as sanctimonious as you are?"

He smiled at her. "You're not talking like such a good Unionist now."

"I didn't think I had to condone arson to be a good Unionist."

"That may be. Nonetheless, Miss Sally, you are a pretty little fraud."

She caught her breath, and real fear flitted into her eyes. "How dare you!"

He chuckled, smug, having the advantage on her. "Don't worry. Your secret is safe with me."

She swallowed, her eyes widening. "What secret?"

"Maybe fraud is too harsh a word. Chameleon may be a more accurate description. Just like you, chameleons change their colors to save themselves."

"Who have you been talking to about me?"

"Nobody. I merely find you easy to read."

"You don't read so well," she snapped.

He lounged against the porch rail, grinning, and took another tack. "How is it you aren't a married lady, Miss Sally Dubose? You're really quite lovely. Charming. Pretty little waist, pretty little hands, and a face like an angel. I'd have thought some ardent Rebel would have snapped you up by now."

She raised her chin defiantly, her vanity pricked. "I'll have you know I've been engaged twice."

He checked his curiosity, sensing dangerous ground. Had her engagements ended in death? Her lovers killed by his own comrades? Best to leave it alone.

"One is too cowardly," she volunteered. "The other one is a soldier."

"A rebel, I'll wager."

"Why, Lieutenant McCord," she smiled. "Surely you must realize there used to be an extreme shortage of Union soldiers in Columbia. Until y'all came along, that is."

"Where is he now? The soldier."

"He's in Butler's Cavalry."

He nodded. "We've been tangling with those fellows."

Her brow clouded. "I hope the two of you never meet. I'd truly hate it if you shot each other."

"You still care for him?"

"Of course not. It's all over with us. Besides that, he married somebody else."

McCord smiled wryly. "The cad."

She sniffed. "Come to think of it, you have my permission to shoot him after all."

He laughed. "Miss Sally, you are so hardhearted."

She lowered her gaze. "You mustn't think that of me. I know how to be sweet to somebody I like."

"I don't doubt that," he breathed. He had been imagining how sweet she could be ever since he met her.

"What if something did happen?" Her concern seemed genuine. "What if you got hurt!"

"I take that risk every day."

"I know what! I'll write a letter for you."

He shook his head. "A letter won't stop a bullet."

"But if you got captured…"

"I hope I don't. Prisoners don't fare well."

"I'll write about how you saved my house and ran off those bad men. Then our men won't harm you if you fall in their hands."

He shrugged. "If that makes you happy, Miss Sally."

She turned, distracted by a commotion, and looked toward the street. "What's that? Who are those soldiers?"

He looked where she was pointing. "Oh, just another of our generals with his escort."

"Like General Howard?" She wrinkled her nose. "He's such a preachy bore."

"Some soldiers believe they have a lot to pray about." He studied the mounted escort. "It's General Kilpatrick with his staff. He runs our cavalry."

"A cavalry general?" She stared hard at the mounted soldiers. "Which one is he? The dashing man with the plumed hat?"

"Yes. That's him. And the muttonchop whiskers." McCord frowned, knowing tough competition when he saw it.

"I have to meet him. Won't you introduce us?"

"I don't know, Miss Sally. He has quite a reputa--"

She whirled to him. "A reputation for what?"

He cleared his throat. "I'd rather not go into it."

"I just want to meet him, that's all."

~ * ~

The road toward Florence was sound, the country flat. Since the weather had cleared, Judith and her companions were making good time, better than 25 miles a day.

Just after starting out on the fourth day, they came across a wagon that blocked the road. A dead horse, all washboard ribs and jutting hipbones, lay in its traces.

Mr. Bagley hauled his rig to a stop and Judith halted Fancy right behind him.

The gaunt-faced young woman sitting in the wagon slowly climbed down, holding a small bundle in her arms. She wore a torn, faded dress and a filthy man's coat. She said in a timid voice to Mr. Bagley, "My horse won't get up. Make him mind, mister. I sure wish you would."

Judith walked over to the girl, an unkempt, plain little thing, who turned dull eyes to her. "He just up and fell down," the girl said. "I whupped him, but he wouldn't pull no more."

Judith shuddered. The starving girl really meant it. She didn't understand her horse was dead. And here she was with an infant. "May I see your baby?"

The girl lifted the blanket for her to see the shrunken little face, the fleshless arms. "He's a real good little young 'un. He don't cry hardly at all."

The baby didn't even squint in the sun's glare. Then Judith smelled the faint odor of death. She looked sharply at the girl. She was smiling timidly, so proud of her good little young 'un.

Chapter
Fifteen

Behind the natural breastwork of a small ridge, Blake set his saddle on the ground and used it as a chair. He munched his supper of a stale crushed biscuit, the inevitable bacon and the last of Mr. Frank's Madeira.

Yankees had tried to push through today, but the boys had stopped them by cutting the mill dam and flooding the path. They held their ground, for a change.

Hunter loomed out of the dark and tossed a wad of blue clothing at him. "See if this fits."

Blake unrolled the bundle, a Federal cavalry private's uniform, coat and trousers. His conversation with Causey had brought results after all.

Matt said, "You ain't going to let him turn you into one of him, are you?"

Blake took off his own jacket and shrugged on the blue coat.

Matt looked him up and down. "Not such a bad idea. Blue suits you. Look good enough to hang."

Blake poked his finger through a bullet hole into his sternum. "Fits all right. What does this mean, Hunter?"

The scout stood, arms folded across his chest. "We're taking a tour through the lines."

"Columbia?"

Hunter nodded, face impassive as usual.

Matt said, "Up to now my company commander ain't shown much inclination to get himself cashiered or captured. Maybe this indiscretion will be my chance at a promotion."

"Dry up, Matt," Blake said. "I'll play Yankee if that's what it takes."

Matt frowned. "Watch yourself. It's a hornet's nest you're stepping into."

"Just keep thinking about that promotion." Blake looked up at Hunter. "When are we leaving?"

"First light. Here are your orders and a pad of paper to tally the damages. Butler puts a lot of stock in you knowing the town. We'll go see him before we leave."

Blake took off his hat and unpinned the palmetto medal. His own equipment was right, a MacClellan saddle and a U. S. poncho. The arm still hurt, but showed signs of healing. "Let's go."

Hunter tapped his finger on the grip of one of the revolvers in his belt. "We don't surrender, no matter what happens. We fight our way out and if we lose, we lose. Period. My neck will never go into a noose."

~ * ~

Blake and Hunter started toward Columbia the next morning. An hour out they met the Yankees.

Dust thrown up by the scuff of thousands of feet hung in the air. Wagon trains and artillery rumbled along the road while the foot soldiers ranged alongside in no particular order. At first Blake and Hunter tried to circumvent them by taking to woods and fields. That didn't work, so they just forced through.

Face-on, enemies swarmed thick as flies on carrion. Shabby and unmilitary in worn-out blue, but dangerous as a pack of wolves, each hefted a rifle and wore a bayonet scabbard. Blake sweated despite the coldness of the morning. His heart rattled against his ribs. Couldn't they look straight through the disguise clear into his gray soul? He pulled his hat down low to hide whatever showed in his eyes, unsnapped his holster stay and held his right hand close to the grip.

He clenched his fist around the reins. Shouldn't be so jumpy. He carried a pass signed by General Kilpatrick, placing him in a Kentucky Union regiment. That would account for the Southern speech in case anybody questioned it. Hunter assured him most Northerners couldn't tell the difference between mountaineer twang and South Carolina drawl. God forbid putting it to the test.

Hunter acted like he didn't give a damn. Whenever a cluster of Yankees blocked his way he pushed through hollering, "Make way! Make way!" He jutted one elbow askew, set an arrogant jaw and dared them to hold him up. The Yankees chaffed the same tired old cavalry jibes he'd heard before and grudgingly cleared a path.

Blake eventually relaxed enough to study his enemies. Smutty faces, stout, robust men, stinking of old sweat and smoke as though they hadn't seen soap since they burned Atlanta. Dirty blue uniforms supplemented with civilian clothes, hats of beaver and straw. One wore a parson's coat, women's jewelry pinned to it in shining rows like medals. Another fool wore a woman's dress and a bonnet and a smirk on his hairy face. He heard snatches of conversation, hard accents he hated.

Bawling cattle, sheep and goats milled with the flow. Herders kept them in line with sticks, bayonets and dogs. Pets, too, picked up along the march. Blake saw gamecocks, an ungainly pointer pup, and a young raccoon digging its claws into a man's coat like a treed cat, rocking along on his shoulders.

All along the road the Yankees had already done their work on the rails. They had built fires out of wooden ties, heated the track and wrapped the softened metal around trees. Sherman's neckties, he had heard them called. They were doing a fine job wrecking what little industry the state had left.

He rode past a charred and collapsed house, still smoldering, chimneys sticking up in the air, monuments to what was once a fine large home. He didn't see anybody he took for the owners. Trees were scorched as far as thirty feet from the house. Killed livestock, left to rot, dotted the yard.

Whatever the Yankees could not consume they destroyed. Orders, or pure cussedness? What had happened in Columbia? He controlled an urge to collar them and demand answers, checked a crazy itch to draw his Colt and punish them.

If only his family had fled ahead of the enemy. At least his wife had escaped this madness. She must be halfway to Fayetteville by now.

Past the thick of the soldiers, he met civilians. Refugees, salvage piled in whatever vehicles they could get, streamed after the Federal army. He spotted a friend of his father's, grimly trudging along. Blake averted his eyes, praying the man wouldn't recognize him in a blue coat. Deep in his own troubles, the man didn't look up.

Then colored people--on ox-carts, buggies, wagons, mule back and shank's mare. Not so grim, laughing, singing, on the adventure of their lives. Behind them a man rode a mule, a nap-haired baby peeked out of a saddlebag. Straggling soldiers mingled with the coloreds.

He caught sight of Chloe, strolling toward him, clothed in one of his mother's old dresses, a bundle slung over her shoulder. He did not speak because a whole squad of Union soldiers trudged up from behind her. He tensed. Would she give him away? No. Not his second mother. But then, everything else had been turned upside down.

She moved her gaze to him, paused in her gait, face set with her opaque look. A smile flicked across her face, then she looked away. He rode by and neither of them said a word.

He turned to watch her receding back, ached to ask her what had become of the rest of his family, but he couldn't even thank her for not betraying him.

He knew he would never have another chance.

~ * ~

Later, Blake and Hunter encountered a cavalcade of Yankees, in columns of four, flags flying, sabers clanking. True to their roles, they had to halt and sit at attention to allow an important officer surrounded by escort and staff to pass by. The pompous-looking man wore general's shoulder-boards and a full beard. His right arm was missing.

"Who's that?" he whispered from the corner of his mouth to Hunter.

"Not that many one-armed generals. Must be O. O. Howard. Old Prayer Book commands half of Sherman's army. Too bad he has so many bodyguards. Wouldn't it be fun to bag a big Yankee like that?"

Blake allowed a small smile of agreement.

Near the general rode a clean-shaven young lieutenant, fine equipment on his horse, martingales in the English style. The only way Blake could get such gear these days was to capture it. The good-looking Yankee looked right at him and they locked eyes. Blake gave him a cool neutral stare. The escort party finally moved through.

He wiped sweaty hands on his trousers, free to continue southward, and he reached the outskirts of Columbia at sundown, what was left of it.

First they came to the railroad depot. From the blasted ruin, the unmistakable stench of rotting corpses mingled with the odor of charred wood. He figured he smelled the looters who blew themselves up just before the Yankees marched in.

On the outskirts of town, a few buildings remained standing. He recognized the Preston mansion and the Theological Seminary among the burned houses along Blanding Street.

But the destruction worsened the closer he rode toward the center of town. The more he saw, the sicker he felt.

His hometown was burned beyond recognition. Chimneys and blackened trees cast long shadows across the road. Leveled houses, ashes and crumbled brick, a collapsed skyline. The business district appeared to be completely obliterated.

Silence. No dogs barked, no children laughed, no vendors shouted on the vacant streets. The people had either left or buried themselves in the rubble.

Stung by the stench of burning, his eyes smarted and watered. A helpless, hollow feeling of grief crept into his gut, along with the dread.

"There wasn't any call to do this. The city was surrendered to them, for God's sake," he said to Hunter.

"Doesn't pay to surrender." Hunter's mouth was a thin line. "I won't."

"Damn them to hell. They don't fight fair."

"Sure they don't." Hunter shrugged. "That doesn't pay either. I quit fighting fair a long time ago."

Blake looked for Sally's house and was relieved to find it intact. He pointed it out to Hunter. "Friends of mine live there. I wonder how they missed the burning."

"You want to stop and talk to them?"

He hesitated, torn. Then he said, "With the house still standing, she must be all right. I have to see about my own family first, then come back."

But on Sumter Street he could not find his house. He looked

around, disoriented. Was this the right block? Where were the landmarks? The picket fence? The trees and shed? He ought to know his own home.

Then he spotted a shoe lying in the yard. He dismounted and picked it up. A leather lady's boot, just like the ones Lexi wore. He gripped it in his fist and looked out at the ruin of his house.

Charred timbers supported the brick chimney and caved-in wall. His own upstairs room, the one he shared with Judith, had fallen into the foundations. The chinaberry tree he and Justin used to climb was shriveled, fire-blighted, dying. The shed was only a black patch amid scorched grass. The fence was gone, the missing posts uprooted, leaving holes in the earth.

"The hospital." Clutching his sister's shoe, he leaped into the saddle and wheeled Magic. Hunter followed.

He reined in a block from the college. The buildings had escaped demolition, but Yankees still infested the area. In the fading light smoky campfires glowed across the street from the campus common. Soldiers lounged around cooking and eating and cleaning their guns, while sentries guarded the gates. Seeing the buildings intact calmed him.

"Provost guard," Hunter said. "We can't just walk in there. They think we're stragglers, they'll arrest us."

"Let 'em try," Blake snapped.

"I could talk to those guards and find out what they're about. Slip in if I get lucky."

"I'll go with you."

"Too risky for both of us, too personal for you." Hunter locked eyes with him. "Besides, I talk Yankee."

"So do I. All I need is a match. Have to see what they've done with my family."

"If there's trouble, one of us needs to be out of it."

"I rank you, Lightfoot, and I'm going in."

"I figured you'd get around to that sooner or later." Hunter took a drag on his pipe. "Tell you what. Just keep quiet so they won't be hearing Southron. We're couriers from Kilpatrick looking for General Howard."

"Agreed."

"You look like a crazy man, so stay in the shadows."

Blake started to snap out an angry reply, but even through his rage he saw the logic in Hunter's plan. He'd better control himself.

They walked their horses to within a block of the campus, by the surviving Episcopal church. The churchyard had been used as a campground, ashes and rubbish scattered about. A candle flickered through a window. A shadow appeared and moved away.

Hunter pulled a flask out of his saddlebag.

Blake laughed harshly. "Where's the party?"

"I hardly ever drink, but I do use the stuff. Watch."

They rode straight to the first guard, who stood at the corner of the fence setting off the campus common. The guard hailed them, rifle ready. "Dismount, one of you advance and give the countersign."

"I'll take care of it," Hunter whispered.

Blake dismounted and led the horses as close as the guard would allow, within easy earshot.

Hunter strolled up to the guard, "We're couriers from Kilpatrick, looking for General Howard. His headquarters around here?"

The Yankee guard, an earnest looking fellow with a tight thin mouth, said, "Hell, no. Rest of the army's gone. What's the countersign?"

Hunter's voice took on the clipped quality of the Yankee's. "Come on, buddy. We're fresh off the line, don't know countersigns. We got passes." He held out his flask. "Here. Hold this while I dig out my pass. Have a smile while you're at it."

The guard was all business. "Don't want none of that stuff, just the papers."

Hunter gave him the pass. The guard struck a light.

The next guard walked up and Hunter offered him the flask. This one took it.

"You'd better not drink on the post, Will," the temperance guard said.

"Why not? Captain's dead asleep, and if the lieutenant comes along, he'll just want some. You ain't gonna snitch on me, are you?" He grinned, a broad, good-natured face, and took a swallow. "Good stuff. You boys looking for General Howard?"

"Yep. Guess we'll have to keep on looking," Hunter said.

"Which way did he go?"

"His wing is headed toward Camden." Will waved vaguely toward the north.

"How come you're still here?" Hunter asked.

"Keeping the peace. But we're leaving in the morning."

"Looks like the boys had themselves a hot time." Hunter pointed his pipe stem toward the campus. "What are those buildings?"

Will wrinkled his nose. "Rebel hospital."

"Do tell. Anybody home?"

"Why do you care?"

Hunter shrugged. "Just wondering."

Will took another swallow, wiped his mouth, but didn't give the flask back. "A few shot-up rebs, a few sawbones. One of them brought his old lady and daughter there." He jabbed the other guard on the arm. "Nate, you seen the girl?"

"I tried to get a peek, but Captain Lyons said he'd buck and gag anybody went inside."

"Well, I did. Blonde, stuck up as hell. Not the best piece of work I ever seen, but I'd shed my boots under her bed any day."

Blake stiffened, held his fury in check. It wasn't easy.

"Look here, boys, you'd better get on down the road," Nate said.

Hunter chuckled. "Old Prayer Book ain't here anyway. Give me my flask back, Wil. See you fine fellows round."

After they rode out of earshot, Hunter said, "Hear that? Your folks are in there."

"I heard what that bastard said about my sister."

"Don't get your drawers in a knot, old chum. She's under protection, and he'll be gone tomorrow."

"Let's go see Sally Dubose."

~ * ~

Blake stepped inside the Dubose home. It had escaped the burning but the front room was in shambles. Soot ground into the rugs, portraits on the walls torn and decorated with drawn-in moustaches. The back of the couch was ripped open, the stuffing hanging out.

The parlor was full of people, their bedding strewn across the floor, refugees, women with their children, who shrank away from him and from Hunter. Fearful whisperings. A child's voice, "Look! Yankees!"

He glanced down at his blue coat. They must not have heard the explanation he had made to Mrs. Dubose. He took off his hat and nodded at them, searching. But he didn't see Sally's face anywhere in the room. "Where's Sally?" he asked her mother.

"She's not here." Mrs. Dubose looked drawn and exhausted. She pulled a handkerchief out of her pocket and daubed her eyes.

"Not here? What do you mean she's not here?"

Mrs. Dubose shook her head, tears welling. "She's gone."

"Gone where?" He stepped toward her, wanting to grab her and shake it out of her. "Is she all right? Where has she gone?"

"A Yankee general carried her off."

"A what?"

Then she broke down, sobbing. One of her guests gave him a hateful look as though he were the kidnapper, embraced her and made soothing noises.

He crumpled his hat brim. Damn the Yankees. Damn them, damn them, damn them. "Tell me. Which Yankee general? I swear I'll kill him."

Mrs. Dubose sat down on the couch. Her lady friend ignored Blake and said to her, "Let it out, dear. Let it all out. There, there."

Blake paced around the room, prowled past Hunter and stopped in front of Mrs. Dubose. He took a deep breath to calm himself. "Which general?"

She turned her face up to him, blinking, clutching the handkerchief. She twisted it in her hands. "Blake, you must find her."

"As God is my witness."

"Kilpatrick. His name is Kilpatrick."

"What happened?"

She told him the story in between fits of crying. Yankee officers took over their house and used it as headquarters. The house was infested with them. General Kilpatrick was a frequent visitor, and he took a fancy to Sally. After Kilpatrick left this morning, Sally was missing, a hostage, taken by force.

"You got to find her, Blake," Mrs. Dubose said. "You got to

save her from that filthy Yankee. Lord knows what he's doing to her."

He didn't need divine insight to picture it, and felt as though he was the one violated. "I find him, I'll find her."

"And your family?" A perfunctory question. "Have you seen them?"

"The house is gone. I believe they took refuge at the college hospital. Yankee guards are still there."

She nodded toward Hunter. "I hope you and your friend will spend the night here. We'd sleep so much better knowing we have male protection."

Blake looked around at the houseful of women and children. Arrangements would be awkward, but he could sure stand to sleep indoors.

She gave him a watery smile. "It isn't such a cold night. There is room on the porch."

"Thank you, Mrs. Dubose." Blake didn't bother to keep the sarcasm out of his voice. "You are truly the soul of hospitality."

Later, he lay on his back under his blankets, his head pillowed on his interlocked hands. He and Hunter had not shed their boots and gun belts in case Yankees came around.

He stared at the porch ceiling. His eyes burned with fatigue, his neck muscles were in knots, and he couldn't seem to come down off his rage.

Hunter sat with his back to the wall, smoking. "Lovely accommodations," he said. "Better than the street, I suppose. Mrs. Dubose--she's a friend of yours?"

"I always figured she'd be my mother-in-law."

"You ought to be thankful she's not."

He ignored the slur. "What do you know about Kilpatrick?"

"Major General Judson Kilpatrick. Chief of Sherman's cavalry, styles himself a lady's man."

"What kind of low Yankee bastard would take a girl hostage like that? No southern girl should be subjected to such insult."

Hunter paused. "I don't know the young lady."

"What's that got to do with anything?"

"I doubt Kilpatrick would have to resort to kidnapping."

"Meaning?"

"Suppose she took a fancy to him, too. Couldn't see her way clear to staying in this pile of ashes that used to be a town. Can't really blame her."

Another slur. Blake levered onto one elbow. "Did I hear that right? Are you impugning her character?"

"Not at all, old chum. Maybe she's the smartest thing around."

"She'd never go with him unless he forced her."

Shrugging, Hunter blew out a lung full of smoke.

"Sally and me, we've been friends for years." Saying it out loud crystallized Blake's thoughts. "Things didn't work out between us, but that doesn't make any difference. She's in trouble, and I've got to save her."

Chapter Sixteen

Next morning, two blue-coated intruders strode into the hospital office. Lexi dived to the desk, yanked open the drawer and snatched out her revolver.

"Lexi, it's me, Blake."

She glanced from him to Hunter. Shocked into laughter, she let go of the weapon. "You're back. Thank God."

Blake embraced her. "You all right?"

She nodded, looking past him at Hunter, his expression never easy to read.

Blake said, "Where are they? Mama and Papa?"

"They're around somewh--"

He whirled out of the office before she could finish, leaving her alone with Hunter.

She grinned. "Come back for me?"

As usual, he appeared amused and detached at the same time. "Even the Yankees couldn't keep me away."

Blake walked in, his arm around Mama, Papa following. Big brother looked grim enough to kill a whole squad of Yankees all by himself. Lexi longed to be like him, and like Hunter too. Dangerous men, tough and purposeful, hands stained from gunpowder, horse and smoke and damp earth smells clinging to their clothes.

Blake handed Lexi her boot. "I found this at the ruins. At least none of you are hurt."

Papa said, "And we have a roof over our heads, temporarily. We managed to save the hospital that night. Guards protected it from a mob the next morning." He looked off. "I'm afraid most of the Yankees behaved quite badly. Disappointing."

"Did you salvage anything from the house?" Blake asked.

"Only what we could carry. We still have our milk cow and my old horse. They didn't want him, but they took the one Lexi's been riding."

"I hope that crazy animal kills the first Yankee tries to ride him," Blake snapped.

"He was scared," Lexi said. "I told them I was the only one who could handle him, but they took him anyway." She paused, not wanting to show hurt. "Chloe disappeared."

"I saw her," Blake said. "She's with the Yankees. Looked like she volunteered."

"I thought as much," Lexi said.

Blake went on, "A Yankee general took Sally Dubose. Forced her…"

Lexi rolled her eyes. "Kicking and screaming, I'll bet."

Blake whirled to her. "I've got to find her. She's in trouble."

Lexi laughed. "That general's got trouble if he's got Sally."

"Why didn't you tell me she wasn't marrying Randolph?" Blake asked.

"How come it matters to you now?"

Mama said, "Lexi, that's enough. I'm sure her mother's half crazy with worry. Son, have you seen our house?"

"What's left. The foundation." His frown deepened.

Papa turned back to Blake looking worried. "Son, wearing that uniform, you could be executed as a spy."

"They've got to catch me first."

"God forbid. Why did you come through the lines like that?"

"To take inventory." Blake smiled tightly, without humor. "We can save time and paper. Just count what's still standing."

"I'm going with you," Lexi said. "I'll go saddle Lightning."

She spun toward the door and Hunter followed her.

Outside, she pointed out the slab-sided cattle nosing around the dry grass in the campus common. "The Yankees stole these cows down the state," she said. "They're too feeble to walk another step. Left them here for the townspeople after they stripped us. Yankee charity."

Hunter surveyed the lot. "You could sit down to eat one whole and get up hungry."

"We don't even have to slaughter them. Every once in a while one drops dead."

They slipped into the shed and she whirled to face him. "Take me away, Hunter. Let me go with you this time."

"No. It'll be some trick to get through the lines and hard riding to catch up as it is."

"Think I'd be a drag on you? I'll have you know I used that revolver you gave me. Shot at two Yankees who were terrorizing Mama and Papa. Ran them off."

"Did you, now." Was that admiration in his eyes, or just amusement? "Still, your brother would never let you come."

She looked down and kicked at the dirt. "I'll be stuck here in this burned-out town forever if you men have your way."

"Lexi, if you knew what it was really like out there, you'd take the burned-out town. The line is no place for a woman."

The set of her jaw told him it didn't matter whether she believed him or not. "Everybody's always telling me where my place is."

Hunter cupped his hands over her shoulders and her eyes came back up, meeting his, surprised. Then she turned on a quick smile, full of life.

He pulled her closer and she snuggled up like she thought that was where her place was.

He had never figured on seeing her again, nor had he expected the unwelcome pleasure the reunion brought. He could picture her riding with him, warming his blankets at night. She was spoiling his objectivity. Should have shaken her off like a duck sheds water. Nonetheless, he wanted her, and he sensed the little innocent was his for the taking. He knew himself pretty well. Not especially kind, nor pure, certainly crafty enough to spot a trap. He could see himself going for the bait and liking it.

~ * ~

Sam had set up camp deep in the woods for the old man and him before the Yankees came. He hid the mule, wagon, and provisions there. Afterwards, he went back alone to watch over the house.

He couldn't save it, not the big house or the cabins that made up the old slave quarters. The Yankees were too burn-happy. They ran him out, fired the place, and tried to get him to go with them.

Make a soldier boy out of him, they promised. Crafty eyes and contempt sharpened their soot-black faces. Even mocked him with their fire-darkened skin. It seemed what they offered was just another form of bondage. After that, he mostly stayed in the tent with the old man. Next set of Yankees might drag him off at gunpoint.

This morning he had slipped back for a look around. The marchers had moved on past so it was safe to come out of hiding. The old man wasn't doing so good sleeping in the woods, needed to be high and dry. Sam dredged enough half-burned timbers from the ashes to make a lean-to. Then he brought back the old man and provisions for the night, planning to go back for more as he needed it. Once that was done, he'd find Roxie.

The old man climbed heavily down from the wagon and stood, hands in his pockets, shoulders slumped, looking over the mess. "They were pretty thorough, weren't they, Sam?"

Sam unloaded a couple of blankets and threw them into the lean to. "I told you." He started back to the wagon.

"I won't have to put up with it," the old man said. "Don't have long to this world. I'm leaving it to you. The land and whatever you can make of it."

Sam halted in mid-stride, then whirled to face him. "Sah?"

"You're my only issue. Who else should I leave it to?"

The old man was half-smiling, enjoying himself.

Sam wiped his hand across his mouth. He knew the whole two thousand acres by heart. He had worked the rich red soil, always treated it as his, even though his only claim on it was the baptism of sweat. Maybe the love of the land was in his blood, the old man's blood that lightened his.

"A land owning free negro, Sam. How do you like that?"

"I like it fine," he whispered. He would go tell Roxie. Jump the broom. No. No broom. Have a regular wedding, like white folks. Standing dignified, in his Sunday shirt and blacked shoes. He would get Preacher Wiggins. He would build a fine house and Roxie'd bear him lots of farm hands and he would be a country squire just like the old man.

"It will take work," the old man said.

Sam squared his shoulders and his jaw. "I reckon I am up to it."

~ * ~

All day long Lexi rode with Hunter and her brother through the ruins, inspecting the Ursulene Convent, the State House, every store, business, factory and government storehouse. Wade Hampton's village-sized estate, Millwood. All wiped out.

People sifted through the ashes of their homes, looking for anything that had withstood the fire. The insane asylum was crammed with refugees, women and children camped on open lots.

She stayed close to Hunter, the two of them touching every chance they got. Blake wasn't noticing. He was busy taking his dismal notes, punctuating them with furious pencil strokes. She mentioned to Hunter that she had a cubbyhole room to herself, even pointed it out to him when they got back to the college. They agreed it would be nice to be alone, later, after the household went to sleep.

That night Lexi lay watching the candle flicker its faint light around the tiny room, not sure what to do with him if he came. Not sure what would be on his mind. What did he expect of her? She figured he would let her know. She did know she liked the way he touched her and how she wanted to be with him.

She wanted a lot of things. She wanted to leave this place that wasn't home any longer. She wanted to be a soldier. She wanted to be just who she was and not have to act prim and proper. Just about everything she wanted to do was not allowed.

Nor was inviting a man to her room at night. But she had done it anyway.

He knocked softly and she opened it, as she had promised. She felt shy, standing there wearing only a thin shift under her robe. "Come on in." She waved toward the mattress with a blanket over it, her only furniture. "We can sit here."

He didn't sit, but stepped close to her, lifted his hands and buried them in her hair, bringing her face close to his. He whispered, "I want to know something. Why did you really ask me here?"

"Because I could. I like having you around."

"That's good, we enjoy each other." His eyes looked into hers, giving nothing back. "If I stay, something is going to happen. Something you can't take back, and you might get hurt."

"Are you that wicked?" she whispered back, sounding surer

than she felt.

"What do you think?"

"You wouldn't do anything bad to me."

He fingered her hair, smiling slightly. "I'm warning you. I'm not interested in permanent attachments."

"Neither am I." She laughed. "Can you imagine me, a married lady?"

"I'm trying to play fair and it doesn't suit." He lifted an eyebrow. "I don't very often."

Tired of the talk, she kissed him on the mouth. He reacted stronger than she expected. His tongue forced her lips open and pushed into her mouth. His hands were moving all over her nightdress, then under it, exploring her flanks and breasts. Wherever he touched her, fire. She put her hands on his taut body, bringing him even closer to herself. She lost herself in the sensations, wanting more and more and more.

They dropped down onto the mattress, rushing to get their clothing out of the way. He mounted her, maneuvering between her legs, flesh to flesh, his motions fitting him tightly into her. It hurt a little but the ecstasy overrode the pain. She had never felt anything like it. She embraced him gladly as he pushed deeper. Swept into his intensity; her body responded. His thrusts grew more violent and he groaned low in his throat before he relaxed, breathing hard.

They lay there for a while, kissing and caressing each other, laughing softly. He seemed grateful, as though she had done him a favor. She felt daring. For once she could do whatever she pleased, and it pleased her to do it with him again. He obliged cheerfully, taking his time, bringing her to new heights of sensation.

After, Hunter reluctantly rolled onto his back, disentangling himself from her arms and legs, well satiated, his remnant of conscience chiding him mildly. He had not lied to her, in fact he had done his best to warn her off, and if he had done her any harm she was not complaining. "I have to get back to my quarters before I'm missed." He kissed her again, got up and hitched up his trousers. "Though I would rather spend the night here."

"You could. I'm not afraid," she said.

"Your brother would kill us both if he found out." Smiling, he cupped her chin in his hand and nuzzled her, affection genuine. "Good night, little soldier."

He stepped into the hallway. Something--a hand--reached from the dark, flung him against the wall and held him there. His knees weakened with shock. He reached for his revolver--wasn't wearing one. Punched empty space with his fist.

"Hold still, Lightfoot, or I'll break your damned neck." His partner's voice, low and menacing.

Stupid, stupid, stupid, getting caught. Hunter held still, not wanting to invite a punch. He had nerve, but Winberry was bigger and stronger. Worse, he was mad.

"What's going on out there?" Lexi whispered from the doorway.

"What the hell was going on in there?" Winberry snapped.

"Oh, for crying out loud," Lexi said. "Y'all get in here before you wake up the whole town."

Hunter slunk back into her room. Winberry followed and shut the door, his breathing harsh. Lexi lit the candle.

The room was far too crowded for Hunter's liking. He stood up against the wall and groped in his pocket for his pipe.

Lexi whispered, "Why are you spying on us, brother dear?"

"Pretty clear what he's doing in your room."

Hunter stuffed tobacco into the pipe bowl with his thumb, taking stock. He could have dropped Winberry in a pistol duel even without cheating if it came to that, but it would be too much like killing his own brother all over again. He knew all about self-preservation--when to advance and when to retreat--and this wasn't the hill he would pick to die on. He sucked in a sharp breath. "What's your satisfaction, Winberry?"

"Marry my sister or I'll kick you downstairs and pound you into the street."

"I don't doubt you could, old chum. But we are not going to fight. We need each other able bodied, at least until we get back to our lines."

"Then marry her tomorrow morning, before we leave Columbia."

"You aren't thinking of her best interests."

"You sure aren't. What if you have gotten her in trouble?"

Lexi said, "Blake, stop--"

"Stay out of this."

"It's about me, not you." She balled up her fist to hit him but he grabbed her arm.

"What, exactly, were you thinking of, Lexi?"

She tore from his grip, jerked out of reach and crossed her arms. "Hunter and I are good friends. We had a lot to talk about."

Winberry laughed, short and bitter. "Do you always entertain your male friends dressed like that?"

Lexi looked down at her shift and back at him, defiant.

Wanting Winberry to leave the girl be, Hunter said, "We're going to get married."

She thrust out her chin. "We don't have to do any such thing."

Hunter shifted his weight on his feet. "In due time. But tomorrow is impracticable."

"It'll have to do." Winberry said.

"Then everybody will figure out why," Hunter said. "What kind of talk is that going to cause?"

"Better than some kinds, a few months from now."

"We must clear out first thing in the morning, no time for ceremony. Let's say we're engaged, then we'll get married properly when time allows. Lexi, I'll give you a gold necklace in honor of my pledge. It's in my saddlebag."

"I know a dodge when I see one," Winberry said. "We'll work it out immediately. I know a minister, and once he underst--"

Lexi said, "I don't want to get married just because somebody's making me."

Winberry turned to her. "You'll accept it and like it."

"Lexi, don't be difficult," Hunter said. "This is the way it has to be."

Outnumbered, her shoulders slumped. She wouldn't look at him.

The crisis was over, for the time being. Hunter lit his pipe and took a calming drag. He wasn't really entangled that badly. He'd go through with the ceremony and he'd be on his way.

~ * ~

Sam woke up abruptly, painfully. Somebody had just kicked him in the ribs. He heard harsh laughter. His sleep-heavy eyes stared into the dark hole at the end of a revolver barrel. He recognized his own gun and was ashamed to be caught so easy.

The Yankee holding the gun was grinning. "We got you, nigra. He, he, he. You and the old man both."

Chapter Seventeen

Lexi didn't get a chance to talk to Hunter alone until after the marrying business was over, next morning. Finally her family granted them a little privacy as newlyweds before he and Blake had to take their delayed start.

She sat down on the bed, feeling sick about the way things had gone. He shut the door and leaned against it, regarding her, his expression unreadable, as usual. She had never taken him for a coward, but she must have misjudged. "Why didn't you stand up to him?"

His voice was calm, rational, as though he did not care what she had implied. "He was in the right, you know."

"Now you're even taking his part!"

"Did you want us to fight over you? I didn't take you for that kind of girl." He gave her a sardonic smile. "I don't lose such fights, and you wouldn't have liked the result, unless you hate your brother."

She stared at him, his meaning sinking in, and grasped that in this case she shouldn't confuse restraint for cowardice. "It really got out of hand, didn't it?"

"Which part are you sorry about? Making love, getting caught, or having to marry me?"

"Oh, Hunter. I never meant to trap anybody. But Blake was so crazy. He said he wasn't telling Mama and Papa what happened, but they have to know it was something pretty scandalous. Whatever Blake did tell Papa, he gave his consent quick enough. After what Blake just put them through with Judith a few weeks ago, they think we've both lost our minds. And that minister. He didn't know what to think."

"At least your brother had the grace not to brandish a shotgun during the ceremony."

She started to giggle despite her misery. "Lexi Lightfoot! Isn't that something!"

He sat next to her and put an arm around her shoulders. Blake might think him a cad, he might know himself to be a cad, but something at his core was good for her. He didn't even seem to hold a grudge about being forced into those vows.

All that rot about obedience, Lexi thought. She was still mad at Blake, but could not deny she was the one he had found in a compromising situation.

Heartened, she said, "Everything's changed. Now can I go with you and join the scouts."

He gave her a squeeze, smiling, humoring her. "Haven't you had enough adventure for one day?"

"It's awful around here. I can't stand it."

He shook his head no, regretfully, she thought. "You'll have to. It's too risky getting through the lines. We would both be so worried about protecting you we're liable to all get killed."

She sighed. No use spending the last little bit of time they had arguing. She snuggled against him and they lay back on the mattress, their kisses and caresses growing urgent. She wondered whether lying down with him would be as exciting now that it was legal.

~ * ~

Sam stood with his hands tied behind him and the noose around his neck. The four Yankees were the meanest, lowest, sorriest looking white men he'd ever seen. Just like the one he had killed, talking nonsense about the old man being rich. He recognized the one named Harry Bell, who acted like he was in charge.

They'd trussed the old man the same way they did him. Ready to hang him, too.

Harry Bell said, "Where's the loot, nigra?"

"I gave you all we had, boss. I already showed you them provisions I hid in the woods. You think I can hoodoo gold and silver out a air?"

"Snipes said Old Man Hughes was loaded."

"No, he ain't, boss." Sam shook his head as hard as the noose would allow. "He lied on us."

"Hang him up."

Two of the Yankees pulled down on the rope. The body weight came off Sam's feet, into the noose around his neck. The rope bit in, squeezing his jaws shut. The joints from his neck down to his spine cracked and popped. Daylight faded, his head about to explode. Over the roar in his ears he heard the old man begging, and somebody giggling.

"Let him down."

The rope relaxed and he settled on his toes, gasping for breath. Eyes about to bust out of his head, neck hurt like fire. Tears rolled down the old man's cheeks. Him knowing he was next.

Harry took another pull at the jug. "You sure set a lot of store by this Sam," he said to the old man. "Fancy that, white man blubberin' over a black buck." To Sam he said, "Tell us where the gold is or you're a dead 'un."

He needed to come up with a good lie, something to make them stop, at least long enough to check it out. He tried to speak, but his hurt throat didn't work and nothing came out.

"Upsy-daisy!" Harry whooped.

The rope jerked him up again, his chin popped up and his weight dragged down on his neck. Harry stood in front of him, grinning.

Let me down. He couldn't get words out of his mouth. His legs kicked. The world spun around and around and around, getting darker.

~ * ~

While Harry watched, Emmett stopped giggling and stared with his mouth open. He touched Harry on the shoulder. "Harry, don't you think we strung him up long enough?"

"Nope." Harry took another swallow of whiskey. Sam's body spun. Eyes going glazed, filling with blood. The kicks weakened.

"Harry, you're killing him."

"Good." He took another slug of whiskey.

"Up to now it's just been good fun."

"This is good fun."

Then Emmett picked up the cavalry saber he had been playing with and whacked the knot where the rope was tied to the tree.

The body dropped like a sack of spuds. Harry slugged Emmett, knocked him to the ground and stepped on his hand, hard. Emmett screamed and let go of the saber. Harry picked it up. He kicked Emmett in the ribs.

"What's the matter with you, boy? Now get up on that wagon and don't say a word or I'll string you up too." He stuck Emmett in the tail with the saber.

Emmett yelped with pain and clapped his hand over his butt, eyes wide and chin trembling. Then he got up and scrambled onto the wagon, blood staining the back of his trousers. He settled on his good buttock, giving Harry that whipped-puppy look.

Harry glowered at the stupid boy. Had to do something about him if he showed another flash of gumption. Maybe he'd shoot him and say it was Rebs.

So far they hadn't seen any. He got the shakes whenever he thought of what would happen if Rebs caught him. He took another pull at the jug to dull the worry. He glared at the darkie he had hung, lying where he had fallen. The buck had started up breathing again, making a little noise. But he wasn't going nowhere, trussed up like that.

Harry had picked up his new partners, Grimes and Smeed, on the streets of Columbia. He liked freelancing better, but it was safer to club with a gang of like-minded fellows. They had helped him snatch a wagon full of loot, but he didn't trust them. Couldn't seem to catch them turning their backs on him either.

Harry kicked Sam in the belly, heard a satisfying grunt. Kicked him again, before he got tired of fooling with him. "Too stupid to tell us anything. Grimes, let's work on Old Man Hughes now. His turn."

Hughes worked his mouth and spat at him. The spit missed, splatted on the ground.

"Go ahead and kill me, damn you," Hughes said in a choked voice. "Go ahead and kill your betters, you damn white trash."

"Our betters!" Harry slapped him across the jowls. "Shut your trap, you--"

Slow hoof beats. He looked over his shoulder. Two blue coated horsemen came around the wooded curve of the farm road at a walk. "Kilpatrick's men," Grimes said. "We better get our guns. They'll want our loot for themselves."

"Ho, boys!" called out one of the newcomers. "Got any whiskey?"

Harry edged toward his rifle. Emmett stared over his shoulder at the cavalrymen, his mouth hanging open as usual.

Then the cavalrymen pulled pistols out from under their coats and started shooting.

Grimes and Smeed tumbled, screaming. Harry dived for the wagon. The startled mules pulled it forward and he crawled on his hands and knees to stay under it.

More shots, another yelp. Foam flecking his beard, Harry launched from the far side of the wagon, into the woods.

~ * ~

Blake charged the one that ran, but the bummer disappeared like a rat in tall grass. He gave up, turned back and rode past a wounded bummer. Hunter had him covered. Blake dismounted by Mr. Hughes and Sam. Both of them alive, Sam barely. He untied Mr. Hughes' wrists and left him free to help Sam. Then he turned to Hunter, who was inspecting the vermin they had caught. "What's the damage?"

"One dead Yankee, two not dead yet."

The dead one didn't matter. A clean kill, didn't even bleed much. The others not so clean. Hunter stood over a filthy bluecoat. The bummer was lying on his side, his hand covering the bleeding place in his hip. He looked at Blake, then back to Hunter, face compressed with pain and terror.

Hunter said, "Name's Grimes, says he's New Jersey infantry. Want to put the rodent out of his misery, or should I?"

"Murdering sonofabitch." Blake's knuckles went white on the grip of his revolver. He took a breath, got his rage under control, though he couldn't think of a reason not to finish him. After he questioned him. "What about the other one?"

"Leg's broke. Just a kid. They start young, I guess."

Blake walked over to him. The boy's wispy reddish beard shadowed his pimply cheeks. He rocked in agony, holding onto his shattered leg, the grass around him beaded with blood. He rolled his eyes and cringed and sobbed.

Blake curled his lip. "What are you?"

The boy gulped. "Private Emmett, 154th New York. It was all

Harry's idea. Swear I didn't have nothin' to do with it. Honest. I'm the one cut the nigra down."

"Who's Harry?"

"Harry Bell. He got away. Please don't kill me."

"You seen General Kilpatrick lately?"

Emmett stared at him, a stupid look.

A gun went off. Blake jumped and whirled toward the sound. Mr. Hughes held a smoking repeater. Grimes convulsed then relaxed and his hand fell away from his hip wound. Half his head was blown away, splattering bloody brains all over the ground.

Mr. Hughes staggered toward Blake and Emmett, sliding the bolt on the carbine to advance the next round. Face gray, breaths coming hard, he opened and closed his slack mouth, pressing one hand to his chest, staring at Emmett as he came on, pulse throbbing fast in his throat.

Emmett mewed like a stricken animal.

Mr. Hughes stopped, wheezing.

Blake stepped out of the way. "You want him, he's yours."

Instead of shooting, Mr. Hughes dropped next to Emmett and laid the rifle on the grass. He whispered, "The boy stopped them from killing Sam."

Emmett fainted, mouth open, lips parted over buckteeth.

Hunter glanced down the farm road. "We have to get out of here. All the shooting might attract a crowd."

Mr. Hughes was breathing easier, ripping pants fabric to expose Emmett's ruined leg. He looked up at Blake and Hunter. "Would you please put Sam and the boy in that wagon?"

Blake reloaded his revolver, then they backed the wagon out of the underbrush and threw out some of the loot, a silver service, blankets, jewelry, foodstuffs, to make room.

They started to lift Emmett, who roused, groaning. Then Hunter froze, looking down the road, where it trailed into woods. "Hear that? Horses. Ten, twelve of 'em. Let's go."

Blake and Hunter dropped Emmett and ran to their mounts. Blake glanced over his shoulder. Bluecoats.

"Halt!" one called out.

Blake bounded into the saddle.

Emmett pointed and yelled, "Rebs! They're Rebs!"

"Shoot 'em!"

Pistol shots cracked out.

A bullet zipped by Blake's ear so close he felt the wind. From the corner of his eye he saw Hunter's horse stagger just as the scout mounted. Hunter spilled with the falling animal, landed free of the horse, but stumbled and went down on his knees.

Blake shouted for him to get on as he wheeled Magic. He turned his revolver on the Yankees and shot at them. Mr. Hughes skittered behind the wagon, repeater in hand. He raised it to his shoulder and fired.

One of the leaders dropped and the horsemen in the rear didn't stop fast enough to avoid colliding with the riderless horse.

Yells, whinnies, snorts and curses, a scattering of gunshots.

Something plucked at Blake's clothes.

He shot the revolver empty, aim so fouled by his dancing horse he couldn't hit anybody. Hunter's dying Morgan thrashed and screamed. Mr. Hughes slumped forward and dropped the rifle, while Emmett wrapped his arms around his head and cried.

Blake looked around for Hunter. Was he shot? Then he felt a hand grapple his coat. He braced himself against the far stirrup to offset Hunter's weight as he pulled up behind him.

He jerked Magic around and kicked her sides. Took a final glance at Mr. Hughes' body drooped against the wagon spokes. Blood enlarged in a red circle on his white shirt.

Magic bolted into the underbrush. Blake lay down over her neck and clung to the mane. Boughs switched him and tore at his face. He felt Hunter's weight on his back, arms circled around his waist, holding on for his life.

He let Magic rush through the woods until she ran off the panic. Didn't hear anybody behind him. He made her slow to a trot, then a walk. Hunter let go of his waist.

Blake sat up in the saddle and looked behind him for a sign of pursuit.

"Don't think they're following us," he said to Hunter.

"They won't chase us into the woods. Afraid of ambush."

"You aren't hit, are you?"

"Banged up my leg, twisted my ankle, that's all. Hate losing that Morgan and all my equipment, but I'll replace them."

Blake rubbed a stinging scratch on his forehead, more scratches on his cheeks. He moved his unsteady hand down, found a bullet hole under his armpit and another in his sleeve to match the old one over his chest. He looked down at himself, but didn't see blood.

He patted Magic's neck, grateful for her speed. Then he laughed nervously. "Lord, that was tight. If they'd been dismounted and steady we'd both be goners." He let out a hard breath.

"We had them confused, didn't know what to shoot at. Your friend helped keep them off balance. And thanks for saving my bacon."

"Oh, Jesus," Blake said. "They killed Mr. Hughes."

"A real tiger. Too bad."

"At least he went out game, like he wanted to. I don't guess the Yankees will have any reason to hurt Sam."

~ * ~

Harry Bell collapsed full-length.

Wheezing, he imagined he could hear pursuers. He'd heard more shots. They were still after him. He hugged the red dirt and squeezed his eyes shut and shuddered. Maybe they wouldn't see him if he didn't open his eyes.

Finally his breathing eased and his heart slowed its pounding. He lifted his head but all he saw was woods. Hell. All the woods looked alike.

Who were those mule turds, anyway?

Must've been Rebs. Rebs in disguise. Won't ever make that mistake again.

Emmett, Grimes and Smeed were no loss, but all he had to show for his hard work were a few greenbacks, silver, and a couple of pieces of jewelry. He stuck his hand in his pocket and closed it around a watch, hard and smooth and reassuring.

He'd taken too many chances staying so far behind the rest of the army. Didn't even have a gun, now. Better find his outfit quick.

He heaved to his feet, guessed which way was north, and stumbled forward.

~ * ~

"You sure were lucky we came along when we did, Mr. Darky," the Yankee was saying.

Another added, "Yeah, those rebs were about to turn you into dog meat."

Sam couldn't answer them. His throat didn't work.

No matter. A black man's word didn't carry any weight with Yankees either. He stared over at the old man's body. Didn't feel like thanking them for killing the only father he had ever known.

~ * ~

Judith opened the gate to her aunt's house and let herself into the yard. She had parted with her traveling companions and the long journey was over. At last she had reached her haven among her own people.

She savored the look of it, a good-sized two-story house with a wide porch. It needed paint and the porch rails looked splintery and broken. Of course the inside would be pleasant and clean and she would have her own bed to lie on and sleep away her travel exhaustion.

The woman who answered the door did not look like any aunt of hers. She had seen a miniature painting of her Aunt Mary, but this woman never posed for it.

"I'm Judith Rogers ah, Winberry. Is Mary Hanover in?"

"She ain't been here for a long time." The woman didn't move aside or invite her in, but squinted past her at her wagon.

"Where is she?"

"Gone. Stayin' with her daughter, somewheres west of here. We pay rent to Mr. Ames, the lawyer, and he sends it on to her."

Judith swallowed past the lump in her throat. "I just arrived in town. Do you know any place I can stay?"

"I got my daddy, and my oldest girl, and my son's wife, and all my grandbabies. Don't look at us to put you up."

The woman shut the door in her face.

~ * ~

Blake passed the ruins of a country house. The odors of smoke and char and rotting animal carcasses stuck in his throat. Swallows of clean water from his canteen did not purge the sick brown taste. He soaked a handkerchief and tied it over his face, but it didn't do much good.

A blind man could track Sherman's army. Failing a sense of smell, he could follow them by feel. Thousands of marching men and their supply trains and artillery caissons left the road cut up. His overloaded horse hopped and stumbled her way through the ruts.

Since they had left the Hughes place the only living things in sight were buzzards. Battalions of them circled and swooped and tore at the bloated dead things until they waddled along the ground, too fat to fly.

Behind him, Hunter straddled Magic with his legs dangling free. He shifted his weight often, unsupported by saddle or stirrups. He had not said much for the past few miles, but smoked incessantly. Blake would not have picked the sneak for a brother in law, but it was done now. He blamed Hunter, who had age and experience on Lexi, and had taken shameless advantage. Of course, Lexi hadn't exactly fought him off. At least the hasty wedding had preserved a vestige of her honor.

They passed Killians, the last place they had bivouacked with their division. Nothing left but trash, cold campfires and dried horse dung. Blake nudged Magic through the vacant campsite. A few hundred yards beyond, Hunter told him to stop, slid off Magic and limped for a few yards. He knelt and inspected a pile of manure. "This is fresh."

"How fresh?"

Hunter hitched forward, studying the ground. "Unshod horses. Two. No, three. Not cavalry horses, farm tackies. I mean to get one. Maybe all three."

"Might be our people."

"Maybe negros, more likely Yankee bummers." Hunter smoothed his moustache. "Not the same cavalry we brushed with, so they won't be onto us. Nothing to it."

Chapter
Eighteen

The savory aroma of roasting pig reminded Blake that he hadn't eaten since morning, and it was almost dusk. He drew rein. "Somebody's cooking."

"Nice of them to fix our supper," Hunter said.

"Yanks?"

"You'd be surprised," Hunter said. "Some of them can cook. Besides that, they have my transportation. We'll have a nice chat with them and get some information, too."

Blake swallowed. The thought of good food made his eyes water. "Let's get the bastards."

"We'll go up all friendly like, take them off guard, get the drop on them. Nice and quiet."

"Fine." Blake dragged the Colt from his holster, hid it under the blue coat skirt and kneed Magic forward.

They found the Yankees camped in a grassy meadow just off the road, rifles propped against a tree a few strides away from them, two horses and a mule tethered nearby. Blake caught another wonderful whiff of coffee and crackling pork and swallowed again. The three men lounging by the fire sat up and watched them approach.

"Howdy, boys. Mind if we join you?" Hunter called out.

A lanky, dark-haired bluecoat stood up. "Who are you?" He wore a corporal's chevron on his sleeve. Eyes narrow, face guarded.

Blake pointed the hidden muzzle of the Colt toward the Yankee's chest, his hand sweaty on the hard grip.

Hunter said, "Taylor and Smith, 5th Kentucky Cavalry. Kilpatrick's Corps."

"Corporal Whitfield. 154th New York. Lose a horse?"

"They don't call us kill-cavalry for nothing." Hunter's voice oozed with camaraderie. "Don't have grub, but we can kick in some oh-be-joyful."

The men by the fire grinned. "Let's see it, bub."

"Sure, sure." Out of the corner of his eye Blake glimpsed Hunter dig into the saddlebag.

He lifted and cocked his revolver at the same time he heard Hunter's weapon clear leather and the snap of its hammer. "Up with your hands or you're dead."

Whitfield jerked his hands to chest level. The other two did the same. "What the hell is this about?" Whitfield said.

Blake aimed right at his chest. "This is all you need to know."

"I'll pull their teeth." Hunter slid off and landed with his weight on his good leg. He wagged his pistol at the Yankees. "Come over here."

They obeyed, sullen-faced, scared.

Hunter limped between them and their rifles, smiled tightly and said, "Take off your clothes. All your clothes. Down to the skin. Toss them over there." He pointed to a spot a few feet away. "I want to see your balls swing in the breeze."

Whitfield's face went dark and he didn't move.

Hunter aimed the Navy pistol at his crotch. "Do it, fool. Do it."

Whitfield's hands leaped to the buttons.

"Hats and shoes too," Hunter said.

The demoralized Yankees rushed to obey.

Blake grinned, starting to relax. "I'll get their things."

He gathered rifles, blankets, sacks heavy with coffee, sugar, meat and meal, and loaded them onto the mule.

He hacked the steaming pig haunch into smaller pieces and stuffed it and the sweet potatoes into haversacks, then tied them onto his saddle. He poured the contents of the coffee pan into a canteen and slung the hot metal container over his shoulder.

"You done?" Hunter said to him. "They've told me enough."

The prisoners were plucked-chicken pale from their necks down, trying to cover their hairy crotches with their hands. Blake said, "Ask them about Kilpatrick?"

"Said he's west of here," Hunter said. "Screening their left

178

wing."

Blake turned to Whitfield, "Have you seen him? Kilpatrick?"

Whitfield shook his head.

Blake looked at the others. "Anybody seen him?"

"Got nothin' to do with Kilpatrick. We're infantry."

Blake tied the clothing into a bundle and packed it onto the mule with the provisions.

"You ain't gonna leave us here without a stitch on?" one of the Yankees said.

"Lie down. Face down," Hunter said.

The Yankees did what they were told.

Hunter stepped closer to them and aimed his revolver at the nearest head. The face turned a little, the eyes cut around.

"Wait!" Blake snapped.

Hunter hesitated, glanced at him and back at the prisoners.

"They surrendered," Blake said. "This is murder."

"We sure as hell can't take them with us."

"We don't kill prisoners."

"They'd do it to you, old chum." A patient look, a teacher waiting for a not-so-bright pupil to catch on. "I'll make it painless. Think they would be that considerate?"

All three Yankees twisted their heads around. Three sets of terrorized eyes imploring.

"No. We leave them like they are."

"After they've burned your town and your house and murdered your friends?"

"We never hurt any civilians." Whitfield's voice was husky.

Blake shook his head slowly.

Hunter said, "Let them go, they'll find their outfit, get new uniforms and re-arm. We'll have to fight them all over again."

"Don't shoot them. That's an order," Blake snapped.

An order? The absurdity struck him. He and Hunter were equals here, except for ruthlessness.

Hunter smiled. Must be thinking the same thing.

"You owe me, Hunter," Blake said. "I'm collecting, now."

Hunter touched his hat-brim in a left-handed salute and stepped back. "My commanding officer has spoken. You boys get off light. Your miserable lives are not worth fighting over."

The first man he'd aimed at closed his eyes and rested his forehead on his hands, mumbling. Whitfield said to Blake, "Thanks, Johnny."

Blake waved his hand and turned away. He had no trouble killing enemies in self-defense, or in the heat of a fight. But he couldn't let Hunter butcher those naked, helpless men like so many hogs. That called for colder blood than the stuff that ran in his veins.

Even if killing them did make more sense than letting them go. Was he being a soft-headed fool?

Hunter mounted a farm tacky. Blake climbed onto Magic and took a backward look at the shivering Federals hugging themselves. His hand reached back to untie a couple of blankets.

Then he pictured the blackened ruins of his home and Sam choked and Mr. Hughes slumped against the wagon spokes, blood spreading over his shirt. He withdrew his hand and kept the blankets. He didn't look back again.

~ * ~

The Yankees wanted to take Sam with them, but what they really wanted was somebody to take care of their horses, cook their meals and take their insults. Sam acted even sicker than he felt, convinced them he couldn't walk, couldn't sit on a horse, might just die on them. After a little while they left him alone to bury the old man and think things over.

~ * ~

Judith found Mr. Ames' office, closed. She climbed back into the wagon, rested her chin in her hands and stared at nothing. She was so tired. Her whole body ached. Sundown already, she would have to spend another night in the wagon. Better find a place to camp.

She started the jaded mule, and the wagon rolled along slowly until she came to a house with a sign in the window. ROOM FER RENT. Shabby, didn't look like much. But the late hour and the prospect of a warm bed made it inviting.

A few minutes later, she followed her prospective landlady up a dark stairwell into a bedroom. A brown-stained mattress took up most of the space. Sooty fireplace, walls covered by cracked and peeling paper, mildew smell. A cockroach crept along the wall and the floor needed a good scrubbing. At least the room was shelter.

"How much?"

The moon face lit up at the mention of money. "Fifty dollars a week, pay in advance. 'Course, I can't provide no bedclothes or provisions or wood for that. Cook in the fireplace and take your meals in here."

"Do you have a place for me to keep my mule and my wagon overnight?"

"Another ten dollars, no fodder. You can leave the wagon in the back yard."

"Now you're raising the price. I wouldn't have had to pay half that in Columbia, including board."

The woman shrugged. "Then go back to Columbia. I hear tell it got burned up anyhow. You don't rent the room, somebody else will."

Judith ran up the figures in her head. She would be completely out of money in a few weeks if she stayed here. "Never mind. I'll just spend the night in my wagon."

She drove to a park and made a campsite where she found wood, built a fire, fed her mule and made a corn cake in her fry pan.

She broke off a piece of the bread, chewed and pondered. Ten dollars a week to feed and shelter the mule, which earned nothing in return. She could sell Fancy to help pay for her living. But she would be sorry if she had to move on without ready transportation. She didn't have much money, and she hated to let go of any.

Maybe she could find a better way, hire out the animal to a hack. Or go back to the old livelihood of making soap. Tomorrow she would make inquiries about where to get suet and lime to make lye from fireplace ashes.

Blake wouldn't like her doing that kind of work. And he didn't approve of her coming to Fayetteville in the first place. But he wasn't around to make objections. Nor was he around to give her support. She took out the daguerreotype and studied his image. Would she ever see him again, or had the Yankees already killed him? God protect him.

Did he know Sally was not getting married? If he did, would he do anything about it?

She had to trust him better than that, no matter what poison Sally had spat.

Rumors about the destruction of Columbia had overtaken her days ago. Her home probably went up in smoke. Maybe she should have stayed to share her in-laws' fate. At least she wouldn't be alone.

Another nagging worry niggled at the back of her mind. Her monthly curse was late, only a few days, but late nonetheless. Probably the hard trip caused the delay. Or else Blake had succeeded in getting her with child. The timing was awful. A baby needed a home with two parents, not a vagabond mother like the poor crazy girl they had found. They had buried the dead baby and taken the mother to the next settlement.

God forbid she should end up like that.

In the morning, she would look for a cheaper room and a way to support herself. Things were not going to get better until she got busy and made them better.

She finished the cornbread and stared at the fire, wishing she didn't feel so alone. She nodded off, then roused herself to climb into the wagon and wrap up in a blanket. She reached for her shotgun and held it close.

~ * ~

Harry Bell followed the three cloaked, barefoot figures for a little way. He recognized his old messmates Whitfield, Morrison and Kramer, hailed them and caught up.

"I sure am glad to see you fellers," Harry said.

"Oh, it's Harry," Whitfield said without enthusiasm.

"What happened to your uniforms? You look like ghosts. How come you're flapping around in them bed sheets?"

"We got bushwhacked," Whitfield said.

"Do tell? He, he, he. Sure is a treat to see the high and mighty Corporal Whitfield brought down."

Whitfield glared at him.

"Two sonsabitches in our uniforms," Kramer said. "Threatened to kill us after we surrendered."

"A dirty Reb trick. Didn't fool me," Whitfield said.

"Sure didn't," Harry said. "That's why you're traipsing around in that fancy outfit. Where'd you get them duds?"

"A colored fella gave us these sheets to wrap up in."

"Them sonsabitches took your guns, too, I see."

"Everything. Where's yours?"

"Lost it."

"You always were careless, Harry."

"You should talk. He, he, he. You even lost your clothes. I ought to let you find your own way, you dumb mule turds."

"We sure as hell don't need you, Harry."

"At least I got my own duds."

They weren't any good to him, unarmed. Why, they didn't even have any grub to offer. But he'd gotten scared bad enough to want to stick with a crowd from now on. Besides, it would be fun to keep deviling them.

"Well, boys, I guess we better stick together 'til we find our outfit."

~ * ~

Blake and Hunter struck the road that ran north and south along the Catawba River. Eventually they encountered horse droppings and hoof-churned earth that signed the recent passage of cavalry.

"Aha. Six nails. Ours," Hunter said.

"I'd better put on my gray jacket." Blake started to unbutton the blue front.

"Mine was on the Morgan," Hunter pointed out.

"Then you can be my prisoner or I can be yours, depending on who we come across."

"You're getting the hang of this, old chum."

"That or get hanged," Blake snorted.

They followed the trail north on the wooded river road until they encountered Confederate pickets. Once Hunter talked his way through the lines, they were among friends.

They found General Butler with the greater portion of his command near a ferry landing on the riverbank. He was sitting on his horse, surrounded by his staff, watching the loading of saddles and other equipment onto a flatboat. Butler's fine features were drawn into a scowl, strong jaw jutting like a pugilist's. He tapped his silver handled riding crop against his cork foot in nervous cadence. Absorbed in watching the loading operation, he returned Blake's salutation but hardly looked at him. "How was it in Columbia, Captain?"

"Pretty bad, sir. More than half the city is destroyed." Blake didn't get a cue to continue.

Butler glanced his way. "I thought as much. Give the report to Captain Causey."

Blake took the report from his saddlebag and handed it to the aide. He wanted to propose to Butler that he wear blue and go after Kilpatrick, but he knew bad timing when he saw it.

Butler whirled to his second in command, Colonel Aiken. "Goddamnit, swimming the horses and ferrying men takes too goddamn long." He swiped his crop toward the river. "The goddamn Yankees are going to catch us right here with our backs to the water and gobble us up if we don't get a move on."

"We'll get across, sir. Here goes now." Colonel Aiken's voice didn't project much confidence.

A trooper eased his horse down the slippery bank and spurred it into the water. A herd of riderless horses followed his lead, soldiers slapping their rumps and shouting them forward. They plunged into the water, sank to neck level and started to swim. Their heads bobbed in the surging brown water as they thrust for the other bank. The current carried them downstream, but they progressed forward as well as sideways.

"So far so good," Colonel Aiken said.

Then one of the horses in front turned in midstream and started back. The rest of the herd turned with it. Dismounted men ran downstream to intercept their animals and pull them out of the river.

Butler swore and slashed at his wooden foot with his riding crop. Aiken's expression was bleak.

"Aiken, can't you tell me why our goddamn scouts can't turn up one goddamn ford across this goddamn river?" Butler raged.

"The citizens who live around here aren't any help," Colonel Aiken said, frowning. "Either they're ignorant or they just won't cooperate."

Hunter cleared his throat. "General, beg permission to be excused so I can look for a ford."

"Have at it, Lieutenant. Captain Winberry, you may rejoin your troop." Butler dismissed them with another swipe of his riding crop. Hunter handed Blake the reins to his pack mule and urged his farm tacky into a shambling canter.

Blake found his troop sitting along the bank waiting for their turn at crossing. His men pressed around him, all talking at once, asking what had happened in Columbia.

And he told them.

Colonel Aiken cantered up. "Captain Winberry," he shouted. "Mount your troop and move them south along the riverbank. The scouts found a ford."

"Yes, sir. Sergeant Frank, get 'em moving."

"Halleluiah. Sprung from the trap," Cheney said.

Simmons grinned. "No prison pen for me."

They hustled a couple of miles downstream and waited their turn at the ford, gun belts hung over their shoulders to keep their weapons and ammunition dry. When their turn came, they rode their horses into the swirling water, up to the saddle skirts. Blake got a soaking by the time Magic clambered up the far bank dripping cold brown water.

Hunter watched them cross from the far bank. Blake kneed Magic up to him and said, "You found the ford? Fine work."

"Couldn't stand to see us go up the spout. The Yanks are crossing both north and south and they would soon have us cornered. We still have to push hard to get to their head."

"At least we've got that chance."

Chapter Nineteen

Blake waited with his troop at the edge of the woods. He had sent Cheney forward on foot to investigate gunfire. Rain dripped onto him from the trees and rolled down his waterproof. Fresh wagon ruts cut the driveway.

They had out-marched the Yankees. Trot, canter, trot, day and night, through the rain. He had grown exhausted enough to fall asleep lying over Magic's neck, trusting her to plod along in column. More than once a hand shoved him upright when he started to slip out of the saddle. He did the same for others so they would not fall and wake up staring into the business end of an enemy rifle.

This morning he felt edgy and alert, forcing his aching spine straight, focusing gritty eyes, expecting no letup. He would rather be hunting Kilpatrick.

He had asked General Butler for a few days' extra duty for the task, but the general curtly told him he did not have time for personal vendettas, and Wheeler's Division was assigned to watch Kilpatrick, not his. Instead, Butler detailed him to take his troop along the fringes of the blue columns, harass them, pick up stragglers, discourage thievery.

Blake had a choice. He could obey orders, or he could desert his command to hunt Sally, destroy his reputation, weaken his unit, and risk a court marshal.

Sally would have to wait.

At least his company and others like them were teaching the Federals a little respect and making them hug their columns for protection. Maybe fewer homes would feel the torch and fewer families would be turned out into the cold to starve.

Cheney trotted back. "Capt'n, maybe fifteen or twenty Yanks

are sacking the house to the other end of this lane. They've stacked their rifles, except the ones killin' livestock to the back."

"What kind of ground? Any cover?"

"Pretty open, just trees along the drive." Cheney shook his head. "They'll see us a ways out if we run at them."

"How far to the house?"

"Quarter mile, maybe."

Blake looked around at his men. Some wore Federal ponchos like his, or captured Federal greatcoats. The wet clothes on those lacking such gear looked dark enough to pass for blue at a distance. Time to borrow a page from Hunter's book.

He said to Matt, "No sense getting our boys shot. We'll outfox them." He lifted his hat. "Attention." He didn't have to raise his voice because twenty men didn't take up much space. "Soldiers wearing coats and ponchos to the front. We're going to ride in easy, talking and laughing like we're going to a picnic. Keep your pistols drawn and cocked, out of sight. Fan out when we get into range, don't fire until I give the order or they show fight. We'll bag the lot without wasting ammo."

"Gotcha, Cap'n." A cackle of hard laughter and a murmur of assent surrounded him.

He heard Simmons' voice. "We runnin' up the black flag, Cap'n?"

Blake gave the troublemaker a hard stare. "We're soldiers, not savages. They want to surrender, let them. Understood?"

A reluctant, "Yes, sir."

Matt started to sort the men by garb. Blake felt the usual anxious stir in his gut. It would go away with the first action.

~ * ~

The yammering woman wouldn't get out of Harry's way. But he didn't dare treat her like he pleased, because Whitfield was just outside. Besides that, Schultz would see and might blab. He'd avoided getting punished for skipping off, but they were watching him closer than before.

He was stuck with the deal because he wasn't going off on his own any more. Not now that the Rebs were dressing in blue and tricking people. He'd have to stick with lots of company and do the best he could.

At least he was back in a foraging party, and nobody would begrudge a good Union man taking a few pieces of silverware from a slavocrat now and then.

Nobody minded but her. She reached to grab the silver spoon from him. "What are you doing with that?"

He snatched it out of her reach and laughed. "Looks like Federal property to me."

"You're nothing but a thief!" the woman squawked.

He shook his head and tut-tutted. "Lord knows I'm sick of this business."

"Then put my silver back."

He took a menacing step toward her. "Shut up, you old bitch."

She recoiled, shock in her eyes. He liked that. If only it was just him and her he could--

Through the window he caught a glimpse of soldiers coming up the drive. He looked sharper and saw cavalrymen riding toward the house, overcoats and ponchos, Federal type.

But Rebs in disguise had almost turned him into dog meat. He squinted at the cavalrymen. Didn't the tall, grim sonofabitch out in the lead look like one of those rebs? He grabbed his rifle and rushed toward the back door.

"What's got into you?" Shultz called after him.

"Rebs!" he shouted over his shoulder.

"They're just Kilpatrick's men, you yella fool."

Harry flung the door open, hearing Schultz's jeering laugh. He hit the yard running, slipped on the wet grass and skidded away.

~ * ~

As Blake led his men toward the house, he noted that Cheney had reported reliably. Well-grazed lawns. Winter-barren shade trees lined the driveway but offered little cover. At the end stood a plantation house and several outbuildings. Bluecoats and colored people were carrying meat from the smokehouse and loading it onto three wagons.

The men fell silent, grim at the sight of plundering Yankees. Some of the bluecoats looked at the approaching horsemen but didn't act alarmed, didn't rush toward their stacked weapons. The only ones carrying rifles were slaughtering animals off beyond the house. Single shots, they had to reload after each kill.

Blake signaled his men to fan out so they wouldn't shoot into each other's backs.

Then a lanky bluecoat split off, ran to the stack and picked up a rifle. He started yelling, "Lieutenant! It's Rebs! C'mon men! Grab a gun!"

Blake whipped out his revolver and shouted "Fire!" He aimed toward the Yankee who was giving the alarm and squeezed the trigger. The air exploded with gunfire all around him. The bluecoat fired, then pitched backwards. Somebody near Blake groaned and slid off his horse. Another Federal grabbed a rifle, spun around and fell. Most of them, caught in the open and unarmed, dropped underneath the bullets.

"I surrender!" one yelled.

"Don't shoot, Reb!" pleaded another.

A few sprinted toward the rear of the house, or toward outbuildings, along with the coloreds.

Matt peeled away, drew several men with him to run down the fugitives, yelping like foxhunters.

"Sergeant Frank!" Blake shouted.

"Here, sir."

"Get three men to take charge of prisoners. Set up two vedettes to watch the drive. Have the rest search the outbuildings."

That would just about use up his little troop. He glanced toward the house. Might be more Yankees holed up in there. He needed somebody with common sense. He whirled around, spotted Cheney. "Come with me."

He dismounted and ran toward the house, pistol drawn, took the porch steps by twos and threw himself against the wall by the open door. Cheney followed and covered the opposite side.

Blake rested there, panting, openmouthed.

He took off his hat, slipped it onto the muzzle of his Colt and stuck it into the doorway. Nobody shot at it. "Anybody home?" he called out.

"Are you Confederate soldiers?" a woman's voice quavered.

"Yes, ma'am. Any Yanks in there?" Blake answered.

"Only one. By all means come in and relieve me of him."

He looked at Cheney and nodded. They stalked into the house, pistols ready.

The inside was vandalized, cluttered with broken furniture and torn-down curtains. Couch cushions slashed open, books swept from shelves, ceramic art broken into shards, rugs caked with red earth and manure.

In the front room, a woman about his mother's age stood, fireplace poker clubbed in her hands. A Federal soldier lay at her feet, holding his hand to his bleeding head, grimacing.

Blake said, "Cheney, put him with the others."

"Get up Yank." Cheney prodded the blue leg with his toe.

"Keep your shirt on, Johnny." The Yankee heaved to a sitting position.

Cheney picked up the Yankee's rifle from the floor and gestured with it. "Get up."

Hand still plastered to his head, the Yankee shoved to his feet and staggered out, Cheney following.

The woman lowered the end of the poker to the floor and leaned on it, her face strained and pale. "When the shooting started, he aimed his gun out the window, so I hit him as hard as I could."

Blake said, "Good. Otherwise he might have killed somebody. Was he the only one inside?"

"There was one other. He ran out the back door." She nodded in that direction.

"We'll catch him."

"I hope so. He was a very bad man, Captain. Much worse than the one I hit. He insulted me."

"You'll point him out, then."

"What will you do to him?" she asked.

"Did he hurt you?"

"I believe he wanted to."

Blake jerked his head toward a movement at the top of the stairs. Two half-grown girls, a small boy and a colored woman looked down at him, big-eyed. One of the girls called out, "Mama, you all right?"

"Everything's fine, but stay up there until I say different."

"Excuse me, ma'am." Blake touched his hat. "I have to go outside and see to things."

"Thank you for saving us from those thieving Yankees. I should like to reclaim what is ours."

"Others are likely to come along and steal it all over again," he told her. "I hope you hide it someplace safe this time."

In the front yard, his men were securing their victory, loading the captured weapons into a wagon and poking through the goods claiming plunder. The prisoners sat in a dejected clump, Simmons and Cheney guarding them. They'd already been stripped of their hats, shoes, coats, anything worth taking. The only officer in the group hunched a little apart from the rest, ashy-faced, elbows on his knees, smoking a cigar. Two lay where they were shot.

One of his troopers--he recalled the man next to him falling out of his saddle--lay on the lawn. David Frank knelt over him.

Blake walked over to see about his casualty. David stood up, grim-faced, shook his head. "Hiers," he said. "Deader'n hell."

A bullet had hit Hiers squarely over the heart. Bright arterial blood wicked through the rain-soaked jacket. Dull eyes, gray face blank of expression.

Blake shook his head. "Shouldn't have lost anybody. Shouldn't have taken the first shot. Have him loaded onto one of those wagons."

The scared black face of a child peeked around the corner of the smokehouse. Across the field, beyond the house, big lumps lay-- dead cattle. His troopers were busy bringing in Yankees who had run, along with the coloreds who had been helping the Yankees. A still blue heap lay between the house and an outbuilding.

He met the woman when she came down the porch stairs. He took her to the prisoners and waved his hand toward them. "See the man you told me about?"

She looked them over and shook her head. "I don't believe you caught him."

"We haven't brought in all the fugitives yet. He might be among them."

The Yankee officer took the cigar from his mouth and stood up. "What's going on here, Captain?" His voice was steady but the cigar trembled in his hand.

"One of your men insulted this lady."

"I don't know anything about it. I don't allow that sort of thing."

"Oh, horseshi--" He broke off, remembering that the woman

stood right next to him.

"I'll see to my things." She pointed to the cluster of coloreds his men had brought up. "Why are my people under guard?"

"They were helping the Yankees. Then they ran. Take charge of them if you'd like."

She walked over to her people and took over.

He turned back to the Yankee lieutenant. "How many of your men got away?"

A bland shrug. "Beats me."

A prisoner was staring at Blake, and he returned the look, recognizing him. One of the blue coats he and Hunter had slickered a few days before. Kramer. Didn't look any less scared the second go-round.

Blake said, "Where are your two friends?"

Kramer pointed with his chin to the shot Federals. "Whitfield was onto you, tried to warn the rest. Morrison caught on too. I was too far away to grab a rifle." He laughed grimly. "Or else I'd be down like them."

Hunter was right about having to fight them all over again. Hiers would still be alive if Whitfield and Morrison hadn't given the alarm.

Quick studies. He had trained them with one sharp lesson, let them go, and Hiers had paid for his generosity. "I should have let him shoot you," he said wearily. "Ought to get a length of rope, hang you this time."

Kramer didn't say anything, just looked even more scared.

Blake walked over and looked at the others. Whitfield's fingers curled as though he still held onto the rifle, his blue coat torn with bullet holes, soaked red from collar to waist.

Morrison exhaled with a moan and blood bubbled from his nose. Blake turned to the Yankee officer. "Detail one of your men to see about this one."

"Go on, Kramer," the officer said.

Kramer shambled forward, looking like he'd rather be invisible.

Matt rode up. "Did you ever see anything like the way them bummers run? We thought up a new name for the sport. Gonna call it 'Bummer Runnin'!' You Yanks fall in with your friends now, there you go."

One of the Yankees he brought in had blood all over his face from a scalp wound and the other was muddy, must have taken a roll. They flopped down with their comrades, breathing hard, heads sinking low.

"We take any casualties besides Hiers?" Blake asked Matt.

"Nary."

The woman organized her people, brought the rest out of hiding and set them to loading goods onto one of the wagons. She came over to Blake and pointed to the wagon, "That is mine. The mules are also mine. Do you have any objection if I have my people bring it off and hide it?"

He shook his head no. "The other wagons?"

"I suppose they belong to my neighbors."

"Do you recognize the other two Yanks my men just brought up?"

"No. He must have gotten away."

"Another one is lying over there between the house and the shed, if you care to look at him."

She shuddered. "I'd rather not."

"No matter. He won't ever bother anybody else." Blake turned to Matt. "Detail four men to take the other two wagons and the prisoners back to the main column." To the Federal officer he said, "Your wounded can ride, the rest of you have to walk."

"What about our dead?"

"We'll bring them along, you can bury them later. Have two of your men put them into a wagon."

"Thank you, Captain." The Federal officer bowed as though he had upbringing.

"Don't go thinking it's out of my love for Yankees. Another party of bummers might come along and find the bodies. Then what would they do to these people?"

Blake looked over the sullen catch of prisoners. Infantry, but it was worth a try. He said to the Yankee officer, "Tell me everything you know about General Kilpatrick."

~ * ~

Judith opened the door to her room, feeling fortunate to have found such a satisfactory home. Her aunt's lawyer, Mr. Ames, had referred her to the landlady, Mrs. Martin. Actually, it wasn't any fancier than the room she had turned down the first night she arrived, but it was cleaner and much cheaper.

She set the basket of provisions down on the hearth. A decent day's ration, bartered for a couple of pounds of the soap she had made.

The landlady's son, Jacob, was earning money for both of them by hauling people and goods in her wagon. They split the fares, and so far her half was enough to cover the rent and then some.

She stacked wood into the fireplace so she could cook her supper. A meal good enough for anybody, sweet potato, corn dodgers with sorghum syrup, and salt pork.

All in all, she was getting along. She had a place to live and enough to eat, and so far had not needed to sell a thing. When she thought back, she had always managed to survive somehow.

She lit the kindling and watched the fire slowly catch.

Mere survival wasn't enough. She ached with loneliness, wanting her husband back in her life.

Chapter Twenty

After crossing to the east side of Lynch's Creek, Butler's division had gained enough distance on the enemy to afford a short rest.

Blake had no orders and asked for none, so a plantation near Kellytown gave him the chance. With clothes sodden from the relentless rain, joints stiff from too many hours in the saddle, throat raw from the rasping air, he was dizzy from lack of sleep. Stinking like a wet dog, he threw himself under the roof of a tool shed and slept until mid-morning the next day. Even the bugler overslept.

Rain was aloft in the clouds, not coming down yet. A southern breeze brought cotton- soft air. After he roused himself Blake cared for his overworked horse, rubbed her down, cleaned her hooves, fed her corn and sweet hay. He got liniment from the farrier to rub on her swollen joints.

After receiving his orders from Colonel Aiken, he still had the afternoon to lounge around a fire David had built outside the shed. His drying clothes loosened and warmed on his body. With his messmates he dined on corned beef and Irish potatoes, cooked together in a hash, and red wine, all captured from a Federal wagon train. He wanted to enjoy the respite although it could not last.

Hunter gimped up. Blake hadn't seen him since crossing the Catawba. He looked exhausted, haggard and pale. For once it appeared the scouting life had been treating him roughly.

"Howdy, old chum," Hunter said. "Leftenant Kirkland." He bowed with sarcastic elegance, and nodded at David Frank.

"Just in time for supper," Matt said. "Ain't we blessed?"

"To what do we owe this honor?" Blake asked.

"Had to check in with General Hampton." Hunter eyed the food.

"Spare me some?"

Blake edged over to make room by the fire. "There is plenty, courtesy of the Federals. They stole it from our people so we stole it back."

Hunter eased himself down and settled with his lame leg stuck out straight. He spooned a portion of the beef and potatoes onto the flatways half of a canteen. "Got hold of some bad meat yesterday. Hope I can keep this down."

"Still riding that farm tackey?" Blake asked.

"Captured a good Yankee horse. Got his rider too. A Yankee officer." Hunter glanced at Blake. "I just now turned him in."

Blake didn't feel like telling Hunter how he had run across the three Yankees they had captured and released. Didn't want to hear him say I told you so.

"We've been catching a few ourselves," Matt shoveled in a spoonful and kept on talking as he chewed. "Bummer running. At this rate we'll soon be outnumbered by our prisoners."

Hunter probed a potato with his fork. "Might have to cull the lot."

"I heard about a fuss," Blake said. "The Yanks threatened to execute some of our boys."

Hunter took a tentative bite of potato, expressionless. "That's so. The generals have been writing love letters to each other."

Matt said, "We can match them if they want to start that game."

Hunter nodded. "Match them double. Wheeler and Hampton both promised to go two for one, starting with their officers. We have more of theirs than they have of ours." He set the potato down and pushed the plate aside as though it had sprouted maggots. "Somebody else eat this."He covered his mouth and belched, then fished his pipe out of his pocket.

Matthew speared the beef with his knife. "What brought it on?" he said around a bite of potato. "This thing gets uglier all the time."

"Yanks found some of their bully boys with their throats cut." Hunter passed his pipe stem under his chin, flashing his teeth in a sick smile. "Seems Wheeler's Texans caught them right after they had raped and killed a girl."

Matt said, "I'd have stuffed their balls down their throats, besides."

Hunter nodded. "That's pretty effective, too."

"Anybody get executed yet?" Blake asked.

"Haven't heard. But don't get yourself captured. Could be very bad for the health." Hunter lit his pipe, the hand holding the match shaky. "You can thank the high water for this little break. Yanks are having trouble crossing Lynch's Creek. Good wet Confederate weather."

"Their trouble suits me just fine." Blake filled his tin cup with wine. "We're supposed to go out on a reconnaissance tonight. See if any are across yet."

Hunter took a drag from his pipe and settled back on his elbows, eyes closing.

Blake drank the wine fast, hoping it would go to his head and numb his mind.

~ * ~

Andrew McCord rode out that night with Captain Duncan and sixty picked men. They had managed to cross Lynch's Creek though the rest of the army was having varying degrees of difficulty. General Howard had ordered him to take a cipher message to Federal headquarters in Charleston, which had recently fallen into Union hands.

The squad picked through the dark quietly, sabers tied down and muffled, singing and loud talking prohibited. The road led through the woods, which added to the murky darkness of the night. McCord sat alert in the saddle, watching and listening for signs that the Rebels were onto them. He whispered, "Captain Duncan, how long do you think it'll take us to get to Charleston?"

"From the map, two days. Three at most."

"You believe the map?"

"No. It probably lies. We got it from a secesh." Duncan shook water off his hat. "Damn this rain. Looks like it's setting in, too."

"Good," McCord said. "Makes it that much darker."

Duncan's low laugh rippled in the dark. "You aren't nervous, are you?"

"Just cautious. All the Rebel cavalry skulking about."

"After tonight, we'll be through the thick of them. Then we can relax a little."

Then the wet darkness was split by the crack and flash of gunfire. Duncan halted the column, waved his pistol and started barking orders.

"Return fire! Fire! Fire! Fire!"

~ * ~

"Ambush!"

"Yanks!"

Blake drew rein, not sure what was going on to his front. Gunfire, and all that confused yelling.

The horse behind him slammed into Magic and the rider broke into an under-the-breath curse, Simmons' voice.

"Surrender!" The voice sounded like Colonel Aiken, somewhere toward the front of the line.

Another volley answered.

Then came the order to trot, and charge, and the columns surged forward, yelling.

The regiment had deployed to find out whether any Yankees had crossed Lynch's Creek yet. Sure found out in a hurry.

Blake drew his pistol, cocked it, and held it pointed skyward until he could see something to shoot at. Then he broke into the open, and fast flashes of gunfire lit the silhouettes of his enemies.

A horse crashed against his leg. Magic staggered and lost stride. Blake swore at the rider. Men and horses surged past him and he pushed ahead, hot to regain the front. He dug his heels into Magic's sides and pressed her forward. A cathartic yell ripped from his sore throat. He came to a crossroad, then a confused tangle of horses and men.

"Who are you?" a man next to him hollered at a shape that appeared to their front.

A carbine flash showed a stranger's face and the man next to Blake screamed, pitching forward. Blake shot into the center of the man who fired. The Yankee made an awful gagging cry and fell away, under scrambling hooves.

A bullet zipped past Blake's ear. A hand grappled at his saber belt, pulling him backwards to unseat him. He lashed his pistol in an arc behind him until it connected, hard. A grunt, and the hand released his belt.

He whirled, snatched the man's wet coat, jammed his pistol against his rib cage and thumbed back the hammer to shoot.

"Don't! Don't kill me, Yank," the man begged.

"Yank? Yank?" Blake held onto him and kept the pistol in place. "Who the hell are you?"

"Tompkins, Company C, 5th South Carolina."

"Why the hell did you grab me?" Though still furious, Blake lifted his finger from the trigger.

"You ain't a Yank?"

"Hell, no." He released Tompkins.

"You like to put my eye out."

"So what? You can't see worth a damn with two of 'em."

The fight moved away from him--the Federals forced back. He hustled forward between riders he took to be comrades.

Not every enemy had quit the field. Two of them stood their ground, calling for their men to rally, firing pistols, lighting themselves like a fireworks display. Blake picked one and aimed his Colt but somebody moved in between.

He rushed alongside--made out Lieutenant Colonel Davis' gray horse. One of the Yankees fired as Davis dashed up to him--Davis fired back. Blake saw the Yankee's stricken face lit by the pistol flashes. Davis spun off in pursuit of the other officer.

The shot Yankee lurched in the saddle but managed to wheel his horse. Blake wanted him alive, to question. He shouted, "Surrender!" and lunged for him, but the rubber waterproof slicked away from his fingers. He lost his balance, then recovered. The Yankee made off into the darkness.

Blake changed his mind, raised his Colt, aimed between the shoulder blades, and squeezed the trigger. The hammer clicked on a misfire. He cocked and tried again. Another misfire. He dug into his saddlebag for a dry cylinder he had loaded in reserve, but by now the Yankee was too far away, unclear in the dark.

To chase headlong into the dark all by himself would get him butchered. He drew rein, then switched cylinders in his Colt by feel. Rearmed, he looked around, orienting himself.

Smoke hung low in the moist air. The Yankees had withdrawn, maybe found another place for an ambush. Ghostly men gathered around him in the road. A wounded horse thrashed, making strangling noises.

He shook his head, clearing his brain, feeling his blood settle. His ears roared from the gunfire. Burnt sulfur raked his throat.

A gray horse loomed out of the dark--Davis. He was holding a handkerchief to the side of his head, saying, "Captain, gather your troop. Colonel Aiken is dead. I'm in charge now." Davis raised his voice. "All company commanders assemble your men. Let's go get 'em."

~ * ~

McCord stuffed a handkerchief into the hole in his groin, panting and trembling and blinking back tears. The bounce of his trotting horse stabbed white-hot pain through his body. "Duncan, I'm shot," he said through his teeth. He slowed his horse to a walk.

Captain Duncan rode closer. "How bad?"

"Bad. Bad. Can't keep up," McCord said through gritted teeth. "The message."

"Give it to me."

He let go of the handkerchief, thrust his shaking hand into his pocket and withdrew the packet. He shoved it at Duncan.

"You have to keep up." Duncan stuffed the paper into his saddlebag.

McCord nodded. He had to keep up or the Rebels would have him. Wounded and in the hands of the enemy. God help him then! He leaned to one side and retched. Somebody held onto his belt so he didn't fall off.

The nausea cost him too much strength. The only thing holding him in the saddle was the hand on his belt. The acid vomit fouled his mouth and he tried to spit it clean. His surroundings seemed to fade but he couldn't tell because it was dark anyway.

Duncan's voice barely penetrated the rush in his ears. "You have to keep up."

~ * ~

After he came to, McCord lay as still as he could. None of the passing horsemen acknowledged him. As long as he didn't move, didn't call attention to himself in the darkness, he could blend into the earth, the grass, and the brush. Then if he died, it was because he was going to anyway, not because an enemy decided to finish him off.

He couldn't recollect his descent from the saddle to the ground, whether friends had lifted him down, or whether he'd fallen like a rotten tree to rest here in his bloody clothes. It mattered little, because they were gone and he was alone except for these hostile men pounding by not twenty feet from his boot-toe. He had to move his thumb into his mouth and bite the knuckle to keep from making a pain-noise.

One of them must have seen the motion because he slowed and stopped his horse, leaning forward, looking. The Rebel called out names--"Cheney, Simmons"--the voice husky as though he were about to lose it. Two others reined in and flanked him.

Distant lightning glowed. McCord lost hope that they wouldn't make him out. He recalled emptying his pistol and never reloading it. He held his breath. Go away.

Another Southern voice said, "Why don't I just plug him to make sure, Cap'n? One less house burner." The hammer clicked.

McCord braced for a flash and the thud of another bullet into his body. Then he spoke up.

"No. Don't."

~ * ~

Blake threw out his hand and pushed Simmons' pistol barrel down. "Wait till I say."

The Yankee said, "Captain--whoever you are--I surrender."

Simmons laughed. "That flushed 'im."

Blake said, "You move, you're dead."

"I won't, I swear I won't." The voice in the dark sounded dispirited and weak.

Blake wished he could see well enough to be sure that the Yankee wasn't going to break his word and pull a gun.

Better let Simmons shoot him.

No, he wanted to find out some things first.

To Cheney, he said, "Dismount and hand off your horse to Simmons. I'll cover the Yankee. You disarm him. Check inside his coat and boots for knives."

Then he approached the Yankee as though he were a rattlesnake.

Cheney knelt by the Yankee, took up his revolver and sniffed it, checking the chambers. "Shot out."

"Who are you?" Blake said while Cheney searched the prisoner.

"Lieutenant McCord. Who--"

"Captain Winberry."

The Yankee grunted and grabbed Cheney's wrist. "For God's sake don't touch me there."

Cheney shook him off. "Don't do that, damn you."

Blake said, "How bad you hurt, McCord?"

"Real bad." His breathing rasped. "I need water. Please."

It wasn't too much to ask. Blake knelt down and supported McCord's head and held the canteen to his mouth so that he could gulp the water down. "Your friends left you behind, didn't they?"

"Couldn't ride," McCord gasped. "Passed out."

Blake squinted at the Yankee, but could not make out much of his face in the dark. "Where are you shot?"

"In the groin."

"I'm going to see for myself."

"No." The prisoner protested as though he had any say.

"I won't hurt you." He took his matchbox from his pocket, struck one and shielded it with his hands so it would not illuminate him for a sharpshooter. He held it over McCord's face, which glistened with rain or sweat or tears or all three. Clean-cut Yankee features, though pain-drawn. He'd seen that face earlier in a pistol-flash, and he'd captured him after all. Maybe he'd seen him before that, somewhere else. It would come to him in time.

He ran the light down the length of McCord's torso, lifted the waterproof and looked under it. The unbuttoned greatcoat was closed against the drizzling rain. He nudged aside the edge of the coat, uncovered the bloodied open trouser-tops. A dark-stained handkerchief was wadded into the hollow between thigh and abdomen.

Most likely the bullet had driven upward into the poor devil's gut and he would bloat like a colicky horse just before he died, an evil fate every Yankee vandal deserved. But he said, "Doesn't look too bad. It's quit bleeding."

The match sputtered out. "I guess that's something," McCord said.

"How long ago did your friends leave?" Blake asked.

"Don't know."

"Where did they run to?"

"They're gone." McCord's strained voice took on a note of defiance. "You'll never catch them."

"Uh-huh. I'll give you that, Yank. They did run pretty good. What were y'all trying to do?"

"Just a scout."

"Found us, didn't you?" Blake rubbed his aching forehead. "We took it for an ambush."

"No, it wasn't." McCord's voice lifted, interested. "Weren't you pursuing us?"

"I don't think anybody knew you were there. Not until the shooting started."

"Then we just collided in the dark," McCord said.

"An accident?" Blake wished he could see his prisoner better, but did not want to use another match. "What was your destination?"

"I can't tell you that."

"How many men in your party?"

"Not enough, or we would've whipped you." McCord's voice again took on that edge of defiance.

"Fact is, you didn't. How many Federals have crossed Lynch's Creek?"

"I do not know."

"The hell you don't," Blake snapped. "You better come clean."

"In my place, you wouldn't."

Blake rocked back on his heels to sit down next to the Yankee. What was he going to do, threaten the wounded man with further injury? Even if it worked, he did not have the stomach for such barbarity. "You're game, McCord. Too bad you weren't lucky enough to be born in South Carolina."

"What are you going to do with me?" McCord asked.

"You're cavalry. Kilpatrick's division?"

"No, Howard's."

Blake pictured Howard and his escort riding out of Columbia. "Old Prayer Book."

McCord hesitated, but owned up. "That's right."

"You're on Howard's staff."

"How did you get to that?"

"I've seen you with him. Never mind how," Blake said. "Tell me about Kilpatrick. You know him?"

"I've met him."

"Did you see a young lady traveling with him since you left Columbia?"

"Why?" McCord asked.

"She's a friend of mine. I heard he took her hostage and I want to make sure she's all right. Pretty, strawberry blonde. Sally Dubose."

McCord paused again. "I've met her."

Blake sucked in his breath and caught it. "You saw her?"

"In Columbia. I stayed at her house. She told me about you. Here. I want to show you something, a letter."

"What did she say?"

"She said you were too brave for her liking." McCord fished the wallet from his coat pocket, took out a folded paper, and handed it to him.

Blake held it close to his eyes under his hat-brim so the drizzle would not run the ink. Then he struck another fizzling match, cupping it with his hand. He scanned down to the signature. Sally Dubose, the familiar handwriting. Then he read the letter.

"You protected her?" Blake said. "Then how come you let Kilpatrick take her hostage?"

"He outranks me. Besides, she's no hostage. She wants to go north with him."

Blake let out his breath. "I don't believe that."

McCord didn't comment.

"Where's Kilpatrick now?" Blake pressed.

"I don't know."

"Close by?"

"I truly wish he were," McCord said softly.

Blake listened to his prisoner's fast, shallow breathing. "It can't be true. Sally wouldn't have gone with that damn Yankee voluntarily."

"Believe whatever you want." McCord's voice sounded weary.

Blake stood up. "We have to get out of here. Can't you sit a horse if we boost you?"

"If I could I wouldn't be here."

"We could throw you across."

"Please don't. It would finish me." McCord sounded as though he did not care if it did.

Now that Blake had made up his mind never to release a prisoner again, he had found the exception. No harm in it this time. McCord wouldn't be able to fight anytime soon, probably never.

"Cheney, get a blanket and let's make a litter. We're going to take him to that farmhouse back there."

He found the last bottle of wine cached in his saddlebag and dug the cork out with his penknife. Then he poured some of the well-shaken, muddy fluid into his tin cup and gave it to McCord.

"I don't drink."

"Take it for the pain. I doubt even a Baptist God would hold it against you."

McCord slurped it down. He swallowed and said, "I'll write you a letter, too." His voice slurred, fading. "In case… you're ever in my… situation."

Thankful that the darkness hid his scowl, Blake upended the bottle and took a lingering swallow. He felt tired and old. He had spent too much life in too short a time and was about to go broke.

He wanted to keep on drinking until he used it up.

Better not. Might have to fight again before the night was out, and dulling his mind would be dangerous. He stuck what was left of the cork into the bottle.

A few minutes later, he banged on the door of the farmhouse until a man's voice said, "Who are you?"

"We're Confederate soldiers. We have a wounded man that needs help."

The door opened a crack. Blake stuck his boot into it so the man inside would not have a chance to reconsider. Then the door swung all the way open.

The farmer held a candle toward him. An empty sleeve was pinned to the front of his shirt, likely a veteran who knew about men needing help. "We heard all the shooting and it scared my wife half to death. Where is he?"

"Bring him in," Blake said to Cheney and Simmons. They dragged in McCord, semiconscious and moaning, jackknifed in the blanket. They set him down.

"A damned Yankee," the one-armed man said.

"That's right," Blake said. "If he's still alive when the Yankees come, he might spare you trouble. They won't be so quick to burn down your house with him in it."

"True enough." The one-armed man sighed. "We'll take care of him. Bury him if we need to. Take him on back and put him to bed."

McCord's face appeared pale in the candlelight, his eyes shut tight, smooth jaw clenched. He grunted and gripped the blanket when they lifted him.

Blake led his men back out into the darkness and the rain. He recalled McCord's pledge to write a Yankee-to-Yankee letter of recommendation, but the wounded man wasn't in any shape to keep such a promise.

Blake shook his head. God forbid he would ever need a letter like that.

Chapter Twenty-one

All night and through the rest of the next day, Blake told himself the rain soaked the Yankees as thoroughly as it soaked him. But the floodwaters of Lynch's Creek weren't obstacle enough to keep his enemies, every last one, from crossing.

After this discovery, his regiment pushed eastward ahead of the enemy to rendezvous with the rest of the division. A 40 mile march brought them squishing into Cheraw, at the North Carolina line.

After settling into camp, he learned a courier line had been established between the fast-moving cavalry division and Columbia. He posted a letter to his family from headquarters and mailed another to Judith from the local post office, without much hope that either would be delivered.

The Yankees were pushing them in the general direction of Fayetteville. Probably he would have a chance to see Judith soon. What would she think of him when she found out he had no home, no money, nothing?

And he still had not carried through with his vow to rescue Sally. McCord's words assured him her life was not in danger, but most of what he'd said did not make sense. Sally wanting to go north with Kilpatrick? Preposterous.

He tried again to persuade General Butler to let him infiltrate the Yankee cavalry wearing blue. Again he was refused.

At present, the chaos in Cheraw reminded him of Columbia right before the evacuation. Wagons moved out government supplies, panicky civilians left town and looters prowled the streets. A consolidation of the Confederate forces had not happened yet, so the Federals were going to have their way all over again.

General Butler ordered him to destroy the military stores they did not have time to haul away. He hated the job. After he made his men roll barrels of flour, cornmeal, bacon and sugar into the open, he let them load their horses with whatever they could carry. When civilians and coloreds snuck off with some of the provisions, he turned his back and did not see a thing.

He instructed his men to fill buckets with water before they applied the torch so they could keep the fire under control. It was hard to watch the flames eat the food intended for many a soldier's empty belly. The smoke stank of scorched flour, bacon grease and the wickedness of waste.

He finished the destruction and crossed the Pee Dee into North Carolina. Yankee artillery opened up and small arms fire answered from the rear guard. The last Confederates clattered across, fired the bridge and left another town to the enemy.

~ * ~

Restless, Lexi strolled to the ruins of her house. Mama wasn't paying her much mind, so she had a little freedom. Papa had ridden Lightning toward Anderson looking for provisions. She did not expect him home until tomorrow.

The Yankees were long gone as far as she knew, even the stragglers, but she carried her revolver, fully loaded, secured on a belt underneath her coat. She almost hoped somebody would try to jump her, anything to break up the boredom.

She spotted a horse, cropping grass in her yard, an unexpected sight. The Yankees hadn't left many behind.

She moved closer, slowly so she would not alarm the animal, meaning to make the stray hers.

But it wasn't just any old stray. It was Scout! She spotted the scar on his neck. The sorrel was saddled, broken reins hanging from the bit.

"Here, Scout. Come on, boy," she crooned. Scout lifted his head, pricked his ears and stared at her, standing his ground. She eased up to him and took hold of his bridle.

She laughed, delighted, and patted his neck. He pushed forward and nuzzled her, looking for a treat. "You came back, all saddled up! Did you throw that nasty old Yankee and come home? What a smart horse."

Papa needing Lightning had kept her from taking him. Now that she had her own horse back, she could leave this blasted, desolate place.

~ * ~

Blake followed General Butler's finger as he pointed to a map spread over the table. "We are here, and we presume Major General Wheeler is about here. In sum, we need for his division to join forces with ours at once, before Fayetteville."

Blake nodded, absorbing the information that Wheeler's command had disappeared somewhere along the banks of the Pee Dee north of Cheraw. He would have to backtrack to find him. It sounded risky and difficult, and he was likely to run into enemies, most likely Kilpatrick's cavalry.

Butler said, "Since General Johnston took over the department from Beauregaurd, he has been trying like fury to get all our forces consolidated. Wheeler is senior to me, so you'll take an order signed by Johnston."

Butler canted his weight to one side, off his cork foot. "I need an officer for the job, but I cannot spare anyone on my staff at present. Lightfoot is sick. He recommended you and I agreed, since you acquitted yourself favorably when I sent you to Columbia."

"Thank you, sir. My horse is lame, so I will see about borrowing Lightfoot's. Then I'll leave, straightaway."

Butler tapped his finger on the map. "Whatever you do, don't get captured with those papers on you."

Blake found Hunter in a nearby house, installed on a couch, his pipe and a bottle of medicinal brandy within easy reach. He was hatchet faced and heavy lidded, but not too ill for the usual sardonic smile.

"So you get to search out the elusive Wheeler, do you, old chum? Good job. I thought you would be getting bored by now hanging around picket lines."

Blake sat on a chair near the couch. "How's the leg?"

"Least of my troubles. I got the quickstep, both ways, from that bad meat. Dr. Thompson dosed me with opium, think it's slowed the system down a little, but not enough for this job."

"Should I wear blue?" Blake asked him.

"Not unless you want Wheeler's boys to shoot you on sight."

"I hear they are trigger-happy."

"One shot a Yankee officer bringing a message under a flag of truce." Hunter's cynical smile deepened. "Guess he didn't notice the flag."

"Kill him?"

"Not quite. The dispatch was about that prisoner-executing business." Hunter smiled, enjoying the irony. "Doctor patched up the Fed and shipped him off on a train back to Yankeeland. Wheeler had to apologize to Kilpatrick."

"Kilpatrick." Blake leaned forward. "I'll be running close to him, then."

"Likely. He and Wheeler are old West Point classmates. I'd hate to be the picket that shot that Yank." Hunter chuckled. "You get captured, maybe you'll see your girlfriend before they hang you."

"My horse has gone lame. You won't need yours for a few days. Can we swap while I make the trip?"

Hunter nodded. "He's not the fastest, but steady. Balky jumper. Keep that in mind. I got him off a picket line. He belonged to an officer, judging from the fancy equipment. Trouble is, he wants to go back to the Yanks."

Blake smiled. "That's pretty far-fetched."

"See for yourself."

"Got any more of those passes signed by Kilpatrick? I might have need for one. And I'll bring the blue coat."

Hunter cocked an eyebrow. "You really are looking for a noose, aren't you?"

Moments later, Blake saddled Hunter's mount, a healthy young gelding with a U. S. brand on its shoulder. He folded the blue coat under the saddle blanket. Then he set off westward to find General Wheeler's command. After he delivered the papers, he could take a little detour and look for Sally.

He tried the horse over felled trees and a worm fence. The animal never hesitated. Blake patted the sleek neck. "Hunter lied on you, old son. You're not a bit balky."

He came upon the Pee Dee late in the afternoon. The river was swift, swollen beyond its banks, and at flood stage. A log rushed downstream and struck a spit of land with a thud. Too dangerous to swim. He hoped he wouldn't have to.

He started south, following the river. Had Wheeler succeeded in crossing his whole division, he ought to find horse spoor.

At dusk he came across fresh hoof prints with six nails printed in the mud. He followed them along the path. The long afternoon light was already fading. He hated tracking unknown riders through the woods. They'd know he was coming before he knew where they were. He took out his Colt and kept it in his hand.

The horse stopped and pricked its ears. "What you see?" Blake whispered. He peered into the bushes, couldn't make out anything.

A voice called from the brush. "Dismount."

He'd walked right into it. God, don't let him be a Yankee. "Who's there?"

"Never you mind," the voice drawled. "Get down or I'll knock you down with this hog leg."

At least he sounded Southern. Blake dismounted.

"Take off your gun belt, partner, throw it over the saddle."

Fuming, he obeyed.

The soldier emerged from the blind, revolver aimed at Blake's chest. He wore a shabby gray coat, red hair stuck out through the rips in his floppy hat, face all insolence and freckles. He shifted a plug from one cheek to the other. "Who might ye be?"

"Captain Winberry, Butler's Division. Who might you be?"

"Edwards."

"Edwards who?"

"I ride with Captain Shannon."

Shannon's scouts worked for Wheeler. Blake let out his breath. "Good. Just the man. Take me to General Wheeler straightaway."

"Wheeler hisself? Do tell." Edwards holstered his revolver, lifted Blake's gun belt off the saddle and buckled it onto his own waist. He mounted Hunter's horse and said, "March."

"Look here, Edwards. I am an officer and I refuse to be treated like a prisoner. Get off my horse and give me back my sidearm."

Edwards laughed. "Ain't you bossy. For all I know you're a galvanized Yank. My rules. Move it."

A few minutes later he came to a house, windows aglow with interior light. A pack of hounds came baying and woofing and snuffling up to him. A line of about a dozen horses were tethered by the house, guarded by another man in Confederate uniform. Edwards dismounted, shoving the dogs aside. He handed Hunter's horse off to the guard, and made Blake go ahead of him to the front door, past another guard.

The inside of the house was warm and smelled of the bacon frying on skillets in the fireplace. A hard looking set of soldiers lounged around. Most wore gray mixed with parts of Federal uniforms, no insignia. Sabers hung from pegs on the wall. They regarded him with suspicious stares. He stared back. If they were the wrong people, they had him plus the papers in his saddlebags and he had really stepped into it.

Edwards saluted a young man with a dark beard who was sitting by the fire. The collar of his plain gray jacket was turned under, showing no rank. The wiry little man looked Blake up and down while he tapped a nervous tattoo on his boot leg. "What have you got, Edwards?"

"Says he's a Captain Winberry from Butler's Division, Private Johnson, sir. He's lookin' for General Wheeler."

"What business do you have with Wheeler, Captain Winberry?" Johnson's speech was brisk, almost Northern, like a Yankee who had lived in the South or a Southerner who'd lived in the North. His authoritative manner suggested he was used to being in charge. The man was no private, and his name likely wasn't Johnson, either.

Blake stared him down. "I'd rather tell him myself, if it's all the same to you, Private Johnson."

Johnson jerked his gaze toward a tough-looking desperado sitting next to him and they exchanged slight nods. He turned back, a modest smile. "I am he. Pray state your business."

Blake sliced his eyes around at the soldiers, or whatever they were. They looked like cutthroats. For all he knew he'd stumbled into a deserter hideout. Or Yankee scouts. Then he took a deep breath and plunged on. "Sir, I must insist upon proof of your identity."

The tough-looking fellow snickered. "Where's yers?"

Wheeler--or Private Johnson--handed him a calling card, then pulled out his collar to reveal a star surrounded by a wreath. Another modest smile. "Will this suffice, Captain?"

Blake came to attention and saluted. "Yes, sir. You don't know how glad I am to make your acquaintance."

"Your business, Captain?"

"The documents are in my saddlebags, sir."

Wheeler turned to Edwards. "Get those saddlebags and bring them to me." Then he shifted his mild gaze to the desperado sitting next to him. "Captain Shannon, keep this man under guard until I make sure he's all right."

~ * ~

Lexi swept her hair up from the floor and threw it into the fireplace. It curled and shriveled to black dust. The odor of singed hair hung in the room.

She studied herself in the looking glass. The lopsided and hacked haircut was the best she could do on her own. The slouch hat covered the mess and made her look presentable. She ought to pass as a boy.

She had stuffed extra padding around her waist to change her figure and looked about right in the Confederate uniform. She had acquired it from a dead patient, then washed and boiled it to destroy the nits. She had found a pair of riding boots under a hospital bed and had traded a gold ring for the hat.

If only the disguise convinced the courier from Butler's Cavalry into believing she was a boy who wanted to join up. Hair short, in a gray uniform, she would be on her way.

She laid a note on the bed to let her parents know she wasn't abducted. She made sure it was misleading enough that they would not know where to look for her.

They ought to be glad they wouldn't have her mouth to feed any more. Oh, heck. That wasn't true. They would be crazy when they find out she was missing, but if she didn't get out of here, she'd go crazy.

She stored her money and the gold necklace Hunter had given her in her pockets, hurried out and saddled Scout. She rode away from the campus and a little ways out Camden Road where it went deserted.

The courier was late. Just when she started to worry she had missed him he rode into sight. She hailed him and brought her horse into step with his, then looked him right in the eye and lowered her voice. "I am going with you to join Butler's Cavalry.

I want to fight the Yankees."

He was an older, weather-beaten man, his right hand curled up like a claw. He pointed at Scout. "Where did you get that hoss, kid?"

"Off a Yankee."

He snickered. "Sure ye did."

"I'm Alex Wilson."

"Lige Hammond. You old enough?"

"Sure I'm old enough."

"Ha. I ought to send you back to your mama."

"Doesn't Butler's cavalry need recruits?"

"Damned right. They're scraping clear to the rind. Even kept me 'cause I can still shoot a pistol with my good hand."

"I already have one." She moved aside her jacket to show him the grip of her revolver.

"C'mon, then." He extended his hand.

"It's a deal." She gripped hard, just as she figured a man would.

~ * ~

Blake exchanged the map and the orders for a receipt signed by Wheeler. Finally convinced he was on the level, Wheeler ordered Edwards to return his side arms.

Blake learned that Wheeler and a mere handful of his scouts had managed to cross the Pee Dee River. The rest of his command, thwarted by the floodwaters, was stuck on the west bank. Wheeler was laying low until the river receded enough for his division to rejoin him.

During his overnight stay at the cabin Blake learned a little about the Yankee General Kilpatrick, nothing very complimentary. Little love was lost between him and Wheeler, and Kilpatrick had a reputation as a womanizer.

He had concluded that Hunter and McCord were probably right. Sally did not need rescuing, and might not even thank him for trying. He was almost persuaded to give up trying to find her.

At first light, Blake left Wheeler and Shannon and headed back, wearing gray so he wouldn't be picked off by a Confederate scout or a local patriot. If he spotted Yankees, he would remove the palmetto emblem from his hat and change into the Yankee coat hidden under the saddle blanket.

Only an hour out, he heard hoof beats and turned in his saddle. Horsemen were following him. Like Wheeler's scouts, they wore a mix of blue and gray coats.

"Halt!" one of them shouted. "Halt or I'll blow your ass off!"

"Halt, you stinking Reb!"

He goosed the horse's flanks with his spurs and it shambled into a perfunctory canter. More shouts broke out behind him, orders to halt. He whacked the horse's rear with his hat and yelled. It plodded forward with a sorry excuse for a gallop.

They weren't shooting. He twisted around to look. They were gaining, no doubt wanted him alive so they could question him.

Get into the woods and lose them. He urged the horse across the roadside ditch and toward a dense stand of pines.

A low fence blocked his way, he'd have to jump it. He lifted the horse, but it balked, dropped its head and shied sideways, too suddenly for him to compensate. He snatched a handful of mane as he flew over the animal's neck. He missed the fence rails but hit the ground hard, knocking the wind out of his lungs.

He stared at the sky, his left foot sticking up in the air, tangled in the stirrup. The horse turned and walked toward the road, dragging him by his leg.

He tried to shout "Whoa! Whoa! Whoa!" but it came out a breathless whisper. He reached along his leg and bent double to free his foot from the stirrup. If the horse bolted... he'd seen men who had died that way. Skinless faces, shredded sacks of oozing flesh.

Hoof beats pounded next to his ear. One of the fake Confederates grabbed his horse by the bridle, pointed his pistol at him and yelled, "You're my meat!"

Blake stilled his hand on the stirrup, making no provocative moves. Captured. Better than being dragged to death. Maybe.

The rest of them surrounded him, laughing.

"Make mine sunny side up."

"When you learn to ride so good, Johnny?"

"He's really a webfoot playin' at it."

One of them disarmed him and freed his foot. "Get up, Johnny."

He stood and rubbed his bruised hip. Nothing broken except his pride.

"U.S. brand." The scout wearing sergeant's stripes patted the horse's rump. "Where did you get this horse, Johnny?"

"Borrowed him."

"Looks to me like he's still working for our side." The sergeant grinned.

One of the mounted men said, "A good loyal Union hoss." More laughter.

Blake glared at the Judas horse.

"What you doing out here all by yourself, Reb?" the sergeant asked.

"On leave. I had permission to visit a friend."

"Who's that?"

"That's my business," Blake said.

"We'll find out." The sergeant was no longer grinning. Pure menace showed in his face.

Blake's captors took his spurs, hat and gloves, went through his pockets and saddlebags, found his watch, wallet containing his commission and addresses, what was left of his money, his wedding picture, the blue calico shirt Judith had made him, and the receipt from Wheeler.

The sergeant pocketed the watch, read the papers and grinned, his hilarity returning. "You have high-up friends. Old Fightin' Joe Wheeler. Captain Winberry, is it? Fifth South Carolina Chivalry. Boys, we have us a full blooded Rebel." He examined the picture. "Who's the good looking fema--?"

"My wife. Give--" Blake reached for the picture but the sergeant jerked it out of his reach.

"You want it?" the sergeant asked.

"Give it back." Blake stood, hands fisted, forcing himself to stay collected.

"Where's Wheeler?"

"Beats the hell out of me."

"Don't lie, you just been to see him." The sergeant threw the picture down. "Hold him," he said to his comrades.

Blake tried to dodge but had nowhere to go. The closest of them grabbed him and clamped his arms behind him.

The sergeant drew a hunting knife from his boot and pressed the blade under Blake's chin. "He's on this side of the river, ain't he? How many men with him?"

Blake jerked away from the sharp edge, but the sergeant seized a handful of hair and held his head still. He had to tell them something, quick. "The whole division. All five thousand." Maybe that would satisfy them, throw them off. He couldn't give away his friends, tell these Yankee scouts Wheeler was stranded with a handful of men less than a mile up the road.

The man behind him pulled his arms so hard his joints hurt. Pain shot through his shoulders.

"The whole division my ass." The sergeant's voice was flat, face expressionless. "You're still lying, bud. How many?"

Blake flinched as the knife cut into his skin. "For God's sake. I just told you." He sucked in his breath. The sergeant didn't let up on the pressure. They would butcher him no matter what he said.

The scout pinning him from behind said, "He ain't gonna talk. Just stick him and let's get out of here."

"Where's Wheeler?"

A drop of blood crawled down Blake's throat but he couldn't get away from the blade. "North. Go north, you'll find him."

"Where north?"

"Anywhere. You can't miss five thousand men."

"He's lying. Stick him," the man holding him urged again.

"Naw. Even if he's lying he's a keeper." The sergeant released his hair and relaxed the pressure on the blade. "Kilpatrick will want him. With his connections he'll make one dandy hostage."

Rubber-kneed and lightheaded, Blake sagged against the brutal arms holding him in place. This would be a very bad time to pass out. He swallowed nausea and watched the sergeant's hand reach down and slide the knife back into the boot.

"Hoffman, Cole, take him to the general."

The man behind him released and shoved. Blake stumbled forward but caught himself before he fell. He touched his neck and bloodied his fingers.

"Mount up, Johnny."

Chapter Twenty-two

Blake rode along the narrow bridle path, hands bound behind his back, unable to deflect branches that whipped his face. One of the Yankee scouts led his horse while the other rode behind, Spencer carbine cradled in the crook of his elbow.

All his wanting to know about Kilpatrick, and he was about to meet him. Maybe Sally, too. Neither possibility brought much cheer.

Farther south, they struck a column of Federal cavalry. His captors asked the troopers for directions to General Kilpatrick.

Yankee soldiers gave him snide, hateful looks as he rode past the columns. One called him a rebel sonofabitch, another wondered out loud how many yellow bastards he'd sired. He sat erect in the saddle, wishing he had his revolver and free hands to fire it.

His shoulders and elbows, pulled into an unnatural position, shot pain through his joints. The ropes dug deep into his wrists and numbed his hands. His attempts to work free only tightened the knots. Whenever he moved his head his high collar chafed the knife-cut on his neck.

Where was it they imprisoned Confederate officers? Most likely Johnson's Island, a cold hell in a frozen lake, if he got that far. Once they discovered the blue coat and the forged pass hidden underneath his saddle he would cease to be an ordinary prisoner of war. They would call him a spy, fit for hanging.

One of the scouts, Cole, cantered forward to overtake a Victoria carriage and its escort. Cole saluted, said something to a passenger and pointed at Blake. The Negro driver dragged back on the reins. The matched bays chomped their bits and stopped. The second scout led Blake's horse up to it. Inside sat an officer wearing general's shoulder-boards, fancy uniform and plumed hat. Kilpatrick himself. And next to him, Sally.

Her hand rested lightly on Kilpatrick's arm. A fur-trimmed stole hugged her shoulders and the neckline of her gray silk dress opened low enough to reveal a diamond pendant and enticing round hints of bosom. She lifted her queenly face toward Blake, a curious stare, then recognition set in. Her jade eyes opened wider, her lips parted and her grip on the general's arm tightened.

He sat still, throat constricted, the scout's repeater pointed at his chest, and didn't let on he knew her.

The general took Blake's papers from Cole's hand and scanned them. Blake tore his attention away from Sally to her companion, Kilpatrick. His features didn't fit together right, a wide frog's mouth, a jutting chin and a big nose over mutton-chop whiskers.

"You are Captain Winberry with the Fifth South Carolina Cavalry?"

"Yes, sir."

"Where is Butler's division headquartered?"

"I do not know, sir. I left them two days a--"

"Where were they then?"

"In camp, sir."

Kilpatrick frowned. "Don't play dumb with me. How many effectives does Butler have?"

Blake shrugged, determined not to give the Yankee general a thing he could use. "Quite a few, I guess."

"Damn you, be specific."

"Never counted."

"Must've been more than three," growled a captain with a dragoon moustache. "Rebels can't count any higher than that."

Kilpatrick scowled. "What was in the dispatch?"

Blake cut his eyes right and left, looking for a way out, but the two scouts and Kilpatrick's escort company had him surrounded. "The envelope was sealed. I wasn't privy to the--"

"Don't give me that nonsense. You're on Butler's staff and you know plenty."

Blake shook his head. "I'm only a line offi--"

"A guerrilla." The captain unsnapped his holster-stay. "Don't you know what we do to guerrillas, Reb?"

"Who you calling a g--"

The captain drew his revolver, aimed it at Blake's head and cocked it.

Sally screamed, "No! Jud! Don't let him!"

"Captain Griffith!" Kilpatrick snapped. "Not here. I won't have you frightening Miss Dubose."

Griffith lowered the revolver, thin-lipped, leveling a look of pure hatred at Blake.

Blake let out a ragged breath but controlled his voice, forcing it low and calm. "General Kilpatrick, I am an officer in the Provisional Army of the Confederate States of America. I am in full uniform. You have my commission in your own hands. You are obligated to treat me as a prisoner of war."

Kilpatrick swatted the papers against his knee. "Obligated, balderdash. I can have you shot in retaliation for the atrocities your people have committed."

"Oh, Jud." Sally looked shocked. "Truly you can't mean that."

Kilpatrick gave her a stern look. "Don't try to interfere, Miss Dubose."

"But Captain Winberry and I used to be neighbors."

"Neighbors?" Kilpatrick drew his eyebrows together.

Sally tilted her head and put on her sweet smile that Blake knew so well, the same smile she always used to get her way. "His mother and mine are best friends. We even went to the same church. He is just exactly who he says he is."

Kilpatrick shook his head. "Sometimes I almost forget where I found you."

Sally withdrew from him, crossed her arms and dropped her smile. "I suppose you consider me an enemy too."

Kilpatrick chuckled. "No, my dear, you've surrendered." He slipped his arm around her shoulders and leaned toward her, an intimate gesture that convinced Blake he had slept with her.

Sally pouted. "Jud, I really would detest you for having him killed."

Kilpatrick harrumphed and turned back to Blake, scowling again. "Tell you what, Reb. Cooperate, and I'll be lenient."

Blake said between his teeth, "What do you want?"

"Where's Wheeler, and how many men does he have?"

If he didn't tell them what they wanted to know, they might tie him to a tree and pump half a dozen bullets into him.

But if he told them where Wheeler was hiding, they would send enough men after the general and his handful of scouts to exterminate them. He would never be able to hold up his head again. He might as well be dead.

He decided to split the difference and offer a vague half-truth. "His division was north of here."

"His entire division?"

"As far as I know. Lots of men." Maybe Kilpatrick would be afraid to tangle with Wheeler full strength. "Five thousand, give or take."

"Where?"

"North. Can't miss them. Just ride north."

Cole said, "Sir, that's what he told us and it just don't hold water. We didn't see signs of that much cavalry this side of the river."

Kilpatrick glared at Blake. "Well, Reb?"

"It's easy to check," Blake told him. "You can feel them out for yourself, but you better tread light, they'll be ready."

"Have it your way." Kilpatrick whirled to a portly, clean-shaven, spectacled officer. "Major Trellis, put this man under a strong guard. We will deal with him tonight." He turned back to Blake and stabbed the papers at him. "Think on it. For the young lady's sake, I shall give you a few hours to change your mind. That is all."

Blake remembered something Hunter had said and lifted his chin. "Hampton says two for one."

"What?" Kilpatrick snapped.

"Starting with officers, sir," Blake replied. "General Hampton keeps his promises."

Kilpatrick waved the papers at Major Trellis. "Get him out of my sight until it's time to shoot him." He turned to Sally. "Sorry, Miss Dubose, but that's the way it is. We can't coddle our enemies."

"Jud, you are such a beast." Sally slid away from him and showed her back.

"Now, dearest." Kilpatrick tried to pull her to him, but Sally swatted his hand away. "Don't touch me. Beast," she snapped.

"Oh, hell." To the driver Kilpatrick said, "I am sick and tired of having my time wasted. Get this thing moving."

The Victoria rolled off.

Trellis dismissed the scouts and told Captain Griffith to assemble a guard detail. Then he said to Blake in a confidential tone, "You don't have to die if you just cooperate."

"I am cooperating."

"You better start telling the truth."

"Y'all don't seem to know the truth when you hear it."

"Be reasonable. I am willing to meet you halfway." Trellis pulled a cigar out of his pocket and offered him one.

Blake shook his head no.

Trellis took his time lighting it and exhaled smoke. "This isn't worth dying for. You people are whipped. It'll all be over with by summer. If you cooperate you'll help shorten the war, save lives."

Whose lives? He would save plenty of Yankee lives by getting his friends killed.

Griffith rode up leading about ten mounted men and fixed his malicious gaze on Blake. "Dismount, scum. I can't let you ride."

Blake stiffened his shoulders. "My name, sir, is not scum. It is Captain Winberry."

Griffith's fist shot out and smashed into his chin. His jaws cracked together, a jolt of pain, and the force of the blow knocked him sideways. Half stunned, he managed to shift his weight in the saddle and right himself.

Tasting blood, trembling with rage, he faced Griffith. "Untie my hands then try that, damn you! "

"I said dismount!" Griffith grabbed his belt and hauled him backwards off the saddle.

Hands tied, he was unable to cushion the fall. He tucked his head and tried to ball up his upper body as he hit the ground.

He didn't know how long he was out cold before he heard an angry voice. "Damn it, Griffith, he can't tell us what he knows if you kill him."

"He's not dead."

A boot kicked him in the side, hard. An involuntary grunt escaped his throat.

"See there?" Griffith's voice rumbled. "Rebs aren't that easy to kill. Bet he can even talk. Get up, Reb."

Blake rolled onto his side. Pain shot through his neck and shoulders and the back of his head, but he heaved up to his knees, dimly surprised that his neck wasn't broken. Somebody grabbed his arm and hauled him to his feet. He stood swaying, groggy and sick at his stomach, but the hand held him in place. He squinted at Griffith's belligerent face looming before him and bristled. He swallowed blood-tinged saliva, wishing for just one minute on equal footing with the bastard.

Trellis moved in between. "Look, Captain Winberry. We've been giving you every chance. You better come clean."

He set his aching jaw and said, "I have."

Trellis sighed and shook his head oh, so sadly. "Think about it. You have a little while to ponder what your life is worth to you." Trellis shook his head again. "A Rebel's sorry life is worth nothing to us."

Trellis addressed the ten mounted troopers Griffith brought to guard him. He ought to be flattered they thought it took so many. "Men, keep him in your midst. Shoot to kill if he tries to escape."

After the officers left, the guards went through his pockets, turning them inside out and removing everything the scouts had overlooked. They left him hatless and bootless.

Bound and boxed in by horseflesh and attentive guards, he trudged barefoot. Dust swirled up from the hooves and wheels and caked the inside of his nostrils. The pain in his head, neck and shoulders settled into a dull, throbbing ache.

The brass had forced him to watch a military execution soon after arriving in Virginia. The hoof beats reminded him of the drum cadence. The provost guard had stood the condemned man in front of a grave pit. The impact of the bullets had knocked him right into it.

The guard nearest him said, "Hey, Johnny. Why don't you run for it? I could use a little target practice."

"Aw, leave him be, Carter," the man behind him said.

"Leastwise he'd have a running chance. That's more'n he'll get tonight." The guard hummed a snatch of "The Dead March."

Blake had made up his mind, he was not going to give in. He would live or die with the consequences.

But he was not dead yet. And Kilpatrick did not seem to like

223

reminders that Hampton would do the same thing to their men. Double. Better keep on reminding him.

Then there was Sally, consorting with the enemy. The angel had fallen far. At least she had stood up for him in her own way. He could use a friend right now.

Soon a guard brought another man in Confederate gray to join him. He wore a first lieutenant's bars on his ragged uniform and his hands were tied. Starved for company, Blake introduced himself.

The newcomer said, "I'm Jack Brewster from Dibrell's Brigade."

"Wheeler's Division?"

"Right-o. Used to ride with John Hunt Morgan, back in the glory days."

"Ah. Morgan. The Kentuckian."

Brewster looked him over. "They been handling you pretty rough."

Blake returned the look. "I see they didn't take your shoes."

Brewster glanced down at his brogans. "That's about all they left me."

"You look pretty sound," Blake observed. "Obviously you haven't met that bastard Captain Griffith."

"Keep it down, you two," a guard said.

Brewster dropped his voice to a whisper. "Went on the Ohio raid in '63, got away clean. Not so lucky this time. Where did they pick you up?"

"Rockingham Road. What about you?"

"Not far from there." Awkward with his hands tied behind him, Brewster stumbled and righted himself.

Odd. Wheeler had said Dibrell's Brigade was still on the west side of the Pee Dee, caught short by the flood-stage river. "When did they get you?"

"This morning."

"I see." But he didn't. None of it made sense. Blake studied him, a lean, stubbled man perhaps ten years older than himself. He spoke with a mountaineer's twang.

Lots of mountaineers were Unionists.

Brewster leaned closer and whispered, "What do you think they're going to do with us?"

"What did they tell you?"

"Something about reprisals for twenty-eight of their men they claim our boys murdered."

"You don't believe them, do you?"

Brewster shrugged. "Who's gonna stop 'em?"

"They'll have hell to pay when Wade Hampton finds out."

"That won't help us. Besides, they ain't gonna crow about it. We're missing and that's the end of it. They're after Wheeler. They tried to get me to tell them where he was, but I wouldn't tell them a thing."

"Bully," Blake said, believing the man less and less.

"I been thinking. Maybe I ought to come clean. Wheeler can take care of hisself."

"I already told them, they wouldn't believe me." Blake let his voice rise. "Said they're going to shoot me. I have been telling them and they are going to shoot me anyway."

Brewster gave him a searching look, then said. "Thank the Lord, I got religion. You better set yourself straight with the Almighty while you got time, Winberry."

Chapter
Twenty-three

Blake did not welcome the night's halt because it was all the time Kilpatrick had given him to live. He watched the general escort Sally into a nearby house. She clung to his arm and tilted her face up at him. As he talked to her, she appeared to be smiling.

He sat down, watching the Federals build cook fires. Brewster sat next to him. They had parried around each other all afternoon, exchanging questions and non-answers. But he had not learned much, and Brewster certainly got nothing from him.

His tied hands had lost their feeling again. His body ached from the top of his skull down to his sore, stone-bruised feet. His throat was parched from the dust he had eaten, yet his bladder was full. If Kilpatrick carried out his threat, soon he would feel none of it.

He asked one of the guards to untie his hands long enough for him to drink water and relieve himself. After consulting with the corporal in charge, the guard untied the ropes. Then two of them escorted him a little way off and stood aside, carbines ready.

Blake buttoned his pants after he finished. "First time I've ever done that at gunpoint."

The guard who untied him handed him a canteen. "Here's some water. I'll make sure you get some grub too."

"Thanks." He took a long drink and washed off his bruised chin and bloodied neck. Then he tilted the canteen up to his mouth for another swallow.

"Course, the boys will say it's a waste of good grub, giving it to a man who's about to be shot, but I say let him die with a full belly."

He gagged on the water, recovered and said, "Damned

considerate."

The guard grinned. "Don't mention it." He and the second guard escorted him back and tied his wrists again, his ankles too. So much for any notions of running.

Trellis strolled up, a blue coat draped over his arm, Griffith at his elbow. Griffith folded his arms across his chest, gloating.

"I was hoping we would have heard from you fellows by now," Trellis said.

Brewster didn't say anything. He glanced at Blake as though looking for a cue.

Trussed as he was Blake could not stand and face them at their level. "I have nothing to tell."

Trellis held out the coat. "Doesn't this belong to you? We found it under your saddle."

Blake shook his head. "No. I borrowed that horse."

Trellis dug into the pocket and withdrew a slip of paper. "And this? Strange you'd be carrying one of our passes."

Blake tried to project innocence. "Never saw it before."

"Come now, Captain Winberry." Trellis smiled. "Or is it Private Taylor, Fifth Kentucky, U. S? We've found enough paper on you to cover our headquarters wall. If it were possible, we could execute you twice."

Blake stared at the forged pass as hope drained out of him. "Nonetheless, I was captured in my own uniform."

"Tell me, are you married?"

"Why? Are you looking for another hostage? You can't have her. She's safe behind our lines."

"What will your wife think of your choice?"

Blake swallowed hard. "I already told you everything I know."

Trellis pulled out a handkerchief, removed his spectacles, breathed on them and wiped the lenses. "It's out of my hands."

"It'll be all over your hands." Blake set his jaw. "General Hampton won't let this go by unanswered."

"You are a very stubborn Rebel," Trellis said. "It's your undoing. I regret that you are forcing me to carry out General Kilpatrick's orders."

"Hampton has lots of prisoners," Blake reminded him. "I personally arrested and turned in five Federal officers just last week. Two for one, Major."

Trellis put his glasses back on. "That all you have to say?"

Blake thought of the letter McCord had been too faint to write. Would it have helped? "One other thing."

Trellis leaned forward, his eyes glittering behind the glass. "Yes. Well?"

"I captured a Lieutenant Andrew McCord, from General Howard's staff. He was severely wounded. I left him at a house, if anybody wants to know where."

"I don't know the fellow." Trellis frowned, and glanced at Griffith.

"General Kilpatrick knows him," Blake said.

"This is pure hogwash. He is stalling," Griffith said.

Trellis said, "Where is this Lieutenant McCord?"

"I can't tell General Howard if I am dead. Call off the execution, then I'll tell you."

"None of that is my concern." Trellis turned to Brewster. "What about you?"

"I don't have anything to add."

Trellis waved to the guards. "You, and you there. Untie his legs and bring him along."

Brewster stared at him, mouth open. "Where you taking me?"

Trellis jabbed his finger at Brewster. "Him first." He pointed at Blake. "You next. Got it?"

The guards grabbed Brewster by his arms and dragged him away. He twisted and thrashed and wept. They took him out of sight. A single pistol shot cracked.

Blake caught his breath. He had misjudged the Kentuckian after all.

After what seemed a very long time, Trellis and Griffith and the two guards came back, without Brewster.

Blake tried to control the trembling, so they would not see his terror. He steeled himself not to carry on as Brewster had done.

Trellis looked down at where Blake sat, wrists and ankles bound. Firelight reflected on the wire frames of the Union officer's glasses. Griffith held a revolver in his hand.

"Well?" Trellis said.

Blake shook his head, sick with fear. "Don't you think I would tell you if I knew anything different? What is it you want to hear?"

"He's wasting our time," Griffith said. He cocked his revolver and aimed it at Blake's face.

Trellis held up an index finger. "One last chance. We'll forget we found the blue coat and the pass if you tell us where Wheeler is hiding out."

Blake forced himself to lock eyes with Griffith, a last gesture of defiance. He smelled his own nervous sweat. He listened to the scrape of his own breathing and the drum of his pulse, soon to end. He tried to pray.

Then a voice spoke up, close by. "Captain Griffith."

Griffith and Trellis turned to another Federal officer, who was standing by a tree a few yards off. Then the three of them walked off a little way, talking in low voices. Blake could not make out what they were saying.

Griffith glanced over his shoulder at Blake. Angrily, he jammed his revolver back into the holster. He punched the air, a frustrated gesture. Trellis nodded and shrugged. Griffith stomped off, out of sight.

Trellis strode back, his hand resting on the grip of his revolver. His expression had changed, gone contemplative. He said to the guards, "Keep him here until you get further orders."

After Trellis left, one of the guards said, "Damn. There goes a good night's sleep."

"Yeah," the other guard said. "I thought we'd be rid of the sonofabitch by now."

Blake sat down just as his knees gave out.

~ * ~

Hunter Lightfoot held Winberry's high-strung mare to a slow walk along the muddy road, seeking a weakness in the Yankee defenses. He was thankful for the cold rain and the darkness that concealed his approach.

Somehow in the rain and confusion of the past two days, Kilpatrick's columns had slipped in between the Confederate cavalry and where it needed to go. Then the Federals had straddled their camps across every one of the three routes to Fayetteville.

A few days' rest, warmth, good food and liberal doses of drugs had repaired his plumbing well enough for him to return to his work. The mare's lameness had also improved.

He halted, listening. Mounted men advanced from his front, careless fools, letting their weapons rattle. He edged closer for a look, then reversed himself and ghosted back to General Butler, who waited with his escort.

Hunter whispered his identity and rode up to the general. "Yankee cavalry, sir. Thirty or so, coming down this road."

"We're going to bag them." Butler turned and said in a low voice to the man next to him, "Open columns. Draw weapons. Pass it back."

Whispers and shuffling and the multiple scuff of metal against leather and the rasps of drawn sabers followed.

Hoof beats and clanking gear approached.

"Halt. Who comes there?" Butler said.

"Picket detachment, Company C, Fifth Ohio, moving into position, sir."

"Proceed. I wish to confer with you."

"Yes, sir."

The Federals filed into the trap. After the last of them marched through, Butler said, "Halt there! You are prisoners."

Hunter grabbed the collar of the nearest Yankee. He shoved the barrel of his revolver against the man's cheek and hissed, "Hands up, bastard."

His prisoner obeyed. All down the line hammers clicked. Gasps of astonishment and curses followed.

Hunter nodded approval. Not a shot fired, no alarm to the nearby Yankee camp.

"Slick. Really slick," he chuckled. "General, you after my job?"

~ * ~

Blake sat shivering in the prisoner's corral, hands tucked under his armpits to warm them. Rainwater soaked through his clothes. Dank hair clung to his forehead and dripped icy trickles down his face, into his collar, down his spine. His throat was sore, his nose runny, and he had wrapped his blistered feet in dirty rags.

He had not seen Trellis or Griffith since the night they shot Brewster. Two days had passed, and they had not gotten around to murdering him yet. No explanation, they just threw him in with other prisoners. Nobody bothered to tie him up after that. He was lost in the pack and thankful for the obscurity.

A fellow prisoner, a North Carolina home guard, had told him Fayetteville was only a few miles away. Judith was there, and soon she would learn he was missing. He would try to get a message to her, let her know he was alive, and that the Yankees had him. He longed to see her and talk to her, but they probably wouldn't let him.

He had been watching for a chance to escape, but the guards were ever ready with their repeating carbines. He always seemed to be smack dab in the middle of the whole Yankee cavalry.

Besides that, the Yankees didn't believe in feeding prisoners. The guard who had promised him supper never did supply it. Blake's belly was tucked flat against his spine and the aroma of bacon and roasting pork was torturous.

He slipped his hand into his jacket pocket and pinched a kernel off the ear of corn hidden there. He had found it on the ground during today's march, and figured the guards would take it away and give it to one of their horses if they knew he had it. Stealthily he moved the kernel into his mouth, chewed and swallowed. Not much, but it gave his mouth something to do.

The prisoner corral was within sight of the house that Kilpatrick used for headquarters. Sally had gone inside with him earlier that day, and had not come out for hours.

Perhaps her influence had saved him. Maybe she had given her all for him.

A raincoated officer came up to one of the guards and said something and both of them looked his way. Then the guard strolled over and said, "Come with me, bub."

Blake creaked to his feet and limped after the guard to the edge of the corral, taking care to step around his fellow prisoners.

Then he looked into the face of an old tormenter. "Good evening, Captain Winberry," Trellis said.

Blake stifled a shiver. "Is it?"

Trellis smiled. "How are you enjoying our hospitality?"

"It stinks. What do you want from me now?"

"We found Wheeler without your help."

"You mean he found you." Blake pulled out a soggy handkerchief and wiped his watery eyes and nose. "I hope he gave y'all a good whipping."

"Not deuced likely. By the way, General Howard's people found Lieutenant McCord days ago, also without your help."

"Alive?"

"Alive enough to tell the surgeon about you. Said you saved his life. General Howard ordered General Kilpatrick to commute your sentence." Trellis turned to the corporal in charge. "I'll take custody of this man. I will require a man from your detail to come along and watch him."

Blake narrowed his eyes. "Where are you taking me?"

Trellis nodded toward the headquarters. "That house over there."

Yankee officers inside the house greeted Trellis and stared at Blake. Kilpatrick, sitting on a couch with his arm around Sally, ignored him. Sally glanced his way, but quickly turned her smile back to Kilpatrick.

Trellis escorted him with the two guards into a room that contained a bed, a dresser and two army cots. Blake stood in front of the fireplace and reached out shivering hands to catch the heat. Steam shimmered from his wet sleeves. He shut his eyes and absorbed the warmth.

He might as well make himself comfortable. No telling how long before the Yankees changed their minds and threw him back into the bull pen or shot his head off.

~ * ~

Hunter, General Butler and his escort proceeded unchallenged after they bagged the Yankee pickets. They stopped along the roadside near the enemy camp. Butler dispatched couriers to have the rest of the division brought up, sent for Wheeler, and ordered his men to dismount but keep their horses saddled. He stationed vedettes along the road, ordered no smoking or talking, and the troopers hunkered down to wait.

Hunter walked through the woods toward the Yankee camp, to the edge of the tented field and paused behind a maple. Big drops of water from the trees plopped all around and splattered onto his hat.

In the camp, cook fires reflected dully off wet canvas tent flies. Hunter inhaled the mingled aromas of pork and smoke. He longed for his pipe, but dared not strike a match.

He noted a house by the crossroads, probably where the officers were staying. A batch of men sat around under guard in an open lot. Maybe Winberry was there if he was still alive. Nobody had seen him since he had left Wheeler and his scouts three days ago.

Another good officer up the spout, General Butler had said.

A man walked toward him from the camp, his manner hurried but unguarded, apparently unaware of the Confederate infiltration. Hunter stood still behind the tree. The Federal came within a few yards before he stopped. He removed his gun belt, unbuttoned his pants, pulled them down and squatted.

Hunter whipped out his pistol and said, "I got you. Don't move or make a sound."

The Federal twisted around to look at him. His voice was an outraged squeal. "Who the hell are you?" He started to rise, pulling at his pants, but fell on his face, hobbled by his own trousers.

Hunter stalked over to him and stuck the cold steel mouth of his Navy pistol against the Yankee's bare ass. "Shut up." He reached down and picked up the Yankee's gun belt. "Pull up your pants. Hurry. We want to talk to you. You can finish your business later."

"I think it's finished me." The Yankee's voice cracked, as though he were about to cry.

~ * ~

Blake dozed, drugged by a full meal and the warmth of the room. He wrapped himself in the blanket and stretched out on a cot after he hung his outer clothes by the fire to dry.

Trellis let him be, sat on the next cot shuffling papers. The guard stood by, armed to the teeth, ever vigilant.

The door opened and two blue-coated captains clumped in, the bullying Griffith and the officer who had stepped out of the shadows to stop the execution. Clothed only in the blanket and his underwear, Blake stood up to face Griffith, who rested his hand on the grip of his revolver and narrowed his eyes. Blake fisted his hands. At least they weren't bound this time.

"Easy, Griffith," Trellis said. "He's our guest for the night."

Lydia Hawke

"Our guest? What the hell is he doing here?" Griffith said.

Trellis sighed. "It's a long story."

The other officer set a jug down on the dresser. His dark beard didn't grow high enough on his cheeks to cover smallpox scars. He raised his eyebrows. "How long a story is it? Shall I pour our glasses full?"

"I sure could use some warming up," Trellis rubbed his hands together. "Fill them to the brim, Tucker."

Tucker unstoppered the jug. "Do you drink, Mr. Rebel?"

Blake shrugged. "I would hate to offend my hosts by refusing."

Tucker grinned. "And you Southrons are polite, aren't you?"

Griffith growled, "They have to be. The rude ones get killed off in duels." The other two Yankee officers laughed.

Griffith said, "Make him taste it first in case it's poisoned."

Trellis produced cups and Tucker poured from the jug and handed Blake one. He sniffed it, suspicious, and sampled a mouthful. Nasty, but it warmed him all the way down.

Tucker took an incautious gulp, then gagged. "Ugh. Tastes like turpentine. What is this stuff, Mr. Rebel?"

"Pine top." Blake took another sip, but the taste didn't improve. "They make it out of pine shoots," he explained. "Only the truly desperate drink it."

"We're all desperate men," Tucker said. "Although you take the prize for looking the part."

They sat down on the cots, all except Griffith, who stood and watched. Blake took care not to make any sudden moves and give the bastard an excuse to shoot him. He longed to reverse their situation.

"Where did you get this rot-gut?" Trellis asked Tucker.

"Impressed it from a farmer. Should've made him pay me to take it off his hands."

"This isn't even fit for white trash," Trellis said.

"Better than nothing." Tucker coughed. "At least it has lots of alcohol in it."

"Along with the turpentine," Trellis said.

"To hell with the whiskey." Griffith slammed down his cup. "What's this rebel doing in my room?"

234

"General Howard wants it this way." Trellis shrugged. "Seems Winberry was kind to one of his pet aides."

"Ha." Griffith glared at Blake. "The bull pen is good enough for him. For that matter, I'd like to see the lot exterminated."

"You and me both," Trellis said. "But Howard outranks us and Kilpatrick besides."

"Then let Old Prayer Book have him," Griffith said.

"Oh, he's getting him all right," Trellis said. "We're packing him off tomorrow. Until then, General Howard wants us to take good care of him. Though I don't feel obligated to clean him up."

"I'll be damned," Griffith said. "He's not getting my bed."

"You are lucky," Tucker said to Blake. "About as many lives as a cat."

"It isn't luck," Trellis said. "He just knows the right people."

Griffith snorted. "You mean that baggage Jud picked up in Columbia."

Blake drew his back stiff. Damned if he'd allow a Yankee to insult a southern girl unchallenged. "I presume you are not referring to the young lady, sir."

"You have something to say about it?" Griffith snapped. "Keep your mouth shut or I'll shut it permanently."

Blake tensed, longing to take him on. Griffith's eyes taunted him, daring him to try it. The guard brought up his carbine.

"Don't be a damned fool, Winberry," Trellis said. Then he turned to Griffith. "Ease up, will you? What am I going to tell General Howard if we deliver a corpse?"

"Tell him to go to hell," Griffith snapped. "We're supposed to kill our enemies, not invite them in for cocktails."

"Tell him that yourself," Trellis snapped. "It'll be your court marshal, not mine."

Tucker cleared his throat. "So, Mr. Rebel. Your friends must be scratching their heads right now wondering what they are going to do about us."

Blake glanced at Tucker, glad for the change of subject. "I guess they'll figure it out."

"We've got all the roads to Fayetteville blocked." Tucker smiled. "They'll have to pay hell to get through."

"Are they close by?" Blake tried not to sound too interested.

"Close enough our people and theirs kept getting mixed up in the rain all day," Tucker said. "Caught a bunch of Wheeler's men who thought we were them."

"We lost a few in trade," Trellis said.

Tucker shrugged. "We'll just have to capture them back."

Griffith said, "Don't talk about this in front of him."

"Hell," Trellis said. "He's not going anywhere until tomorrow. Then he'll be General Howard's problem."

Chapter Twenty-four

Blake startled awake, raised his heavy head and let it back down. Was that Rebel yell part of a dream?

His furry mouth tasted like that evil blend of alcohol and turpentine. His bloated head felt as though somebody had pumped his ears full of air. Captain Tucker had kept on filling his cup, and he had let him. He was so hard up for friends he had gotten tight with a Yankee officer.

Not quite dawn yet, the window admitted a faint glow of gray light. The three Yankee officers were dark lumps on their cots. The guard ordered to watch him looked out the window. Maybe he had heard something too. There it was again, yelling. And gunshots.

"What the hell?" the guard said.

Blake started from the floor to look outside, but Griffith bolted out of bed and beat him to it.

"We're under attack!" he shouted. "Trellis, Tucker. Get up. We are under attack!"

Blake groped for his trousers, tugged them on still damp, pulled on his shirt and reached for his jacket.

Griffith stuck a pistol in his face. "Try to slip off and you're dead." Then he said to the guard, "Watch him while I get my things."

Blake buttoned his shirt, listening to the crackle of small-arms fire. Sweet music. His friends were coming to set him free. Lord, how he wanted a gun so he could help them do it.

The guard trained the repeater on his chest. Tucker moved hangover slow. The yells and shooting were closer. Blake's bare feet felt vibrations on the hardwood floor from the pounding of hooves outside. A rider flashed by the window.

"Ready." Trellis buckled on his saber belt and stuck his head into the hallway. "Come on."

"Take the Rebel along. Kill him if he so much as twitches," Griffith ordered the guard.

The hallway was full of half-dressed Federal officers, looking worried. Griffith's scowl blamed Blake for the raid.

An officer pulled a suspender over his shoulder. "By God, how did they get by our pickets?"

"Where's General Kilpatrick?" another officer wanted to know.

"He's not in the house. Must've already cleared out."

Sally huddled on the couch all by herself, clutching her hands together. She looked like she had just awakened, hair rumpled, face pinched with fear. Where was her general now?

She set imploring eyes on him, but he couldn't do a thing.

Trellis said, "Great God. What happened to the pickets? Why didn't we get any warning?"

Tucker stammered, "What about the horses? Did they get the horses?"

"Can't tell," came a reply.

Blake knew the voice. He jerked his head around to find the speaker. Brewster, in a blue uniform, knelt next to a window.

Then it sank in. They hadn't killed him after all. Brewster was one of them, his execution only an act.

Was he madder for believing they killed Brewster or finding out they hadn't?

Brewster said, "I'm not waiting for the damned Rebels to storm in. I'm running for it."

"Him first." Griffith shoved Blake toward the door. "He's good for something. Let him take the first volley."

The guard poked the carbine into his back and said, "Move it. You go ahead."

A bullet splintered through the wall ahead of Blake and a window shattered in the front room. He was just as likely to be hit as one of the Yankees, more likely if they made him go out first. But it was the only chance he had seen yet to escape.

Somebody threw the front door open. He slowed down on purpose. The stampede of Yankees swept him outside, through cold mist and powder smoke. Gunfire cracked to his right.

The guard lunged past him, watching the action to his right. Blake threw his weight into the distracted guard, grabbing the carbine. The guard grunted, lurched sideways. Blake kicked him in the gut and wrenched the carbine out of his hands.

The guard recovered and charged, cursing. Blake swung the barrel around, found the trigger and squeezed. The kick jolted the stock into his belly. The Yankee threw up his hands and fell backwards, blood exploding from his face.

Blake advanced the next cartridge as he whirled, lifting the repeater's stock to his shoulder. Griffith stopped and turned toward him, raising his revolver.

He fired just as Griffith's revolver went off. The breeze of the bullet fanned his ear. Griffith clutched his stomach and dropped his revolver. He turned to run but stumbled and fell on his hands and knees.

Blake scooped up the revolver, then rushed over to Griffith and crouched over him.

Griffith snarled at him like a wounded wolf, blood pouring from between the fingers squeezing his abdomen, not asking for quarter. "Finish me."

Partly because Griffith wanted him to, he didn't. Bullets still whined overhead, so he ducked lower.

"What's the matter with you?" Griffith's face contorted with pain. "Get on with it."

"You're not worth losing my self-respect over." Blake reached for Griffith's waist. "Move your hands. I need your gun belt."

"Damn you. Damn you to hell," Griffith snarled between clenched teeth.

"The way you're bleeding, you'll likely get there first." Blake yanked the belt off Griffith and fastened it onto himself. He heard Sally call his name and whirled toward the house. She stood in the doorway, panic on her face, then started toward the Victoria, which was parked beside the house.

"Get down!" he yelled.

She looked around as though it just struck her that no horses were hitched to the carriage.

Blake jammed the revolver into the holster and leaped to his feet, carrying the carbine. He lunged for Sally, grabbed her arm and dragged her away from the house, toward a ditch.

"Get in!" he shouted.

She balked. "I'll ruin my dress!"

"Now!" He pushed her into the gully. He fell in with her and she clung to him, whimpering and shaking.

The firing slowed and soldiers rode up. The early morning light was just enough to show their jackets, butternut and gray. But their revolvers were pointed in his direction.

"Friends!" Blake shouted and lifted one hand.

"Hold your fire," the lead man said. Wild-looking, ragged soldiers, Wheeler's westerners, must have finally made it across the Pee Dee. "Who are you?"

"Captain Winberry, Butler's Division. I need a horse."

"We've captured a few. Any Yanks in that house?"

"There were, better check." Blake glanced at the guard he had killed. Griffith was still alive, holding his belly, staggering away. "Fetch that Yankee officer. He's trying to escape."

The corporal in charge sent two of his men to search the house, and another to take charge of Griffith.

Sally finally lifted her head and stared at the corporal, mud smeared on her face. He grinned and touched his hat. "Need any help with your lady friend, Captain?"

"I'm with Captain Winberry," Sally said.

"More's the pity," the corporal snickered.

Gunfire intensified again, off to Blake's left. "Sounds like the Yanks want their camp back." He rubbed his temple, aching from too much pine top whiskey. He said to Sally, "I have to find my command. Stay right here."

"I've heard that before." She stood up and latched onto his arm.

"Get down, Sally. They're still shooting."

"Promise you'll take me with you, Blake. Promise."

"Lady, if he don't want you, I'll take you," the corporal said.

Horror filled her eyes. "Please, Blake."

She had been consorting with the enemy, but she needed him now.

"All right, Sally. I will"

~ * ~

Judith awoke to the rumble of distant artillery.

Although Fayetteville was clogged with Confederate soldiers the day before, she wasn't able to find out anything about Blake. She gathered that in some way, Butler's Division was cut off from the rest of the army.

Was he involved in the battle she was hearing? She threw herself down on the bed and prayed for his safety.

~ * ~

Later that morning, Blake rushed a captured horse past Wheeler's columns along the road to Fayetteville. The Texans stared with curiosity and admiration at Sally clinging behind him.

The Yankees had rallied and beat off the Confederate attack. Still, Blake managed to re-equip himself with boots that fit tolerably well, greatcoat, poncho, gloves and a black felt hat with a New Jersey regimental insignia before he had to withdraw.

His hand and blistered feet hurt, his head ached and he still tasted turpentine. He couldn't sit straight for fatigue, and he still hadn't found his troop. Sally had delicately confirmed that he smelled moldy and expressed the fear that she would catch bugs from him. But he was alive and breathing free air.

Sally's warm weight against his back and her hands around his waist added to his distress. He wished she didn't affect him so, and he tried not to let on that she still had that kind of power over him.

She leaned closer and whispered into his ear, "I did save your life, you know."

"How'd you manage to persuade Kilpatrick?"

"Never you mind."

He shook his head, feigning disbelief. "I figured they were afraid of reprisals."

"No, they weren't. It was all my doing."

"Just for me? Thanks," Blake snorted.

"Beast." She whacked him between the shoulder blades. "You could at least act grateful."

"What happened to Kilpatrick?"

"He left through a window." Her voice sounded bitter.

"The window to your bedroom?"

"Blake, how dare you!"

"Your mother spun me quite a tale. I pictured Kilpatrick dragging you off kicking and screaming. She begged me to save you. Instead, I find you cozy, enthroned next to that damned Yankee like royalty, wearing jewelry he stole."

"You came for me?" Her voice lifted. "Is that how you got captured?"

Time was he would have come for her, but not now. Let her think what she wanted.

"That's so sweet. Gallant." She tightened her arms around his waist. "You really came just for me? You do still care!"

He got a vague feeling that he had just given her a weapon, and tried to take it back. "I thought he took you against your will."

"He did," she said. "Really and truly. I was a prisoner of war, just like you were."

"I would like to believe you, Sally. But I heard you wanted to go north with Kilpatrick."

"That's a lie. Who told you that?"

"Your other Yankee friend, Lieutenant McCord."

"Poor Andrew. They told me he was wounded. You shot him, didn't you?"

"As it happens, it wasn't me that shot him. I picked him up after." He scratched his chin. "What am I going to do with you, Sally?"

"I want to stay with you."

"You need to talk to General Butler. You've been so tight with the Yankees, you might have information he can use. You haven't turned into one, have you? You will tell him what you know?"

"Certainly." She sounded indignant.

"After that, I'm going to find space for you on a baggage wagon."

"What? After all I've done for you? I don't want to ride like baggage. Besides that, I'm afraid of the drivers. They swear and smell bad."

He snorted. "That's what you said about me."

"I didn't say it was your fault. They kept you in those awful pens for three days." Her lips brushed the nape of his neck. "I care for you, Blake, very much. I realized just how much when I thought they were going to kill you."

He closed his eyes and tried to shake off the effect she had on his body. "I have to find my troop. Then, when I get to Fayetteville, I have to find my wife."

He felt Sally draw back. "Your wife?"

"Yes, Sally." He glanced over his shoulder at her, smiling. "Remember her?"

"Oh, just forget about her. You don't even have to let her know you're in town."

"What are you suggesting?"

She smiled that silky taunting smile of hers, and her hand stole down his hip to his thigh, fingers caressing. "You love me. You came looking for me, and you found me. I thought you wanted to keep me."

"Things have changed." He tried to ignore the sweet agony her touch created.

"You still love me. Admit it."

He caught her hand and stilled it. "Don't."

She pouted and jerked her hand away.

He turned from her to face the road ahead. "She's staying at her aunt's house. I won't leave her to the Yankees. I'm taking her with me."

"You aren't planning to leave me to the Yankees, are you?"

"Don't you want to stay put and wait for your general?"

"Beast. I hate you." She whacked him between the shoulder blades again.

He slowed the horse as he passed a clump of Yankee prisoners marching under guard. "See anybody you know?"

"Jud got away, but I wish you'd caught him. Just what he deserves for carrying me off."

Blake scanned the sullen faces. "I don't see Trellis or Tucker, they must've escaped too." Griffin's wound had looked fatal. He was probably dead by now.

"Take me with you when you leave Fayetteville. Please don't let Jud get his hands on me again. You don't know what I went through. It was terrible."

"Oh, yes. You appeared to be suffering such agonies."

"Don't you even care? After all we've meant to each other?"

"All right, Sally." He let out a long breath. "I won't leave you."

"I knew I could count on you," she murmured.

He found General Butler and left Sally in the care of his escort. Then he promised to come back for her after he located his troop and straightened out army business.

He continued to ride outside the columns until he saw David Frank, Simmons, Cheney, the Caldwell boy and the rest of his troop.

"Well lookit what the cat drug in," Simmons sang out.

Jimmy Caldwell whooped.

"Glory be. We done give up on you, Cap'n." Cheney grinned.

"Gave up too soon." Blake felt a surge of affection for the powder-blackened men. It was good to be welcomed back to his own.

David Frank saluted, relief on his face.

"How goes it, Sergeant Frank?" He looked over the troop. "Where is everybody? Where's Lieutenant Kirkland?"

"Uh, he got hit, sir."

"Hit? How bad?"

"Gut shot. We brought him off, he's in an ambulance."

Blake felt as if he'd just been hit in the gut too. "Oh, God."

"Jones is killed, Hoffman slightly wounded. He can still ride. He's with us. We got caught pretty bad when the Yanks rallied and came after us."

Blake shook his head, reeling inside, trying to picture the scenario. "That was infantry they brought up."

"Whatever it was, we couldn't stand for it. They had repeaters." David cleared his throat. "I'm really glad to see you, sir."

It was too much to take in. Blake gripped David's shoulder. "Carry on, Sergeant. I'm going to see about Lieutenant Kirkland." He rode back to the wagon train, afraid. Hardly anybody survived being gut-shot, a hard way to die.

He made inquiries of the drivers until he found the ambulance containing Matt. He handed the horse to a wagon guard and climbed inside among the broken men. Stepping between them, he could not avoid the blood pooled on the floor. The space under the duck cover smelled of raw meat wounds and bone and waste from men who had lost control. Every bump and jolt wrenched grunts and moans from the passengers.

Matt sat on the floor with his head propped against the side of the ambulance. His jacket was loose around his shoulders and a blood soaked dressing covered his stomach. It was darkest right over the wound where the blood still leaked out. Blake knelt next to him and Matt opened his eyes halfway. Blood matted his moustache and beard. He held his mouth ajar as though it cost too much effort to keep it closed. His face was waxy and gaunt and damp with sweat.

Matt smiled weakly. "Hey. Never thought I'd see you again." His voice was labored. "Where you been?"

"I was a prisoner. The attack cut me loose."

"Good. Good. We did something right."

Blake smiled to encourage him. Maybe it would help. Anything. "Y'all gained the road, cleared the way through to Fayetteville."

"Guess you're happy."

"Sure am. What can I do for you?"

"Water. And I want a chew. Cut me a chew." Matt grimaced. "Can't do it myself. Here in my pocket."

Blake found a canteen and gave him a drink. Then he fished out the tobacco and penknife, cut off a hunk and poked it into his friend's mouth.

Matt rolled it around to his cheek. "Sell my horse, give the money to my folks."

"Sure. It'll be a while before you can ride anyhow." He tried not to look at the blood-soaked bandage. Gut shot.

"Oh, hell. Don't humor me. I'm not that dumb." Matt went into a spasm, coughed up a mouthful of blood, started to tremble and went wild eyed. "Something busted loose."

"What can I do?"

Matt coughed again and another trickle of blood oozed from the corner of his mouth.

Blake circled his arm around Matt's shoulders. If only he could reach inside and fix what was wrong.

Matt's noisy gurgling breaths quit. His eyes dimmed and his body relaxed.

Blake rested his head back and closed his eyes. He was tired of watching friends die.

A voice quavered to his left. "Cap'n, can I have the water and the rest of that plug?"

Blake gave the wounded man the canteen and the tobacco. Then he arranged Matthew's body so it would stiffen respectably straight. It took longer than it should have because his hands were shaking.

Chapter
Twenty-five

Later that morning, Blake rode through the military traffic into Fayetteville, Sally perched behind him. Crowds of soldiers and refugees jammed the town, leaving no decent accommodations for a lady. He had no choice but to bring her on to where Judith was staying and hope she could find space to sleep there. She had money for the night's rent. Good thing, because the Yankees had all his.

He tried to focus his blurry eyes on the forwarding address Judith had left with her aunt's tenants. Apparently the plans to stay there had fallen through. At least she'd made it to Fayetteville.

He reeled in the saddle, dizzy from fatigue. He had tried to improve himself, picked off lice and washed his face and hands in an ice-cold stream. But the war-dirt seemed to have worked all the way inside.

He looked like a desperado, and couldn't blame Judith if she recoiled from him. Now he was coming to her broke and half sick. He wasn't sure how she would take to his ex-fiance's presence. Surely after he explained what he owed Sally, she wouldn't object.

~ * ~

Judith sat on the front porch of the rooming house, her knitting in her lap. She had picked the spot giving her the widest view of the street. Although various army units gathered in and around town, none of the officers she asked could tell her where Butler's Cavalry might be. How could a thousand men and their horses just disappear? Did the enemy somehow swallow them up?

Cannon fire this morning, toward the southwest, had filled her with dread. What if Blake's whole division was simply blown out of existence?

No use trying to knit his new socks. She didn't dare look away from the street for fear of missing her first glimpse of him. Somehow, despite her worries, she knew deep in her soul that he was on his way to her.

An odd sight drew her attention, a soldier and a woman riding double on a horse. A cavalryman, the same lean build as Blake, looking her way. But the horse was lighter in color than Blake's bay mare, and the girl…

She set the knitting aside and stood up for a better view. The soldier waved at her, grinning, then turned to say something to the girl seated behind him.

"Blake!" She started laughing, so relieved and happy that tears sprang from her eyes and rolled down her cheeks. She threw down her knitting, jumped up and ran down the steps into the yard to meet him.

He jumped from the horse and turned to lift his passenger down. Then Judith recognized her. She stopped halfway across the yard, holding her breath, shocked. What on earth was that witch doing here? New fear clutched at her throat.

Blake slapped the reins around a fence post, strode to the gate and paused, his smile wavering. He said, "How are you, Jude?"

Sally stood next to him, looking her over with that half scornful, not quite rude smile of hers.

Just exactly what was that woman doing with Blake? Was she trying to steal her husband?

But he had come to her safe just as she had hoped and prayed, and she would give him a proper welcome. No Sally Dubose was going to ruin it.

She lifted her chin, smiled, and strode the rest of the way to the gate.

He swung the gate open and caught her in his arms. She laughed and kissed him and hugged his stale-smelling body, refusing to acknowledge Sally. "Oh, Blake. It's really you. I've missed you so much. I was afraid something awful happened. You look exhausted. Are you all right?"

"I'm fine. Fine." He held her so tight it almost hurt, and she reveled in the hard vital feel of him. "Let me see you," he said. He released her, then grasped her shoulders and held her a little apart from him. She gazed up into his face, studying him. He was thinner than when she had last seen him, gaunt of face, eyes deeply shadowed by the hat brim, but his smile was warm.

She laughed and tugged his beard. "You need a bath and your clothes smell like you used them to wipe down your horse. But that's all right. We have lots of soap. I'll take good care of you."

"I know you will," he said softly. "And you're still just as beautiful as I remember."

Sally cleared her throat. Blake turned, and Judith looked over his shoulder at the unwelcome visitor.

"You two look so sweet." Sally was smiling, except for her eyes. "Don't let me interrupt anything."

Blake glanced back at Judith, his expression strained. "Uh, Judith, this is Sally Dubose. Sally, my wife."

Judith's hands were still on Blake's waist, and she tightened her grip. "We've already met."

"Sally was with the Yankees," he said. "They were going to shoot me, Jude, but she persuaded them to desist."

"Good heavens!" Sally daubed at her eyes, woebegone. "I wasn't with them by choice. I was a victim. That scoundrel Yankee general kidnapped me. Then there was a battle, and Blake rescued me."

It was too much to take in all at once. Judith stared at Blake. "You were a prisoner?"

He nodded. "I was. But that's done."

"Thank God," Judith breathed. George died a prisoner, but Blake didn't. She leaned into him, grateful for the miracle of his presence.

"You ought to thank Sally, too," he said.

Judith squared her shoulders. She didn't understand what this was all about, but she had better act gracious. Swallowing her dislike, she extended her hand to Sally. "Thank you for saving my husband."

Sally took her hand, smiling mistily at Blake the whole time. "Actually, he was quite the hero. He wouldn't tell the Yankees a thing, no matter how they threatened."

"Please, Sal, I don't want to discuss it right now." Blake's jaw tightened, and he turned back to Judith. "Does your landlady have room for an extra boarder tonight? Sally doesn't have anywhere else to stay."

"I don't know." Sally staying in the same house with them? What next? "I'll ask."

Judith reminded herself again that she was the one married to Blake, and Sally was the outsider. He would be coming to her bed tonight, not Sally's. She nestled against him, saying, "Darling, come inside before we scandalize the neighbors for carrying on like this."

She glanced at Sally. "You, too, of course."

Then Judith smiled at Blake. "I better introduce you to the landlady so she'll know what strange man I'm taking up to my room."

The three of them started toward the porch. Blake offered his arm to Sally, but slid his other arm around Judith's waist. He said, "Jude, we have to pack your things. Come morning you're both coming with me."

~ * ~

Later, Judith closed the door to her room behind them and whirled to Blake, pretenses over. "She's coming with us tomorrow?"

He tossed his hat onto the bureau and looked at her, his brow knitting into a frown, his eyes narrowing, annoyed. "Does that present a problem?"

"Can't she ride in one of those army wagons? What a fine threesome we'll make! It's a good thing Mrs. Martin has a couch for her to sleep on tonight. Otherwise, you'd feel obligated to invite her into our room. Maybe even our very bed."

The muscle over his jaw tensed; his gray eyes flashed anger. "Is that some kind of accusation?"

"I trust you, but not that Sally girl."

"She's coming, and that is final."

She bit her lip, suddenly realizing she could not win this one without making herself appear small and ungrateful. All the terrible, fatal things she had pictured happening to him came back into her mind. He had brushed close to death, but now he stood before her, unharmed. And he had told her it was somehow to Sally's credit.

"You will be hospitable," Blake added.

She lifted her chin. "Just like a long-lost sister."

"Good girl." His shoulders relaxed slightly. If he had caught her sarcasm, he was ignoring it. "Just until I can get both of you situated somewhere safe." He unbuckled his gun belt and set it on the bureau next to his hat. Then he shrugged out of his jacket and dropped it on the floor. He nudged it with his boot-toe. "My clothes could stand a good boiling. Is there a laundress I could hire?"

"I'll wash them." She crossed the room and caught his hands in hers. "I told you I'd take care of you."

He drew her hands up to his chest, and some of the tension left his eyes and the corners of his mouth. "I want to hold you, to lie down with you, but I'm dirty. And I picked up a few passengers besides Sally."

She studied him, noting the new lines around his eyes, the cut on his neck. He really did have a bad time, and it showed. Probably would not let on how much he needed her tender concern. She would bite her tongue over Sally and hope this new involvement with her was innocent, at least from his standpoint. Of course, there wasn't an innocent bone in Sally's body. "I'll heat some water and draw you a bath. Just rest."

He let out his breath. "I really am glad to see you, Jude."

She rocked up on her toes and kissed him. "And you, darling, are a wonderful sight." Then she laughed, smoothing the hair from his forehead. "I'm not afraid of your passengers. Any of them."

~ * ~

Sally stood in the parlor, hands on hips, looking over the old horsehair couch made up with a sheet and a blanket. "Fine. Dandy," she muttered. She laid out the few possessions she had managed to bring out of the Yankee camp, a change of clothes and a little jewelry.

She glanced up the stairs toward the room where Blake was staying, behind a closed door with his wife.

She realized how much she still cared for him when that nasty Captain Griffith offered to shoot him dead, and she had to pitch a fit to save him.

Jud didn't like it when she refused to speak to him or let him touch her, but that was what it took to keep him from having Blake shot. Then she had rewarded Jud with a loving he shouldn't forget for a long time. She wrinkled her nose at the distasteful memory of the things she'd done to please him. And after all that, he'd dived out that window and left her. She hoped he'd gone to blazes.

If only Blake hadn't been in such a hurry to marry that widow. Things would be like they were before, and she could simply take him back as though there was no Randolph and no Jud.

She closed her eyes, recalling how it used to be. Long walks and deep kisses and impassioned promises. He had awakened her, touched her with sensations that neither Randolph nor Jud could provide. Why did she just now realize he was the one made for her? Didn't he feel that way, too?

She heard a door open and close. Blake and his wife descended the stairs, hand in hand. Disgusting.

He paused, looking toward her. "Need anything, Sal?"

Silly man, silly question. She needed him and he knew it, but the woman hanging onto him was in her way.

She waved her hand, forcing herself to smile. "My accommodations are adequate, thank you very much."

He nodded. "Fine. I have to take care of my horse and some other things." His wife, for instance.

Sally kept on smiling. "I won't be going anywhere."

He and that woman set about their business, leaving her sitting on the couch, fuming. She watched him carry a hip tub and a couple of buckets of water up the stairs. He was going to bathe and make love to Judith. And there wasn't a thing she could say or do right now to stop him. He was out of her reach, the man she wanted but couldn't have.

She had first claim on him. That other woman had no right to him.

And he still loved her. She knew it.

She could still get between them.

Chapter Twenty-six

❝…So I left that disgusting place and the greedy landlady and camped out one more night," Judith said. "Good thing I found this rooming house the next morning. I went into partnership with Mrs. Martin's son, Jacob. He's been driving people and cargo around in my wagon and we split the fees. I've been making soap to sell--I'm going to rinse now, shut your eyes."

She poured the pan of water over Blake's head and swished it through his hair.

He sputtered and wiped his face with the washcloth.

Laughing, she rubbed his head with a towel. He took it from her and stood dripping into the tub, wiping himself down.

She touched his ribs. "Poor darling. You haven't been getting enough to eat."

"Enough to stay in fighting weight."

She traced the cut on his neck. "What caused this? And there's a fresh scar on your arm."

He clasped her hand, stopping it. "Nothing very important."

"Thank God you're here. I love you so much."

His voice husky, he said, "I've been living for this moment, when I could be with you again." He stepped out of the tub and took her in his arms.

She lay with him long after his breathing lengthened in sleep. So many nights she'd longed for his warmth beside her, his arms around her, and it was hard to pull herself away from him even for a few minutes. Something might come between them again. The war. Maybe Sally.

What had been going on between them? Perhaps nothing, but

253

she didn't trust Sally to keep her hands off him. Could she really trust him not to give in to Sally? He had turned to her right after Sally jilted him, before he had a chance to get over her.

Judith sat up and watched him. In his sleep, the stern lines of his face softened, tension gone. He had come to her in alarming condition. But he was alive, not seriously ill, and all seemed right now.

He had made love like a man who had saved up for weeks. She smiled and kissed his forehead. She had better keep on loving him, use him up, leave no leftovers for anybody else.

She had not told him yet, but he had another reason to be pleased with her. Up to now, her growing certainty that she was pregnant only added to her worries. But he had made it plain he wanted to father a child, and she was going to give him one. Maybe the timing wasn't so bad after all.

No, she didn't need to concern herself with Sally. All her advantages made Sally seem a very poor rival indeed.

And weeks of not knowing were over. She'd often wondered whether she was a widow and didn't know it yet. Here he was, safe in her bed.

Then why did she feel so uneasy? Worry must be a hard habit to break.

She slipped out of bed and started to pack, humming softly. She wasn't sorry to leave this place and there was something romantic about being carried off, Sally or no Sally. Just like the first time she saw him, when he saved her from the deserters, he was taking her out of reach of the Yankees. He wouldn't leave her to face the trouble all by herself, not this time.

He slept through the afternoon despite her stirrings. Toward sundown, the room grew colder. Time to cook supper, so she added logs to the fire. One of them crunched through the charred wood from the previous night's fire, waking him up.

~ * ~

Blake rubbed his eyes and propped himself up on one elbow. He was in a clean warm bed, and Judith was in the same fire-lit room, bending over the hearth. She straightened, smiling at him, her dark hair loose over her shoulders. A radiant dream? Then he recalled his reunion with her, the sharp words over Sally, and the sweet lovemaking. He wanted her again, and here she was right in front of him.

He sat up in bed. "Is it night? How long did I sleep?"

"All afternoon." She sat next to him and combed his hair back with her fingers.

He shut his eyes, enjoying her gentle touch. Life was good again. He did not want to think about the enemy headed their way, or about how on earth he was going to protect Judith and Sally. But he had better prepare. "You know what time it is?"

"Not exactly. About seven. Where is your watch?"

"Lost it." He sat up. "Better pack the wagon. Where are my clothes?"

"You don't have to get up yet, the wagon is already packed. Just rest while I fix supper."

"You let me sleep while you loaded the wagon? Should've gotten me up before now."

"Darling, you'll get sick if you don't get some rest."

He cleared his throat. "I'm not sick."

She opened the trunk and handed him a union suit. "Here. I brought these with me for safekeeping."

"Good thing." He slipped on the undershirt, picked up the drawers and stared at them. "Jude, I lost other things besides my watch. When the Yankees had me. They took my wallet and all my money. That fine shirt you made me. Even our wedding picture. About the only thing they didn't want was my toothbrush."

She touched his arm. "Thank God you're safe."

"Anyway, I'm broke. I wrote you a letter. Didn't you get it?"

She shook her head.

"The house is gone. I can't even give you a place to live."

"That's all right. I've been houseless before. Anyway, we're together now." She moved to the hearth, reached into a basket and picked up an egg. "Don't you want an omelet for supper?"

"An omelet?"

She smiled, picked up a pan, and broke three eggs into it. "I have a half dozen eggs and they won't travel very well. I can fix half for supper and save half for breakfast."

"You are really something." He sat down next to her, slipped his arm around her and squeezed. She sidled against him while she beat the eggs. She accepted the setbacks better than he had any right to expect. As though she cared more about him than his worldly goods. He said huskily, "You are spoiling me rotten."

"I hope so," she murmured.

"Didn't those eggs cost a lot?"

"I traded soap for them." She dolloped a spoonful of bacon grease into her skillet and set it on the fire. The crackling fat smelled good and smoky. "I still have the two hundred you gave me."

"You managed to hang onto that?"

"The hack business was pretty good. Hardly anybody has any draft animals left."

"I figured you'd have spent it all by now."

She poured the eggs into the skillet and added a square of corn bread she had stored in a tin food safe. "I've been getting along all right."

He let the honest admiration slip into his voice. "You're a smart girl."

She flashed him a glowing smile. With her, he felt content. Loved. She took him as he was, gave him what he needed. He had come to her exhausted, but she had worked her wonderful magic to his spirit, and he was starting to feel whole again.

Judith served the eggs and cornbread onto china plates and handed him one, along with a fork. He held the fork up to the firelight. "Silver."

"We still have a few nice things, might as well use them. How are your friends? How is Hunter?"

"He and Lexi got married."

She laughed out loud. "You must be joking."

"It's true. But I'm not sure it's a satisfactory match."

"People were probably saying that about us, too." She looked away, thoughtful. "She's an odd girl. One thing I can say about Hunter, he accepts her on her own terms. Hardly anybody else does."

He wolfed the eggs.

"What about Matthew?"

"Dead."

"Ye gods. The poor man. When?"

"This morning."

She laid a shaking hand on his arm. "Dear God, it could have been you."

He covered her hand with his to still it. "Don't be scared for me. It won't help."

She shivered, then gave him a brave smile and said, "I have something to tell you."

He set down his empty plate. "What, sweetheart?"

"I believe I'm expecting."

"Expecting what?"

She smiled and patted her stomach. "You are going to be a father."

"Jude!" He threw his arms around her, joyous. "How shall we celebrate?"

"Just hold me," she murmured. "Love me."

"I do." He kissed her cheeks, her eyes, her mouth. "Never, ever doubt it."

~ * ~

Lexi warmed herself next to the campfire, listening to another of Lige's stories. She removed her gun belt and set it aside to make herself more comfortable. That was all she would take off, even for sleeping, except her boots. The less of her female anatomy the courier saw, the better.

They had traveled together for three days now, successfully avoiding the Yankees. Lige said they made about a hundred miles so far, within spitting distance of North Carolina.

Her legs were stiff and sore from all those hours in the saddle, but she proved to herself she could stand it as well as a man. Lige treated her like a kid brother, or maybe one of his boys. He hadn't figured out she was a girl by now, others wouldn't either.

"I'm telling you, Alex," Lige continued, "We shot that horse out from under that Yank and I figured we shot him too. He ain't moving, nohow. A real gold mine. An officer with nice new boots, spurs, a fancy hat. I get down off my horse and go through his pockets. Damned if he don't start shakin'. Then he busts out laughin'."

"Laughing?"

"That's when I figured out I wasn't prowling no corpse. I ask him what's so funny. After all, he's supposed to be dead, and since he wasn't dead, he was a prisoner. "'You're ticklin' me, damn you,' the Yank says. 'Cut that out.'"

Lige scratched his chin with his claw-like hand. "Sometimes I wonder how that Yank's doin'. Whether he's still laughing after a spell in Libby prison."

~ * ~

Harry Bell crouched in the shadows, watching. The campfire and the smell of cooking had drawn his attention, and the two horses tethered nearby were more interesting yet.

He had rejoined his regiment, the only man in his foraging party who didn't get killed or captured. Soon after, things went sour. Worst luck, Emmett had survived, minus a leg. After he recovered enough to talk, he told all kinds of lies to General Howard about his buddy Harry Bell. Harry got wind of it and skipped off before Old Prayer Book got a chance to have him arrested.

He was really on his own now. On foot for days, and the country so picked over he couldn't find enough grub to stop his stomach from complaining. Couldn't even find a fleabag horse to ride, not until he spotted these two Rebs.

He took his time, watching and listening. His rifle was only a one shot, and he didn't like the odds here. He could shoot one, then bayonet and club the other if he got close enough, but he didn't want to take a chance on getting himself hurt.

Better wait until they went to sleep, then sneak up and take the horses. They would never catch him.

But that mule turd just talked and talked and talked. Didn't he ever sleep? Harry felt like shooting him just to shut him up. That Reb had his back to him, but the other one sat in profile, a kid no older than Emmett. The boy he could handle if he had to. Sick of waiting, maybe he'd better plug the older Reb and bayonet the kid.

He cradled his rifle, listening to them talk.

The older Reb said, "Alex, I been thinking about you. What you really gonna do when you get to the army?"

"Join up and fight. What else?"

"They ain't takin' girls."

Harry caught his breath and studied the kid. A girl?

The kid said, "Who you calling a girl?"

"You, Alex. What's your real name?"

"Alex, just like I said."

The older Reb shook his head, grinning. "You don't feel like a man. I knew from the time you stumbled back there and I caught you. And you don't walk like one. Too much sway. Short hair and men's clothes don't fool me, not for long."

Harry hardly believed he heard right. He needed a wench almost as much as he needed a horse. He licked his lips. How could he just take the horses and leave that piece undone?

She said, "I mean to join the army, Lige, and you're not going to stop me."

"Don't you know what they'll take you for?"

Silence.

"I've studied on it," the man continued, "And I don't take you for a loose woman. But some fellows will."

"I'd sure have something to say about that," she said.

"I ain't gonna let it go that far. I'm gonna leave you at the next settlement with proper folks who'll help you get yourself home. What's your name, for real?"

"Alex Wilson."

The man shook his head. "No. For real."

A pause, then she said distinctly, "Lexi Winberry Lightfoot."

Another damned Winberry! Was this the same girl that shot at him and ran him off from the doctor's house in Columbia? Damn, he'd like to get back at her for making him look bad in front of Emmett.

Harry's cock was getting stiff, just from him thinking about how he would use it. He was horny as hell, and she could fix that, and he could put her in her rightful place. Underneath him.

Now that he found out it was just one man and a girl, he figured he could take them, easy. Get the man out of the way, and she was all his. He aimed his rifle at the man's back and pulled the trigger.

~ * ~

Lexi heard the rifle-blast and saw the flash to her right. Lige said "Oof," and pitched forward, into the fire. She screamed his name and lunged for him.

Her hand gripped his wet coat. Bloody. Shot. Then a dark shape loomed out of the shadows, grabbed her around her throat and shoved her to the ground. The attacker climbed atop her, one hand pinning her right arm, the other at her throat cutting off her air, his knee grinding up into the soft place between her legs.

She struggled and fought and clawed with her free hand. Her gun belt and dagger--where were they? Then she remembered taking them off and setting them aside. Out of reach.

"Quit, bitch." His fist slammed into her face. "Hold still or I'll kill you."

He could strangle her with his bare hands. She stopped fighting, tasting blood from her hurt lip, the rank animal odor of the man mingling with the reek of scorching cloth and flesh.

Oh, God. Lige was burning in the campfire.

The man lowered his face close to hers, his matted beard prickled harsh against her face, his eyes reflecting red firelight. "That's better. You do what I say."

He let go of her throat and thrust his hand between her legs, poking and prodding, and grabbed her so hard she cried out.

"Hehehe. No guns. No cock, either. That Reb was right about one thing, and I do love to pleasure the gals. We gonna have us a hoppin' good time, sugar." He groped upwards, under her shirt, explored her breasts, pinched her nipples. "Not more'n a mouthful, but it'll do. Take off them men's duds."

"No," she said between her teeth. "Get off me."

He raised his hand, threatening.

She flinched, remembering how hard he had hit her. "All right. I'll take them off."

"That's better, sugar. We can both have fun if you do what I say."

She unbuttoned her jacket, very slowly. He lifted off her, fondling his crotch. Kneeling, he fumbled with his pants.

He didn't notice her gun belt and dagger in the shadows not three feet from her head. Why didn't he search her more closely for weapons? Not very smart. He must think she was just a helpless girl. She would show him not to underestimate her.

He shed his coat, unbuckled his belt, unbuttoned his pants, and dropped his drawers to his knees. In the dim firelight his organ shined red against the crotch hair. Then he grabbed her hand and stuck it over the thing. "Feel that, sugar? Feel what ol' Harry's fixin' to pleasure you with."

She sat up. Gritting her teeth in disgust, she forced herself to take hold of his organ and stroke it. He let out a moan of pleasure. "That's the way, sugar. Keep it up." He sighed, licking his lips, grunting like a happy pig, stiffening within her fingers.

Then she squirmed her hand lower, seized his cods, squeezed and pulled down. He howled and grabbed for her hand. She held on with all her strength and twisted. He smashed his fist into her face. Her grip broke and she fell backwards. Then she rolled sideways, grabbing the gun-belt, her hand closing on the hilt of the dagger.

"Bitch!" he screamed. He tackled her and crushed her to the ground, face down, pinning her hands and the gun belt underneath her.

His hands clamped around her neck, choking her again. But he must not have seen her weapons. She raised enough on one elbow to grab for the holster-stay, but the dagger was all she could get to. His fingers pressed into her throat, hurting. She couldn't suck in any air. He was killing her.

Somehow she twisted around, dagger in hand, and hit him in the side. Hard bone stopped the point. He reared up, yelled and let go of her neck to grab her hand.

"You stuck me, damn you! Now I'm gonna kill you, bitch! Then I'll fuck you!"

He pried the dagger from her hand. With her other hand she managed to unsnap the stay and slip the revolver partway out of the holster. She pointed the gun upwards, toward his head, not yet clear of the holster, thumbed back the hammer, and jerked the trigger back.

The gun roared and the flash lit him up, the bullet's shock lifting him slightly off her. He sighed and settled atop her, quivering.

She wriggled out from underneath, rolling him aside. He flopped onto his back, blood all over his face, his pants obscenely down around his knees. His erection had already gone limp and pale and small.

She swallowed past her bruised throat and lowered her shaking gun-hand. She rubbed her neck and touched her battered cheek. Ought to check him for a pulse, but she couldn't bring herself to touch his filthy body again. She had shot him in the head. Surely that was enough to kill even a monster like him.

Lige. She crawled on hands and knees to him and dragged him by the arms out of the fire. He was limp and lifeless, his hair singed, his face blistered and blackened. Smoke curled from his clothing.

She searched for a pulse, but there wasn't any. The bullet had torn through the middle of his back and out his chest, right through his big, simple, honest heart. Tears rolled down her cheeks.

"Lige," her voice a whisper. "I got him." She shuddered and glanced toward the body of the man she killed. She had to bury Lige, but the thought of touching the murderer made her feel ill. She would just leave him be.

"I'm sorry you're dead, Lige. I'll miss you." She sniffed and wiped her nose on her sleeve. "But I guess you aren't going to tell on me now."

Chapter
Twenty-seven

Blake sat on the horse alongside the wagon, fuming at the delays. The string of ordinance, baggage and ambulance wagons started and stopped every few feet on its approach to the Cape Fear River bridge. Pistol fire cracking behind them, in Fayetteville, sounded like trouble. If the train didn't get a move on, he'd be caught on the wrong side of the river with his women.

Judith's eyes were anxious, but she was bearing her fears quietly.

Sally turned on the wagon-bench and looked toward the fighting, also uneasy. "It's not going to be like yesterday, is it, Blake?"

"Of course not," he said. "It's probably just some fools hurrahing the town."

"Thank goodness." Sally sighed. "That was enough excitement to last me awhile."

"I'm not sorry I missed it." Judith, looking fresh and alluring in the sky-blue dress she'd made, as yet showed no outward signs of the changes going on inside her. Blake's responsibilities had increased with prospective fatherhood, yet another loved one to protect and defend. He welcomed the tender weight, even though it bore heavily upon his shoulders.

Sally was stunning, as always, strawberry blonde sausage curls bouncing with every movement of her head. She wore the gray silk dress that showed plenty of bosom. The sight of his first love still excited Blake, though he wished it didn't. He tightened his hands on the reins. Having her with him all the time was going to be a trial, but what else could he do?

He turned his attention where it belonged, to Judith.

He had volunteered his troop for wagon-guard so he could personally protect his wife. General Butler had permitted it, saying he was entitled to a day of easy duty after being wrung through hell by the Yankees. His men, sneaking glances at the women, were on their best behavior. He had not heard any swearing all morning. He looked for Matt, and it hit him again. The company bled afresh after every contact with the enemy. How long before all of them were gone without a trace?

He had detailed the reliable Cheney to drive their wagon until all the Confederates crossed the river and fired the bridge and the immediate danger was past. After that, he would give up the mobility of the horse and drive the wagon himself.

The wagons in front started to roll as the train closed and spread like a squeezebox. After they cleared the bridge, Hunter Lightfoot came alongside the wagon riding Magic, wearing a clean uniform, fit and well, the color back in his face. He looked over the women, smiled, and raised a questioning eyebrow.

"Howdy, old chum. Heard you were still in one piece, came to see for myself. Morning, Mrs. Winberry." Hunter bowed from the saddle. "Ma'am…" He let his eyes linger on Sally.

She smiled back at him, fingering her curls. "I don't believe we've met. Such a fine gentleman, too." She held out her gloved hand. "I'm Sally Dubose."

"Ah. Miss Dubose." He took her hand, shifted his gaze at Blake and back to her. "Hunter Lightfoot, at your service. My, don't you two ladies make this dreary old wagon train so much easier to look at."

Judith said, "I heard something exciting about you and Lexi. I'm sorry I couldn't be at the wedding."

Hunter gave her a crooked smile and stroked his moustache. "I guess we're all family now."

"That's wonderful, Hunter." Judith's delight appeared genuine, as Blake had not told her in detail how Hunter and Lexi came to be married.

Sally looked from Judith to Hunter. "Wedding? Family? What happened?"

"What's all the gunfire?" Blake said.

"Federal recon," Hunter said. "They found us."

"The Yankees are that close?" Judith's dark eyes widened in concern.

"Don't worry," Hunter said. "Only a squadron. We routed them and you'll be in the clear soon. Once we fire the bridge, the Yankees will have fits trying to cross that nice mushy swamp. Ought to stop 'em for a day or two."

"Oh, thank goodness," Sally gushed. "I do feel ever so safe with all these brave men around."

Magic pushed forward and nuzzled Blake's pocket. He dug in his saddlebag and found a bit of hardtack to give her. He affectionately ran his hand over her forelock and pulled her stiff ears. Her swollen joints were almost back to normal. He said to Hunter, "That sorry piece of crowbait you loaned me refused a jump and got me caught."

"I warned you about him, remember?" Hunter nodded at Blake's Yankee horse. "Suppose you'll be wanting to swap. Any vices?"

"This one doesn't seem to care if he's Confederate as long as he gets what he wants." He caught himself before he added, "Just like Sally.

~ * ~

Harry woke up with the sun on his face, dried blood in his eyes, feeling like hell. He lifted his hand and felt the tender place on his scalp and found a long graze.

His pants hobbled him around his knees. He was cold, his head and balls ached, and the puncture in his side hurt. He started up, but his head throbbed. He eased himself back down, rolled over on his side and hitched his pants back up. He would lie here a while until he was able to get up on his pins again.

He looked around. He was alone. The girl was gone, and so was the dead Reb.

That bitch got the better of him for the second time. Sure she was the same girl who shot at him in Columbia, and this time she damn near killed him. Next time, he wouldn't stop to pleasure her. He'd kill her first, before she had a chance to pull any tricks.

~ * ~

A half hour after they crossed the bridge, Judith looked behind her and spotted smoke. She pointed it out to Blake.

"Our people must be burning the bridge," he said. "You'll be

265

safe. Yanks can't pursue us now."

He flashed her a grin. Clean, fed and rested, he cut a trim, handsome figure, the gallant cavalry officer, straight and at ease astride his mount. The news that she was expecting had energized him.

"Good," Sally said. "I've had my fill of those beastly Yankees."

"I'll make sure." Blake rode back down the line, leaving Judith alone with Sally and Private Cheney.

Judith noticed Sally watching him ride away, also admiring his looks.

"It certainly is a relief to be back among friends," Sally said.

That prissy tart sure was assuming a lot. But Judith was determined to be civil to her even if it took every shred of her will power. "And just how awful were the Yankees?" She leaned toward Sally, pretending interest. "Did they really mistreat you?"

"You've no idea." Sally dropped her gaze and shuddered. "I shouldn't like to speak of it. They were so cruel. Heartless. And they were going to kill Blake."

"Do you have to keep bringing that up? Anyway, it's all over now."

"And to think he was willing to sacrifice himself just for me." Sally sighed wistfully.

"Oh?" Judith blinked, startled. "How is that?"

"Didn't he tell you?" Sally's green eyes locked onto hers, a little smile curling her lips.

"Tell me what?"

"He came to rescue me. That's how he got captured in the first place."

Judith shook her head. "He told me he delivered a dispatch to General Wheeler and was on his way back--"

Sally spread her hand, examining a fingernail. "He was on his way to find me. My mother told him about the fix I was in, and he was determined to save me from those despicable Yankees."

He had not mentioned that part. Was it true? He had told her about returning to Columbia after the Yankee occupation and the destruction he had found. He must have heard about Sally then. Did he really risk his life to chase after his old lover? Judith felt a touch of nausea and was not sure whether to blame her condition or Sally's smug words.

Blake returned, riding alongside the wagon. "We're in the clear," he said. He excused Cheney, tied Magic and climbed in next to Judith.

She laid her hand possessively on his sleeve. That Sally certainly had a habit of saying unsettling things. At the depot in Columbia, that woman had claimed Blake married her out of spite. Now she said he chased after her when he found out the Yankees had her. Just like he was still in love with her.

Maybe he was. The looks she caught him giving Sally from time to time were anything but brotherly.

Was it so terrible for him to strive to rescue a girl who used to be his fiance?

As though Sally really was in trouble! A hostage? More likely she had something to gain by sticking with the Yankees.

Why didn't Sally stay in Fayetteville and wait for them? Or did she prefer running off with Blake?

Blake popped the reins. "This old mule is still poky."

"Don't pick on my mule," Judith snapped. "Fancy always gets me there."

"This fine mule, then." He took a hand off the reins and slipped it over hers. She linked her fingers through his and held on to him. Shouldn't feel so panicky, better keep her head, better not let Sally spook her. Losing her temper or getting whiny wouldn't gain her anything.

Blake had spent all of yesterday and last night with her, his wife, not Sally. And that was how she was going to keep it.

Fight for him, hang on, never let the vixen get a pry-hold.

~ * ~

Blake grabbed the handle of his saber and gave the chunk of beef impaled on it a half-turn. Fat dripped into the fire, sizzled, and flames licked higher. He was hungry enough to eat it raw, make up for the three lean days he had spent as a prisoner.

He glanced at Sally. She sat on a campstool, deep in conversation with General Butler. Captain Causey stood at her elbow and three other staff officers hung around like puppies begging for scraps. But her eyes were locked on the general's face, a pouty little smile on her lips, fingers twirling the ends of her hair. She covered her mouth and giggled at something he said.

Blake sat down next to Judith on one of her trunks, and she cocked an eyebrow his way. "Looks like Sally found a new interest or two. I take it she fancies generals best."

"She's just being sociable. Besides, General Butler is married," Blake said.

Judith raised an eyebrow. "That doesn't seem to make a whit of difference to her."

He scowled. "There you go again. I told you to be nice."

"Ha. I've been sticky sweet, just like molasses."

"Jude--"

"I know," Judith said quickly. "We're beholden to her."

"I have to make sure you're both safe," he said. "Women don't belong in an army camp. I need to get you situated."

"I like it here." She touched his arm. "This way we can be together. That canvas cover you rigged on the wagon will give us plenty of privacy."

He stared through half-shut eyes into the flames. With his peripheral vision he watched Sally flirting with Butler. If the general's wife were present, would she be as bothered as Judith seemed to be? He gave her no cause to think he wanted Sally back. Or did he?

What the two women thought of each other was the least of his problems. It was up to him to keep them safe, regardless of their petty differences.

After he ate his fill of beef and corn-dodgers, he took time to check on Magic and Fancy, make sure Wheeler's men didn't swipe them.

He gave the animals an extra handful of corn and a muzzle-rub. After seeing to them he started back. He veered into a stand of pine to relieve himself.

As he buttoned his pants back together, he heard a light step behind him. He jerked his hand toward his revolver grip and whirled toward the sound. A figure moved toward him through the shadows, a skirted silhouette. "Blake?" Sally's voice.

"Don't ever sneak up on me like that again." He moved his hand from his gun and fixed the last button on his fly.

She laughed softly. "But I wanted to talk to you." She came right up to him, touching close. "Hardly ever get a chance any more. Judith is always around."

Sally's violet scent swirled about his head. "You've gathered quite a following," he said. "Besides that, Judith is my wife. Why do we need to talk?"

"Don't you know?"

"We talked yesterday. Nothing has changed since."

"You're right, it hasn't. We still care for each other. Very much." She nestled closer.

"What of it, Sally?"

"We could go away together. Resign your commission and we'll go where there isn't a war." She circled her arms around him.

"The hell you say," he snorted.

"You could. You'd be free." Her hands moved down his back and stole around under his waistband. She stood on her tiptoes and offered her face for a kiss.

~ * ~

Judith noticed Sally leave her admirers and wander off roughly in the direction Blake went.

All day she had played the outsider, listening to those two talk and laugh about good times and mutual friends back in Columbia. Such fine boon companions. She was ignorant of their shared history, could not join in or contribute a thing.

Now what was Sally up to? Judith set off to find out for herself. She didn't intend to be sneaky, but caution and guilt made her steps stealthy. She slipped through the woods toward the horse picket, couldn't see much in the darkness but the outlines of trees, barely enough to keep her feet on the path.

She heard low voices off to her right. Sally's, and wasn't that Blake's whisper? She paused, listening, and started toward the voices.

There they were, embracing.

Sally said, "You could be free."

Judith froze.

He was still in love with Sally, and acting upon it, here and now.

Stunned, she couldn't gather her thoughts, couldn't decide

whether to make herself known or continue to watch from the shadows.

Sally said he could be free. Free from what? His wife? Was he going to take Sally, right here in the woods? She couldn't stand to bear witness to her husband's betrayal. She retreated before the lovers could sense her presence.

~ * ~

Blake gripped Sally's shoulders and pushed her to arm's length. "Stop."

"Why?" Her voice was indignant.

"It isn't right."

"Ha." Sally's anger came at him in waves. "Mr. Duty and Honor. Do what you really want for a change!"

"Sally, just leave me be." He shook his head. "It's too late for us."

"No, it isn't. I didn't save you just so your wife could have you."

"She does have me," he insisted.

"I don't believe you. It's me you love." Sally broke through his restraining hands and stepped forward. "You have to send her away."

"No, Sally. We're going back to camp. Now."

He took her arm, but she slapped his face, shook off his hand, and whirled away. Head high, she walked stiffly, hands fisted, not toward camp, but in a different direction.

He rubbed his stinging cheek, staring after her. A woman had no business wandering around an army camp unescorted. And she was still his ward, even if she was being so cussed difficult. He had to make sure she didn't get into trouble. Although by now he was convinced Sally was the trouble. Keeping Sally close to him was proving to be dangerous, a constant temptation to betray his wife. Was he really honor-bound to watch over her forever and ever?

Did he still want her? His body sure responded as though he did. Why shouldn't it? He had dreamed of her for a very long time, and it was hard to give her up.

But he must leave her be. Judith was the one carrying his child. And he cared for her. Deeply. Comfortably. She offered a warm, healing kind of love that nurtured and didn't sting and burn like

Sally's lightning. Judith took him for what he was and did not make unreasonable demands.

Sally hesitated and looked around as though she heard him coming up behind her.

Blake spoke up. "Are you ready to go back to camp now?"

"Oh, it's you. Why are you following me?"

"I thought you might need protection." He started to laugh. "Perhaps I am mistaken."

"I ought to scream and say you tried to rape me," she snapped.

He stopped laughing. "What's that going to get you, Sal?"

"Wouldn't your wife think a lot of you!"

"She would never believe it." Blake noted the petulance in Sally's voice How could he love her and dislike her at the same time? "Don't be that way, Sally. It doesn't become you."

Her shoulders drooped, but he did not trust that she had given up on causing him trouble.

"Let's go," he said softly.

He led Sally to the ambulance General Butler had provided for her quarters, left her there, and looked for Judith. She wasn't in sight, must have retired to their wagon for the night.

He climbed inside and reached for her in the dark, eager to make love to her and calm his inner turmoil.

She drew away from him. "Don't touch me," she snarled.

He jerked his hand back as though she had burned it. "What's the matter?"

"I saw you and Sally together," she whispered harshly.

"Spying on me, Jude?" Indignation rose in his chest. "Taking sneak lessons from Lightfoot? I'm surprised at you."

"I just wanted to find out what she was up to. Well, I sure did."

He sat down next to her, not quite touching, trying to calm down, be rational. "Just exactly what was it you thought you saw?"

"You kissing and loving on her like it was her you married instead of me."

Damn, damn, damn. "All right. She wanted me to kiss her. That is all."

"All?" That single word carried a world of fury.

I'm sorry." He rubbed the ache starting in his temple. "I won't get that close to her again. Never."

"Should I believe that?" Judith held the blanket close to her throat. "You made love to me, wanting her the whole time. You called me Sally the night we married. Remember that?"

"I didn't." Did he? He shook his head, bewildered. "I honestly don't recall."

"She told me you married me to make her jealous." Judith's words came in a rush. "And you chased after her when the Yankees had her. You got her, too. Why did you even bother to come to me?"

"She told you all that?" It struck him that most of it was half truthful, and he felt ashamed.

"It's her you wanted all the time. I'm just a substitute." Judith whispered.

"No." He stared at her in the dark, wishing he could read her face. "I married you because I wanted you." Blake let out a long breath. "Maybe I was confused once but I have it sorted out now and I don't want anything to do with Sally any more."

"That's not what I saw."

"Jude, I walked away from her. If you'd spied on us long enough, you'd know that yourself."

"Now you're acting like I'm the one who did something wrong," She snapped.

"I haven't broken our vows, Jude, and I won't." He touched her cheek. "I love you and I need you."

Judith studied him, wanting to reach to him, to trust him. She had so much at stake. She loved him even if he was bossy and still attracted to Sally. And she was going to bear his child. "I want to believe you." Her voice sounded tremulous in her ears. "I want to believe that your worst fault is too much loyalty."

His face came closer, within inches of hers. "I have never lied to you, not once."

"But you didn't tell me everything. And just exactly what do you expect me to think, after seeing you and Sally like that?"

"Like what?" His arms came around her and drew her to him. "Like this?"

She held her body rigid, resisting. "Do you intend to claim your husbandly rights on me right now?"

"No other woman can know me this way, Jude. I haven't

betrayed you and I won't."

How she wanted to believe him. She felt his lips brush against hers. She yielded, relaxed, let her own lips part to accept his. He moved his body over hers, covering her with his warmth, reminding her that he was here and not with Sally. If she drove him away, where might he go? She brought her arms around his hard lean shoulders and drew him in.

He paused, whispering, "You don't object, do you?"

She let out a sigh. A groan, really. "I never could refuse you."

Chapter Twenty-eight

Next morning, Judith sat on a trunk embroidering the last leg of a W on a handkerchief. A farm dog sunned itself near her wagon, and off to her right a picket of horses stomped, gnawed at their ropes and flicked their ears and tails at flies. The camp smelled of dirty socks, horse dung and low-hanging campfire smoke. Male voices, shouts, sometimes laughter or singing, crackled through the camp. Jingling spurs, buckles and rattling sabers warned whenever soldiers walked near her campsite.

But Sally's approach was silent, a sneak attack. She sat down on the trunk. "Where's Blake?"

Judith pretended to keep her attention on the needlework so Sally wouldn't see her eyes. The tart must not know she saw them together last night. "Why do you care?"

"I want to talk to him."

"There's an inspection," Judith snapped. "He's busy with that."

Sally wrinkled her nose. "Isn't this a dreadful place? It smells."

"If you hate it so much, why don't you just leave?"

"I don't have any place to go," Sally said in a pitiful voice.

"Camp suits me fine," Judith finally looked at her. "The soldiers have all been perfect gentlemen, and my husband is here."

"Have they now?" Sally raised an eyebrow. "I thought you ought to know, for your own good, how Blake's been behaving. Not such a perfect gentleman."

Judith stabbed the needle into the handkerchief. "I thought you two were on the very best of terms."

"He must have thought so too." Sally laughed shortly. "He came after me last night and made indecent proposals. And you sitting not a hundred yards away."

"More likely the other way around."

"I had to defend my honor." Sally's voice took on the pitiful note again.

"Didn't hear you calling for help."

"I was too dumbfounded."

Judith tried to manage the next stitch but pricked herself instead.

"He's been after me for a long time." Sally spread her claws like a cat and studied them. "I told you why he married you, just to make me jealous. It's me he's been wanting, all the time."

"Is that so?" Judith smiled, showing her teeth. "I guess that's why he loved on me all night long. Didn't get much sleep, but I'm not complaining. I do enjoy my wifely chores. And by the way, did he tell you I'm expecting his child?"

Sally started and blinked. She laughed, covering her mouth. "So soon? Quite the broodmare, aren't you, dear?"

"That's enough." Judith threw down her sewing and stood up so she could look down at Sally. "I have been enduring you because you helped him, but this is the last!"

"I didn't save him for you." Sally rose to her feet.

"That's clear. But you can't have him."

Sally started to walk away, but turned and shot back, "I always get what I want."

Judith strode after, grabbed her by the shoulders, spun her around and shook her. "Stay away from my husband, you conniving little witch." Sally's astonished face swayed before her. Judith let go with one hand and slapped her, hard. "If you so much as look at him again I'll twist off your head and spit in the hole!"

Sally cried out, broke free and whirled to escape.

Judith balled up her fist and hit her on the back.

Sally lunged away and ran.

Judith chased her, wanting to claw her face bloody, but her legs tangled in her skirt and she almost tripped. She recovered and looked up just in time to see Sally slip out of reach and disappear behind a stand of trees.

Judith looked around. Most of the men were gone, busy with

the inspection, but one trooper was watching, leaning against a tree. He grinned at her. Her face burned in embarrassment. She rubbed her stinging hand, and returned to her trunk and snatched her spilled sewing off the ground.

~ * ~

Sally fled to the headquarters tent, hoping to find friendly staff officers there. Things weren't going like she had planned.

Last night was humiliating. She knew Blake wanted her, he responded just as she had expected, but he suddenly thrust her away. No man ever turned her down before. How dare he scorn her so?

Must be that wife of his had a stronger grip on him than she realized.

She touched her cheek, fearing a mark would show where Judith had slapped her. But a high flush would be ever so becoming. She slapped the other cheek, making sure they matched.

Captain Causey met her at the entrance to the tent. He smiled and bowed. "Miss Sally! What a pleasure. Is there something I can do for you?"

"Where is everybody? General Butler and the others?"

"Inspection. They left me here to hold down the fort."

"Well, I certainly am glad you stayed." Sally gave him a flattering smile. "Now I don't have to be so lonely. May I sit with you for a little while?"

Captain Causey almost tripped over himself getting her a campstool. She settled down on it, beaming up at him. Not a bad sort, really. Well-tailored uniform. Might even have money.

More than Blake had. Maybe she was foolish to want him back. He wouldn't bring much with him but his own sweet self. Ha. Right now she was furious with him for treating her as he had last night. And his precious Judith! Unspeakable creature.

"Captain Causey, I hope you're not busy."

"Not at all."

She lowered her eyelashes modestly. "I want to know everything about you. Just everything."

For the next half hour Sally listened to Causey's life story, pretending rapt interest. Just when she was beginning to think she couldn't bear the sound of the man's voice for another minute, soldiers rode up.

Officers. She scanned the crowd, delighted to pick out General Butler, his staff, and a few company commanders.

Blake was with them. He dismounted and strode up to her, watching her, jaw line set hard, eyes wary. He saluted Causey and bowed to her, unsmiling.

To Causey he said, "Thank you for entertaining Miss Dubose."

"My pleasure."

"May I borrow her for a moment? There's something we have to discuss."

"Certainly, Captain Winberry," Causey said. "Provided you don't keep her too long."

She allowed Blake to lead her aside, hoping he was going to apologize and beg for her favors. "What is this all about?" she whispered, licking her lips. "Are you planning to make more indecent proposals?"

"Behave yourself, Sal, or I'll wring your pretty little neck," he said between his teeth.

She faced him. "How dare you!" She wouldn't make it easy for him. She wanted him on his knees, and she would dictate the terms for his surrender.

"I've been making inquiries." His voice was cold, his expression controlled. "I've finally figured out what to do with you and Judith."

She pouted. "I know what you want to do with me, but you have made me very angry and I shan't allow it."

"Listen," he said, ignoring her words. "Smithfield is about twenty five miles from here. You and my wife can take the wagon up there--I'll arrange an escort--and catch a train on to Raleigh. Find a place to stay after you get there."

Sally recoiled. "I'm going nowhere with her."

"You're not safe here."

She looked off toward headquarters. She would make him jealous. That would work. She smiled up at him. "Captain Causey has very kindly made arrangements for me to stay at a house," she lied.

A smile twitched up the corners of his mouth. "Did he, now?"

Sally opened her mouth to counter the protest she expected.

He nodded, looking relieved. "In that case, you're all set."

She shut her mouth hard, catching the inside of her cheek painfully. Where was his indignation?

"Tell you what, Sally. I'll walk you back to Captain Causey, and leave you in his care. I have to go see about my wife now."

Stunned, Sally took the arm he offered.

How could he have turned her down? Certainly he couldn't be in love with his wife. What did she have to offer? Just wait until the woman's swollen belly sagged between her legs. How charming would she be then?

Sally lifted her chin and prepared a smile for Captain Causey. Of course he would be glad to help her find a place to stay. Men were always happy to do things for her.

~ * ~

Judith didn't see any more of Sally that morning, but she wouldn't put it past her to cry to Blake how his mean wife had mistreated her.

Blake finally returned to their campsite, his horse's hooves thumping softly on the sandy soil. He greeted her, dismounted and tied the animal.

She set down her work and walked over to meet him. He slipped his arm around her waist, and they walked together to the trunk she used as a seat.

"How did your inspection go?" she asked.

He let himself down onto the trunk. Frowning, he said, "Broken down horses, ropes for bridles, rusty sabers and holey uniforms. Nobody in their right mind would want to show off a troop that looks like mine."

"They still have valor."

"That's wearing thin, too." He hunched his shoulders, dug in the earth with his boot-heel, staring across the camp. Then he looked down at her project. "What are you making?"

She gave him the pair of handkerchiefs. "I monogrammed these for you."

He held them up, smiling. "Spoiling me rotten."

"I traded a pound of the soap I made for them."

"They're beautifully made. Too pretty to use." He kissed her.

"I love you," she murmured.

"I am a fortunate man to be so honored." He grinned, but quickly went sober again. "Look, I've been thinking. This isn't going to work."

"What isn't?"

"You can't stay in camp. It's too dangerous."

Judith swept her hand toward the campfires. "I've never had so many protectors in my life."

Despite her brave front, he knew how afraid she was of Yankees overtaking her. "If the Yankees come after our camp like we went after theirs, something could happen to you."

"They wouldn't shoot me, would they?" she asked.

"Bullets don't mind who they hit." He shook his head. "I have to get you out of here. There's a depot at Smithfield, you can take the train on to Raleigh."

Her hands twisted the front of her skirt. "You want to send me away?"

"I have to. It's best--"

"What about Sally? Does she get to stay?"

"She's planning to stay in a house not far from here."

"I'm the one that has to leave?" Judith's brow clouded like a building storm.

"She made her own arrangements," Blake said. "Captain Caus--"

"I suppose you'll want me to sell my mule and wagon, go to that strange city all by myself where I don't know a living soul and start all over again."

"I don't like it either, but that's the way it has to be."

She lifted her face to him. "You're all I've got. What if you got hurt and needed me?"

"Better than if something happened to both of us." He spanned his fingers across her middle. "And our child."

"I can make my own arrangements, too. Find a place close by."

"The Yanks only stopped in Fayetteville to destroy the town and re-supply. Once they decide to move all hell--"

"That's why I want to keep my rig. I can leave when I have to. In the meantime, we can see each other whenever you have time." She rested her hand on his arm. "Please don't make me leave you."

"You're not taking this the way I--"

"Won't General Butler let you have a few hours off to find me a place to stay?"

"He's tired of cutting me slack. I'm supposed to be getting up a reconnaissance right now."

"I'll go by myself, come back and leave word where you can find me." She said it with an air of finality.

He was not convinced. "You need to be a long way from here."

"What difference does it make? If I went to Raleigh, the Yankees would follow me there. They're everywhere."

"You don't know that. Even Lightfoot doesn't know where they're headed. Jude, I'm trying to do the right thing by you."

"Quit trying so hard. I'll find a place to stay near the camp."

"Here we go again." He shook his head, his jaw tense. "I'm going to regret it, but have it your way."

~ * ~

Ever since her encounter with the Yankee, Lexi was wary of others who might do her harm. Even though she was armed with her revolver, Lige's revolver, and the Yankee's rifle, she didn't want to use them on her own countrymen. She avoided the few Confederates she met headed the other way, taking them for deserters.

She found it easy to keep track of the Union army by the smudges on the horizon. She skirted the smoke columns and rode through the desert of burnt-out forests, fields and houses. Only after she emerged on the other side of the belt of destruction did she find citizens who were able to sell her provisions.

Yesterday she took a flatboat across the Cape Fear River. The ferryman said the Yankees were in Fayetteville, same as her sister-in-law. He suggested she head north and east to avoid them.

She was a mess with her smashed lip, swollen jaw and bruised throat. What would Hunter think of her now, battered, hair cropped close?

It didn't matter. She was going to be a soldier. Their being married was only a formality.

~ * ~

A few days after she left the cavalry camp, Judith took advantage of the fine spring weather and sat on the porch repairing a hem that had come loose. The air was fresh and the ground was wet from the latest deluge. It would take more than one sunny day to dry the puddles and harden the roads. Nonetheless, a stream of carts and wagons persevered east toward the nearby settlement, away from the armies.

A high-pitched shriek made her start and jerk her head up. Her landlord's youngest was screaming and chasing chickens around the yard. She let out her breath.

He ran right through a puddle, spattering up a spray of brown water. He laughed and the chickens squawked, scattered and fluttered out of reach.

The door banged open. "Billy!" shouted Mrs. Oliver.

Billy giggled and ran behind the house. His mother said, "Young 'uns. That boy ruined one good set of shoes, now he's out to ruin another." She went back inside and slammed the door.

A cavalryman turned in at the gate and rode his horse through the yard. He sat slouched in the saddle, watching the chickens run away from his horse.

He rode up to the porch, removed his hat and bowed. She recognized Hunter Lightfoot.

Her hands stilled in her lap. She feared news, but he was smiling. "Good morning, Mrs. Winberry. Your husband asked me to call by."

"He couldn't come in person?"

"He's attracted the notice of General Hampton. The favor of a general means more work. He sent you a letter." Hunter searched through the papers in his saddlebags.

"I've stayed close by, but it hasn't done a bit of good. I haven't seen him since I left camp." Judith stood up and reached for the note.

She ripped the envelope open and scanned the hasty scrawl.

March 17 '65 - 7 a.m.

Dear Judith,

Hope this letter finds you well. I am all right. Think of you constantly with affection. Sorry I haven't been able to see you in person, but I have been on patrol watching the enemy.

Yankees are moving toward the coast and I fear they will pass through Bentonville. Hunter has agreed to escort you as far as Smithfield. Get your things together and go with him, rid yourself of the mule and wagon, and take the next available train to Raleigh.

God willing, I shall find you in Raleigh at the first opportunity.

Your loving husband,

Blake W.

She stared at the note. Once again he made plans and expected her to jump.

Hunter said, "I have official business at General Johnston's headquarters, at Smithfield, so I can take you there. Shouldn't be difficult to find a buyer for your rig."

"Come inside," she said. "It won't take me long to get ready." She turned and laid her hand on the doorknob and looked back at him over her shoulder. "I know exactly how much time it takes to pack."

~ * ~

Hunter settled onto a couch and pulled out his pipe. Good upholstered furniture, rugs on the floor, a scent of prosperity about the place. The landlord, Mr. Oliver had done well for himself despite the war, or maybe because of it.

"What's going on?" Mr. Oliver said. "Are the Yankees coming this way?"

"I'd say so. Maybe Goldsboro."

"Are you sure of that? And here we are not a mile from the Goldsboro road."

"We've been watching their right wing march this way. General Hardee took on their left at Averasboro, now that lot is turning toward us. I'd say their head isn't fifteen miles west of here."

Mr. Oliver looked uneasy. "I'm no soldier, no sons old enough to be in the army. Make my living in the peaceable timber and turpentine business. The Yankees have no cause for complaint with me. I always had Unionist sentiments anyhow."

Hunter allowed an ironic smile. "Think that will save you? You aren't just a fool, you're a damned fool."

Mr. Oliver blinked. "Come again?" Must be too shocked to be insulted.

"Maybe you'll make out all right." Hunter waved his hand. "They've let up a little since they cleared South Carolina. I guess they heard about all the North Carolina Unionists. But they sure play hell with the turpentine business. Forest fires everywhere."

Mr. Oliver's fat Adam's apple bobbed. "I'd better stay here and protect my interests."

~ * ~

Upstairs in her room, Judith opened one of her trunks, snatched up the pictures of Blake and George and tucked them inside.

She hesitated. Was Sally still around? What would the little tart be doing while she was miles away in Raleigh? How much temptation could she expect Blake to bear?

Besides that, the thought of leaving gave her an unexplained flutter of fear, right in her center. As though something terrible was going to happen if she left. It was even stronger than her fear of the Yankees.

She couldn't go to Raleigh. She just couldn't.

She wrote a note to Blake on the blank side of the letter and stuffed it into the envelope. That complete, she drifted down the stairs. Hunter sat on a couch talking to Mr. Oliver, but looked up when she came into the room. She said, "Hunter, can't we go outside?"

On the porch, she walked to the rail and looked out over the yard. Turning back to him, she said, "Hunter, please go on without me."

He waited, gave her time.

"I have this feeling," she said.

"There's trouble coming," he told her. "Your husband is frantic to have you out of the way."

"If there's trouble, he might get hurt and he would need me. I won't leave until the last possible moment."

Hunter's brow lifted. "The fellow has a temper."

She shrugged, countering his sardonic smile with a brave one.

"I guess he'll have to be mad. He's been mad at me before. I have a good mind to ride over to camp and tell him myself."

"Don't. You won't find him there anyhow. He's been on patrol. And it's getting dangerous. The Yankees are closing in."

She handed back the envelope. "I wrote him a note. I have to find a soldier passing through to take it to him, unless I go myself. Are there any couriers?"

"Give it to me. I'll find somebody by the time I pass through yonder little settlement." Hunter nodded in that direction. "Bentonville, is it?"

~ * ~

Harry Bell took help along the way from nigras who were happy to feed a Union soldier. They didn't have much worth taking besides food. His wounds weren't serious, only festered up a little bit.

He finally caught up with the Union Army at Fayetteville. He told the cavalry pickets his name was Harvey Smith, and that he escaped from a Reb prison camp. He told them of his original capture in Virginia, cleverly forgetting to mention his late connections to Sherman's army. Wouldn't do to have Emmett's lies catch up with him.

Another hero's welcome. The cavalrymen swore him into their company, gave him a revolver and a good horse they'd taken from a farmer. He was back in business.

~ * ~

Lexi struck a main road north of Fayetteville and found the Confederate Army, or at least a fair portion of it.

Although she was wary of the stringy, grimy, powerful-smelling hikers, she made Scout and Lige's horse fall into step with them. Mounted, she could outrun them if they offered trouble.

She spotted a dusty man she took to be an officer because of his bearing and the tattered gold braid on his sleeves. "Whose command is this, sir?"

"Cheatham's. Whose you in, boy?" He squinted up at her.

"Nobody's. Do you know Lieutenant Hunter Lightfoot?"

"Is he in the Army of Tennessee?"

"Hampton's scouts, Butler's cavalry." She lifted her chin. "I'm joining up, going to be a scout."

"A scout? Ha." He ran his gaze over her and the horses. "Anyway, you're well armed. Where did you get the army rifle?"

"I killed a Yankee. He murdered my partner." She set her jaw. "So I killed him."

"You don't say." The office's eyebrow shot up, disbelief. "Get off that nag and swear in. We're gonna need all the trigger fingers we can muster."

"But I must find General Hampton." She pointed to the saddlebags on Lige's horse. "I'm carrying mail."

"We're going east to catch the Yankees. We'll see Hampton's people by and by." He jerked his thumb toward the rear of the column. "Broke-down soldiers are having trouble keeping up. Give them rides on those two nags, you can keep one."

Joining this infantry unit wasn't what she had pictured, but at least they would guide her where she wanted to go, and no Yankee straggler would bother her. "Sure." Lexi started to turn Scout.

"You mean yes, sir."

"Sure. Uh, yes, sir." She gave him what she meant to be a snappy salute.

Chapter
Twenty-nine

Judith looked out the window at two canvas-topped ambulances halted in front of the gate. The passengers had not yet been brought into the house. Could they be anybody she knew--soldiers she had met at the cavalry camp--maybe even her own husband?

Downstairs, she found Mrs. Oliver trying to reason with the doctor. "Sir, don't you understand we have a houseful of little children? If you bring sick men into our house my babies will catch their death."

"Oh, we don't have any sick, unless you count lead poisoning as a disease." Dr. Thompson tied an apron over his black-trimmed medical officer's uniform. "Your children won't catch anything from a few men with gunshot wounds."

"A few?" Mrs. Oliver arched a brow.

"Just two men. The other ambulance contains medical supplies."

"Are you expecting a battle?" Judith said.

"Can't say for sure, madam, but we have been ordered to prepare field hospitals in case one occurs. "Dr. Thompson didn't look her in the eye. "We aren't asking anyone to vacate the premises. I'm sure there'll be plenty of room for the family upstairs."

Mrs. Oliver ordered her housemaid to roll up the rugs throughout the first floor and cover the sofas and chairs with sheets.

The stretcher-bearers brought in a man who was moaning from pain. A ribbon of blood marked his passage across the room. Judith looked into the stranger's gray face. His eyes, squeezed shut, popped wide open when the attendants set him down on the floor. He screamed, cursed and struck out at the nearest man.

The attendant grabbed his wrists, held his arms still and snapped, "Stop, dammit." A fresh torrent gushed from the writhing man's abdomen. The other attendant ripped open the soaked shirt.

Dr. Thompson bent over the soldier. He was hurt the same way Judith's brother was. He was dying.

Overwhelmed, she ran outside, past another bloody man who'd wandered in unassisted and leaned against the doorframe. She barely made it past the porch before she lost her breakfast in the hedge.

She held on to the banister, panting and trembling, spitting out the vile taste. She had little else to bring up--she was eating light on account of her recent queasiness. But she had to do better than this. What if they brought Blake in hurt and bleeding and she was too ill to help him?

She gathered her nerve to go back inside but had to pass through the parlor to go upstairs. The room smelled like a butcher shop. The man on the couch was quiet and still. Was he already dead? The doctor worked on the second casualty, slumped into Mr. Oliver's stuffed chair. Blood all over his chest, he breathed hard through his mouth. She paused to see if she recognized him, but he was a stranger.

"Aha, there it is, "Dr. Thompson said, satisfaction in his voice. He reached for his scalpel and cut into the cringing man under his armpit. The victim flinched away from the knife and yelled, "Goddamnit, I'm already wounded!" Blood oozed from the cut.

"You're lucky, sonny." Dr. Thompson clunked the lead ball into a pan. "It whizzed around the outside of your rib cage, didn't hit anything matters much. You'll be good as new." He pressed a wad of cloth onto the incision while he reached for a sponge with his free hand. The soldier panted. His face glistened with sweat and his eyes rolled upward. He slumped in the chair.

Dr. Thompson glanced up at Judith. "Why don't you make yourself useful? Start filling every bucket and pan you can find with clean water. Men come in dying of thirst and covered with blood and dirt. All the water you can get."

She steadied herself, resting her hand on the back of a chair. A big battle, lots of hurt men. Soon the house was going to be full of them and their leaky wounds, stench, noise and suffering.

She swallowed down another wave of nausea. She could stand it if they could.

The doctor said, "You don't look so well yourself. You aren't a swooner, are you? Can't be bothered with bringing out the salts for a bystander."

"I've worked in hospitals before," Judith told him. "I'll do whatever I can. I'm just a little sick to my stomach right now."

"Maybe I've got some medicine that'll help that."

"What I've got has a long cure. It'll just have to run its course."

~ * ~

Lexi's messmates divided their rations with her so she didn't have to go to bed hungry. She had taken up with the rag-tag end of the column. Her new friends, Tennessee soldiers, had been a long time on the road, all the way from Mississippi, mostly on foot. They looked and smelled like it. Some had no shoes, all were footsore and weary. She had given them turns on Lige's horse all day to help them keep up. She had dared them to ride Scout, who bucked off everybody but her.

Captain O'Donnell, the first man in the division she'd met, strolled up. "Still with us, Wilson?"

"Still here, sir." She grinned at him, proud of herself.

"I told Colonel Bagwell about you. He directed me to swear you in."

"No, sir." She shook her head. "I've got to take these dispatches to the cavalry."

"I'll turn them in for you."

"But I'm holding out for Hampton's scouts."

"Wilson, you don't get it. You're conscription age. You got to serve."

"I will serve, but not in the infantry."

"It's the law. You're in the army now."

Her grin faded. She didn't want to join this sorry outfit. All foot soldiers, and Hunter nowhere in sight. She could get out of it by telling him she was really a girl. But she was doing so well, not making any of the mistakes that gave her away before, just had them believing she was fanatical about her privacy.

If she told them she was a girl, would they make her undress to prove it?

"Come on, Wilson," Lewis said. "You don't want to be in no sissy pony outfit."

"Kick in with us," another soldier said.

Lexi shook her head. "You just want my horses."

"The hosses are good, but you're all right too," the soldier allowed.

"What if I'm not really eighteen yet?" she asked.

"You said you were," the captain said.

"Maybe I lied."

"We're not that choosy."

Out of excuses, she jerked her hand up to take the oath. So far she was getting along fine with her new friends, and they were headed in the right direction. Letting them know she wasn't really one of the boys would only spoil things.

~ * ~

Blake hunkered down behind a pine tree. This part of North Carolina needed respectable timber. Little bitty trees weren't much use for stopping bullets. After fighting the vanguard of Sherman's left wing all day, his ears buzzed from the banging guns and his clothes smelled burnt from the powder.

He rearranged his captured hat and pulled it lower over his eyes. He had removed the New Jersey emblem and replaced it with a palmetto medal to represent his own state. If the feds captured him again, he'd better not be wearing one of their hats. He cradled the Enfield rifle. Today he wasn't just officering. The ranks were so thin he had to help flesh them out. He had gotten in as many long-range shots as any private and believed he had dropped his share of bluecoats. His shoulder ached from the heavily charged rifle kicks.

His little force had been pushed clear to this scrubby wood on a little rise overlooking a field, but he was through letting the Yanks drive him. Hampton's trap wasn't scheduled to spring until tomorrow, when Sherman's hordes wouldn't be up against civilians, militia, or a handful of cavalry, but thousands of veteran infantry. All the scattered units in General Johnston's forces, what was left of the Army of Tennessee, and the coastal garrisons coming together, a real convention. The Yankees were in for a big surprise.

He hoped they choked on it.

Good thing Judith was off to Raleigh by now, away from the prospective battle-site. She would be safe there. If only he'd had one more chance to see her before sending her away, one more chance to atone for his stupid obsession with Sally, one more chance to assure her of his love.

Cheney jerked his chin at the battery concealed in the brush to their right. "Ol' Hampton's playin' a bluff game, and if he don't mind Sherman'll call him."

"He's trusting us to keep the guns safe." David Frank sure was full of himself since his field promotion.

The noise of small-arms fire made the back of Blake's neck tingle. Then came the vedettes, flying for safety as fast as horseflesh could carry them. One of them turned in the saddle and emptied his pistol, leaving a defiant trail of smoke behind him.

Blake spotted the first bluecoats jogging toward them in a jagged skirmish line, fixed bayonets gleaming. "Steady boys," he called out to his men. "Wait till the battery softens them up, then we'll give 'em a volley."

David repeated his order, walked down the line. Did he think that a commission brought immunity to bullets? Blake waved him down and David slipped behind a pine tree. Blake pressed the stock of the rifle against his shoulder and sighted toward the oncoming blue uniformed men.

From his left he could hear artillery officers barking orders. A throaty boom and the ground shuddered. The battery threw out a load of canister and the Union skirmishers faltered. Some of them fell. Those still on their feet broke into a forward run to get through the danger zone.

"Fire!"

"Fire!"

The attackers went to earth under the volley and began to shoot at the puffs of smoke that betrayed the Confederate line. Blake peered around his pine tree, found a target and pulled the trigger. Too much smoke to tell if he hit anybody. A few balls thunked into trees and earth. He opened another cartridge, emptied it down the barrel and rammed it home. He swallowed bitter gunpowder and looked for another target, not wanting to waste a charge.

The Yankees moved back out of range. The smoke drifted off and he saw a man hobbling away. Another turned, raised his rifle and gave a parting shot. One slapped his butt in contempt. A rifle snapped from the right. The butt-slapper pitched forward and fell. He didn't rise.

"Sonofabitch won't do that again," Simmons cackled. He reached for another cartridge.

"They believed the bluff and didn't call," a relieved Blake said to Cheney. He looked down his part of the line. Intact, no casualties he could spot, thanks to their good position. His brand new lieutenant knelt stiffly behind his own stunted tree, looking down at his arm. He sagged, swayed and crumpled to the ground.

Blake ran to him and dropped onto his knees next to him. David blinked up at him, grimacing. He pointed to his bloodied forearm. "I think it's broke."

Simmons laughed. "I swear, this troop is hell on lieutenants." He propped his still-smoking rifle against a tree and wiped his hands on his pants. "I ain't lookin' for no promotion. No sir. Not me."

"No chance of that," Cheney grunted.

Bright red blood welled up between David's fingers as he clutched his hurt arm.

"Let go, let me have it." Blake took out his penknife and cut the sleeve away from the wound. The flow was steady, not dangerous. He found two sticks to form a splint, pulled the two handkerchiefs Judith had given him from his pocket and tied the sticks to the arm.

He looked over the field, making out several blue heaps that had stayed behind. One raised a hand heavenward, then dropped.

The daylight was fading. The Yankees probably would not attack again, not today. They didn't seem that determined. They didn't have to be, because the main force would eventually catch up.

"Cheney, go look around that thicket and see if any more blue is headed this way. Bring in the haversacks if there's anything good in them. Caldwell and Simmons, gather up the rifles and ammo they dropped."

A courier rode down the line to him, stopped and saluted. "Sir?

I'm looking for Captain Winberry."

"I'm Winberry. Fetch a stretcher crew for this man."

"Yes, sir. Orders from General Hampton." The courier rifled through his packet. "Oh, yes. Here's that dispatch Lieutenant Lightfoot gave me. I've been carrying it around since yesterday."

Blake took the letter, smearing a bloody thumbprint on it. He recognized Judith's handwriting, no doubt a farewell note.

~ * ~

Judith filled every container she could find with water. Finally, overcome by tiredness and nausea, retreated to her room and threw herself onto her bed.

Now that her hands weren't busy she began to worry about what would happen when Blake found out she refused to go to Raleigh. He was going to be furious. Would he ever trust her again?

Worse, a battle was about to take place on her very doorstop, and Blake in the fight. The image of her brother's dead body being lowered to the hospital floor replayed inside her head and she opened her eyes to drive away the picture. Sally was suddenly the least of her troubles.

She could still leave. She had counted on using her wagon and mule to avoid getting trapped behind enemy lines, but she would be traveling alone. It was getting late, almost dark. Better wait until morning.

She stared at the ceiling. One of the boards appeared to be loose. It was a little out of line and showed space between it and the next plank. It gave her an idea. She needed a place to hide her belongings. An increase in traffic through the house might bring undesirable characters. No one was likely to check the ceiling for something to steal.

She stood on the bed and pushed the plank. It yielded, so she moved it aside and dislodged a cloud of dust that made her cough. She stood on her tiptoes and looked around inside, finding a crawlspace. Her valuables ought to be safe there unless the house burned.

She hitched up her skirt, took off her money belt and laid it on top of a rafter. What else should she stick up there? Her shotgun. No, she would keep it handy. Her silverware, hard money, Blake's spare clothes, one after another she tucked each item into the hiding place until she filled it. She replaced the plank. The telltale space vanished once the plank was re-aligned.

The dinner bell rang. She was over feeling sick, might keep it down this time. She needed all the strength she could muster.

The family was already seated at the supper table, and Judith noted an extra place setting. Mr. Oliver and his wife looked fuming mad. Their youngest sons, Joe and Billy, wriggled, giggled, jostled and punched each other. "Stop fidgeting or I'll whip you," Mr. Oliver snapped. "Bow down your heads and we'll ask the blessing."

Dr. Thompson strode in and sat down before Mr. Oliver intoned the "Amen." Ignoring the family, he piled his plate high with food even though he had just been wrist-deep in gore. He poured amber liquid from a flask into his water glass and took a sip.

Billy sculpted his mashed potatoes with his spoon and said in a loud voice, "There's a dead man in the back yard. I seen him."

Mrs. Oliver paled. "Billy! Hush."

"Never mind, Edith. The boy brought it up, so I might as well get on with it." Mr. Oliver glowered at the surgeon. "Sir, just what do you intend to do about the corpse?"

"Fatalities will be carried off for burial. We'll see to it tomorrow."

"Tomorrow ain't soon enough," grunted Mr. Oliver.

"It's the best we can do." Dr. Thompson took a bite out of a drumstick and talked as he chewed. "By the way, we have to take down some of the planks in your fence so we can bring ambulances right up to the house. You better secure your livestock."

Mr. Oliver banged his fist on the table. "You are vandalizing my property and I will not stand for it!"

"We'll replace the fence when we're finished. It won't help to get worked up over it. All for the greater good, you know." Dr. Thompson shoveled another forkful of mashed potatoes into his mouth.

"Greater good be blasted!" Mr. Oliver stood up, throwing his napkin down onto the table. "Who is your commanding officer?"

"General Hampton," said Dr. Thompson.

"Where is he?" Mr. Oliver demanded.

Dr. Thompson swallowed. "Cole house."

"I'm going to see him about this outrage."

"Have at it." Dr. Thompson took another drink and helped himself to a chicken breast. "Might as well wait until after supper, though."

Mr. Oliver must have thought that was good advice because he sat back down and attended to his dinner plate.

Judith picked at a wing. The mashed potatoes seemed to settle comfortably inside her stomach. Maybe she wouldn't lose this meal.

"Didn't you hear the big guns just about sunset?" Mrs. Oliver shuddered. "The windows rattled so, I thought they would shatter. And the cries of that poor dying man." Her voice caught and she daubed at her eyes with her napkin.

"I should go to Raleigh like my husband told me," Judith said.

"It's too late now," Dr. Thompson said. "The roads are jammed. Impassible with troops and wagon trains."

"I didn't figure on that." The chicken she had eaten felt like a lead sinker.

An attendant came to the dining room door. "Fresh meat, Dr. Thompson."

Chapter
Thirty

After dark, Judith sensed Blake coming into the parlor. She heard his boot-tread, his low, hard-controlled voice saying "Judith."

She stood up and turned to face him. No blood, thank God. He scowled and the black powder stains looked like war paint. She smiled nervously. "Are you all right?"

His gray eyes narrowed. The muscles tightened over his cheeks and his hands balled into fists. "Why the hell are you still here? Are you out of your mind?" His voice hit her in staccato blows.

"Not so loud. You'll wake him up." She pointed to David Frank, who lay sleeping on the couch, drugged with laudanum. His arm, bound in a fresh bandage and sling, rested across his waist. Seepage dyed the dressing bright red.

She picked at her skirt, wanting to talk about anything but herself. "The doctor's trying to save his arm, but the bone's all splintered. He'll decide in the morning whether to amputate."

Blake stared at David and not at her, so she chattered on. "He asked me to sit with him. Remembered me from camp. He gave me your handkerchiefs. The ones I monogrammed. I'm going to wash them out. The opium is letting him sleep--"

He shook his head, looking dazed. "We aren't going to have this discussion in front of people. Let's get some privacy."

Judith picked up a candle and led him upstairs, his boot steps thudding behind her. She slipped into the bedroom and Blake slammed the door. "Jude, what in God's name--"

She swallowed even though her mouth felt dry. "You aren't mad, are you?"

"Mad? What is the matter with you? Why can't you do what I

tell you? Just once, for a change?"

She took a deep breath and met his fury face on. "I thought it would be better if I stayed," she said calmly.

"You thought it would be better?" She sensed more anguish in him than rage. "Look around you. Is this better?"

"I was going to do what you said, but after you left I just couldn't. I had this feeling--" She shrugged, unable to articulate what she felt.

"You've really done it up big this time." His voice was weary. "Not only did you defy me, you've endangered yourself, and our child. Why didn't you go when you had the chance?"

"I need to stay close to you, in case something happens."

"It already has."

She crossed her arms over her chest. "I can still leave if I need to."

"You'll never get through. Not with thousands of troops headed this way."

Dr. Thompson had said the same thing.

"This isn't about Sally, is it?" he said.

Judith lifted her chin. "Has she been after you again?"

"I've been watching the Yankees, not women."

"What's become of her?" Judith asked.

"Unlike you, wife, I presume she had sense enough to clear out."

Judith bit her lip to keep from lashing back.

"I have had nothing to do with her," he continued. "I think she went to Raleigh. Colonel Causey made the arrangements." He sat down heavily on the edge of the bed. "Jude, something awful could happen to you." His voice broke.

She sat next to him and slid her arm over his taut shoulders, understanding that his concern for her added to his troubles. "It wasn't Sally I was worried about. I was afraid you would get hurt, and I wouldn't be able to do anything about it. Or even know, so far away."

"Next time you have a chance to clear out, take it, will you?"

She nodded, meaning it.

"We have to work together on things." He raised his hand to his temple and rubbed as though soothing a headache. "From now on, just do what I say."

Again she held her tongue, although she longed to tell him what she thought of his one-sided idea of working together.

"You'd better be gone the next time I come back," he told her.

"I'll do my best." She took a deep breath, not wanting to burden him further. "But how will you find me?"

"I will. I'll find you." He shut his eyes. "I am so tired. I'm tired of fighting, and killing, and being half crazy for worry. Now the Yankees are upon us."

"At least you know where to find me now, and I can hardly ever say that about you," she pointed out.

"You can this time. Right in between you and the Yankees."

A fresh jolt of fear shot through her. "Darling, no," she breathed. "Don't take risks. Not for my sake."

"Don't take risks?" He gave her a wry smile. "I'm a soldier."

"I mean it."

"I know how to take care of myself."

She rested her head on his shoulder. "How long before you have to go back?"

"Not long."

She ran her hand down, over his thigh. "No telling when we'll get to see each other again."

His warm hand covered hers completely. "I'll take the time."

"Hold me," she said, and nestled against his war-scented body. His arms came around her, and everything seemed all right. She longed to memorize the feel of him wrapping himself around her, sheltering her.

~ * ~

The next morning, Blake felt like the worm on the end of a hook. The trap better be ready to spring, because the little force of cavalry in his charge--the bait--couldn't hold off the quarry any longer.

He retreated toward the Confederate lines and ordered his men to check their mounts to a taunting, slow trot. Simmons rushed past him. "Hold up, damn you, Simmons!" he yelled. "If the Yankees don't get you, I will!"

Simmons obeyed, glancing over his shoulder at him. Blake's authority held for the moment, at least. It was hell trying to keep men like Simmons from bolting, using fleet horses to get away from danger.

The fight had become more and more a personal matter. Judith was stuck only a little way behind the lines. He had to do his best to keep the Yankees from getting to her.

He passed the Cole farmhouse, until this morning Hampton's headquarters. He continued through the fortifications. On either side of the road the infantrymen hunkered down behind their barricades, rifles ready, waiting for the gray horsemen to pass through, searching with hard veteran eyes for their blue targets.

"Come on, come on, I'll get you," one of them chanted as he sighted along his rifle barrel. A florid officer, saber uplifted, voice quavering, told his men to be steady.

Blake waved the troopers through the works. After the last one passed, he rode into the dew-misted screen of woods before he paused to look back. The bluecoats jogged forward, heads thrust forward like bulldogs, sun glinting off their bayonets, cheering their deep, measured hurrahs.

Fire and smoke spat from rifles all along the line, spraying lead into the thick of the oncoming Yankees. A battery positioned to the right boomed and spewed canister shot into the crowd. A triumphant howl arose from the works.

Blake turned Magic and cantered to report as ordered. He asked his way to where Hampton and Johnston and their aides had stationed themselves. They sat on their horses watching the action.

Hampton lowered his field glasses when Blake rode up and returned his salute. "Commendable, Captain Winberry." He looked relaxed, as though supervising the laborers on Millwood, back in the days before Sherman's men destroyed it. Payback time today.

Hampton waved toward the action and said to Johnston, "Hoke's men broke the charge. See there, sir? The fugitives are hiding in that ravine."

"They won't let it go at that." Johnston sat erect in the saddle. "They will mass for a real assault. Can't expect Hoke's Division to hold them off without assistance." Taut-faced, he said to an aide, "Major Falconer, ride back and find General Cheatham and ascertain why in the devil his troops haven't arrived. Impress upon him the urgency of having his division in place immediately."

Falconer wheeled his horse and rushed away. Blake said to Hampton, "Orders, General?"

"Stand by. We may need your men to fill in the gaps."

~ * ~

Lexi tripped and fell forward. She pushed herself up, withdrew her hands from the clammy muck and wiped them on her trousers. She grabbed the rifle she dropped, just saving it from getting stepped on. She pushed to her feet and pressed forward through the clinging underbrush that shredded her clothes and crisscrossed her stinging face with scratches. Captain O'Donnell shouted something in between swear words about getting a move on.

She caught up with the others when they went to ground and started digging with bayonets, cups and plates. She set down her rifle and imitated them, infected by their haste and by the spattering of gunfire to the left, where the Yankees were assaulting another part of the line. The men grabbed fallen limbs, small logs, whatever wood they could find to build up the breastworks.

By the time they piled enough earth and timber in front of them to absorb bullets, she still hadn't caught her breath. She was dirty and muddy from her short hair to the soles of her boots. Even her underwear was gritty as sandpaper.

She grabbed a cartridge and chewed on the paper to rip it open so she could load the rifle. Mentally she went over the steps. Lewis told her if she didn't remember to shoot every time she loaded, she would blow her fool head off.

"Here they come," called out Captain O'Donnell. "Hold your fire until you hear the order."

Lexi stuck her head up over the top of the earthworks. Her throat went dry when she saw the solid line of blue striding toward her, banners flying, moving with the athletic ripple of a single beast, intent on killing her.

"Ready! Aim!"

Lexi leveled the rifle barrel on the pile of dirt, toward the middle of the batch of oncoming soldiers. She concentrated on aiming at gut level. They closed in, convincing her they were going to come down on her before she could do anything to stop them. She waited for an order for what seemed like forever, didn't dare shoot, her fear building. She held onto the rifle tight so her hands wouldn't shake so much and snugged the stock hard against her shoulder to absorb the kick.

"Fire."

She squeezed the trigger and the stock rammed into her shoulder. The crash of rifles numbed her ears. Smoke puffed in clouds, obscuring her vision so she could not even see what she had shot at. She yanked the rifle down, fumbled to reload it, fingers shaking. She could hardly see what she was doing through her watery eyes.

She brought the rifle up to fire again. The smoke lifted a little and the fragmented blue beast reassembled and surged forward again in a cheering mass. She fired, opened another cartridge, jammed down the ramrod, panted, grimaced, dimly aware of her comrades. Again and again and again, she fired and reloaded.

Through the cloud of white smoke she made out a look of horrified disbelief on one man's face. His mouth formed in an O, he stumbled forward and let himself down easy, as though only lying down for a rest.

She saw arms thrown up, legs sliding out from under Yankees. Men screamed, stricken. A flag drooped as its bearer fell, popped up when another man seized it, fell again. Only then did the Yankees break and run for cover. Some dropped before they reached it.

"We got 'em on the run," yelled a Confederate. "We whipped 'em."

Lexi rasped in a deep breath and looked around. Captain O'Donnell lay on his side clutching his stomach and vomiting blood. Other men had fallen in the ditch. Smoke drifted upwards from the field, strewn with blue heaps.

She hugged the hot rifle barrel to her chest, closed her wet eyes and shuddered. She couldn't stop shaking. The captain's choked groans echoed down into her center. Her ears rang, her shoulder felt battered and she coughed from the smoke.

Lewis slapped her on the back and laughed wildly. "Good going, kid, steady does it. Now you seen the elephant."

~ * ~

The distant crackle of gunfire awakened Judith early. She found work to take her mind off her worry, making pallets for the wounded by stuffing feed sacks with straw.

She carried them past the man Dr. Thompson had carved on yesterday afternoon. Well enough to walk around and do for himself, he sat on the front porch listening to the guns. Inside, David Frank lay on the couch and watched her arrange the pallets on the parlor floor.

He wasn't doing very well. Eyes sunk in their sockets, his face rigid, denying the pain. His swollen, oozing arm was still attached, but it wouldn't be for long.

"Can I get you anything, David?" she said.

"A new arm, maybe? The doctor acts like it's nothing. Like I'm a salamander that can grow a new one after he chops it off."

The surgeon strode into the parlor with his assistants and said, "Take down both those doors."

The noise of the demolition brought Mrs. Oliver storming into the room. "Doctor, what on earth are you doing?"

"We'll lay those doors across sawhorses," the doctor explained, his voice enthusiastic. "They make dandy tables."

"What? You are destroying my home."

"Madam, we have to make do with whatever is available. We aren't going to hack them up, and we'll leave all the outside doors intact."

"If only Mr. Oliver were here, he would keep you from doing that." She folded her arms and inclined her head. "He went to see your General Hampton about removing you and these men from our home."

The surgeon shrugged and turned to his assistants. "Set up one in here, the other can go outside in that tool shed." He walked over to David, who blanched even paler at the sight of him, picked up the wrist of his sound arm and timed the pulse with his pocket watch. "Good and solid. Won't be long now, sonny. I want to get you done before the rush hits. You'll be well rid of that mess. I can even leave you the elbow joint."

After Dr. Thompson had David taken outside, the first ambulances of the day brought in a few more wounded. Judith gave each of the exhausted men a drink of water. All strangers this time, thank goodness, reeking of blood and dirt and the excrement that caked their bodies. She expected to be sick again, but after a few turns her stomach settled.

She supposed she could get used to just about anything.

The cannons boomed so close they rattled the windows.

Mr. Oliver ran into the parlor white-faced, eyes wide and rolling like a buggered horse's. "Edith!"

"Yes, Henry. You needn't shout," she said from the next room. She came to the doorway. "Did you see General Hampton yet? Are we going to get rid of all this?"

"Never got that far. I like to got killed. A shell came down near me and spooked the horses." He ripped a handkerchief from his pocket and mopped his brow. "Gather up the children and the servants. We're leaving."

"Now? Where?" Mrs. Oliver asked.

"I don't know and I don't care. Jump, woman."

"The doctor said we'd never get through," his wife protested. "All the soldiers coming this way."

"Don't give me no lip!"

The Olivers, their offspring and housemaid scurried in all directions to pack and load the family carriage. Judith started up the stairs to gather her belongings and pack her wagon. That was the only sensible thing to do. Clear out.

She paused half way up the stairs. Attendants were carrying David Frank back into the house, surgery finished, injured arm a bandaged stump. His head wagged from side to side, but when he caught sight of her he stilled and he kept his eyes on her. Better go tell him goodbye.

She bent over him. He gave her a wan smile and raised his remaining hand. His fingers trembled with weakness. "Would you mind very much sitting with me a minute?" he whispered. "I don't feel so good."

Mr. Oliver hustled by, shouting orders to his servants who were struggling with steamer trunks. They would soon be gone and if she didn't quickly pack her belongings into her wagon and go she would miss her chance to travel in their company.

She looked into David's face, full of desperation and need. What if they brought Blake to the house hurt and needing her and she was gone to Raleigh and couldn't do a thing, wouldn't even know…

She was only making more trouble for herself, but she couldn't help it.

"All right, David. I will stay as long as you need me."

~ * ~

Lexi stared out across the field, at the blue bodies clumped along the high-water mark of the Federal assault, some still moving. Stretcher-bearers had removed Captain O'Donnell. Behind the breastworks, the living shoved aside the dead to make room. Spurts of gunfire broke out at random. Somewhere to her left a regimental band was playing "Marseillaise."

Couriers cantered their horses up and down the line. An officer she didn't know rode by on a buckskin horse, saber aloft, haranguing the troops about liberty and home and mother and such as that.

She made sure her rifle was loaded, fixed the bayonet and adjusted the cartridge box on her belt. No quitter, she made up her mind to see the thing through. But her hands still shook.

A bugle pierced the air, sounding a charge. She followed her comrades, vaulted onto the other side of the barrier and started running toward the Yankees.

A yell burst from her insides, spewing excitement and fear from her system. Regimental flags flew close together. Regiments mustered company-size in this army.

She ran over dead Yankees, leaped and stumbled to avoid them, accidentally stepped into a yielding body, kept going. She narrowly missed one who was still living, caught a glimpse of fear-crazed eyes and heard yells as her foot pounded the earth next to him.

She ran on, cradling her rifle in her arms, toward the booms and rising smoke of Federal artillery. A shell chuffed down to her left. The explosion blew dirt treetop high and she caught a glimpse of an arm and a shoe flying upwards. Lewis sprinted past her. She struggled to balance the heavy rifle, elongated by a bayonet. As much as getting shot, she feared she would trip and get trampled.

Puffs of smoke from enemy rifles marked their position along the woods. Now and again a head poked up, taking aim. A soldier near her cried out and fell, disappearing. Another shell exploded to her left. She felt hot wind and heard awful screams. Gasping for breath, she kept going on rubbery legs, falling behind, minie balls singing past her.

Now one of the Yankees leaped up, showed his back and ran. Others followed his lead. She felt a savage thrill and wanted to pursue.

The first Confederates to reach the works shot and clubbed and jabbed the few bluecoats that would not run or give up. She paused and leaned against a tree, panting, as bayonet wielding Confederates herded together prisoners. A few dead men, most of them wearing blue, drooped along the line of the works.

She looked behind her at the gray bodies scattered along the path of the charge. A man was crawling in circles on his hands and knees. Something hung from his middle. Gutted. She jerked her eyes away but afterward she saw him no matter where she looked.

Lewis gave her a comradely shove. "They done showed us some good running, kid. Now we'll run 'em clear out of the country. Less go."

She nodded, and unable to speak, picked up her rifle and followed Lewis. A shell come down in front of them and exploded, a storm of wind and dirt and heat and wetness and pressure. She fell backwards and the world went black.

~ * ~

Judith did whatever she could think of to soothe David Frank. She propped what remained of his arm on a pillow, gave him brandy and water, bathed sweat off his face and urged him to eat fried chicken and light bread she raided from the deserted kitchen. After he settled down, drowsy, she took a bucket and cup outside to water thirsty men.

The Oliver house was in such a convenient location that other surgeons besides Dr. Thompson had set up shop there. The house overflowed with wounded men, doctors and attendants.

She glanced toward the outbuilding where the surgeons were doing their cutting just in time to see a leg chucked out the window. It landed atop the pile of human flesh and slid downward to rest on the ground. Someone inside the building was whimpering.

She gritted her teeth, refilled the bucket from the well and turned to looked over the wounded who lay out in the yard unattended. Hopeless cases? The doctors seemed to think so. Some struggling, others quiet, all suffering. She decided to do something about it.

The first one she came to was slack-jawed and vacant-eyed and dead. She passed him and went to the next soldier.

He was a captain, the same rank as her husband, gore all over his face and middle. Shot in the stomach, he shouldn't drink. But what did that matter now? She dipped just enough water into the cup to wet his mouth, raised his head and gave it to him.

"More, please," he whispered.

"The way you're hurt, too much isn't good for you."

"I don't want to die." He grabbed her hand. "I'm not ready."

She hesitated, her throat constricting, then found her voice. "After I've attended to the others I'll get a doctor to look at you."

What was the use? The doctors decreed he must die and were making sure of it. No one had bothered to dress his wound or tend to him until she came along.

She had to pry his hand off hers before she could move away. She passed by a man who was unconscious, but every breath made a gurgling moan as the air blew in and out of the gap in his chest. Another had raw meat where his under jaw should have been. His tongue hung slack, unsupported. She averted her eyes so she wouldn't faint or throw up and poured water into the mouth-hole. Somehow he managed to swallow some of it.

She gave water to the last of the dying and sought out Dr. Thompson. She found him tying off a leg wound. The jetting artery sprayed blood all over his apron. Red ran down and dripped on the floor.

"A man over there," she waved toward the outcasts, "Wants somebody to take a look at him."

"It would be a waste of time."

"He wants to live."

"I can't help that." He rubbed his chin and left a bloody smear. "Nobody wants to believe they're going to die."

"I'll dress his wound." She picked up a handful of lint and a swatch of linen.

"Suit yourself." He reached into his medical kit, pulled out a bottle and unscrewed the lid. He sniffed the contents and took a swallow.

Outside, she refilled the bucket, walked over to the captain and knelt by him. He lay quiet, eyes shut. She started to open his shirt to expose the wound, then realized he was no longer breathing. Her fingers stilled on the buttons and she shivered. She hadn't realized he was that close to gone.

She couldn't do a thing for him now. She dipped her ladle in the bucket and moved to the next soldier.

Chapter
Thirty-one

Lexi struggled to consciousness in the dark. A weight bore
down on her chest. She groped to shove it away. She felt
around until her hand connected with something fleshy: not smooth
skin, more like cool moist meat. Above that, hair. Somebody's
head. Good thing she couldn't see it, but she imagined it mangled
and torn. She pushed the corpse and it fell away stiff.

Lanterns and heat lightning silhouetted moving figures and
ambulances with their teams. From the darkness came moans.
Someone prayed, another cried. The voices sounded very far off.
Her ears rang and her head hurt. She held a shaky hand to her face,
caked with damp dirt, found a cut on her forehead. She felt herself
from the neck down, but found no other hurts.

The shell blast must have stunned her. "Lewis," she whispered.
She reached for the body, then withdrew her hand. He had taken
the explosion and the shrapnel into himself, shielding her.

No more Captain O'Donnell, no more Lewis. No idea where
the rest of Cheatham's Division was, or whether any of them were
still alive.

She swept her arm out, found her rifle and closed her fingers
around the barrel. She found her slouch hat, put it on, and stood
up. Her legs worked, but they were stiff.

She walked to the lanterns and the ambulances, into a circle
of light. Someone shined a lantern in her face. She blinked in the
glare.

"How bad you hurt, boy?" His voice sounded distorted, as
though her head was under water.

"Not too bad, I think."

"You're all bloody. You sure?"

"Blood?" She touched her face. "I don't think much of it's mine."

"You a Yank or a Reb?"

She tensed. Could he be an enemy? She squinted, dazzled by the lantern, couldn't make out what color uniform he was wearing.

"It don't make no difference to me, boy." His voice was gentle. "I'm a chaplain. Nobody's enemy. But if you're a Yank I got to take your weapon."

"I'm not a Yank." She tightened her grip on the breech of her rifle and drew it close.

"Fine," he said. "Don't have ambulance room for anybody that can walk, but you can sit over there and rest, then follow us to the hospital."

"Did we win?"

"We still got the ground, don't we? We pushed 'em a good ways before they stopped us."

"Good." She started toward the ambulance, but hesitated. Couldn't let any doctors look at her. They would send her back to Columbia.

She wasn't ready to quit. Not until she found Hunter, and she would make up her mind what to do next.

~ * ~

Next morning Lexi stood behind a tree outside General Hampton's headquarters, watching busy couriers and staff hustle about. She didn't speak to them for fear they would ask too many questions. They seemed preoccupied with running the war, uninterested in a scruffy young private.

If she stayed long enough, Hunter was bound to turn up. She might even see Blake, but could not let him spot her. She did not dwell on the possibility that either of them could be dead.

Judging from the intermittent sounds of rifle and artillery, much thinner than yesterday's, the battle was at a standstill. She didn't try to seek out the Tennessee company that had left her for dead. Because she would not give her real name to the ambulance personnel, and pretended to be too dazed to remember her unit, she assumed she would be listed as missing in action under the name of Alex Wilson.

Last night she had stuck with the ambulance for want of a better plan and followed it to the field hospital so she could get something to eat. She also had found water and washed herself. She figured she could avoid the doctors because they would be busy working on men who were hurt worse than she was.

But she didn't count on running into her sister-in-law drawing water from the well. She slipped away before Judith recognized her.

From there she wandered into Bentonville, washed off in Mill Creek, and took up with soldiers who had a fire going. She spent the night trying to sleep so she could blank out what it was like to wake up wearing the brains of a friend.

She found her horse where she had left him but did not try to reclaim him because she would rather stay missing. Maybe Hunter would be able to get him back.

Her ears still rang and she hurt all over, even her eyeballs. Before, she had imagined Hunter would be glad to see her. Now she wasn't so sure.

~ * ~

Judith picked her way through the groaning, bleeding bodies carrying two empty buckets. The wounded weren't coming in as fast as yesterday, but even a few were too many. The authorities were starting to evacuate those who could be moved. Progress was so slow it didn't seem to make a dent in the numbers.

She walked to the well and cranked up the pail. An ambulance pulled into the yard, blood dripping from the floorboards, but such a sight no longer excited her alarm, or even much interest. Attendants wearily hauled the passengers out one by one, placing them on the ground near the porch.

She filled the buckets and carried them toward the newly arrived wounded only a few steps away. Lately she had thought a great deal about how many steps it took to go anywhere, because her feet and legs ached so.

She saw a soldier leading Fancy, hitched to her wagon, around the house into the front yard. She set down the buckets, ran over to him, and grabbed the reins.

"What are you doing with that mule?" she demanded.

"Let go, lady. I got orders."

"Whose orders?" she demanded.

"All the way up to General Johnston."

"Stay right there until I get back." She hurried into the house and found Dr. Thompson bending over the table in the parlor, suturing together a hole in a man's side.

"Dr. Thompson, they are taking my mule!"

He didn't even look up. "I'll see that you get a receipt."

"I don't want a receipt, I want them to leave my mule alone. Once they take it, I'll never get it back."

"I can't do a thing to help you." He poked the needle through the man's flesh and drew it out deftly, knitting the gap closed. "We need all the vehicles and draft animals we can find. Must remove these men."

"Not my vehicle."

"Mrs. Winberry, I can't do anything for you. That's just the way it is." He tied and snipped the horsehair suture, then looked up at her, not unkindly. "I know it seems like a harsh blow, especially in view of how hard you've been working for our wounded, but the greater good..." He shrugged.

"Never mind. I've heard that speech before."

~ * ~

Hunter dismounted in front of Hampton's headquarters. The Confederates were already calling yesterday's business a success despite their losses. God save them from such brilliant victories.

The intelligence he had gathered this morning revealed that the Confederates were about to snatch defeat from the jaws of the so-called triumph. So far they had been tangling with the surprised and disorganized Federal left wing. After Sherman had caught on, he sent the rest of his army to the fight. By afternoon there would be twice as many Yankees closing in on Bentonville.

He looked up from tying his horse and noticed a slight, beat-up soldier at his elbow, looking as though he got the worst of a fistfight.

"Hunter..."the soldier's voice was familiar, and something about the face.

"Lexi." He stepped toward her, but stopped. "What the devil are you doing here? How--"

"Aren't you glad to see me?"

She looked at him expectantly. Cut face, bloodstained clothes, holding a Springfield rifle in the crook of her elbow. She was a mess, battered and exhausted. He absorbed what she had done. What it must have cost her to get here was one mystery, but why was the bigger one.

He hated admitting it to himself, but he had missed her. Seeing her again was a sweet shock. "You astonish me, Lexi."

"I want to join up."

"Come." He grabbed her arm and escorted her around the corner of the house, away from sight and hearing of anyone, then he turned her around to face him.

"You are looking to get yourself killed," he said. "Appears you almost succeeded. I ought to notify your brother you're here."

"Why?" She grinned bravely. "He's just my brother. You're my husband, remember?"

He had almost forgotten that detail. "Then it's up to me to send you packing."

Her grin didn't falter. "You're not going to do that."

He smiled back. "I must admit you went to a lot of trouble to track me down."

"I want to ride with you, do what you do."

He shook his head. "Just what I need."

Her eyes flashed blue fire. "I'm a good soldier. Yesterday I fought and shot straight and didn't show the white feather."

"I never said you weren't brave. That has nothing to do with it."

She lifted her chin. "I can pull my weight."

His respect for her grew. "You have a horse?"

"He's with the supply train. I need you to get him back."

She would be a comfort to have around if he could figure out how to keep her from getting killed, or getting him killed. He nodded. "I guess you've earned the right, at least for the time being. First I'll attend to my business with General Hampton, then we'll steal your horse back."

~ * ~

That night Blake persuaded another officer to spell him for a couple of hours. It was his first opportunity to see Judith in the past two days, but he would rather find her missing, gone to Smithfield.

The Yankees weren't likely to attack after dark, just toss a few shells into the Confederate lines so nobody would sleep for fear of waking up dead. Hampton had placed him in command of a skinny extension of the left part of the line and he had spent the day waiting for a Yankee assault that did not come. But he had heard that Sherman's whole army was drawn together now, three Yankees to every Confederate.

As he neared the Oliver house, the odor of gore made Magic balk. In no humor to fight a skittish horse, he tethered her a long way from the house. Tents covered some of the wounded men strewn in the front yard, the rest shivered in the rain. Lanterns burning on the porch cast light through the windows of the house, and lit the open door of an outbuilding. Inside, a doctor bent over a table, trying to save a man's life by mutilating him.

He walked through a narrow passage on the porch between bloodied men lying in rows and entered the house. In the hallway, he held his breath to avoid inhaling the stench of vomit, urine and dying flesh.

Pools of blood, fresh and dried, tainted every square foot of floor that wasn't covered by a wounded man. His gaze was drawn to a writhing, bloody man, hands moving, moving, moving, clawing at the bandages covering his eyes.

Red smeared the wallpaper waist-high. A brittle hopeless laugh crackled over the low chorus of groans and whimpers. An attendant staggered by carrying a pail.

Blake found Judith in the ruin of the first floor gallery. She was sitting on the floor beside a man whose hands were bandaged, spooning gruel into his mouth. Her eyes and her cheeks were hollow, her hair stringy and unkempt. An apron protected the front of her old dress, but the hem had dragged through blood.

Involved, she didn't look at him right away. He paused, seeing her in a new way. "Jude," he said.

She jerked up so quick she almost dropped the bowl. "You aren't wounded, are you?"

He shook his head no. "I was hoping you were out of here by now."

They were standing apart. Between them, the man she was feeding looked up at him, wary. He was a big, strapping fellow, blue coat draped over his shoulders. Judith helping a Yankee?

"Couldn't leave." Her shoulders drooped. "They confiscated Fancy and the wagon." Her words slurred with exhaustion. "Said they didn't have enough ambulances to take the wounded to Smithfield."

"Didn't you tell them they belong to a Confederate officer?"

She shook as if weeping. Ragged laughter. "Now you claim that ratty old mule!"

The room went quiet, everybody listening. Blake said, "Let's go to your room."

"My bed is full of wounded men."

"For God's sake, Jude. Where are you going to sleep?"

"I'll just pick a spot on the floor. I'm tired enough to sleep anywhere."

He stepped around the prisoner, took her hand, and led her through the doorway, as far away from the other men as he could manage.

She swayed as though dizzy. He caught her by her arms. "Look at you, Jude. You're working yourself into the ground."

"Whenever I stop, somebody dies."

"Oh, Jude." He slipped his arms around her and gathered her to himself.

She nestled against him, breathing a deep sigh, and they stood supporting each other for a long moment.

"They moved David to Smithfield this morning." She pulled two handkerchiefs from her apron pocket and pressed them into his hand. "Here. I tried to get the blood out but I suppose they're ruined."

He stuffed them into his pocket without examining them. "Thanks. It doesn't matter."

"It's going slow--the evacuation--that's why they took our wagon. Too many wounded, not enough ambulances, bad roads and only one bridge. To think grown men plan these things."

"We ought to be withdrawing early tomorrow," he said. "I'll come get you if you haven't found a way out by then."

She nodded. "You'll be careful, won't you? I'm terrified for you."

"That won't help anything."

She rested against him. "I love you. More than anything in the world, I want to keep you."

"I love you, Jude," he murmured into her ear. She held onto him fiercely. He lingered until the last possible moment.

~ * ~

Lexi followed Hunter into the darkness behind a screen of brush, away from where the other scouts had bedded down. He had explained her presence to them in sketchy terms. She had gone along with the story, trying to convince them. All day long she and Hunter had remained at arm's length so they wouldn't give themselves away. He had not cut her any slack, maybe trying to convince her she had better give up, not reckoning on her determination. Life as a soldier was turning out to be even harder than she'd expected, but she was proud to be holding up her end.

She helped him lay a waterproof on the wet ground and spread a couple of blankets and another waterproof over the top. A tough day had followed a hellish one and she could stand a few hours' sleep.

"We won't get too wet unless there's a flood," he said. "We're behind the picket lines so the Yanks won't surprise us."

She crawled between the damp blankets without taking off her clothes and he crawled in next to her. Nobody would think anything of it. Soldiers slept in pairs to conserve blankets and body heat. She curled against his wiry body, glad she could talk freely. "I shocked you pretty good this morning, didn't I?"

He nuzzled her neck, no longer keeping his distance. "I stood it all right."

"I think J. C. knows. He's been looking at me right funny, and when we went off together, I thought he was going to follow us and--"

"I'll handle him."

She felt his hand under her shirt, fondling her breast, his mouth coming down on hers. He smelled of stale sweat and tobacco smoke, and that was all right.

No matter they had the preacher's blessings this time, they had to do it fast to lessen the risk of somebody catching them. She worked aside enough of her clothing to let him get to her. His active weight bore down on her bruised body but she didn't try to stop him because she wanted him even if it hurt. She forgot caution and let out an excited cry. He moved his hand over her mouth and the only sound either of them made after that was their hard breathing.

Chapter
Thirty-two

Mid-afternoon the next day Blake was still waiting for the order to pull out. He dug a square of hardtack out of his pocket. The dampness had softened it enough to make it edible. He hunkered inside his dripping poncho and gnawed on the cracker, listening to the incessant crackle of gunfire.

"Hear that?" Cheney said. "It's getting closer. Over to the right."

He glanced down the overgrown farm road his squadron straddled, saw nothing but black jack oak, slash pine and the stream at the bottom of the slope. He had dismounted his men and posted them in a skirmish line about ten feet apart in two tiers, a third held in reserve, horses tethered at the rear.

"Wheeler's men to our right," he noted. "I guess they're catching hell about now."

"If the Yanks are looking for a weak spot, they'll sure find one here," Cheney said.

"Maybe the reinforcements I applied for will come."

"Don't think I'll hold my breath." Cheney took off his hat and knocked off drops of rainwater. "Line's thin as a politician's promises."

"Yeah," Blake grunted. "And our part is the thinnest."

The artillery opened up, close enough for him to feel the vibrations. He stuck the unfinished hardtack into his pocket and reached for his Enfield.

Hampton had ordered him to hold the line at all hazards. Hold it or die trying. He understood the critical nature of his position. If the Yankees broke through, they would discover the entire line was an empty eggshell, nobody inside to stop them. Once they took the bridge across Mill Creek, they would have Johnston's whole Army of Tennessee surrounded. Along with his wife, who was still stranded in that house turned hellhole.

He turned to Jimmy Caldwell. "Jimmy, shin up that tree and tell me what's going on."

Jimmy pulled himself up the oak until he was about ten feet in the air. "Yanks, sir. They're coming right at us across the field, on the other side of the woods."

"How many?"

"Lots. Hundreds, maybe thousands."

"How far away?"

"Couple of hundred yards. I can make 'em out pretty good beyond the trees."

"Do you see flags?"

"Yes, sir."

"Count them."

"One, two, three…"

When Jimmy got to six regimental flags, Cheney said, "We are really in for it now."

Blake said, "That's enough, Jimmy. Come down."

The boy jumped from the lowest branch. Blake told him in a forcibly level voice, "Get your horse and split it back to General Hampton or whomever the hell you can find and tell him we're under strong attack. We must have reinforcements immediately if they expect us to hold."

Jimmy took off at a run and Blake ordered his reserves to the line. He cradled his rifle and crouched behind the biggest tree he could find. Gut and brain said run for your life. But duty did not leave room for common sense. The tic under his eye came back.

He looked over his thin line of men. How steady would they be on their fourth day of fighting? He was asking a lot. He cleared his tight throat. "Boys, hold your fire till I sing out. Make every bullet count. Let's make a lot of noise, like Gideon at Jericho."

Patches of blue moved through the woods, started down the far side of the slope, into the stream. A few stealthy riflemen slipped from cover to cover on each side of the road. His men cocked their rifles and pistols, prepared to defend themselves.

Blake took aim at the chest of one of the leaders, a dark blue smear half hidden in the brush. "Fire!" he shouted and squeezed the trigger. His target disappeared into the rifle smoke. He threw down the empty weapon, drew his Colt, cocked and fired, again and again and again.

The bluecoats cheered and pressed forward, shooting as they came, close enough for him to pick out belligerent faces. A small branch, shot loose, fell on his head, swept off his hat and raked his hair. The bluecoats splashed across the stream and poured down the road. He pointed toward them with his saber. "That way, for God's sake! Shoot that way!"

Several broke through untouched, then they were upon him, nothing but air between him and their rifles. He raised his revolver and fired at the nearest Yankee. It clicked. Empty.

"Kill that goddamn officer!" yelled one of the Yankees.

A rifle swung toward him. He gathered himself to spin away, felt the blast and the heat of the explosion in his face.

He heard the thud of the bullet hitting his chest, felt a heavy blow. Deep, searing pain sent shock waves through his body. He dropped his revolver, spun in mid-stride, lost his balance and fell forward. Tried to push up--too heavy. Clutched a handful of loam, cheek pressed against wet leaves, sensed enemy feet pounding toward him. Couldn't fight back, couldn't even get up.

He went limp, played dead, staring ahead, letting his mouth fall open, trying not to breathe. The bullet hole burned like a hot poker all the way through his body, front to back. A spasm ripped through his chest. Against his will he coughed, tasting blood.

He saw the smoking rifle barrel from the corner of his eye, poised over his back, bayonet fixed. One short lunge would bury the rusty blade between his shoulder blades and pin him to earth. He twisted around and lifted his hand to ward off the thrust, saying "No."

The Yankee paused, blinked, expression hostile but uncertain. He took a step forward, brandishing the bayonet. "I'm taking you prisoner."

Blake dropped his hand. "I guess you are." He let out a shuddering breath that brought more blood into his mouth.

His captor swung the bayonet aside. "I'm the one shot you. You had it coming." He knelt down, picked up the revolver, took the sword belt and gun belt and buckled the prizes around his own waist.

Another coughing fit seized Blake. He levered onto one elbow and spat onto the wet leaves then settled back, spent. He blinked through the rain at his captor. He inhaled, sucking cold air through the hole in his chest. It made an awful whistling sound.

He lay in the midst of the Yankees. They busied themselves reloading their rifles, pants muddy halfway up their thighs. His Yankee stood over him, possessive. Wasn't going to let anybody else finish him off. His right.

"What you got, Lowery?" an officer said.

"Reb captain."

"Good work."

"I got him good, but he's still alive, sir."

Warm blood soaked into Blake's clothes front and back. Shot clear through. Spitting blood. Lung shot. Sucking air. A prisoner. Got good, all right.

A group of officers pushed their way along the road with their mounted escort. Soldiers moved aside to let them through. Horses passed so close the muddy iron hooves just missed him. The officer who had just spoken saluted the general at their head.

"Well done, Colonel Curtis," the general said. "Any prisoners for me to question?"

"They skedaddled, General Mower sir, except for this officer we tumbled and a dead Reb over there. We got a bunch of their horses too."

"Can the officer talk?"

"He's still breathing, sir."

Mower tossed his reins to an aide and dismounted. A handsome, powerfully built man with a heavy beard. He knelt on one knee, rested his elbow on the other knee and looked over Blake with quick mobile eyes. "I see you're badly wounded. I regret that."

Blake whispered, "Thank you, sir." He was absolutely sure he out-regretted the general.

"You in charge of this part of the line?"

He nodded.

"Cavalry. Which one? Is this your hat? A palmetto. Hmmm. South Carolina cavalry. How many more people do you have tucked away in those woods?"

He could still fight, after a fashion. Let them think they were walking into a trap and they might get cautious, slow down. "Lots of 'em." Talking was a great effort.

"Who? What corps?"

Another cough shook him. The pain centered in his chest quivered through his whole being. He clamped his jaws to keep from screaming in front of his enemies.

Mower drummed his fingers against his thigh. "Don't expire before you tell me," the general ordered. "Which corps?"

"Stewart's. Cheatham's. Hardee's. Hampton's…"

One of the staff officers said, "General, we're dealing with Joe Johnston again, and he's got a new trick up his sleeve for every day of the week."

Mower sprang to his feet. "I'm not afraid of him. What's the matter? You scared?"

"No, sir. Of course not." The cautious officer looked around and reddened.

A muddy soldier ran up, saluted the officers, and announced that companies delayed by a bad swamp would be up in a few minutes.

"Have them double quick here," Mower said. The man ran off and the general turned to his staff, fist on hip. "Gentlemen, let us advance as soon as our forces unite. We can smash the rebels today."

Mower sure had it right. Blake said, "General, if you succeed… My wife is at our hospital. Please… see that she's protected?"

Mower whirled. "Your wife? Why in hell? You people. Colonel Curtis, have someone take this man out of the road. Later on we'll bring him along if there's anything to bring."

"Lowery," the colonel said. "You plugged him, you move him."

Lowery bent over him. "C'mon Johnny. Put your arm around my neck, throw your weight on me."

They passed close to a blood-basted Confederate Blake recognized. Simmons didn't cut and run this time. At the edge of the woods Lowery eased Blake down next to a tree. "You want to sit or lie down?"

"Sit."

One of the Yankees led Magic by. Patted her neck, gentled her as if he knew horses and liked a good one. Maybe he would treat her all right.

Dizzy, Blake closed his eyes. He coughed again and the violent movement rent him. Panic ran in tandem with the pain. Was he dying? How was he supposed to know? God, please no. Too much to lose.

He ran his left hand up to unbutton the coat and reveal the damage. His fingers trembled, weak and blunt.

"I'll do that, Johnny." Lowery brushed his hand aside and opened the waterproof and the jacket. He ripped the pullover shirt, peeled the soggy fabric off his shoulder and uncovered the weeping hole above his breast.

A few threads led into the purple wound. Blake tugged on them and pulled out a plug of saturated cloth. A new flow oozed out. Wasn't pumping or spurting, maybe he could stop it. Lowery took out his own handkerchief and pressed it against the wound. "I'm not sorry I shot you, Johnny, but I'd rather killed you outright."

Blake pulled the handkerchiefs Judith gave him out of his pocket. "Can't reach my back..."

Lowery took the handkerchiefs out of his hand and wadded them into the hollow between shoulder blade and spine.

Everything Lowery did to stanch the bleeding sent pain through his chest. He shut his eyes and bit the inside of his cheek hard enough to make that bleed too.

~ * ~

"Yanks!"

Yells and gunfire sounded close by. Judith roused herself from her exhausted stupor, opened the door and looked out. The guards were gone.

Gray soldiers splashed through the puddles in the road, running like sheep before a pack of dogs. One whirled, knelt, raised his rifle to his shoulder, fired and spun away.

Wounded men rushed through the doorway past her to stagger after their running comrades.

"Where you going?" she said to one of them.

"Don't want to be captured. You better come too."

More yelling and shooting, louder, closer. She shrank against the wall.

Where was Blake in all this? She prayed he was safe.

Some of the wounded men stumbled back. A panting fugitive threw himself on the porch floor, a trapped look on his washed-out face. Fresh blood reddened the bandage on his leg. He said, "I reckon I'm cotched."

A horde of bluecoats ran past along the road. Judith said, "It's got to be safer inside." She helped him into the hallway and left him lying against the wall. The house wasn't as crowded today. Most of the wounded and surgeons had already evacuated to Smithfield. She hadn't been able to hitch a ride on vehicles crammed with so many passengers the skinny draft animals could hardly pull them.

She rushed past the wounded Yankee prisoners who watched the door with glad anticipation. Of course they were satisfied at the turnabout, liberated while their captors were made prisoners. The one with some of his fingers shot off, Pearson, got up and followed her into the parlor.

She found Dr. Thompson standing over a table, picking splintered bone from the thigh of a sweating man. He glanced at her without pausing in his work. He had been hard at it for the past four days and nights. Eyes looked bruised, face shadowed with stubble, hands shook unless he steadied them on something. "What's going on? Are we getting unwelcome company?"

"Yankees. Our soldiers are running away."

"Prudent fellows."

"What should we do?"

"Invite them in, I suppose." He reached for a bottle of medicinal brandy and took a swig. "Otherwise they'll just break down the door."

"I have a shotgun upstairs--"

"Leave it there, unless you want to get us all killed."

The man on the table wiped his forehead and said, "Ma'am, would you please give me my coat? That one right there with the stars on the collar. Might as well let them know my rank."

She draped the gray coat over his middle and he clutched it to himself like a talisman. The doctor kept working and didn't seem concerned.

Pearson stood by her. He said, "You treated me kind and I'll see to it nobody bothers you, ma'am."

She nodded, glad to note how big the man was. She had observed little about him up to then, except that his hands were ruined and he couldn't feed himself. She guessed she would have helped a hurt wolf, too. Everywhere she turned there was somebody needing help and Yankees bled just as red as anyone else.

Heavy shoes tramped on the porch and the door banged open. Liberated prisoners cheered. Muddy bluecoats clumped into the parlor, rifles ready, looking around, jumpy. They paused, dripping rain from their waterproofs. She stared back at them, afraid to move or speak. Pearson slipped between her and his comrades.

Dr. Thompson said, "Put those guns away. This is a hospital. Didn't you see the yellow flag? "He scooped up a handful of lint and arranged it on the wounded man's thigh. The colonel was paler than ever, breathing hard and sweating.

One of the Yankees stepped forward. "It's ours now and you are my prisoner."

Dr. Thompson didn't bother look up. "You're not an officer, are you? I want to see an officer."

"Officer, hell. This is all the authority I need." The soldier raised his rifle and cut his eyes at Judith. Show-off.

Pearson laughed at him. "What a fightin' man! They got a chaplain you can gobble up while you're at it. Watch out, he might brain you with his Testament."

The soldier scowled.

Pearson stepped forward, serious now. "Leave the doc alone. He's been patching up our boys too."

The muddy soldier stalked off, grumbling.

Dr. Thompson wrapped a bandage around the colonel's leg as she watched from behind the shield of Pearson's big shoulders.

~ * ~

Lexi sat on her horse next to Hunter. They were with General Hampton not far from Johnston's headquarters. She had spent the day riding reconnaissance.

A courier galloped up, his horse's hooves scattering mud. He sawed the animal to a stop and yelled, "Sir, the Yanks have got through our left!"

Hampton turned to an aide. "Go back to that Georgia brigade and the battery we just passed and fetch 'em double quick. Lieutenant Lightfoot, round up all the mounted men you can find to hit 'em with."

Lexi followed Hunter at a gallop until they came to a small band of Texas cavalry that had been held in reserve. The ranking officer, a captain who didn't look any older than she was, hustled his troopers toward the rest of the men Hampton gathered. She did not know much about battles, but from the harassed look on Hunter's face they must be in serious trouble.

She waited for the order to charge the Yankees. Heard their noise, shooting and cheering, only a little way off. She pulled out her revolver, a weapon that made her any man's equal in deadliness.

Hunter looked at her and shook his head. "No. Stay here."

"Lieutenant--"

"That's an order."

"They'll think I'm scared."

"Don't argue with an officer."

She glared at him. "You're starting to sound just like my brother."

"Go on," he said in a gentler tone. She'd never seen him look that way, almost tender. "Report to General Hampton, tell him we got up some cavalry and we're going to charge the enemy skirmish line."

An officer called out, "Right face." She watched Hunter move into position. Then she kicked Scout into a canter and hurried to where she'd last seen General Hampton.

~ * ~

Judith was relieved to see a Federal officer strut into the hospital, aides at heel. She did not trust his intentions, but at least authority should bring order. During the long minute or two that the Federals had occupied the house they had ransacked the place and confiscated all the liquor and other medical supplies they could lay hands on.

The soldiers came to attention as the officer walked through, a good sign.

"Who's in charge here?" he said.

Dr. Thompson finished dressing the colonel's thigh. "I believe I am the ranking surgeon, Major." He wiped his hands on his apron before he saluted. "Captain Thompson, at your service. I ask permission to continue my work."

The Yankee major nodded. "Carry on, doctor. We'll be removing our wounded." He looked from Judith to Pearson, who didn't budge from his place in front of her. "Don't just stand there. Go on outside, private."

"Thank you for protecting me," she told Pearson. "I'm all right now."

The Yankee major nodded at her and touched his hat brim. He swept his eyes onto the sweating Confederate colonel. "You'll be coming with us as well."

"This man should not be moved," Dr. Thompson said. "The ball grazed his femoral artery and he'd likely bleed to de--"

"That's not my concern. Too high a rank for leniency."

"At least have one of your own surgeons certify--"

"Go through and make sure all the rebel officers are brought out," the major said to an aide.

"Sir, I protest." Dr. Thompson balled his bloody hands into fists.

"Protest too much, doc, and I'll take you too."

The yelling and gunfire increased again, closer. A Federal soldier ran into the house and shouted, "Rebs! They're attacking and our boys are running!"

"No. Can't be." The Yankee major looked out the door, then whirled and shouted, "Let's go! Move! Clear out of here and fall back."

The Yankees ran out of the house without stopping to carry off the colonel. Guns fired in the yard, a windowpane cracked, a whining ricochet sound followed.

"Get down." Dr. Thompson yelled. He dropped to the floor and so did Judith. Yells and gunshots split the air and the boards vibrated with running men and horses.

After the noise moved away she sat up and looked around. Not one blue uniform in sight. The colonel wiped his brow with a shaky hand. Dr. Thompson pulled a bottle of liquor from under his apron and took a deep swallow. He handed it to the colonel. "To our health and freedom, sir."

Chapter
Thirty-three

Lexi didn't stay with General Hampton's escort very long. He made a courier of her, sent her off in one direction after another on her tiring horse. Better than sitting in one boring place being an observer. After the small and hastily gathered Confederate units somehow beat the Federals back, she got to carry the news to General Johnston.

When she reported back to Hampton at dusk, Hunter was there, muddy and worn. He held himself without showing strain and didn't appear hurt. She wanted to throw her arms around him. Wouldn't that cause a stir!

Hampton excused him and she followed him to their campsite. She told him, "General Hampton about had me run Scout's legs off."

"He found a job for you, then?" He sounded preoccupied.

"We did it. We beat them."

"They thought it was a trap. I talked to some we captured. They are afraid of Johnston and his tricks. That's the reason they turned back."

"Ha. They ought to be afraid." Lexi felt a glow of pride.

"I found out what happened. Dismounted cavalry fell back and let them through. Later that same squadron rallied and helped us drive them out."

She felt like celebrating, but didn't like the somber way he was looking at her. "What's the matter?"

"Your brother was in charge of them. I didn't see him, so I made inquiries. His men said he was shot down."

"Blake? Oh, God. Dead?"

"Couldn't say. They were in such a big hurry to get away they even left some of their horses behind. They didn't have his. If he isn't dead the Yankees have him."

She lifted her hand to her mouth. Mustn't cry out. Hold the pain inside.

The last time she saw Blake she was furious with him. But he was the only brother she had left, and she did love him. "What can we do?"

"Not a thing. I can't get to him through the lines, not with a battle going on."

"Maybe I can."

He shook his head no. "Slipping through is my trade. I know what I'm talking about."

"Does Judith know?"

"I doubt it."

"Somebody has to tell her," Lexi said.

"So tell her."

"I'd give myself away. You have to."

The muscles in Hunter's cheeks went taut. He didn't want to, but she knew he would.

~ * ~

By dark, most of the wounded had left and Judith had her room to herself again. All evening, soldiers marched down the road and across the bridge, the army moving out. Where was Blake? He had promised to come for her. Fear beat her insides like dragonfly wings. She assured herself his duties were probably detaining him.

Dr. Thompson had promised her transportation on the next ambulance. She carried a lantern upstairs to gather her things so she would be ready. Blake would want her to take the chance to escape.

Although the wounded men were cleared out of her room signs of them remained, the mattress and bedclothes blood-soaked and grimy, the floor quilted with patches of red and dark brown. But she was leaving soon and would not have to endure it much longer.

She stood up on the bed, removed her valuables and Blake's clothing from her ceiling cache and crammed all she could fit into a carpetbag.

A soft knock on the door startled her. She slammed the carpetbag shut. "Who's there?"

"Hunter Lightfoot. May I come in?"

She hurried to unlatch the door. He walked in, wet and powder-smudged, hat in hand.

"Hunter, I'm so glad to see--"She broke off when she got a look at his grim face. Fear wasn't fluttering any more--its claws sank into her throat.

Hunter fingered his hat-brim and glanced about the room. "You're getting ready to leave?"

"It's Blake, isn't it?"

He nodded.

Weak-kneed, she sat down on the bed and waited.

His words were blunt and brutal. "When the Yankees advanced he was shot. That's all anybody knows. Dead or alive, he's in their hands."

Surely he was mistaken or confused. She stared at Hunter's angular face, searching for a change of expression, anything to give the lie to his words.

No. If Blake were all right, he would have come by now. "I have to find him." The prospect of taking action calmed her. "Tell me what I must do."

"Nothing, until daylight. You would get yourself shot by pickets in the dark. The lines will shift by morning, we will be gone and you'll be behind Union lines."

She shuddered at the notion of searching for him among the Yankees. Thousands of them, and she would be on her own. What was to keep them from doing something vile to her?

Hunter said, "Maybe you can get some big Yankee officer to help. See if you can get a pass."

Steeling herself into a show of calmness, she forced her voice out level. "Where did it happen?"

"There's a little farm road off to the left, down this road a quarter mile or so. It leads down a ravine with a creek at the bottom. His squadron was stationed just this side."

"That's where I'll start."

Hunter gave her an approving nod and pulled out his wallet. "I'm buying his horse and equipment. A hundred dollars U. S.

ought to be a fair price."

"Why, Blake won't want to sell that mare."

He folded the greenbacks into her hand. "I'll have you sign a receipt so I can take possession."

"What if he wants her back?"

Hunter shrugged and gave her an odd smile. "In that case, I'll sell the mare back to him."

~ * ~

Blake awoke alone in the drizzling dark. The sounds of fighting had died out except for an occasional comment from a battery or a sharpshooter.

He was cold and feverish at the same time. His chest felt as though it were on fire, and inhaling pained him. His windpipe gurgled and he was thirsty beyond reason. He drank from the canteen Lowery had left him. Creek water, rich with silt from the woods tasted earthy, sweet life itself. He drained the last gritty mouthful.

He set the canteen down, spent from his drinking orgy, but better. The water had cleared his throat and breathing was less troublesome.

Trying to make his sluggish brain work, he sorted with effort through his frazzled thoughts. Was he still a prisoner, or had the ground changed ownership while he slept? He seemed to recall hearing movement on the road, footfalls and talking, but he could have dreamt it.

Had the Yankees passed him by, assuming him dead?

He hurt too much to be dead.

"Hey. Anybody there?"

The weak voice couldn't carry far. Nobody answered. Groaning, he shut his eyes.

He must find the Confederate lines. Was Judith still there? She would know what to do. Like when he came to Fayetteville filthy and worn out. She had even put up with Sally. He felt a sense of shame for ramming Sally down her throat.

Clinging to the tree trunk, he pushed himself to his feet, pausing whenever he felt faint until he was upright. He stood still to catch his breath. Some of the air went directly through the bullet hole into his lung and made those deadly sucking noises. He picked his direction, stepped off and hung onto the next tree.

Careful not to fall, he worked his way from tree to tree, making a little progress before he blacked out. He came to, lying on the wet ground, staring at bare branches netted across the night sky like spider webs. Despairing, he moved his hand over his chest, trying to stop fresh bleeding. He was going to die alone. He'd always figured he would end this way.

~ * ~

Judith turned down the ambulance ride to Smithfield and spent the night in her room listening to the medical staff evacuate. Before dawn, a wagon hauled out the last of the wounded that could be moved. How she wanted that wagon to carry her out of her enemies' reach! But she couldn't desert Blake. If he was alive he needed help.

She imagined him in trouble, in the hands of enemies who did not care whether he lived or died. How did the Yankees treat wounded prisoners? Would they taunt and torment him? Would they even lift a finger to save him? Would they let her help him? Yet she could do nothing but wait until she came under their dominion and hope they did not interfere.

At dawn she stood at the door watching ordinance wagons careen down the road. A squad of gray horsemen came after, wheeled and formed a line in the road facing the rear. They sat on their lean horses for a few minutes, pistols drawn, then turned and cantered away.

Federal troops filled the void. Hordes of them rushed past the house and many more filed in behind. Rifle fire cracked from the direction of town. Weren't they ever going to stop the killing?

The firing eventually ceased. All at once the house and the yard filled with Yankees. They stacked their guns, loitered on the porch, laughed and joked and smoked. One of them fixed a rude stare on her. Hadn't he ever seen a woman before? Or did he lose whatever manners his mama had taught him? He said, "You got any tobacco, lady?"

He was a soot-stained young man who might have been handsome after a good scrubbing. The Confederates were just as grimy but she felt sorry for them. On him it looked like a moral defect.

She shook her head. "I have nothing you would want."

He grinned. "I doubt that." He moved past her to the couch, where a man lay struggling to breathe. "Had enough, buddy?"

"Leave him alone," she said. "Haven't you any decency?"

"Just checking our handiwork." To her surprise, he adjusted the pillow. "That better, buddy? Got any tobacco?" He did not get an answer and moved on.

The only other able-bodied Southerner at the house was a chaplain who had volunteered to remain behind. He ignored the Yankees and their jeers and went about his tasks. After a while they decided he was no fun and quit pestering him.

She tried to get a pass. Although soldiers infested the house she could not find anyone who would point out an officer. As usual, she was on her own. She returned to her room to get her carpetbag and found a soldier going through her trunks. "Get out of there," she snapped.

He paused in his looting and gave her a menacing grin. "What Reb belongs to this?"

"This Reb, and you can keep your filthy paws off it." She beat off his hands and banged the lid shut.

He laughed and lounged back on the bloodstained bed. Ignoring him, she checked the carpetbag, found Blake's clothes, a canteen of water and the flask of brandy Dr. Thompson gave her, still inside. Thank goodness she had rescued it in time. She stuffed in a blanket the Yankee had pulled out of the trunk.

The shotgun. She glanced up at the loose rafter, still in place. But she dared not haul it out in front of the Yankee. If he caught her with it they would confiscate it and arrest her.

She took the carpetbag downstairs. How could she go anywhere in the midst of these terrible men? She pushed her way through the soldiers to the chaplain. He was straightening the body of a man who had just died.

The Yankee who was looking for tobacco had found it. He puffed on a pipe and stared at her.

"Reverend Mullis," she said. "I'm going to go look for my husband now."

"Yes, of course. I hope your quest has a happy result."

She glanced at the Yankee, and back to the chaplain. "I wish you'd go with me."

"I'm afraid my duties won't allow me to leave these men."

The Yankee wasn't coy about eavesdropping. What if he followed her? The pit of her stomach went hollow. "Please."

"I'm very sorry," the chaplain said.

The Yankee said, "I'll go with you, lady. Where you goin'?"

She glared at him. "All the way to General Sherman, if I have to."

She walked out of the yard past two dead men no one had taken time to bury and started down the road. She looked over her shoulder but did not see anybody following her. She had to move against the tide of the oncoming Federal soldiers. If they couldn't recognize her fear, maybe they wouldn't come after her. The rain had stopped and the sky was light, clearing except for a smudge of smoke from the direction of town.

~ * ~

Scouting ahead of the rest of the burial detail, Harry Bell discovered a dead Union soldier. He dropped onto his knees, turned the pockets inside out, found a wallet with a few dollars in it and dropped it into his own pocket. He checked the dead man's stiff fingers, a gold ring. "You won't be needing none of that no more, buddy," he said to the corpse. He tugged on the ring, but it wouldn't come off.

Harry took out his penknife and sawed off the finger at the joint closest to the hand. Ground the blade through sinew and gristle, twisted the finger off. Not too messy, the blood had congealed in this corpse hours ago.

He shook the ring into his palm and dropped it into his pocket along with the money. He threw the useless finger into the bushes.

Joining the cavalry sure was a good move. His unit had missed most of the fighting in this battle. Afterwards he got to be on the burial detail, a big opportunity. All he had to do was make sure nobody spotted him plundering corpses, at least the ones wearing blue. Nobody would care what he did to dead Rebs.

"Smith!" one of his comrades called out. "Where the hell are you?"

A good deal, except everybody wanted to order him around.

Harry slipped away from the corpse and came out of the woods. "Over here!"

"What the hell are you doing?" the sergeant said. "How come you're not digging? Get a shovel and get to work or I'll have you flogged."

Harry tried for a way out. "I can't dig without no shovel."

"Get one off the wagon. If I catch you throwing off on me one more time, I'll hang you by your thumbs besides."

Grumbling under his breath, Harry headed for the supply wagon, freshly reminded why he had skipped off every chance he got.

Chapter
Thirty-four

Down the farm road Judith came upon a burial crew of Union soldiers. She hung back and watched. Two men carried a corpse, stiff and ramrod straight between them. They dumped it into a ditch behind a breastwork.

The morning was mild. The soldiers were bare from the waist up, pausing occasionally to brush off flies. This part of the woods didn't smell much of death despite the presence of a few bodies. Must be fresh kills. Yesterday's.

The two men looked her way. "What you doing here, lady?" one of them called out. He strolled toward her.

She stood her ground, knowing she had to start talking to them sometime. "I, uh, I'm looking for somebody."

He wiped sweat off his face with the back of his hand. "Hell of a place to be looking for a body, if you'll pardon my saying so." He grinned like a hyena.

"He's a Confederate officer."

The soldier went serious. "Here?"

"Have you seen any?"

"A couple of noncoms, that's all. Course, we're not the only ones working this duty."

"Can you direct me to an officer?"

He pointed down the road. "Captain Tucker."

The officer was easy to find, leaning against a tree, smoking a cigar, watching his men work. A wagon full of implements stood nearby and a burly soldier was dragging a shovel out of it. The sleek horses were well equipped with leather bridles and military saddles. Smoke from campfires mixed with the aroma of coffee and the reek of the officer's cigar.

He drew himself straight and jerked the cigar out of his mouth when she came up. Dark beard, pitted face, but his uniform was reasonably clean. Must not do any of the digging.

"Excuse me, sir. Are you Captain Tucker?"

"At your service, madam." His eyes, bright with curiosity, looked from her face down to her bloodstained skirt.

"I'm looking for someone, and I wondered if perhaps you could help me. Have you found any Confederate officers?"

He took a puff from his cigar and studied her. "A relative?"

"My husband. He's a captain. In the cavalry. Missing." Her voice broke. She took a deep breath and clenched her fists. Can't fall apart.

"Wait here." He walked over to where some of his men were working, talked with them, and came back.

"One. Only one Rebel officer, unburied as yet. Come with me." Captain Tucker glanced at the brutish soldier who was still standing by the wagon, leaning on the shovel. "Smith, don't you have a job to do?"

"Yes sir," grunted the soldier. He turned and trudged off.

Captain Tucker paused, watching him go, then shook his head and started walking.

Judith followed him to where several dead men lay in a row like logs in a corduroy road. All strangers. Relief rushed through her. "He's not here. My husband has light hair and a beard. He keeps it trimmed short."

"What else can you tell me?"

"Shot. Yesterday. Near this place, I think. There's supposed to be a little stream."

"Haven't come across a stream yet. We didn't come the same way as Mower's crowd did yesterday when they broke through. Too swampy. Came off the Goldsboro Road instead."

"Where would they take him if he were wounded?"

"Our field hospital. You have to go back out this road and around. Don't try a short cut--a swamp is in the way. You have any kind of pass?"

She shook her head.

"You should secure one."

"How do I... I haven't been able to..."

"Provost marshal. Never mind. I'll write you one. Might do, I'm on General Kilpatrick's staff."

She waited while he took stationary and a pencil from a saddlebag and watched him date the top of the paper.

"Your name, please?"

"Mrs. Judith Winberry."

He started to write, paused and looked at her hard. "That's an unusual name."

"Is it?"

"I met a rebel captain called Winberry. We captured him a little over a week ago. He must have escaped, never saw him after the Rebs attacked us. Light hair and a beard. You must be his wife."

She didn't know whether it was good or bad that Captain Tucker knew Blake, but useless to deny it. Tentatively, she nodded.

"Nice meeting you." He started writing again. "Hope you find him in good shape." He handed her the pass.

"Thank you so much, Captain Tucker." Courtesy was the last thing she'd expected from a Union officer. Her lips quivered into a smile. "I better look around first, then the hospital."

~ * ~

Harry managed to stay within earshot, digging slowly.

He recognized the woman right off. Good thing she didn't notice him, identify him and tell tales to Captain Tucker. She was the woman he and Dink and Snipes had jumped. Back when that soldier came down on them and killed Dink. A Captain Winberry. Her husband must be the same bastard. Plus, the girl that shot and stabbed him almost to death was a Winberry.

That Winberry pack had given him more trouble than anybody had call to put up with.

It wouldn't be too hard to get hold of that woman, set things straight. He licked his lips, liking the idea. And her sorry Reb husband, too, if he wasn't already stiff.

He hoped he wasn't. He wanted the bastard to know what was happening to him.

He threw down the shovel and started to follow the woman.

"Smith," the sergeant yelled. "Where the hell you going?"

Harry hesitated and turned toward the interfering sonofabitch. "I gotta go take a leak."

"You haven't done a nickel's worth of work all day. You're gonna get back to work right now, I don't care if you pee in your pants. Pick up that shovel."

Harry glared at him. He'd like to get that bastard off by himself, too.

"Now, dammit," the sergeant roared, and took a step toward him.

Harry swore and reached for the shovel. He'd have to play along for a while, then he'd catch up with the woman.

"Just you wait, Sugar," he said under his breath. "Just you wait."

~ * ~

Judith kept going and found a stream at the bottom of a slope. Soggy paper cartridges were ground into the earth. Might be where it happened.

She cast about the area, looking around for some clue, anything. The path was cut up and muddy from the passage of many soldiers' feet.

Need a system. Walk in circles, start small, make them bigger to cover every foot of ground.

What's that, on the ground next to that tree? She picked up the bloodstained handkerchief. The monogrammed BW on the corner was her own work--there was the place where she had dropped a stitch and covered her mistake. Blood. She leaned against the tree to steady herself. This was the right place, after all, where he was shot. Where is he?

Dead. Whether she found him would make no difference. He would still be just as dead.

She blinked her eyes clear and turned the grisly relic in her hand. If only it could tell her what happened, where he had gone. Wet linen in a wad, as if it was used to stanch a wound. Nobody would have bothered to wipe up the blood on a dead man. He was alive, at least for a while. Bleeding. Hurting.

The first time she'd seen him, he seemed indestructible, came out of nowhere and saved her from those thugs. But he was only a man after all. Mortal flesh and bone and blood, subject to death.

She crumpled the handkerchief in her fist and looked around. She walked in a wider loop. Called out, "Blake!" He didn't answer.

Of course not. No use.

She spotted a still heap lying on the ground and rushed to it. The soldier's clothes were pitifully sodden from the rain, his face as gray as his jacket. He was not Blake, but she recognized a man from his troop.

She couldn't hold back the sobs. Her shoulders shook and stinging tears blinded her.

Cry it out. Get it over with. No good all in pieces.

She shook herself, wiped her eyes, recovered enough to leave the body and push forward. Probed the brush, parted the scrub so she could pass through. It clung and tore at her skirt. Maybe they had already taken him away and all this was for nothing.

A sticker vine grabbed her clothes. She stopped to untangle. The thorns tore at her and pricked her fingers and drew blood. Even nature was against her. Frustrated, she yanked the vine away, ripped her skirt. Freed, she lurched out of the thicket.

Useless. He can't be here. Go to Captain Tucker and ask for passage to the Federal hospital. Looking for him there made more sense than wandering blind through the woods.

She paused to get her bearings, try to think.

No. Walk one last circle, farther from the path.

Why do this? Wasting time. Need help. Never find him here...

Finally she spotted him, long body across a scattering of wet leaves, upturned face still and white, eyes closed, blood soaked jacket open, exposing a purple bullet hole in his chest.

"Blake!" She made it to his side just before her knees failed. She dropped her carpetbag as she collapsed and choked back a wail as she seized his hand. Limp and cool, blood caked around his fingernails. She beat the air to drive away flies wheeling around the wound. Touched his cheek and stroked the wet mussed hair off his forehead.

She pressed his hand against her lips and groaned with pain too deep for words. Too late.

She felt a slight press from his fingers.

Was she wanting it bad enough to imagine it?

She cupped his hand in hers and stared into his face, afraid to hope. His eyelids moved. His damaged chest rose in a shallow breath. He moaned and coughed.

She thrust her hand into the carpetbag, found the canteen, unstopped it, brought the mouth of the bottle to his lips. She poured a little water into his mouth to moisten it but not enough to choke him. He didn't swallow. The water rolled out into his beard.

"No. Don't do this. You have to swallow." She plugged the canteen, pulled out the flask and dribbled a little brandy onto his tongue to sting him awake. He turned his head aside and closed his mouth. His Adam's apple moved as he swallowed. His eyelids slitted open, showed a slice of gray iris, then closed.

"Better, better. Now you're trying." She gave him a few more drops of brandy and cajoled a little water into him.

Alive, just. He looked terrible. Fragile. His face colorless, translucent, unknowing. Chilled from lying in his wet clothes all night. His wound untended and flyblown--a very dangerous wound--even she knew that.

She set her jaw. She would fight for him as long as there was a scrap of life left in his body.

Judith peeled off his woolen jacket and flannel shirt, heavy with rainwater and gore, and found the second bullet hole in his back. Clotted blood plugged both openings. She looked for other wounds, but didn't find any. She tore off a strip of bed sheet and wrapped it around his chest as a dressing.

She double folded the blanket she'd brought and tucked it around him. She dampened a rag and washed blood and dirt from his face. Gave him more brandy.

He swallowed easier, with less coaxing. Breathing shallow but even, except when it caught in a groan. If only she could move him to a bed in a warm dry place. Somehow she had to get him to her own room at the Oliver house.

His eyes opened again and fixed on her face briefly before they slid shut. She said, "It's all right. I'm here. Just rest. I'll take care of you." She stroked his face and watched him breathe.

How could she move him to the house? She wasn't strong enough to carry him. What about the chaplain? Had the Yankees dragged him off as a prisoner? Even if he could help, how would they get him to the house? Neither of them had a wagon. The armies had certainly taken every civilian vehicle or draft animal within ten miles of Bentonville.

339

The only other quarter from which she could ask help was the enemy. Captain Tucker was civil, even helpful, and he had wagons. She didn't know of anyone else as well equipped. He was her only hope.

"Darling, I'm going to get help." She pillowed his head on the carpetbag, took a deep breath and hurried away. Once she broke free of the woods onto the road, she ran. She stumbled, panting, to Captain Tucker, who left his post by the tree to meet her.

He must have read the desperation on her face. "You found him?"

She collected herself enough to talk. "Barely alive."

Tucker threw down his cigar stub and shouted, "Sergeant Kilcullen, get three men and a stretcher double quick."

~ * ~

Blake opened his eyes, but he was too tired to keep them ajar. He let them slide shut. It hurt to breathe. Too much trouble. Wanted to quit. He could have sworn he saw Judith, but how could she find him out here? Must have been dreaming.

He was cold and wet but the blanket over him was dry. His mouth tasted of liquor. How it got there was too much for him to figure out unless she gave it to him. Where was she? Why didn't she stay?

Footfalls. Men gathered around him and lifted him sideways onto a stretcher. The motion reawakened the soreness of his wounds and he tried to raise his hand in protest. It was too heavy. Blue uniforms. Yankees. Finally came for the game they'd bagged, just about in time to bury it. Satisfied, bastards?

Judith bent over him and tucked the blanket under his chin. Beautiful sight. Frantic. What's she doing with a pack of Yankees? At their mercy, just like him?

"There you go, buddy," one of them said.

"One, two, three, hup."

They bore him up and carried him a distance, but he slept through most of it. When they set him down it jarred him awake. She hovered over him and cupped her warm hand on his cheek and told him he had to hang on. This time it was too real to be a dream.

He felt her love, a tangible, flowing force. He absorbed it like a drug.

~ * ~

Judith accepted the coffee from Captain Tucker. She almost wept with gratitude. "Thank you. It's just the thing," she managed to say.

"I put lots of sugar in it."

She sampled the bittersweet liquid. Warm, not hot enough to burn. She pillowed Blake's head on her lap and held the mug to his lips. He was functioning just enough to drink it a little at a time.

"I'm sorry you found him in such low condition," Tucker said.

"Oh, I think he seems better already." She tried to sound cheerful, believing Blake was aware but too weak and exhausted to respond. "It's good for him to stay calm and rest."

"Sometimes lung-shot men live." Tucker sounded breezy, as though he were only humoring her. "You know, we got pretty friendly that night. Did he tell you about it?"

She shook her head. "He keeps war things to himself."

"Had too much to drink, both of us. General Howard wouldn't have liked that. I doubt that was what he had in mind when he instructed Major Trellis to treat him right. Old Prayer Book runs the religion in our army. He would treat you better than one of your own generals."

She restrained herself from informing him that no Confederate general had shelled her house in Atlanta. "I need to take him to my own room where I can care for him."

"Don't think so. We have to take him to our field hospital."

She had spent the past several days in a place like that, watching doctors sort out the wounded. Would the Federal surgeons bother with a prisoner as critically hurt as Blake? Or would they coldly cast him aside to die unattended?

"In the hospital, will they let me stay with him?"

Tucker shrugged. "That's not my department."

A few minutes later she climbed into the wagon with Blake. She arranged the blanket to cushion him during the ride and supported him with her arms to keep the jolting wagon from pitching him about. The motion was still hard on him. By the time they reached the Goldsboro road he was coughing and gasping and groaning. They would be riding like this over miles of broken rutted road to the Federal hospital. New bleeding would finish him.

They came upon the Oliver house and Judith called out, "Captain Tucker, why don't you just take us over there and leave us?"

He rode his horse closer to the wagon. "That's not our hospital."

"It used to be ours. He can't take this bumping. We have to stop."

"He needs to be seen by a doctor."

"There won't be anything for a doctor to see if he has to endure this any longer. Can't you have one sent to us?"

Tucker looked down at the wreck of her husband and scratched his forehead. "This is irregular. Letting off a prisoner isn't what I'm supposed to do."

"What difference can it make? He's no threat to your army or your bloodthirsty republic, either one. Besides that, your soldiers have been all over this house since morning. It's within your own lines."

"Nonetheless--"

"Captain Tucker, I refuse to let my husband get beat to death in this wagon."

"You refuse? Ha. As if you have any say."

She let her chin tremble and tears roll out of her eyes. "You've been so kind. Please let us--"

Tucker frowned and turned away. "Driver, let's go over to that house. At least we'll know where to find him when we're ready to pull out."

"You don't mean to take him with you?"

"That's not up to me.

Chapter Thirty-five

Judith led the Federal soldiers carrying Blake up the stairs to her room. She swept the bloodstained sheets off the mattress and covered it with a blanket, and they set him down.

As soon as Captain Tucker and his men left she locked her door and went to work on Blake. His wet clothes must go--they were keeping him chilled. The leaves, sand and blood clinging to his body quickly soiled the clean blanket. She pulled the boots and clammy pants from his legs, toweled him down and worked dry drawers onto him. He mumbled and stirred under her hands. She talked to him, hoping he could hear and understand she was there and fighting for him.

Captain Tucker had said something about knowing where to find him. If the Yankees were cruel enough to take him with them he wouldn't survive the wagon ride. Even with the best of care he might not survive the day.

But he was still alive, and she wouldn't wear mourning clothes until she must.

She knew enough from her hospital experience to grasp the complexity of his problems. He needed warmth and cleanliness, but bathing would keep him chilled. However, too much warmth would encourage more bleeding. His wounds were still seeping--she dared not wash them for fear of starting them again. She didn't have lint for packing, used folded bed sheet linen instead. The doctors dosed their patients with opium and applied cool wet compresses on wounds such as his to slow internal bleeding. She could manage the compresses, but she had no drugs.

She ought to try to feed him, but she had no food or anything else. No medicines, no magic, no great medical minds to counsel her. Only her tired hands and common sense and her wish that he would recover so she would still have her husband and the father of her child.

Maybe she should have let Captain Tucker take him to the hospital. No. He wouldn't have made it that far. The bumpy wagon ride would have killed him.

"You must live," she whispered into Blake's ear.

He didn't respond, but the blanket moved as he inhaled. Air rattled through the blood inside his pierced lung. Never before had watching someone breathe seemed all-important to her, and she hung over him for a little while to make sure he kept doing it.

Dizzy with tiredness, she dragged the wicker chair beside his bed and sank into it. As she looked around at her surroundings she realized for the first time what a shambles the room was. Clothes ripped out of the trunks and strewn about, ashes of her sheet music smoldering in the fireplace. The Yankees must have hunted for valuables, but the ceiling board was still in place.

She had passed guards at the front door on her way into the house. Maybe the sacking was over. She heaved to her feet and ventured outside for fuel, food, water and whatever else she could salvage.

Columns of blue soldiers were walking east along the Goldsboro road, skirting puddles left from the two-day rain. One waved at her. Another shoved a comrade. They scuffled and punched and laughed. Striding along, holding rifles casually as for a long hike. Maybe they were leaving for good. Not soon enough for her.

The sun was high and the warmth would speed decay of men and horses lying unburied. Already the thick brown odor stuck in her throat. She avoided the blackening pile of discarded arms and legs under the window of the outbuilding. She swatted at the flies that hovered around her head and realized with a sickening sensation what they had been feeding on. One caught in her hair, buzzing, and she shook it out. Tomorrow and the next day millions more would hatch, nourished by the plentiful food supply.

She filled a bucket at the well and found a few sticks of firewood. The blue-coated guards nodded politely as she returned, must be under orders to behave themselves.

The Yankees had not dragged off the chaplain after all. She found him in the parlor tending the men left in the house. It was wonderful to have an ally.

"Mr. Mullis, I found my husband. He's upstairs in my room."

"How is he?"

"Terrible. He was shot through his chest and left out in the rain all night." Her voice quavered. She took a deep breath. "Do we have any medicine? Opium?"

He shook his head. "We are out of everything."

"What about food?"

"I have applied to the Federal authorities, no word yet."

She set down the water bucket. It had grown too heavy.

Mr. Mullis said, "I'm not a doctor, but I've tended to enough wounded to know a thing or two. Would you like for me to take a look at him?"

"Oh, please."

To her relief, Blake was still breathing. Mr. Mullis bent over him, felt his wrist, looked at the wound without touching it. "It's a very dangerous wound."

"What can I do for him?"

"I can't do more than you have. Keep him warm and clean. Love him."

"Instead of help, you give me platitudes? What good is that?"

"Pray."

She started to snap off another sharp reply, but something resolute in his benign face checked her. "I have been. Constantly."

"It's the best you can do." The chaplain clasped her hand, then left her alone with Blake. He felt warmer to her touch than when she had first found him, so she arranged wet dressings over the packing on his wounds. She placed the sticks in the fireplace. When it got cold tonight the unburned bits of sheet music could serve as tinder. And the house contained plenty of wood furniture.

She sagged into the chair and stared at the clothes that the intruders had dragged out of the trunk. Ought to fold them and put them away. Too much trouble. Had to save her energy for what was important, keeping Blake alive. Her vision blurred.

Even through the closed window, she could hear the shouts and the tread of marching Yankees. How could she persuade them not to take him? Maybe she could buy them off. She would gladly exchange everything she had hoarded, and clung to, for her husband.

~ * ~

Harry tethered his horse near the house that used to be the Reb hospital and scouted it out. Some of the boys had said that was where Captain Tucker took the woman and the Reb captain. He had volunteered to haul him in, but the sergeant made him stay and dig instead. Maybe that wasn't so bad. The woman still hadn't fingered him.

He didn't plan to rejoin his unit. He knew plenty of places to hide, until the army was gone, that sorry sergeant too. And nobody would tell him what to do. He was damn sick of everybody ordering him around.

Right now, he felt like getting a woman and killing a Reb. Maybe he would kill the whole lot that was left in the hospital. That would be fun.

He studied the house. Guards at the door. Shit.

But they weren't going to stay there forever. Not with the army pulling out. All he had to do was lay low, wait a little longer, maybe until dark, and he could get a couple of Winberrys back for all the trouble their kind had caused him.

~ * ~

Boots clumped up the stairway. Somebody rapped and Judith jumped to her feet. "Mrs. Winberry, open the door."

The voice wasn't familiar, a clipped Northern accent. Drat, they even knew her name. Maybe Captain Tucker sent a doctor after all. "Who are you?"

"Provost officer. Mr. Mullis said you have a Confederate officer in there."

Traitor, turncoat, big-mouth. She couldn't even deny it. They'd never believe her.

"Open the door."

They'd kick it down if she didn't, then be mad as everything. Nothing to do but let the Federal officer into the room.

"Wait for me in the hall," he said to the two soldiers with him.

"What do you want?" She stood between him and Blake.

The provost officer brushed by her, turned down the blanket

and exposed the damp dressing on Blake's chest. It was pink with diluted blood. He shook him by the shoulder, making him groan in his sleep.

She grabbed the Yankee's arm. "Stop that. Leave him be."

"Don't get excited. I have to wake him up to sign this." He started to scribble on a writing pad. "What's his name, rank and unit?"

She told him and said, "Please don't take him. It would kill him." She slipped her hand into her pocket and wrapped it around the folded hundred dollars that Hunter gave her. Enough for a bribe?

"I don't want him. Looks like a goner anyway. If he gives his parole by signing this, we'll be done with him."

"A parole? What does that mean?"

"He is prohibited from taking up arms against the United States until he's legally exchanged. Only a formality, I'd say."

She took her hand out of her pocket. "Give me that." She placed the pen between Blake's limp fingers and wrapped her hand around them and wrote his name on the pad. She thrust them back at the provost officer. "There. He signed it."

The Yankee looked from the pad to her face and shrugged. "So he did." He made a copy, tore it off and handed it to her.

"Did you bring a doctor?"

"No doctors. They're all dropping with exhaustion, enough of our own people to tend."

"What about food and medical supplies? Your soldiers took what little we had."

"You'll have to talk to the commissary people. Failing that, I expect you'll have to improvise. Good day." He bowed and closed the door behind him.

~ * ~

Blake opened his eyes. Walls. Ceiling. Daylight. He recognized Judith's room, though he had only seen it once by candlelight. How did he get here? He tasted the salt of his blood and heard the bone-saw rasp of his own breathing. Pain was always present to one degree or another, and he was very, very tired.

Gradually he recalled the rough movement when they'd carried him. The hard floor of a wagon, being hauled up stairs.

This was much better. An actual mattress, dry and warm except for the coldness of wet dressings over his wounds.

Where was she? Had she left him? No, she wouldn't do that. Not even when he insisted. If she'd done what he told her, he'd be dying alone in the woods. He longed to hear her voice, to feel her presence, craved the calming touch of her hand. Helping him to endure.

The door opened. She set a tray down on the table next to the bed. "Oh, you're awake." She looked surprised, smiled, bent down and kissed him. Her face was haggard and drawn, her eyes bloodshot. She was no less beautiful.

He tried to smile back but didn't speak because just breathing took all his strength.

"I fixed you supper. Can't you eat a little?" She sat on the edge of the bed, stroked his cheek and smoothed the hair from his forehead. "The chaplain, Mr. Mullis, is still here. He talked the Yankees into leaving a little food behind and asked me to cook it. They're gone now, thank goodness."

She slipped her arm under his shoulders and elevated him a little, supporting his head against her breast. She spooned a brownish-white mound toward his mouth. He wasn't hungry, but accepted the mouthful of food because he wanted to live. Potato mashed with bacon tasted better than it looked.

She wiped his mouth with a cloth. "Good. You need to eat so you can get your strength back." He swallowed the potatoes with the water she gave him, hoping he would keep it down.

"Captain Tucker let me bring you here. He was nice, for a Yankee. Said he knew you from when you were a prisoner, before you came to Fayetteville. Here's some brandy. The only stimulant we have." She poured a little into water and stirred honey into it. "I was pretty mad at Mr. Mullis for telling that Yankee provost officer you were here but it turned out all right. Mr. Mullis knew he was going to take your parole."

He started to feel a little stronger, more alive. The food and drink had washed the taste of blood from his mouth. The pain was still there but farther in the background, not as important, and he was out of the hands of his enemies.

He must remember to tell her, if ever he was able, that he'd thought of her the whole time he lay in the woods. Nobody but her.

He fell into a deep sleep.

~ * ~

Judith awoke with a start, found herself sitting in the dark beside Blake. She lifted her chin from her chest and rubbed her sore neck. The inside of her mouth felt sticky. Blake, outlined in the dim glow from the embers in the fireplace, was mumbling, restless. He moved his hand to his chest and plucked at the bandage over his wound.

"No." She captured his hand in both hers. "You'll just make it worse."

He quieted a little after she spoke. She touched his cheek, finding it fevered. His rattling breath lengthened as he settled into a calmer rest.

She closed her eyes and drooped, so very tired, not but a few hours of sleep in days. She had been breaking her heart and her back trying to save lives, no time to rest. Now the most important life of all was in jeopardy. Blake needed her full attention. Strength sapped, she wasn't sure she was equal to the demand.

She must rest, but what if he needed her and she didn't awaken? She slipped off her outer garments and climbed into the bed with him. Careful not to jostle him, she stretched out full length alongside him. Touching, his movements would likely awaken her if he came into distress.

His hand sought hers and closed on it. She took heart that he was aware of her.

Grateful, she closed her eyes, praying that he would still be alive come daylight.

~ * ~

Harry walked across the starlit yard to the front porch. The army was gone, guards with it, and all he had to do was open the door and walk in. The country people that lived here didn't even have locks on their doors.

The Union Army wouldn't have let the Rebs keep anything deadlier than a pocketknife. He had a rifle and a cavalry-issue revolver, so he was sure to outgun anybody there. He had been watching the house all evening, and saw only one man well enough to walk, a preacher type he could bust in two. Through an upper window, a corner bedroom, he had spotted the woman moving around, so he knew just where to find her when he got upstairs.

"Who's that? Who's come in?" He heard a man's voice, then somebody walking through the dark house toward him. The preacher.

Harry flattened against the wall behind the door.

"Who's there?" The preacher sounded nervous. He paused, eased up to the door, closing it with Harry inside.

Harry brained him with his rifle-butt, knocking him to the ground and kicked him in the ribs. The preacher moaned, not dead yet. Harry raised his rifle butt to smash the head, finish the job. But he caught something else from the corner of his eye and turned from the preacher, peering into the house.

He couldn't make out anybody, but a creepy feeling crawled up his back, like a warning. He felt like the something that spooked him was still watching. He said to the preacher, "I'll get back to you later," then stepped over him and entered the house.

Other Rebs, disabled and defenseless, lay about the inside of the parlor, just waiting for him to fix them. But he was primed for the woman, didn't want to wait any longer.

After he finished with her and her worthless Reb husband, he could come back down and take his sweet time making every half-dead sonofabitch all the way dead.

He found the stairs and crept upwards. A wooden plank creaked, and he paused, but nothing happened. He climbed to the head, got his bearings, figured out which was the right door, the one at the end of the hall. He threw it open.

He didn't see the woman right away, blinked, then made her out near the window. In the bed, a few feet away, Winberry lay flat on his back. All his. Harry licked his lips, anticipating a night of pleasure.

~ * ~

Judith faced the stranger in the dark. Something she had heard, or perhaps some intuition, had roused her in time to get out of bed and face him. "Who are you? What do you want?"

"I want you, Sugar." The man started toward her, menacing.

She backed up into the corner, remembered leaning her shotgun there. "Go away. Leave us be."

The man sidled to Blake's bed and stood over him. "Captain Goddamn Winberry. He won't save you this time, Sugar. Can't even save hisself."

"Who are you?" She crouched downward, finding the cold metal barrel, drawing it toward herself, hoping the darkness would cover her actions. "How do you know my husband?"

"Just wanted to have a good time." The man's growl curled into a whine. "His kind is always messing me up. But I got you both now. I'm gonna fix him good, then I'll work on you." He raised his rifle and pointed it at Blake, who lay unconscious.

"No!" She snatched up the shotgun and jammed it against her shoulder. The man turned toward her.

Determined not to repeat a mistake, she pulled only one trigger, bracing herself for the recoil. The explosion roared, lit up the room and rocked the man backward. He grunted, staggered, still clutching his rifle.

"Why'd you do that, Sugar?" His voice was a sob. "All I want is a good time."

She held the wavering shotgun as steady as she could manage. Only one barrel of shot left. Blake moved, aroused by the noise.

"I don't want to shoot you again," she pleaded. "Leave us."

The man groaned again. His breathing was labored, panting. Why didn't he fall like a wounded man was supposed to?

"Goddamn you." He growled like an animal and jerked his rifle up, straight toward her. She pulled the second trigger, heard the double boom, saw the flashes of her shotgun and his rifle going off at the same time. The window behind her shattered. The man dropped his weapon. It clattered to the floor and he collapsed.

Judith stood frozen. At last she lowered the shotgun, amazed that she'd suffered no blow from a bullet, no pain of a wound.

The man let out a long dying groan. Blake struggled to rise, crying out.

"Hush," she whispered harshly. "Don't hurt yourself worse."

She held her breath. Was the man dead? Were there others? She set down the used-up shotgun and groped in the dark. She found his rifle, trust it aside, and her hand connected with wet clothing. Smelling blood and urine, she gritted her teeth and ran her hands

351

up and down the body. The leg kicked once, making her start. She told herself snakes did that too, after they were dead. She found a gun belt, a holster, the grip of a revolver.

Footsteps on the stairs. Sobbing, she ripped at the holster-stay and dragged out the weapon.

Someone was coming down the hall. She lifted the revolver and pointed it at the door. "Who's there?" Her voice was choked, couldn't have carried far.

A man lurched into the doorway, cradling his head in his hands. She thumbed back the hammer, slippery with blood. "Who's there?" she repeated.

The man leaned against the doorframe. "It's me. Mullis," he whispered.

She lowered the revolver, and started to tremble all over. "I almost shot you. Where have you been? God forgive me, I killed a man."

"Thanks be to God." Mr. Mullis slid down the doorframe, all the way to the floor.

Chapter Thirty-six

Hunter had finished with the prisoners. He had learned that Sherman's army cleared out of Bentonville and was headed toward Goldsboro. He committed the information to a sheet of paper and folded it in half.

The two Yankee stragglers sat in their underwear, listening, eyes fearful, as J. C. concluded his story. "I took that shotgun and blowed his leg clean off. And I tell you another thing, he must've been made out of blood..."

Lexi's face showed a mixture of fascination and disgust. "Did he die?"

"Not till I blowed his head off with the other barrel to stop the hollering."

Hunter handed the dispatch to him. "All right, J. C., we're impressed. Take this to headquarters along with these good-for-nothings."

One of the stripped bluecoats said, "You ain't gonna put that maniac in charge of us, are you Lieutenant?"

Hunter didn't give a damn whether the prisoners made it to Smithfield alive or not, but for appearances he said to J. C., "Don't get careless and lose 'em."

J. C. grinned at Lexi. "I want Alex to go with me."

"You don't need him. Get going."

J. C. turned his hard grin to the Yankees. "You heard him, boys. Go it." He headed off with the two half-clothed prisoners trudging in front of his horse.

Lexi chewed on her thumbnail. "If J. C. ever looks at me like that again, I'll punch him."

"That's something I'd like to see."

"He's onto us."

"If he touches you, don't ask my permission. Just shoot him. Now put on that blue coat and mount up. We've been ordered back into Bentonville."

"To look for Blake?"

"I am to determine what damage we did to the Yankees, since they haven't volunteered the information. But we'll see about him while we're there."

The village was not far away, just across the bridge over Mill Creek. But Hunter was cautious, took his time. He had been doing things that way lately. He was losing his edge. Ever since she joined him he was avoiding trouble, staying away from fights, hedging his risks.

He glanced at her, swallowed up in the too-large Federal coat. Her face, unguarded at the moment, was somber with tragedy over her brother's misfortune.

Damn it all, he cared for her, more than he had ever believed possible. He ought to shake her off like an unbroken horse throws a rider, but he did not have the strength. She had a grip on him. And he had gotten far too used to enjoying his marital rights.

He saw no enemies loitering in the village. He wrinkled his nose at the obscene stench. No wonder they cleared out in such a hurry. From the way Bentonville stank and buzzed in the morning calm, the dead had not been buried fast enough. He dismounted in the yard of the Oliver house, noticing a horse tethered nearby, outfitted with Federal gear. He drew his Navy Colt and handed his reins to Lexi.

She shook her head and threw the reins back at him. "I want to see for myself."

"We find Judith, she will recognize you," he pointed out.

"Who's she going to tell? She's behind the lines now, cut off." Lexi shook out a handkerchief and tied it around her face so that only her eyes showed. "Just say I have to keep out the smell."

~ * ~

Judith saw the two blue-coated soldiers ride into the yard. Now she heard a commotion in the hallway. More Yankees. When would she see the last of them? She gripped her shotgun and walked across the room, avoiding the bloody places she had tried and failed to clean up. She glanced at Blake, who lay asleep, pale and quiet, and stationed herself by the door, ready to defend both of them as many times as necessary.

A familiar voice sounded in the hall. "Mrs. Winberry. It's me, Hunter Lightfoot."

"Thank God." The relief was so draining she had to lean against the wall for support. She pulled aside the chair she had jammed under the doorknob and opened the door.

In walked Hunter, eyes roving from Blake to the bloodstain on the floor and back to her, his face unreadable. With him was a slim soldier, bandanna around his face. Only haunted blue eyes showed, fixed on Blake. The soldier struck Judith odd, but she had more important things to worry about.

Hunter said, "The chaplain told me what happened last night."

She closed her eyes and nodded.

"You improved the Yankee breed a bit," Hunter said. "By culling from the bottom."

He introduced the stranger, without further explanation, as Private Wilson. The boy nodded but did not speak. Maybe the handkerchief covered a disfiguring injury. But something about those troubled eyes was familiar.

"Where did you find Blake?" Hunter said.

"About where you said to look…" Judith's knees went wobbly again. Overcome by exhaustion, she let herself down on the chair next to the bed. It was a luxury she could afford now that Hunter was here.

"How bad is he?" Hunter asked.

Judith shrugged helplessly. "I don't know whether he can live. All night long, he was delirious whenever he wasn't unconscious." She did not break down. She was out of tears.

Hunter and Private Wilson exchanged glances, and Hunter said to Judith, "Do you have enough provisions?"

"The Yankees left a little behind, but it's about gone," Judith said. "I have the federal money you gave me for Blake's horse, as if there's anything to buy."

Hunter smoothed his moustache. "Tell you what. I've got investigating to do, but Private Wilson can stand guard and take care of Blake while you get some rest."

Judith turned doubtful eyes to the young soldier, who had not spoken once.

"Absolutely reliable," Hunter said. "Used to work in a hospital."

Before she could raise objections, Hunter stalked out the door.

Judith turned to Private Wilson. "I guess I have to trust you too," she said.

The young soldier nodded, looking at Blake.

Hunter, her brother-in-law, had given his recommendation. And she was too worn out to turn down a chance to rest. "All right then," Judith sighed. She spread a blanket in the corner, stretched out on it, and pillowed her head on her arms.

~ * ~

Lexi flopped into the chair Judith had planted next to Blake's bed, turned the blanket down and lowered her ear to his chest. The pulse seemed strong enough. His respiration rasped through the blood in his wounded lung, but he was not drowning, not so far. She lifted the dressing and sniffed at the puffy, oozing wound. It had not gone bad yet, didn't reek with the sick smell of infection. Still, his kind of injury killed all but the lucky and the strong.

Her brother was strong, and he was lucky too. He had Judith, who had found him, brought him to shelter and guarded him like a mother bear.

Lexi had seen the body downstairs, recognizing the same Yankee that killed Lige. The one she thought she killed. But there he was, ripped to shreds by the shot from Judith's gun, his horse still waiting for him outside. He wasn't going to come back to life this time.

No wonder Judith lay on the floor sleeping like a dead thing. And the load wasn't going to get any lighter for her, stuck here with Blake half dead, with no help but the chaplain. The man was still woozy from a busted head and babbling about an angel of the Lord delivering him from death.

No help but her.

She stuck her thumbnail under the bandanna, between her teeth and gnawed it. Hunter would return soon, expecting her to leave with him. But she couldn't desert her own brother and her sister in law after seeing the fix they were in.

She changed the bloody dressing on Blake's wound, substituting a clean cloth she found in a little pile on the nightstand. His eyes fluttered open and fixed on her face, questioning.

He sure didn't need the shock recognizing her would give him. Avoiding his gaze, she lifted his shoulder, removing the wet pad underneath, substituting a clean one. The back hole was open, draining clear pink fluid. Good. Anything that came out wouldn't clog his lungs.

"Judith?" he whispered.

Lexi nodded toward the corner, where she lay. He turned his head to look at her and closed his eyes.

Maybe he hadn't caught on who she was yet, but if she stayed, he or Judith would figure her out sooner or later. Not that he was in any shape to do anything about it. And whom would he tell?

Blake needed her, desperately. She would give up anything to save her brother, even her hard-won freedom.

She sat watching both of them sleep for a long time before the door quietly opened and Hunter slipped inside.

Lexi jumped up, caught his hand, and led him back to the hallway. She said, "I can't leave them. I have to stay and help for a little while at least."

Hunter seemed to expect it. "Do they know who you are?"

She shook her head no. "Maybe I can keep it that way."

"I'll make sure Hampton knows he's here. I found fifty more of our poor wretches at another house. One family trying to take care of the whole lot." He allowed a sardonic smile. "Maybe our grateful country will see fit to send a doctor and provisions. But I wouldn't count on it."

Lexi accompanied him outside, to where they had tethered their horses. "As soon as they don't need me any more, I'll catch up with you," she told him.

He shrugged. "As you wish."

"Don't you want me to rejoin you?"

He untied the reins, ignoring her. Sometimes he was like that, cold and indifferent. At other times, she could swear he loved her. All she knew was she liked being with him better than anybody else, and she didn't mind being married after all. It seemed most of the time he didn't mind either, though they had not been free to talk about it much. Their lovemaking was silent, furtive and thrilling. She knew he liked that part.

She stroked Scout's neck, remembering something Hunter had said. She grinned up at him, sitting on the horse. "Slick piece of horse-trading, Hunter."

"What are you talking about?"

"Buying Blake's horse, the one the Yankees have. You do have a heart."

He narrowed his eyes. "Tell anybody about that and I'll--"

She laughed out loud. "I can keep a secret."

~ * ~

Judith awoke when Private Wilson closed the door behind him and walked across the room toward Blake, who was asleep. The young soldier took his place again in the chair by the bed, not paying attention to her. It struck her that he moved more gracefully than most boys, and that he certainly did look familiar. He wasn't looking in her direction, but she could see the profile. She could swear she'd seen those eyes and that brow before.

It couldn't be. She shook her head. Impossible.

She sat up and said, "Lexi."

The soldier startled and stared at her, looking trapped.

Judith exhaled. "I don't care why or how. I'm glad you are here."

The girl reached behind her neck and untied the bandanna, letting it fall from her face. The change in her was startling, her face sharp and shadowed, a healing cut across her brow, the mouth set more obstinate than ever. "I'm not going back to Columbia," she said.

"I'm not sending you anywhere." Judith gave her a tired smile. If she had the energy, she would be ecstatic. "I need you right here. Who knows besides Hunter?"

"Just you. I guess that means Blake, too."

She shrugged. "We don't need to worry him with that right now."

Lexi glanced at him. "He has been resting easy. I think he's got a good chance."

Fresh tears stung Judith's eyes. Didn't know where they came from, thought she was cried dry. Lexi came over, knelt down and put her arms around her. Judith gratefully let go, sobbing into her sister-in-law's shoulder.

~ * ~

Two days later, Blake endured an examination by Dr. Thompson. The high command had sent the doctor with ambulances and supplies back to Bentonville to treat the wounded still there. An afterthought, prompted by Hunter's report.

Blake had recognized Lexi, her soldier's disguise only fooling him until his mind cleared. She was a great help to Judith, taking short foraging trips and bringing in enough food to keep them from starving. She was a skilled nurse and had always shown more interest in learning from Papa than her brothers. Blake had considered reporting her but gave up the idea. The girl was going to do whatever she wanted to anyway. She'd already slipped off again to join Hunter. She was his wife, his problem.

Finally there was the matter of the money Hunter had given Judith, supposedly for his mare that was in possession of the Yankees. Blake regarded it as a loan and resolved to repay him.

"Stick out your tongue, Captain Winberry." Dr. Thompson looked rested and sober for a change.

Blake submitted to the doctor's probing, chest-thumping and ear-to-chest listening. He coughed bloody phlegm into a handkerchief and showed it to Dr. Thompson. "What do you think of that?" he asked.

"To be expected," came the unsatisfactory reply.

"Out with it, Doctor, am I going to live?"

To his relief, Dr. Thompson smiled. "For being lung shot, losing all that blood and spending a night in the rain, you're doing pretty well. Only a little inflammation, no sign of pleurisy yet. The fluid in your lung ought to work out in time, but I expect you will always be a little short winded. You'll have a long convalescence, but you'll recover if nothing goes wrong. Has a surgeon done anything for you?"

"No surgeons." Blake smiled at Judith, who was standing by the doctor's elbow, watching his every move. "Just my wife."

"That's all right. A Yankee quack might have bled you to death trying to control internal bleeding, or he might have poked bone splinters into your lung with his dirty fingers." The doctor nodded to Judith. "Your wife is wiser than that."

Judith said. "I was just about afraid to touch him."

Blake caressed her face with his gaze. "She went through the whole Yankee army to find me. Even got them to help. I have a very brave and resourceful wife."

"Brave? I was scared to death," Judith said.

"Only a fool wouldn't have been," Dr. Thompson said. "No doctor, no medicine. It's enough to keep a physician humble. But then, your work at the field hospital taught you a thing or two. I can take credit for that much." Dr. Thompson turned back to Blake. "We'll get you out of here. You're all right to move as far as the hospital in Smithfield."

"I can't wait to leave this awful place," Judith shuddered. "Flies. I've been picking maggots out of his wounds every morning, in there squirming and driving him wild. Disgusting."

"A few maggots never hurt anybody," Dr. Thompson went contemplative. "Curious thing, flyblown wounds don't often turn gangrenous." He shook his head and shrugged. "We don't know why, but it's true. Anyway, you won't find the Smithfield hospital much of an improvement. It's short of everything except patients. And flies."

"Will they let me stay with my husband?" Judith asked.

"They better," the doctor said. "Last I heard, they weren't turning down any help. I'll certainly recommend it."

"I'd rather go home, if it were possible." Blake's jaw tightened at the thought of his destroyed house, his family living in a public building. But it wasn't a house he needed to see. He wanted to make sure his family was all right.

"Nothing but bad roads, Yankee raiders and bushwhackers between here and Columbia," Dr. Thompson said.

"I still have the receipt for our mule and wagon," Judith said. "The army owes us. I want them back."

"Good luck getting anything," the doctor said. "Tell you what's better. I'll help you turn that receipt into a train ticket. Let him rest up a day or so in Smithfield, then take him to a private home in Raleigh or Greensboro to convalesce. You will have to go that far to find a decent place."

"What are the Yankees doing?" Blake said. "Are they headed toward Raleigh?"

"They are still in Goldsboro," Dr. Thompson said. "We don't know what they are plotting."

Judith shrugged, feeling more resignation than fear. "I expect they'll just follow us, like they always do." She looked around the room at her belongings, and Blake's. This time she would leave behind the broken china she had carried all the way from Atlanta. She didn't need to hang onto useless reminders of the past any more. Time to start traveling light.

~ * ~

Northwest of Raleigh, Hunter watched the road with J. C. and Lexi. She had rejoined him when the medical department came for her brother. Against his better judgment, he let her stay.

In truth, he had been delighted to see her. She knew it, too.

Horsemen approached. Dust obscured the color of their clothes. Their emaciated horses staggered under them. Most likely Confederates, riding down from the north, the wrong direction.

He alerted Lexi and J. C. then hid behind a screen of bushes, pistol drawn. He must find out for sure what was behind the appearances of these intruders. He called out, "Halt there."

The five men stopped and looked around, dazed expressions, dirt streaked faces. "What the hell?" one of them said. His second lieutenant's bar was almost obliterated by grime. His hand started toward his pistol-handle, then hesitated. "Who says halt?"

"Who are you?" Hunter said.

"We're from the Seventh South Carolina Cavalry."

"That won't work, boys. Seventh is in Virginia."

"Was." The lieutenant glanced at his bedraggled cohorts, befuddled.

"You trying to desert? I'll run your asses in to the provost."

"No, no, that ain't it. Lee's army is gone up. We came down here to join up with Hampton's Ca--"

"Gone up? Say you're lying." Hunter's gut knotted and his mouth went dry. He had been pushed clear to the Virginia line by the Yankees coming up from the south. A few days ago he had heard the Yankees captured Richmond. And here this man was claiming that the north boundary of the Confederacy had fallen through as well.

The dusty lieutenant shook his head. Big tears welled from his eyes and traced lighter tracks down his smudged face. "I wish I was lying. Lee surrendered the whole damn army."

"The hell you say. When?"

"How long? Two days ago, I think. I lost track. We cut our way out and we been pushin' so hard we ain't even stopped to sleep." He wiped his sleeve across his face, smearing the dirt.

The newcomers wore the threadbare uniforms of the Army of Northern Virginia, talked right, must be right even if it did seem impossible that Lee would ever give up.

Telegraph would have carried the news to headquarters by now. Sure they would keep it secret. Otherwise, it would send a shock wave through Johnston's whole army, just as it sent one through him. Disorder and mass desertions would result.

He ought to shoot them so they wouldn't be able to speak of it again, spread their poisonous news. But others would come.

He had gambled everything he was. Now he could see it all going up and he could not do a thing to stop it.

He held his bitterness inside. "All right, boys, come on in. J. C., show them to headquarters."

Lexi emerged from cover and stood next to him, peering at the weary men who had refused to surrender. She chewed her thumbnail and said in a low voice, "It's as good as lost, isn't it? What are we going to do, Hunter?"

"I can't surrender. There's a price on my head."

She turned her quick blue eyes at him from under her hat brim. "Then I can't surrender either."

"Don't be stupid. You can just go home. Something else I can't do."

"I'd die of boredom." Her eyes fixed on him, steadfast. "I want to stay with you."

"The game's up. You ought to be able to get our marriage annulled. Find yourself a nice boy instead."

"I don't want anybody else."

"I've just been using you. Haven't you figured that out by now?"

She shook her head, refusing to believe his hard words. "You're brave and clever and you haven't ever let me down. We do real well together."

He swallowed to moisten his parched throat. Did she really think that of him?

She touched his hand. "If you don't want me, just say so. I never was out to snare you."

He took out his pipe and stuffed tobacco in the bowl while she stood watching him, as though waiting for him to say something. The bruises on her face from the beating and the shelling had healed. Constant riding had made her body taut with flat muscles like whipcords. She had grown boyish in appearance, tough and positive, not exactly his ideal woman, but all woman under the façade. Their inside joke. "You did a damn fine job anyhow."

She grinned, all optimism. "We can hold out against the Yankees forever."

"Johnston is no fool." Hunter struck a match and lit his pipe. "He knows he can't go on without Richmond, without Lee, not with Sherman and Grant boxing him in. If he kept it up he would be squeezed to death between the two Yankee armies. Not Johnston. He never was much for futile bloodshed."

"What are we going to do?" she pushed.

He took a long, burning drag. She was willing to stay with him, under any conditions. And she made no other demands. What was so bad about that? Why was he so determined to keep her at a distance? He had not succeeded.

He took the pipe from between his teeth and exhaled the smoke. "Better leave before Johnston gives up. Before J. C. gets a notion to collect a reward. West. Maybe I'll go west. It's a big place, I'll get lost out there."

Lexi grinned. "Just what I always wanted to do."

"I ought to take you straight back to your mama."

Her grin didn't fade a bit. "I know you better than that."

"It'll be hard," he warned. "We'll be on the run."

"I'm not afraid."

"Guess not. You never did have good sense." He shrugged. "I could stand some company." Then something inside him gave way and he was truly glad he hadn't been able to thrust her away. He smiled sardonically. "How did you do it, Lexi?"

Her brow crinkled with puzzlement. "Do what?"

"Tell you what." He stuck the pipe stem in his mouth and sucked in another lungful of smoke and breathed it out. "It might work out. We do all right together."

She laughed wildly. "Say it, Hunter."

"All right," he snapped. "I need you, Lexi. I care for you. I want to keep you. Is that plain enough?"

"It'll do for now."

He wrapped her in his arms and she softened to him, just like a woman.

Chapter Thirty-seven

Blake sat on the porch of the Raleigh boarding house, waiting for Judith to return from the post office. Never before had he witnessed such a lovely spring. All around, winter was waving surrender flags. Trees colored with fresh growth--dogwoods, red maples, oak leaves. Azalea hedges around the house budded pink and yellow, their perfume soft on the air. He drew energy from the morning sun like a growing shoot.

He had recovered just enough to be restless. Earlier, he had walked Judith partway into town, as far as his strength would allow. Forced to let her manage their affairs for the past few weeks, he was spoiling to pick up the reins again, take the burden off her.

He was still sore and weak, but he improved a little every day. He could get around if he didn't move too fast and he could make love to his wife. Small accomplishments. But he was thankful--amazed--to be alive. He owed it all to Judith and her contrariness.

And her steadfastness. Sally would never have faced the whole Yankee army to save him.

He and Judith had met Sally at the depot when they arrived in Raleigh. Surprised all three of them. He didn't hide his indifference, not that she cared. Sally was traveling by herself to Charlotte, but denied she was going to look for Randolph there. Judith seemed satisfied with the encounter, even a little smug. He guessed she finally believed his interest in Sally had died.

He shifted uneasily in the rocking chair. She was overdue. If she didn't return soon, he'd have to go find her, whether or not his strength allowed it.

At last he spotted her, walking fast along the sidewalk toward the boarding house. He stood up, held onto the banister and eased down the steps to meet her. She took his arm, too tightly, the old anxiety in her eyes.

He said, "What's the matter?"

"The Yankees--"

"What about them?"

"I heard talk at the post office. They're headed this way."

"Have a habit of doing that, don't they?"

"I went to the depot and got tickets to South Carolina, Chester, as far as the line goes," she said in a breathless rush. "Yankees tore up the tracks from there to Columbia. We'll get down there somehow. The hack will pick us up at three, take us to the depot."

He felt a twinge of annoyance. "Jude, you should have consulted me first."

"Surely you don't want to stick around--"

"That's not the point--"

"There wasn't time. What did you expect me to do? Run back here to get your permission, then run all the way to the depot? Space on the train would have sold out by then. Don't you want to go home, even if it's a few days sooner than we planned?"

He didn't want to be angry with the woman he adored, his best friend. Besides, her logic was sound and the controversy wasn't worth fighting over. He would have suggested she do exactly what she did anyway. He was well enough to stand the trip now and he didn't trust the Yankees to honor his parole.

Still, he would rather have been in on the decision.

"It's all right," he said.

Her eyes searched his face. "Are you mad?"

"No, but next ti--"

"I will. Promise."

"I've heard that before." He laughed softly. "You'll never change. But if you didn't have that cussed mind of your own, I wouldn't be here." He couldn't look at her without remembering dying but for her soothing, yet determined touch.

His eyes stung. Nerves still raw, bled easily.

Her voice took on a teasing note. "You must be feeling better. You're getting bossy again."

"Like me better when I was at your mercy?"

"It's good to have the old Blake back." She laughed and gently pulled his whiskers. "Even if he is a martinet."

He grinned and teased back. "If you were a soldier I'd have you arrested for insubordination." He slipped his arm around her waist and they stepped up onto the porch together.

"Packing will be easy," she said. We don't have much left, especially since I got rid of the things we don't really need."

"You mean that broken china?" He had noticed the useless stuff, but had never asked her about it before. His wife was entitled to her quirks.

"I used to think I needed it," she said.

"Now you don't?"

"Memories are best carried in the heart. You are the present, and I can touch you."

He gave her a squeeze.

"I'll be glad to see your family," she said.

"My folks are probably still staying in that hospital building. It won't be a bad place to live until we can rebuild."

"We'll make do, now that you don't have to go off and fight again."

The sadness weighted him down, as it did every time he thought of defeat.

"Blake, there's something else."

He waited.

"There's a rumor going around that Lee has surrendered."

It was a heavy blow. Just a few weeks ago, he would not have believed it possible. Now it had the ring of truth. "If that's so, we are finished."

She took his hand. "At least the fighting will be over."

He led her into their room and shut the door. More than anything he wanted to close out the rest of the world and surround himself with her warmth. He circled her still-slim waist with his hands. "How much time before the train leaves?"

"Hours." She lifted her face to him.

He bent down to kiss her, tasting the sweetness of her mouth. She rested her head on his good side and he buried his face in her lavender-scented hair. "I love you, Jude," he murmured.

She lifted her face and gazed at him, smiling, dark eyes damp with tears. I have loved you from the first moment I saw you."

The worry started gnawing at him again, as it did every time he started to believe he was happy. How was he going to support himself, a wife, and a little one on the way?

"Everything's going to be fine," she said, as though reading his thoughts.

"I'd better come up with some way to make a living. Real quick."

She touched his cheek, ran her fingers down his beard. "You're smart as everything. You went all the way from private to captain. Whatever you set your mind to, you can do."

"Maybe I'll find a way to go to medical school. I always was a quick study, liked the books. I can apprentice with my father until then. I got over being squeamish a long time ago."

She smiled, wistful. "Once the mail is running again I can find what's left of my folks, back in Tennessee."

"That's right." He chuckled. "I have a mother-in-law I've never met. Don't we own land in Atlanta?"

"A vacant lot."

"Plenty of those around." He thought of his burned-down home.

She gripped his hand. "If only the Yankees will leave us be, let us live."

"Oh, I don't think they have enough prisons to hold all the has-been Confederates. But things really are going to be different anyhow. We will have to learn how to tolerate Yankees. Might take a lifetime."

"That's all right." Judith gave his hand a squeeze. "You have one of those, now."

Meet Lydia Hawke

Lydia Hawke is a native Floridian born in St. Augustine who has always been avidly interested in Southern history. She graduated Summa Cum Laude with a BA in Communications from the University of North Florida. Lydia's fiction work has finaled in several literary contests and she writes for Civil War Courier and Clay Today Newspaper. She breeds and shows champion Collies and competes with them in agility events. She owns an electrical contracting business with her husband Larry, and they have one married daughter. Lydia enjoys horseback riding, scuba diving, training her dogs, and is a licensed amateur radio operator. An officer in the Greater Orange Park Dog Club and the Greater Jacksonville Collie Club, she is also a member of the Collie Club of America, Pals and Paws Dog Agility Club, Orange Park Amateur Radio Club, United Daughters of the Confederacy, Orange Park Community Theater, EPIC, First Coast Romance Writers and Romance Writers of America.

Printed in the United States
76212LV00003B/67-180